Two Wrongs
Make a *Right*

Two Wrongs Make a Right

CHLOE LIESE

BERKLEY ROMANCE
NEW YORK

Berkley Romance
Published by Berkley
An imprint of Penguin Random House LLC
penguinrandomhouse.com

Library of Congress Cataloging-in-Publication Data

Names: Liese, Chloe, author.
Title: Two wrongs make a right / Chloe Liese.
Description: First edition. | New York: Berkley Romance, 2022.
Identifiers: LCCN 2021061992 (print) | LCCN 2021061993 (ebook) |
ISBN 9780593441503 (trade paperback) | ISBN 9780593441510 (ebook)
Subjects: LCGFT: Romance fiction. | Novels.
Classification: LCC PS3612.I3357 T86 2022 (print) |
LCC PS3612.I3357 (ebook) | DDC 813/.6—dc23/eng/20220118
LC record available at https://lccn.loc.gov/2021061992
LC ebook record available at https://lccn.loc.gov/2021061993

First Edition: November 2022

Printed in the United States of America
1st Printing

Book design by Kristin del Rosario

For the strength inside me that I found when I had to.
And indomitable hope.

For which of my bad parts
didst thou first fall in love with me?

— WILLIAM SHAKESPEARE,
Much Ado About Nothing

Dear Reader,

This story features characters with human realities who I believe deserve to be seen more prominently in romance through positive, authentic representation. As a neurodivergent person with (frequently) invisible chronic conditions, I am passionate about writing feel-good romances affirming my belief that every one of us is worthy and capable of happily ever after, if that's what our hearts desire.

Specifically, this story explores the realities of being neurodivergent—being autistic, having anxiety—and navigating the vulnerable gift of life and relationships. No two people's experience of any condition or diagnosis will be the same, but through my own lived experience as well as the insight of authenticity readers, I have striven to create characters who honor the nuances of their identities. Please be aware that this story also touches on the topic of recognizing and healing from a toxic relationship.

If any of these are sensitive topics for you, I hope you feel comforted in knowing that only healthy, loving relationships—with oneself and others—are championed in this narrative.

XO,
Chloe

· PLAYLIST ·

ONE

Bea

A word to the wise: don't have your fortune read unless you're prepared to be deeply disturbed.

> *Wrong is right and right is wrong.*
> *I foresee war—merry or misery, brief or long?*
> *A mountain looms built on deception.*
> *Surmount it and then learn your lesson.*

See what I mean? Disturbing.

I tried not to get anxious. But the morning after my grim fortune reading, I woke up to an ominous daily horoscope email. The cosmic warning was loud and clear. Duly noted, universe. Duly noted.

Quaking in my Doc Martens boots, I decided to beg off the party. That didn't go so well, seeing as this party is my twin sister's doing and my twin is hard to say no to. And by "hard" I mean impossible.

So even though the universe has all but warned me to *buckle up, buttercup,* and the air crackles like ozone before a storm, here I am. I reported for duty at the family home—wore a dress, donned my crab mask, made a cheese-and-cracker plate. And now, like any self-respecting scaredy-cat, I'm hiding in the butler's pantry.

That is, until my sister sweeps in and blows my cover. The swinging door flies open, and I'm caught in a beam of light like a crook cornered by the cops. I stash the peppermint schnapps behind my back and slide it onto the shelf just in time to prove my innocence.

"There you are," Jules says brightly.

I hiss, throwing my arms across my face. "The light. It hurts my eyes!"

"No vampires in this costumed animal kingdom. That crab mask you're wearing is scary enough. Come on." Taking me by the arm, she tugs me toward the foyer, into the jungle menagerie of masquerading guests. "There's someone I want you to meet."

"JuJu, please," I groan, dragging my feet. We pass an elephant whose trunk clips my shoulder, a tiger whose eyes hungrily trail my body, then a pair of hyenas whose laugh is spot-on. "I don't want to meet people."

"Of course you don't. You want to drink in the butler's pantry and eat half the cheese-and-cracker plate before anyone else can. But that's what you *want*, not what you *need*."

"It's a solid system," I grumble.

Jules rolls her eyes. "For eccentric spinsterhood."

"And long may those days last, but I'm talking about my anxiety."

"Having been your twin our entire lives," she says, "I'm familiar with your anxiety and its bandwidth for socializing, so trust me when I say this guy's worth it."

The peppermint-schnapps-and-hide trick *is* my social anxiety lifesaver. I'm neurodivergent; for my autistic brain, engaging strangers isn't easy or relaxing. But with the trick of a couple of covert swigs of schnapps—buzzed, calmer—I find the experience less overwhelming, and my company finds me not only passably sociable but minty fresh. At least, that's how it typically goes. Not tonight. Tonight I have grim cosmic warnings hanging over my head. And I have a bad feeling about whatever she's dragging me into.

"Juuuuules." I'm that kid wailing in the grocery store. All I need is a smear of chocolate chip cookie on my cheek, a rogue untied shoelace, and I am typecast.

"BeeBee," she singsongs back, glancing my way and failing to hide how disturbing she finds my papier-mâché crab mask. She tugs it up off my face and nestles it into my hair. I tug it back down. She tugs it back up.

I glare at her as I tug it back down again. "Lay off the mask."

"Aw, c'mon. Don't you think it's time to come out of your shell?"

"Nope, not even for that dad-level pun."

She sighs wearily. "At least you're wearing a hot dress—oops, hold on." We stop at the bottom of the steps before she yanks me behind the banister.

"What?" I ask. "You're letting me go?"

"You wish." Jules cocks a smooth dark eyebrow as her gaze dips to my dress. "Wardrobe malfunction."

When I peer down, I see my dress gaping along my ribs. Thank you, universe! "Pretty sure it's busted. I should go check it out in the bathroom."

"So you can hide again? I don't think so." She slides the zipper up my ribs, the sound of my fate being sealed.

"It could be on its last little zippery legs. Shouldn't chance it. A boob might pop out!"

"Uh-huh." Clasping my hand, Jules launches me forward. I'm a meteor hurtling toward catastrophe. As we approach our destination, sweat breaks out on my skin.

I recognize her boyfriend, Jean-Claude, and Christopher, next-door neighbor, childhood friend, surrogate brother. But the third man, who stands with his back to us, a head above them, is a stranger—a tall, trim silhouette of dark blond waves and a smart charcoal suit. The man turns slightly as Jean-Claude speaks to him, revealing a quarter of his profile and the fact that he wears tortoiseshell glasses. A molten ribbon of longing unfurls inside me, curling toward my fingertips.

Distracted by that, I catch my toe on the carpet. I'm saved from a face-plant only because Jules, who's used to my body's abysmal proprioception, grips my elbow hard enough to keep me upright.

"Told you," she says smugly.

I'm staring at a work of art. No. Worse. I'm staring at someone I want to *make* a work of art. My hands crumple around the fabric of my dress. For the first time in ages, I ache for my oil paints, the cool polished wood of my favorite brush.

My artist's gaze feasts on him. Impeccably tailored clothes reveal the breadth of his shoulders, the long line of his legs. This man has a body. He's the jock of your dreams who forgot his contact lenses and had to wear his backup glasses. The ones he wears at night when he reads in bed.

Naked.

The fantasy floods my mind, red-hot, X-rated. I'm a walking erogenous zone.

"Who *is* that?" I mutter.

Jules stops us at the edge of their circle and takes advantage of my stunned state, lifting up my mask as she whispers, "Jean-Claude's roommate, West."

West.

Oh shit. Now, thanks to my recent deep dive into hot historical romance, I've got even higher expectations for the guy, with a name like *West.* I picture a duty-worn duke, thighs stretching his buckskin breeches as he walks broodingly across the windswept moors. Braced for ducal grandeur, I fight a swell of anxiety as Jules breaks into the trio, as *West* turns and faces me.

Stunning hazel eyes lock with mine and widen. But I don't linger on his eyes long. I'm too curious, too enthralled, my gaze traveling him, drinking in the details. His throat works as he swallows. His hand grips his glass, rough at the knuckles, his fingertips raw and red. Unlike nonchalant Jean-Claude, whose stance is arrogantly loose, his tie looser, there's nothing relaxed or casual about him. Ramrod-straight posture, not a wrinkle to be seen, not a hair out of place.

His eyes travel me, too, and while I'm poor at reading facial expressions, I'm excellent at noticing when they shift. I observe the record-scratch moment as his features tighten. And the heat previously flooding my veins cools to a chilly frost.

I watch him register the tattoos swirling over my body, starting with the bumblebee's dance down my neck, across my chest, beneath my dress. His gaze drifts upward to the frizz of my just-showered hair and messy bangs. Finally, it wanders over the family cat Puck's white hair stuck to my black dress. There's a rather aggressive tuft on my lap area, where Puck parked himself before I nudged him off. Mr. Prim and Proper looks like he thinks I forgot the lint roller. He's absolutely judging me.

"Beatrice," Jules says.

I blink, meeting her eyes. "What?"

After twenty-nine years of twinning coexistence, I know that her patient smile plus my full name means I zoned out, and she's repeating herself. "I said, this is Jamie Westenberg. He goes by West."

"Jamie's fine, too," he says, after an awkward beat of silence. His voice is deep yet quiet. It hits my bones like a tuning fork. I don't like it. Not a bit.

He's still scrutinizing me, this man I've decided most definitely doesn't get to ruin hist-rom *West*s and is instead getting called Jamie. Judgy Jamie suits him much better.

His eyes are back at it, traveling the tattoos along my neck, over my collarbone. His critical gaze is an X-ray. Heat flares in my cheeks. "See something you like?" I ask.

Jules groans as she steals Jean-Claude's drink and throws back half of it.

Jamie's gaze snaps up to mine as he clears his throat. "Apologies. You looked . . . familiar."

"Oh? How so?"

He clears his throat again and slides his glasses up the bridge of his nose. "All those tattoos. They reminded me of . . . I thought you were someone else for a moment."

"Just what someone who busts their ass on designing highly personal tattoos wants to hear," I tell him. "They're so unremarkable, they're easily mistaken for someone else's."

"I'd think you're accustomed to being mistaken for someone else," Jamie says, glancing toward my twin.

"Thus the *highly individual* tattoos," I say between clenched teeth. "To look like myself and no one else."

He frowns, assessing me. "Well, no one can say you lack commitment."

Christopher snorts into his drink. I rub my middle finger along the side of my nose.

"Maybe West recognizes those tattoos because you two *have* bumped into each other in the city . . . somewhere . . . at some point?" Jules says hopefully.

"Doubtful," I tell her. "You know I don't go out much, and definitely not to places that someone as stuffy—I mean, *serious*—as him would like."

Jamie narrows his eyes. "Considering that club Jean-Claude dragged me to last year was a den of chaos, complete with an inappropriately handsy woman who projectile vomited on my shoes, I'm reassessing. Perhaps it was you."

Jean-Claude rubs the bridge of his nose and mutters something in French.

I smile at Jamie, but it's more like baring my teeth. "Chaos dens aren't my speed, but whoever the poor soul was that bumped into you, then upchucked, I imagine puking was an involuntary response to the misfortune of making your acquaintance."

Jules elbows me. "What's gotten into you?" she hisses.

"I remember that night and it definitely wasn't her," Jean-Claude tells Jamie, before he directs himself to me. "West is determined to die a miserable old bachelor and has grown crotchety in his solitude. You'll forgive his rusty manners."

Jamie's cheeks darken to a splotchy raspberry red as he stares into his half-empty lowball glass.

A determined bachelor? That means I'm not the only one who's been avoiding romance. Dammit. I don't want camaraderie with Mr. Bespectacled Stick Up His Ass.

"Bea, too," Jules adds, like the nosy mind-reading twin she is. "She hissed at me when I found her hiding tonight. The determined spinster's turned feral." Smiling up at Jean-Claude, she tells us, "But I'm just as determined to see her put away those claws and be as happy as I am."

The two of them share a lovey-dovey look, then a long, slow kiss that makes the cheese and crackers I ate crawl up my throat. As their kiss becomes kiss*es*, Christopher adjusts his watch. Jamie studies his lowball glass. I pick Puck fur off my dress.

Glancing up from his watch, Christopher gives me a meaningful lift of his eyebrows. I shrug my shoulders. *What?*

He sighs before turning toward Jamie. "So, West, you and Jean-Claude go way back, right?"

"Our mothers are friends," Jamie tells him. "I've known him my whole life."

"That's right," Christopher says. "You went to the same boarding school?"

"Our mothers did, in Paris, which is where they're from. Jean-Claude's family didn't move stateside until we were teens, and then we didn't cross paths academically until we went to the same university."

I roll my eyes. Of course Jamie's one of those people whose *French* mother went to *boarding school*. I bet Jamie did, too. He's got prep school written all over him.

As Christopher asks him another question, Jamie drains the rest of his cocktail. It smells like bourbon and oranges, and when he swallows, my gaze dips from his lips to his throat.

I stare at him as they talk, telling myself I don't have to like *him* for my artist's eye to love observing how the soft lighting of my family home knifes down the long line of his nose and caresses the angles of his face, revealing sharp cheekbones, a sharper jawline, a tight slash of a mouth that might be secretly soft when he's not pinning it between his teeth. A stuffy stick-in-the-mud shouldn't be allowed to be this beautiful.

"Well, Miss Crabby," Christopher says, nudging my crab mask and rudely dragging me back into the conversation. "Did you make this yourself?"

"But of course," I tell him, feeling Jamie's eyes on me and hating how that makes me blush. "I'm not even going to ask you, Christopher. This brown bear disguise is clearly store-bought."

"Sorry to disappoint. Some of us are too busy working to make our own masks for Jean-Claude's masquerade birthday party."

"Well, at least you're color coordinated." Christopher's dark hair and amber eyes are the same shades as his bear mask. I sink my fingers into his neatly styled locks and purposefully mess them up.

He flicks my ear. "Ever heard of personal space? Back up. You reek of peppermint schnapps."

I dodge the next flick. "Better than having bourbon breath."

Jamie watches us in silence, a notch in his brow, like he's never seen two people good-naturedly tease each other.

Before I can make some jab about that, the lovebirds break apart on a loud lip smack, leaving my sister breathless and pink-cheeked.

"The things Juliet comes up with," Jean-Claude says on a sigh as he stares down at my sister. "A masquerade party, full of people I have to share you with." Tucking her tighter against his side, he adjusts the neckline of her wrap dress so her cleavage is covered. "When all I need is *you*."

Jules smiles and bites her lip. "I wanted to make it special. You always have me to yourself."

"Not enough," he growls.

Something about Jean-Claude's intensity with my sister makes my skin crawl. They've been together for a bit over three months now, and rather than mellow out after the first frenzy of infatuation, like the people Jules has dated before, Jean-Claude just seems to be ramping up. It's to the point that I can't even walk around the apartment in a bathrobe because he's *always* there, on the sofa, in our kitchen, in her room. My gut says it's too much.

But Jean-Claude works at Christopher's hedge fund, and he's recently been promoted, meaning Christopher trusts him, which says a lot. More than that, Jean-Claude seems to make Jules genuinely happy. I don't understand it, but I can't deny it. That's why, so far, I've kept my concerns to myself.

"Well." Jules smiles. "Seeing as we're hosts, we should mingle, Jean-Claude." Next, she elbows Christopher, raising her eyebrows. "Mind making sure there's enough ice at the bar?"

Christopher frowns at her before his expression clears. "Oh. right. Bar duty. Gotta run."

Leaving Jamie and me. Standing together. Alone.

The air drips with tension.

If I were feeling mature, I'd make myself scarce. Be helpful. Serve drinks. Refill appetizers. But I'm not. I'm feeling my competitive streak overriding logic. I'm feeling perversely invested in proving to Jamie that he's wrong about me. I'm not someone to be mistaken for a chaos demon with unmemorable tattoos who puked on his shoes in a dingy bar months ago.

Well, I'm a bit of a chaos demon, but it's hardly my fault that I'm a little clumsy. Everything else, he's got me pegged all wrong, and I'm going to out-civilize him just to prove it. Only problem is, that requires something I'm very, very terrible at: small talk.

"What . . . are . . . you . . . drinking?" I ask. Because, you know. Small talk.

Jamie glances up and gives me a guarded look, like he's not sure what I'm up to. That makes two of us.

"Old-fashioned," he finally says, his words as neat and tidy as his looks. Then he peers at my empty hands. "Not partaking?"

"Oh, I am. I just hit the schnapps pretty hard in the kitchen. You know, a little social lubricant."

His eyes widen. I die inside.

Lubricant. I had to say *lubricant.* So much for out-civilizing him.

"I see." He adjusts the lion mask that rests on top of his impeccable dark blond hair.

My *lubricant* bomb threw the conversational waters into sky-high swells. We're seconds from drowning, but Jamie just threw me a little rescue floaty in those two words. So I grab on and throw him one, too. "Nice mask," I tell him.

"Thank you." He examines mine. "Yours is . . ."

"Gruesome?" I stroke a pincer of the papier-mâché crab mask. "Thank you. I made it myself."

He blinks at me like he's trying very hard to think of something nice to say about it. "That's . . . impressive. It seems . . ." He clears his throat. "Complicated?"

"Ah, it wasn't too bad. Besides, I'm an artist, so I like hands-on creativity." And then, because I'm feeling extra juvenile, I add, "Like my tattoos."

He swallows and blushes spectacularly as his gaze darts down my neck to my breasts, following the bumblebee's trail. Not sure what he has to blush about, since there's hardly anything to see. My black dress runs low, but unlike Jules, I was not blessed in the chestal department. The curse of fraternal twinship: similar face, different boobs.

Jamie is silent in the face of my latest move. It's gloriously rewarding. Now I'm the one smiling politely, and he's the one letting our conversation die a slow, awkward death. I'm about to declare victory when Margo pops her head in.

Smiling up at me from her diminutive height in a burnt orange jumpsuit and a fox mask that pins back her tight black curls, Margo says, "Need a cocktail, sweet cheeks?"

"God, yes." I take the glass from her, appreciating its deep red complexion and enticing aroma. Margo is a mixologist who makes the best drinks. I'll take anything she gives me. Like nearly everyone else at this party, she's also one of Jules's friends, because my twin is the nucleus of our social cell, unlike me, who's happy existing on the edge of the semipermeable social membrane.

I have friends but only through Jules, which is enough for me. Jules is how I know Margo, who's married to Sula. And because I met Sula, whom I now work for, I once again have a job as an artist that pays a living wage. My sister's social strategizing can be exhausting, but it's also made my life better. Without Jules tugging me inside her sphere, nudging me to make connections, I'd be lonelier and a lot less gainfully employed, especially since things took a nosedive nearly two years ago.

In keeping with my prove-non-chaos-demon-status campaign, I'm polite and make introductions as Margo offers Jamie her hand. "Jamie," I say, "this is Margo."

"Actually," he says, taking her hand, then releasing it, "most people call me—"

"West!" a voice yells from behind us, startling me so badly, I jump half a foot and send my bright red cocktail straight into his chest.

Jamie's jaw tics as he steps back and shakes off the liquid dripping down his hand. "Excuse me," he says, eyebrow arched in censure. *See,* that eyebrow says, *you* are *a chaos demon.* Then he turns and disappears into the jungle of guests.

I beg the ground to swallow me up.

But the universe is silent, so here I remain. The meteor that's just made impact, hissing in its crater.

Jamie

Jean-Claude gives me a confused once-over when I reach the bottom of the steps. My wardrobe change took place in a second-floor restroom—well, one of them. This house reminds me of my parents', in size, at least. That's where its similarities end. This house feels like a home.

"What happened?" he asks.

I adjust my cuffs until the buttons are halfway across my wrists. "Beatrice. Thankfully I packed a backup shirt."

He pats my back and sighs. "You would be that neurotically over-prepared."

"I always have a change of clothes. I'm a pediatrician, Jean-Claude. Do you have any idea how many times per week a baby vomits on me?"

"Fair enough." He sips his drink and gestures toward the large living room where the cocktail explosion took place. "I hope you won't write her off," he says quietly.

"Who?"

He glances around, then switches to French. We're both fluent, thanks to our French expatriate mothers, but he only uses it when he wants to gossip around others. "I'm talking about Bea. I know she's rather . . . odd, but she's sweet once you know her. In her way."

"I'm not writing anyone off. There's no need to, when she and I won't be crossing paths again." I was at my socially anxious worst, which I know isn't when my most endearing qualities come out. Beatrice made sure I knew it, too. After that disaster, why would we ever seek out each other's company?

"Perhaps not tonight," Jean-Claude concedes as we stroll toward the foyer. "But you'll be seeing plenty of her in the future."

I stop abruptly. "What?"

He flashes a wolfish grin and pats his pocket. "I'm going to propose to Juliet."

"Propose? It's been three months."

Jean-Claude looks perturbed. "Long enough to know that I want her to be mine forever. Not everyone moves at your glacial pace, West."

That stings, but I let it roll off my back, like I always do with him. "Right. I meant no offense. I was just surprised."

His gaze settles on Juliet mingling among the guests, not even an exotic swan's-feather mask obscuring her wide smile. "West," he says, eyes still on her. "You've been alone for too long, indulging in this bachelor nonsense. You're lonely and miserable. Why not let that change tonight, eh?"

"I'm not lonely or miserable," I tell him, reverting to English, a signal that this little private chat is over. "I'm busy."

No time to miss a relationship when you're drowning in work. And yes, perhaps I'm working so much to avoid meeting someone or dating at all costs, but if your last relationship ended the way mine did, you'd be single by choice, too.

It flashes through my mind at warp speed, from the moment I met Lauren at a local fundraiser, to the day she ended things. I thought I'd found someone who made perfect sense for my life, who wanted exactly what I wanted—a meaningful career in medicine, a routine, tidy life. Turns out, I'd just found someone who saw me as useful for a time, and then perfectly easy to leave behind when I no longer suited her purposes.

I've cited the rough breakup as an excuse to decline social situations for the past year, when really I'm simply too weary to even think about trying with someone again, only to not be enough, to once more have the rug pulled out from under me. No, a long, uneventful bachelorhood is all I need, and avoiding socializing best accomplishes that. Unfortunately, it seems my breakup-recovery excuse has expired with Jean-Claude, who pulled the *It's my birthday, I'm your roommate, and it's rude not to come* card.

He knew it would work. He was right.

"If you're not miserable, then why are you wallowing?" he asks.

"I'm not wallowing."

"You are." He swirls his drink, pale blue eyes narrowed on me in analysis. "And it's time for you to have some fun."

"Fun?"

"Yes. Fun. Like tonight. This is fun."

"Hmm." I scratch my cheekbone where the mask is aggravating it. "Must 'fun' involve being so itchy? This is polyester, isn't it?"

Jean-Claude rolls his eyes behind a rather chilling cobra mask, then turns and examines himself in the hallway mirror, fussing with the tousled style of his brown hair, which he spends a heinous amount of time on every morning, making it look like he spends no time on it at all. "I don't know what the mask is made of. But I do know you make a very good lion. Now we just have to find someone to make you roar."

"Get out of here. Go. Mingle."

He claps my back. "We're going to enjoy ourselves tonight! Love is in the air, the wine is flowing." He grins, backing away. "You never know what will happen."

My stomach sours. That look. I know that look. It's mischief.

I want as much distance from it as possible. So I wend my way through the crowd, searching for an isolated corner of the house to sit in, where I can pull out my phone and read. Just for a bit. Thank God for smartphones to sneak-read e-books.

"West! Hello again." One of Juliet's friends hooks an arm in mine. I only just met her, the one with dark curls and a fox mask. I need a moment before I can recall her name.

"Hello, Margo."

She smiles. "Looking for something?"

"Just somewhere quiet to sit."

"I know the perfect spot for you. Here." Guiding me toward the back of the house, she gestures to a cozy corner that looks lived-in but tidy. Twin mustard-yellow armchairs, a slim side table, a Tiffany-style lamp whose stained-glass shade casts kaleidoscopic jewel-tone colors around us.

"Thank you," I tell her.

She smiles again. "Happy to help."

Sinking into one of the armchairs, I stretch out my legs, unearth my phone from my pocket, and start to read. It'll only be a minute or two. Just enough time to finish the chapter that was interrupted when my cab arrived.

It's quiet back here, peacefully removed from the party's chaos. A window is cracked, and the scent of autumn whispers in the air. It's one of those moments that's absolutely perfect.

Until Bea walks in through a swinging door on the far side of the room that I didn't know existed and scares the life out of me.

I shoot upright in my seat and almost knock over the fancy lamp. "Beatrice."

Her eyes widen behind the elaborate papier-mâché mask. "James."

"Jamie," I correct her, though why the hell I told this aggravating woman she could call me by my given name in the first place, when only a few people in my entire life have earned that intimacy, is entirely beyond me.

"Bea," she parries. "You call me Beatrice, I call you James. What are you doing here?"

Language evades me for ten eternal seconds. I've always been like this, tongue-tied when my anxiety gets the best of me. But it's worse tonight. With her.

I stare at Bea, starting with her long legs and the subtle flashes of black ink on her skin, up to the neckline that's torturously low yet reveals so little. Her hair is dark except for the tips at her shoulders, which are bleached white-blond. But it's her eyes that made every word fall out of my head when I first saw her. Blue-green irises ringed with striking cloud gray, like ocean waves churning under a stormy sky.

"Margo showed me to this spot," I finally manage. Uncomfortable while sitting because it makes me much lower than her, I stand. Now I'm towering over her. That's even more uncomfortable. "What are *you* doing here?" I ask.

"I was sent here to make sure no guests had missed champagne before Jules gave her toast to the birthday boy."

"Ah." I clear my throat.

That's odd. Why would Juliet's—and I suppose they're also Jean-Claude's—friends send us both to the same corner of the house after the disaster that just happened?

"Have one," Bea says, lifting the tray of fizzing coup glasses closer.

I take an involuntary step back.

"It's champagne, James, not a Molotov cocktail."

"Drinks in your hand are not just drinks, Beatrice. They're projectile missiles."

"Wow," she says. "You're one hell of a—"

Before Bea can finish whatever insult she was about to throw my way, the swinging door opens right into her. Instead of insults, she throws six glasses of ice-cold champagne straight onto my pants.

———

After *another* wardrobe change, I round the corner into the kitchen with my wet pants in hand, startling when I see Beatrice standing at the counter, a catlike intensity lurking in her eyes.

Tugging the lion mask over my face, I slip the champagne-drenched pants into my messenger bag, then straighten my cuffs. "Despite being an apex predator for the night," I tell her, "I'm feeling hunted."

"Trust me, this isn't how I wanted to spend my night, either." She slides a wedge of gooey Brie between two crackers and crunches on them, then says around her bite, "Whose idea was the lion mask?"

"I picked it up in the foyer. Your sister had a collection for guests who didn't bring their own."

Bea stops chewing. "I don't get you people and your soulless, impersonal disguises. Homemade masks are the only good thing about this night."

"Well, you're an artist. You'd think that. I haven't touched tissue paper or glue since the early 2000s, and I'd like it to stay that way."

"What a sad existence. Getting messy is one of life's greatest pleasures. Besides, how else could I celebrate being a Cancer?" she says, tapping her crab mask. "Nobody even sells crab masks."

"I wonder why."

"Oh, burn. At least I'm wearing my proper sign. Why's a textbook Capricorn wearing a lion? That's what I want to know."

I blink at her and adjust my glasses, which are pushed down by the mask. "How did you know?"

Not that I put credence in zodiac signs and all that nonsense, even if technically, yes, my birthday places me in the astrological map as a Capricorn.

She snorts. "James. If you were any more of a goat, you'd be mountain bounding as we speak."

"That's not actually an answer."

"It is," she says, crunching on her cracker again. "It's just not the one you wanted. Anyway, are you done?"

"Yes. Though why you waited—"

"Jules is waiting for *you*. I'm on orders to bring you out and give her a signal so she can make her toast." She frowns, her eyes traveling me. "Did you *change*?"

"Yes."

"Of course you have backup wrinkle-free slacks." She crunches another cracker. "You're a Capricorn."

"Little did I know how wise it would be to come ready for disaster, seeing as, tonight alone, you and open-container alcohol have an oh-and-two track record."

A soft growl leaves her. With those feline eyes and the jarring crab mask, it's bizarrely alluring.

It must be the unreasonably flattering dress she's wearing. And my lengthy abstinent streak. That'll make anyone see attractiveness when they should be running the other way.

Smoothing my hands over my cuffs, I tug them down, once each wrist, then meet her eyes again. "I forgive you, by the way."

She smiles, but it's more like baring teeth. "How generous. Or you could forgive *Jean-Claude*, who barged through the mudroom door without knocking, like a one-man elephant stampede."

"Seeing as he's a man, he'd be a one-man *man* stampede."

She blinks at me, clearly annoyed. "Let's go. I can't take this anymore."

"Hey, you two!" Margo says warmly as Bea and I walk into the foyer together. "What a lovely sight." She gives a signal to Juliet, who smiles and lifts her champagne glass. "Come on. Jules is about to give a toast; then it's time to play!"

"Play?" I ask weakly.

Beatrice leans in and says, "It's this thing people do sometimes, James. To have this thing called . . . 'fun.' "

She can't know how on target that barb is. Like an arrow meeting a bull's-eye, the word lands in my chest with a sickly *thud*.

Fun.

Fun is hard to have when you have lifelong anxiety, when new places and people make your throat close and your chest tighten, when everywhere you go, you're told you carry a family name and its reputation on your shoulders, that there'll be hell to pay if you fail it.

My anxiety is better managed now than it was when I was a child, but the accusation hits a tender old bruise, scrapes open a wound that's never quite healed.

I have no witty response to her barb about my stodginess, no stinging riposte. Beatrice seems surprised by that, her brow furrowing as I glance away and stare longingly at the cocktail in Margo's hand. God, do I want another drink, but with Beatrice nearby, is it worth the risk of wearing it?

"West." Making my decision for me, Christopher offers me a glass, a copy of the one I had earlier. His mask sits up off of his face, nestled in his dark hair, and I take that as silent permission to do the same with mine.

I'm eager for a nice swig of my drink, before I think better of it. First, I discreetly put another solid foot between me and Beatrice. "Thank you," I tell him.

Christopher nods. "It's the least I could do after startling Bea. She turned you into a Pollock painting of Margo's jungle juice."

"I'm here, remember?" she snaps.

He tweaks her hair affectionately. "How could I forget?" Then he lifts his glass and clinks it with mine. "Sorry again."

"Not at all," I tell him. "Cheers."

We both take long drinks.

Beatrice glares at me. "So you can't be bothered to drink the bubbles I offer, but you'll take Christopher's manly bourbon drink."

"It's nothing personal. I just don't particularly *like* champagne. And that's quite sexist of you, to masculinize bourbon."

Her sea-storm eyes flash with lightning.

Christopher laughs. "Ah, c'mon," he tells her. "That was funny."

"Don't start with me, Papa Bear."

"Papa Bear?" I ask.

Bea glares up at Christopher and tugs his bear mask back down over his face. "He's the brother I never had."

Christopher slides it once more up on his head. "Someone has to keep an eye on you Wilmots."

"We grew up together," Bea explains. "His house is next door."

Christopher grins. "I have many embarrassing Bea stories."

Her eyes narrow dangerously. "Don't even *think* about it."

Before it can escalate, Juliet whistles, drawing the crowd's attention. "Okay," she says, standing on a chair near the front door. "Thank you for being here tonight! I'm so happy you could come to celebrate Jean-Claude. Before we move on to all the fun, I'd like to give a toast," she says, lifting her glass.

"Actually." Jean-Claude steps forward and drops to one knee as he opens the ring box. "I had something I wanted to say first."

"What the *fuck*?" Bea says.

Christopher elbows her. "Shh."

"They've been dating for *three* months!"

"Bea." He looks at her sternly.

When I refocus on the proposal up front, Juliet is already nodding fervently, hands over her mouth.

To hoots and cheers and applause, we raise our glasses, toasting an engagement and then a birthday. Bea stands, stunned, as people swarm the happy couple with congratulations.

I have no idea what to say.

"Now!" a new woman says, jumping up on the chair Juliet was occupying a minute ago. Her hair is bright blue, a perfect pairing with her peacock mask. "For those of you who don't know me, I'm Sula, Juliet's friend!"

Margo wolf-whistles from the middle of the crowd, and Sula gives her a wink.

"Our first game of the night begins now. Let's get started and give the newly affianced a few minutes to themselves. Jules and Jean-Claude, you'll lead the search. But first, everyone else, hide. Nowhere is off-limits. Once you're found, you join the search party, and the last person found wins the grand prize! Go!"

THREE

Bea

I'm extremely competitive, and the point of this game is to be the last one found. But that's not why I'm using my ultimate hiding spot. I just want to be alone for as long as possible. For once, I couldn't care less about winning.

There are a dozen little closets in my parents' big old Georgian. But Jules doesn't know about this one on the third floor. She's been too scared, ever since our menacing little sister, Kate—who's currently halfway across the world and missing this stomach-turning development, the lucky duck—made up a ghost story when we were kids about the third floor that terrified my twin.

If Jules comes up here at all, it will be a desperate last resort, and she definitely won't be alone.

The broom closet is halfway down the hall of the third floor and blends into the three-quarter wood paneling. But if you have an eye for detail—and I do—you notice the seam along the wood. That's how I found it twenty years ago.

Pressing softly, I feel the door give, then quietly drag it shut behind me. A tiny plug-in night-light bathes the small space in a faint glow. It smells like lemon furniture polish and sachets of citrus potpourri that Mom nestles into the house's many nooks and crannies "to keep the place fresh" when they're gone, which is often. My parents love to travel and spend lots of the year exploring warm corners of the world. They passed that wanderlust on to Kate, who hasn't been home for longer than a few weeks since the day she graduated college. What I'd give to be in her shoes right now—thousands of miles away from this nonsense.

I mean, engaged. After *three* months. I know I sound like a cranky old biddy, but come on. Three months!

Taking off my mask, I shut my eyes as I settle onto a box of toilet paper, then hike up my dress so I can spread my legs. It's too quiet in here. I like ambient quiet—a gentle breeze, the rhythmic crash of ocean waves. But this quiet is empty and painful. The kind of quiet that leaves nothing for me to hear but my too-fast breathing and my pounding heart.

Juliet's *engaged*. I rub my hand over my aching chest. It feels cracked open, like there's no glue to fix it.

Just as the first flood of tears fills my eyes, footsteps tread down the hallway. Soft and steady. They stop right outside the door, and my ears perk at the sound of a hand smoothing over the wood. Seriously? This can't be happening. No one should have found this.

The door pops open, then slides shut. The closet now brims with the tall, lean form of the last person I expected or wanted to see.

Jamie.

He spins and slaps a hand to his chest when he sees me. "Christ," he hisses, shutting his eyes. Backing away, he bumps into the built-in shelves, causing an audible *thunk*.

"Shh," I whisper-yell. "If you're going to crash my hiding place, at least be quiet. How did you find this anyway?"

"Everyone's scared of third floors. It's a logical place to go." He adjusts his cuffs until the buttons are exactly halfway across the underside of his wrists. "And Sula—I think it was? Blue hair?—might have mentioned the third floor would be a good option."

I grit my teeth. It's got my friends written all over it. They've been pushing and nudging us the whole night, since Jules forced our introduction, then Jean-Claude and Christopher hightailed it with her, leaving us alone. Then Margo sent me to the back room on that errand with champagne. Jules put me on Jamie-babysitting duty before her toast. Now Sula's got him following me after she must have seen me sneaking upstairs. "Those meddling meddlers."

"Beg your pardon?"

"Nothing," I tell him. "I'll go hide somewhere else." Standing, I reach past Jamie and feel for the small groove in the door that will give me leverage to open it. Except when I try to pry it open, nothing happens.

I try the door again, tugging harder.

And suddenly a wave of warmth, the scent of something much better than furniture polish and potpourri, washes over me. I shut my eyes for just a moment. Damn him. Why does Jamie have to smell like . . . like walking through a dense forest on a cool, foggy morning? Like sage and cedarwood and rain-drenched earth.

Swallowing, I glance back at him. He's standing close behind me, frowning at the door.

"What is it?" he says quietly. His breath whispers along my neck. Orange zest and bourbon, the cocktail he had.

I swallow again, feeling the room grow smaller by the second. "It's stuck."

"It's *stuck*?"

"Yes," I mutter sourly. "Thanks to you."

"How? All I did was shut it behind me."

I spin and face him, which is a mistake. It places our fronts flush against each other, and in this tiny space, there's nowhere to go. Jamie's sudden inhale makes his ribs expand, his chest brush against mine. I grip the wall as unwelcome heat floods my veins.

"If you shut it too hard," I tell him, not bothering to hide the accusation in my voice and trying really hard not to notice how my heart's now pounding even harder, "it jams sometimes."

"How was I supposed to know that?"

"You weren't! You weren't supposed to *be* here." I grit my teeth, battling frustrated tears. I just needed to be alone. Instead, I'm stuck in a closet with this condescending, pretentious, irritatingly attractive tight-ass whom I've embarrassingly spilled booze on not once but *twice* in the same night that my sister got herself engaged out of *nowhere* to someone I still don't feel sure I can trust.

And now I'm going to cry in front of him because I honestly can't take it.

"Are you all right?" Jamie asks softly.

I blink up at him, at a loss for words. Is this . . . kindness? From the cranky Capricorn?

He peers down at me. "Are you claustrophobic? If I need to, I can probably shoulder it open."

Shit. Now there's no chance of holding back tears. I was not prepared to be treated gently. Not by this six-foot-lots-of-inches prickly bespectacled pear. Not when I was hurting and I needed it most.

A squeak slips out. Another squeak. Then a sob that I stifle just in time, clapping a hand over my mouth.

"Oh no," he whispers, as if to himself. He rips off his mask from the top of his hair and tosses it aside. "Just . . . please . . . d-don't cry."

Sobs wrack my chest. I hold a hand over my mouth, but it's a waterfall now. The little makeup that I wear is a drip painting down my face. My nose is running. I am the portrait of emotional disaster.

"I c-can't stop."

"All right." He looks at me with so much concern, it makes me feel even worse. I cry harder. "What—" He swallows nervously. "What will help?"

A hug. A hard squeeze. But I can't tell him that. I can't ask him to hold me. So I wrap my arms around myself and tuck my chin, hiding the worst of my tears.

Suddenly he's closer, the heat of his body pouring over me. "Can I hold you—that is . . . Do you need to be . . . held?"

I stare at the ground. Self-conscious. Determined to handle this myself. But I'm shaking with the need for the relief that pressure gives me, the blissful calm that washes over me with a hard, squeezing hug. Reluctantly, I nod.

Without a moment's pause, Jamie wraps me in his arms, tight to his chest, like he understands exactly what I need. He doesn't rub my back. His grip isn't half-assed. The insistent buzzing of my skin starts to ebb. Already I can breathe a little easier, smooshed against him, in a vise grip, my ear over his heart tuned to its drumming beat.

He looks calm and unfazed, but that thundering *lub-dub* of his heart says he's feeling far from it. It makes me wonder, if Jamie is that good at appearing fine when he's actually freaking out, what else is he hiding beneath that pristine surface?

Well, it *was* pristine. Now it's a mess, thanks to me.

Pulling back slightly, I dab my eyes and nose, then paw uselessly at his shirt, stained with my mascara, snot, and tears. "Sorry about your shirt," I whisper, suddenly realizing how close he's still holding me, how everything in us lines up a little too well.

Jamie seems to have noticed the same thing. His breathing's changed. So has mine. Faster. Shallow. "What?" he asks, sounding dazed.

"Your shirt," I tell him, trying to take a steadying breath and immediately regretting that decision, seeing as it forces my breasts to brush against his chest. "I'm sorry about ruining your shirt. This one . . . and the last one . . . and your pants."

An almost smile tugs at his mouth. "That's all right. I came prepared."

"Very Boy Scout of you."

"You're looking at one." His tone is as serious as ever, but there's a faint sparkle in his eyes that's new, a warmth that matches the kindness he's just shown me.

It makes me wonder what might have been if we'd seen this side of each other first, if we hadn't started off so catastrophically. Looking at him now, I experience an odd, absurd hope that in some parallel universe, where the timing wasn't all wrong, Alternate Bea and Alternate Jamie got it right and are hidden in a little broom closet for the right reasons.

Silence fills the tight space, and it feels like the world spins as our gazes lock for a brief, suspended moment. Jamie's expression softens. The sharp furrow in his brow fades. The hard, flat line of his mouth surrenders to a faint lopsided tilt. But it's those eyes I can't stop staring at. His hazel eyes are a September night—bonfire-smoke rims, irises the color of golden firelight dancing on the last green leaves of summer. They are unfairly lovely.

This is so strange. I'm wedged into a broom closet with the guy I've done nothing but clash with all night. And he's holding me pinned against him. He's given me comfort.

I wonder if I've swapped bodies. If I'm now in that parallel universe, if we're Alternate Bea and Alternate Jamie, because I'm leaning into him, my hands sliding up his chest, as Jamie exhales slowly—a concerted, steady breath, grappling for control that heats me from head to toe. His grip is tight on my waist, tucking me close.

I have the epiphany amid the lusty haze that Jamie might not just be prickly but maybe a little promising, too. Maybe he's like my pet hedgehog, Cornelius. I just need to run him a bubble bath, then watch him unfurl and turn cuddly.

Shit. My brain is scrambled now, my legs noodly, picturing that.

Jamie's nose grazes my hair, and he breathes in like he can't breathe me in enough. I glance up as he glances down, and our mouths almost brush. Our eyes lock. Are we going to kiss? We're not going to kiss.

Oh God. *Are* we?

My gaze shifts to his mouth. His hand slips lower down my back and pins our hips together. He groans right as I whimper.

And the sounds lurch us back to reality, wrenching us from whatever the hell that was. Staggering apart, we ricochet like repellent magnets, Jamie smacking his head on a shelf as I stumble backward and make a pile of towels rain down on us.

"So sorry," he mutters, staring at me wide-eyed. "I don't know . . . I don't know what I was thinking—"

"Me neither," I whisper, my cheeks hot with embarrassment.

Before he can respond, the door flies open, Jean-Claude smiling triumphantly with Jules and a crowd behind him. "What is this, eh?"

"Nothing," Jamie says, not once looking at me as he steps out of the closet like he can't get out of there fast enough. "Excuse me." Heading straight for the stairs, he disappears down them.

Nothing. Even though it shouldn't, his dismissal stings.

I thought I couldn't be any more humiliated tonight. But, of course, Jamie Westenberg has once again proven me wrong.

· FOUR ·

Jamie

Home in the dark, I lie in bed, staring up at the ceiling. I can't sleep. When I shut my eyes, all I see is Beatrice in my arms. Those sky-blue-slivered-with-grass-green eyes, cloud gray swirling the perimeter. That delicate ink sweeping over her trapezius muscle, disappearing beneath the plunging neckline of her dress. The fabric cinched at her waist that my hands ached to unzip, to feel every rib, the slope of her hips, then draw her close and—

Meow.

I peer down at my cats at the foot of the bed, twin pairs of lantern eyes in the dark.

"You're right," I tell them. "Best to nip that thought in the bud. That woman is a tattooed tornado of flying cocktails and unsolicited astrological commentary. We could not be more different or unsuited."

And I almost kissed her.

God, what was I *thinking*?

"I wasn't thinking," I explain to the cats. "That's the problem. All the more reason never to see her again."

The cats let out another pair of *meows.*

"Well, that's a fair point. With Jean-Claude and Juliet engaged now, I'm bound to see more of her." I sigh and scrub my face. "I'll just have to stay very, very busy with work."

The cats have no reply to this. I have no answers, either, for this di-lemma or for what happened in that closet. We could barely hold a conversation before we were trapped together, and what we did manage was a model social crash-and-burn.

So why did I want to kiss her?

And why did it feel like she wanted to kiss me back?

Groaning, I shut my eyes and begin cataloging every bone of the human body. Usually it puts me right to sleep. A physician's version of counting sheep.

But even that doesn't work. Because as I name each one, I picture where they belong on Beatrice.

Clavicle. Shadows kissing her collarbones.

Mandible. Her jaw clenched, pursing her soft lips.

Metacarpal, proximal, middle, distal bones. Her deft hand clasping a champagne glass, assembling crisp crackers and snow-white cheese. One solitary finger sliding through her mouth, sucking off ripe Brie with an erotic *pop.*

"All right," I mutter to no one in particular. Definitely not to my cats, still watching me with disapproval in those eyes that remind me of another feline gaze, glowing with disdain.

I throw back the sheets and stand. "Time for a cold shower and refreshing my Latin."

FIVE

Bea

"Beatrice Adelaide." On a delay, I process the sparkling jingle that heralds the shop's door opening and the voice that just said my full name.

Glancing up, I frown at Jules. "What are you doing awake this early?"

"There's this thing called coffee," she says. "And an alarm clock."

Her smile is innocent as she saunters through the Edgy Envelope, Sula's custom stationery shop, which I manage and design for. But I know my sister better than anyone, and I sniff mischief on her as much as the pastry shop she visited on her way here. She's up to something. I don't know what it is, but after a week of poor sleep since that god-awful party, I'm too tired to force it out of her. So I slump back over the antique glass display case littered with my sketchbook and colored microtip pens.

Monday mornings are slow, and I usually spend them doodling, brainstorming new ideas. When a customer comes in, I simply slide my artwork off to the side, and no one's the wiser that Bea, who works at the register, is also the store's most purchased artist.

"He looks familiar," Jules says.

"What?"

She nods to the paper beneath my pen. "I said, he looks familiar."

I peer down at my drawing, then slap my palm over it. It's the profile of a person who's not at all responsible for my fitful sleep, whom I definitely haven't dreamed about every night since we were stuck in a tiny closet together. Whose hands wrapped around my waist, dragging me against his body, which I absolutely have not re-created in my sleepy brain or woken up to the thought of, on the edge of shattering relief.

Because I would never dream about a person who made me feel like dog dirt from the moment of our clashing introduction to his hasty exit, which made me look like a fool.

My sister's hand creeps toward my sketchbook, and I yank it farther away. "No snooping on my art," I tell her.

Grinning, Jules spins and wends her way toward my corner of the shop—the Prurient Paper Collection. She picks up a card featuring an intricate floral design and squints. "What's this one?" she asks.

"Hey, butterfingers, put the card down."

She flips it over. "Don't know what you're talking about."

"I can hear parchment paper crinkling in your pocket and you smell like a chocolate croissant. If you didn't nab one from Nanette's before you came here, I'll buy an underwire bra."

Laughing, she flips the card back again and turns it sideways.

"JuJu," I warn, "you smudge it, you buy it."

Sighing, she snags an envelope along with the card and brings them to the front desk. She slaps both down, leans her elbows on the glass, and sweeps her fingers through the delicate chains hanging from a necklace display.

I swat her hand away. "Must you touch *everything*?"

"Says the most tactile person I know. Now, tell me"—she taps the card with one perfectly manicured finger—"what is this one?"

I don't need a second look at the design. Once I conceptualize a piece, it's in my head forever. "It's a vulva."

"No, it's not!" She spins the card, trying to catch it at an angle that allows her to see the hidden design.

I'm used to this routine. It's been a year and a half since I expanded my work as an erotic artist, selling private commissions, to my bread and butter: the Prurient Paper Collection. An extensive line of card stock, stationery, and other paper-based art, my Prurient Paper designs include everything from lush nature scenes to abstract geometric art that secretly contains a sensual image.

It started off as a joke when I got outlandishly drunk one movie night with Jules, Sula, and Margo. Sula, who owns the Edgy Envelope, fell in love with the idea of a stationery line that you could gift to your pearl-clutching relative who'd never know what they'd been gifted, as much as to the lover you wanted to know *exactly* what you were thinking. Now it's the Edgy Envelope's bestselling line.

"You're so good," Jules mutters. "Think you can work them into my wedding invitations?"

We're already onto wedding invitations? She got engaged *a week ago*.

"No chance. Mom's too quick at spotting them."

"She doesn't mind, though. In fact, I'm pretty sure she wishes she could brag about you over ladies' card night. Even Daddy likes your art."

"Because he's hopeless at spotting what's in it and remains blissfully ignorant."

Jules smiles. "Exactly. So I won't take no for an answer. My wedding invitations will be Beatrice Wilmot originals."

I add her card to my tab on the store's iPad, which we use for transactions, and charge it to my account. Slipping the card and envelope into one of our slim recycled-paper bags stamped with the Edgy Envelope's logo, I peer up at Jules, who is indeed sneaking bites of chocolate croissant from her pocket.

"Well, now that we have this bogus purchase out of the way," I tell her, "to what do I owe the honor of an early Monday morning visit? Shouldn't you be sleeping still, given you and Jean-Claude were moaning like pandas in heat until three in the morning?"

Jules smiles sheepishly and licks her thumb clean of a gooey fleck of chocolate. "Sorry about that. It's been a while because our work schedules weren't syncing. And when I'm keyed up like that I get—"

"Really loud? Yes. Yes, you do. Now, let's move on from your sex life."

"Well, you won't have to know about my sex life much longer. Jean-Claude and I are going to start looking for our own place."

My stomach drops. "Already?"

"Don't worry," she says quickly, clasping my hand. "We'll figure out a roommate solution for you before I move. You know me—how picky I am, plus how tough it is to find a decently priced rental around here, it'll take a while for us to find something we both like."

I take a deep breath that feels like swallowing too-hot tea. "Right. Of course."

"We'll figure it out together, okay?" Jules smiles gently.

I want to tell her it's hard to feel like there's still a "we" when her boyfriend—excuse me, *fiancé*—is dragging us apart. But I'm probably just being typical Bea, reluctant to accept change, especially when I'm eons away from her priorities of marriage and babies and riding off into the sunset.

"Yeah." I nod and force a smile.

Releasing my hand, Jules smiles wider, then clears her throat and says, "So, why I'm here: I want to talk. You've been sullen since the party. Is this about what happened with West?"

"*Jamie*. And yes, it's your fault, all you hooligans. You pushed and nudged us together until I ended up locked in a closet with him!"

Where we came really fucking close to kissing.

I keep that to myself. I'm not admitting that we almost kissed before he thought better of it and bolted. I've been humiliated enough.

"We didn't plan that!" Jules says, searching my eyes. "Why were you upset? Did something happen?"

"I told you it didn't!"

She lifts her hands in surrender. "Okay, okay! You just seemed flustered. You still do."

"Because it was a terrible, awful, no-good, disastrous night."

Jules shuffles her foot, scuffing her high-heeled Mary Jane on the store's wide wood planks. "I don't think he meant to offend you by leaving like—"

"He'd just escaped close quarters with a rabid animal?" I offer.

"He gets nervous. Jean-Claude told me West is really hard on himself, and he gets anxious in social settings."

"Welcome to the club. You don't see me acting like that, and I'm socially anxious, too."

"No. You just throw cocktails at people's clothes."

I glare at her.

She arches her eyebrow. "I'm not shaming you. I'm making a point. You both had a bit of a rough start. That night didn't bring out the best in him. It certainly wasn't you at your best, either."

I have no comeback for that. Because she's right. Which is very rude.

"Let's move on," I tell her. "To what you really want, coming in here."

Jules gives me one of her long, incisive twin stares, a small notch forming in her brows. "I . . . have something for you."

Ooh, I love gifts. Hate surprises, though. "What is it?"

Her expression clears as she holds out her hand. "Give me your phone and you'll find out."

I slap a hand on my skirt pocket instinctively. "Hell no. Last time I gave you my phone, my lock screen changed to your only tattoo, and we both know where that is."

Jules bats her eyelashes. "I was intoxicated when I did that. Right now I'm sober as a saint, and trust me, you want this."

"Explain yourself, JuJu."

Turning, my sister examines the bottles of perfume lining the wall alongside candles and incense that are based on signs of the zodiac. I blame Sula for my newfound obsession with all things astrological.

"BeeBee, I know you don't like me to tell you your business, but there are some things that only the older and wiser understand. And I *am* older than you."

"By a whopping twelve minutes!"

"Firstborn wisdom is innate," Jules says serenely. "Twelve years or twelve minutes, it makes no difference." Spraying a mist of perfume, she walks through it.

"That's not even your sign," I grumble.

She ignores me, replacing the cap. "Listen, I just want you to be happy, and you're not happy. You don't date anymore. You haven't gone out in ages—"

"I'm happy *because* I don't date anymore, *because* I haven't gone out in ages."

Jules lifts an eyebrow. "Oh really?"

"Yes! That's the truth."

Well, the partial truth. I'm happy that my heart's not getting crushed. And my heart can't get crushed if I don't give it to someone. I do miss sex, though. I just don't want my feelings tangled up in it, not when they're even more sensitive than my body. Casual hookups are the ideal solution, but finding someone who's up for that isn't easy when I can't find it in me to socialize beyond my group of friends, all of whom are either partnered or pseudo-siblings.

In short, I'm backed into a corner: for me, sex generally happens in relationships; I don't want a relationship, and I won't do what it takes to have sex outside of one.

Inspecting her perfectly manicured nails, Jules says casually, "Okay, if you're so happy, when's the last time you got laid?"

I glare at her because she knows the answer to that. We're twins. We tell each other nearly everything. "You know I'm enjoying an extended abstinent streak."

Jules snorts loudly and drops her hand. "*Enjoying?* BeeBee, honestly."

"Okay, fine!" I mist the glass top with Sula's homemade cleaning spray and angrily wipe it down. "I'm happy *except* for the fact that I haven't had a lay in forever."

"Right. Which means you're really not happy at all. And that's why I need your phone. I have a solution."

I clutch the essential oil–based glass cleaner, hoping against hope. "You've found me a sexual partner who wants to do the emotionless mattress merengue with frequent reckless abandon?"

"Sex? Yes. Emotionless? Probably not. He doesn't strike me as the casual type."

My hope pops like a balloon shot out of the sky. "Which means you expect me to date this guy. And I do not date anymore, Juliet."

"You do this Saturday." She unearths her own phone from her jeans and leans away so there's not even a contortionist's chance that I can read her screen as she types. "Just *one* date," she says, before pocketing her phone, then holding out her hand again. "That's all I'm asking of you. Starting at ten a.m. The park bench across the street from Boulangerie."

I stare at her in disbelief. "I'm sorry?"

"No need to apologize. I knew it would come to this. You go through a bad breakup *two years* ago—"

"Eighteen months, I'll let the record show!" I breathe deeply through my nose. "Jules. We're misunderstanding each other. I'm not going on a date, not on Saturday, not on a bench, not at a bakery that's—"

"French?" she says sweetly, bopping my nose with the tip of her finger. "Okay, Dr. Seuss. Except you are. Because you're unhappy, and that's got to change."

I batten down the hatches. Gird my loins. Wear my scowliest scowl. "You are despicably pushy, you know that, right?"

"Of course I am. I'm the oldest."

"Not this again!" I yell.

"BeeBee, hand over your phone. I'm giving you his number. He's being given yours as we speak."

"What?" I sputter. "How could you just pass out my number to some stranger—"

"He's not a *stranger* per se." Taking advantage of my shocked state, she lunges and deftly plucks my phone from my skirt pocket. "He's someone who's right for you. A One True Pairing, I can feel it. Do you understand how many romance novels I've read? I know what I'm talking about."

"Well, with that robust expertise guiding you, how could I say no? This is absurd. I'm not going on a date."

Jules is already into my phone, fingers flying over the screen because her smarmy face works for my Face ID unlock. Damn near-identical fraternal twinship. If only I weren't incapable of memorizing numbers for a password. Every time I think I have it down, I get myself locked out of my phone. Numbers and names, they jumble in my brain, then drop through like it's a sieve.

I lean on tiptoe and watch as she types. "Ben?"

"Benedick," she says. "That's his middle name, but call him Ben. He'll know you by yours."

"I *hate* the name Adelaide."

"Which is why he'll call you Addie."

I shut my eyes and take another deep breath. "This is ridiculous."

"Actually, it's brilliant. Everyone agrees."

My eyes snap open. "Everyone?"

"Well . . ." Jules tucks a smooth chocolate brown curl behind her ear. "I mean, everyone agrees with me that he's a great fit for you. Even Margo."

"Margo?" My jaw drops. Margo is notoriously hard to please.

"Who's talking about my honey?" Sula slams the back door and drops her bag, which she hangs over the back of her bicycle. "I fucking hate drivers, by the way."

I peer at her over my shoulder. "Who almost ran you off the road today?"

"An asshole trying to make a point with his lifted truck."

We both groan sympathetically. Sula removes her fuzzy hat, rubs her buzzed cerulean-blue hair, and uncuffs her pant leg, which she rolled up for bicycling.

"I'm over it. Anyway." Sula smiles at me. "So, how are we feeling about this date—"

Jules clears her throat loudly, and something unspoken telepathically exchanges between them.

Sula smiles awkwardly, backtracking toward the office. "I, uh . . . I gotta get on the phone with the plumber, who still hasn't called back about that leak. Stationery shops and water damage do not mix." Then she disappears down the hall.

I turn back to Jules. "You guys are real subtle."

Jules sniffs, returning her focus to typing on my phone. "Okay, so here's the plan, Operation First Date with Ben—"

Except he's not really Ben. He's some guy I'm supposed to text, only knowing his middle name and that my sister and my friends think he's great for me. Who is he? And how does everyone know him except me?

Jules pokes my phone, sending it skating across the glass top separating us. "Text him. Today. Talk to him. All week. No outside details, in case it doesn't pan out. Just you and him. Get to know each other."

I glance from my phone to her. "You're serious."

"Very." She wraps my hand in hers. "Listen to me. I know romantic love isn't everyone's cup of tea, but I've seen you happy and in love before, Bea."

I flinch, hating the reminder.

"Love *is* your cup of tea," she says softly. "And just because you got burned once, doesn't mean you can't find the perfect pour that's just right for you."

"Wow."

"Okay, I stretched the limits of that metaphor. But my point stands. You want love. You deserve love. You get love."

"Well, that's all I needed to hear. Now I just magically believe in happily ever after again!"

Jules is unfazed. "Talk to him. Be yourself."

"Juliet—"

"Beatrice, I'm going to level with you." She leans her elbows on the counter and holds my eyes. "You are one of the best, warmest, dearest, most beautiful people I know. But you are so damn stubborn. You're lonely. You want a relationship. And you're terrified to give someone a chance. I'm trying to find a way to help you take that chance and feel safe doing it. Especially because soon, when I'm living with Jean-Claude, if you haven't found someone, you'll be alone. I hate that."

My stomach drops. There's a lump in my throat at the thought of those changes. "I'll be fine."

Her eyes search mine, smooth, placid blue-gray-green that we inherited from Mom. "I know you'll be *fine*," she says. "But life's too short to be just *fine*."

"You're a romantic. You're in love," I tell her. "Of course you think that."

I don't say, *When your heart gets broken, you'll understand just how damn important "fine" becomes*. Because I wouldn't wish that pain on anyone, least of all Jules.

"Bea, I know you. Deep down, beneath all that hurt, you think that, too." Straightening, she releases my hand. "Text him. If you don't, he'll be texting you."

I peer down at the phone. This is unbelievable. "I'm just supposed to text a stranger?"

"Not a total stranger, remember? He's someone I think is good for you."

Sighing, I shove the gift bag with her Prurient Paper card and envelope into her arms. "Get out of here."

"Yes, dear," she says, backing away, an impish glint in her eyes. "Remember. Text him. Be yourself. So when it comes time, you'll be comfortable on your date . . . ?"

"This Saturday," I finish wearily.

"That's right. Oh, and you know how Boulangerie has chess tables?"

"Sister dearest, please. I know every chess table in the city."

She smiles. "Apparently he likes chess, too."

"Hmm." I slide my fingers along the surface of my phone and mull that over. I guess he can't be all bad if he likes chess.

"Promise me one thing, come Saturday?" Jules says.

"What?"

She opens the door and steps across the threshold. "Keep an open mind."

SIX

Jamie

This is serious. Not even a week's worth of brutalizing runs in my favorite weather—foggy, cool autumn mornings—can make my head
stop playing a loop of what happened with Beatrice.

My hands are on the blender, which is whirring my breakfast into a
palatable smoothie, but my mind's in the Wilmots' third-story closet.
Snagged on the moment when I realized how close I was holding her,
when the world became the glow of her skin in faint light, the curves of
her shoulders and hips.

I still can't believe I almost *kissed* her.

Shutting my eyes as the blender whirrs louder, I remember breathing her in—a wisp of mint on her breath, the sensual spell of sugar-
sharp fig and earthy sandalwood that clung to her hair.

Jean-Claude shuts the front door behind him, snapping me out of
my thoughts. He winces at the sound.

"Feeling all right?" I ask.

He gives me a sour look and drops onto a stool at our breakfast bar.
"Too much wine last night. Coffee?"

I pour a cup and slide it his way. "Drink up."

He chugs half of it in one gulp, then sets it down and gives me an
assessing glance. "You should have come last night," he says. His phone
buzzes, and he pulls it out, frowning as he reads, then types a response.
"Juliet insisted on friends joining us, and some of them were of the attractive female variety."

"I had a patient emergency." It's my default lie. No one questions a physician when they say they're answering the call of duty.

"Bullshit," he says before another sip of coffee. "You weren't on call. You were being avoidant."

I pour my blender's contents into a tall glass tumbler. "If I *was*, I'd say I'm justified, considering the last time I was in a group social situation thanks to you, I ended up stuck in a closet with the same woman who'd already doused me in liquor. *Twice.* I had an entire wardrobe change because of her."

And you nearly kissed her, my mind whispers, *without overanalyzing, without worrying or second-guessing yourself.*

Which is nonsense. I only almost kissed Beatrice because I was . . . turned around. Holding her close, feeling her lean into the comfort of my arms as she broke down, it was disorienting. Like navigating an unfamiliar town in the dark and taking a wrong turn down a one-way street. Just because holding her wasn't entirely unpleasant doesn't mean that it was wise or that we'd make any kind of sense.

"West, listen. You won't get over Lauren if you bolt whenever you come close to liking a woman."

"I haven't done that. There's been no one to bolt from."

He pockets his phone. "Then this is long overdue."

"What is?"

"Dating again."

I groan. "Jean-Claude, no."

"West, yes. You need to date again. Have a fresh start."

"With whom, exactly?"

"Someone who's right for you. Come on." He holds out his hand. "Give me your phone."

"For what?" I ask warily.

Jean-Claude gestures to hand it over. "I'm giving you Miss Right's number. Juliet has the perfect person for you."

"I don't have time to date right now."

"No one's asking you to get married and settle down," he says. "It's just a date. One date. Juliet already set it all up. You two are scheduled for this Saturday, meeting at the park bench across the street from Boulangerie, ten a.m. sharp."

I gape at him. "You scheduled a date for me? Before even asking?"

"Well, technically Juliet did that." Spotting my phone on the charger, which is much closer to him, he lunges and gets to it first.

"Jean-Claude—"

"West." He punches the number into my phone, adding it to my contacts. "There. Until Saturday, text her. And no talking about other people. Keep it as anonymous as possible."

"Why?"

He shrugs. "In case you don't connect. Then you can part ways without it being awkward when you bump into each other again."

"I know her?"

He sips his coffee and gives me an enigmatic look. "If you did, I wouldn't tell you."

"This makes no sense."

"It makes perfect sense. Whether it's someone you've met or someone new, you'll get a fresh start and you'll have anonymity if it doesn't work out. Share only about yourself, become familiar with her. You'll do better that way, texting. No chance of your awkward silences, that stiff way you are in person."

"Of course. It's so much better texting, when I have ample time to overanalyze every sentence I write, rather than overanalyze it through in-person conversation."

He sighs. "I forgot how much hand-holding you need."

"We aren't in college anymore, and I certainly don't need you to wingman for me. I'm simply stating a fact. I tend to come off—"

"Cold? Stern? Exacting?" he offers. "Yes. But once you're familiar with someone you're not so bad. Just relax and be yourself."

"I can't believe this. You're giving me a strange woman's number. Worse, does she have mine?"

"She's not strange. Well . . . not too strange," he mutters.

"How comforting."

He gives me a look. "Juliet has passed along your number and your middle name, shortened. She'll know you as Ben. Keep it that way until you meet."

"What?"

"As I said, if you two stay anonymous until you meet, it's easier to end things comfortably should they not work out. Conversely, if you get along, you clear things up when you meet in person."

I rub my eyes beneath my glasses, massaging the bridge of my nose. "I already have a headache."

Jean-Claude slides the phone my way, and my curiosity wins out. I stare at the number, then the name above it. *Addie.*

"Addie. How does Juliet know this *Addie*? Or whoever it is for whom Addie is a pseudonym."

Jean-Claude scratches his jaw and glances off. "Oh, they have lots of history. Since childhood. Juliet swears she's been saving her for someone good—the right person. She thinks you're it."

"And she believes this woman will want me? How does she even know who suits me?"

Jean-Claude makes a very French noise in the back of his throat before having another drink of coffee. "I don't think *you* know who suits you. And don't say Lauren, she was terrible."

"She was exactly right. I mean, not *her* specifically, but her type. Organized. Even-keeled. In my profession—"

"Yes, yes." He waves his hand. "I know how boring you are about this. You think you need someone just like you, but you don't, West. You need someone who knocks you on your ass."

"That sounds terrible."

He sighs, standing with his coffee. "As long as I've known you, all you've done is play it safe. Try something new. See where it takes you. Even if . . ." He grins wickedly. "Even if it's just to work out some frustration, eh? It can be as much or as little as you want."

Halfway down the hall, he turns and says, "Oh. And . . . she likes chess. So, that's something."

Damn. I can't entirely dismiss a prospective date with a woman who likes chess. Groaning, I stare down at the number.

And when I settle in at the office thirty minutes later to prepare for the day, I'm still staring at that number. Sipping my green tea, I read through the first few patient charts of the day and try to avoid it.

But then I glance at my phone again, contemplating messaging her. It's a text. Just a text.

But it feels like so much more. It feels like I'm about to step out of my *Groundhog Day* life and risk introducing something new. Am I ready for that?

For nearly a year, life's been a blur of sameness, which isn't the downer Jean-Claude says it is, not to me. I love sameness and routine. And yet, maybe Jean-Claude's not entirely wrong, either. Maybe I have played it a little *too* safe. Lately I've felt the depth of my days' predictability wearing thin. Life's begun to feel a tad empty, a bit washed-out.

Perhaps I am a little lonely.

Even if I don't know precisely where texting this *Addie* might take me, I realize I do want to explore it.

Try something new, Jean-Claude said. *See where it takes you.*

I take a deep breath and type.

· SEVEN ·

Bea

Halfway through this quiet Monday morning, my phone buzzes.

I glance up from my sketch pad and read it.

NRB: Why do chess players use dating apps in Prague?

My phone tells me it's Not-Really-Ben, "NRB," as I've labeled his number. I wait to respond, thinking maybe his texts came out of order. But nothing follows, no predictable introduction, no formulaic *Good morning!* He's diving right in, which is how I love to communicate. My relief is a long, slow exhale. I don't have to pretend. I don't have to engage in mind-numbing introductory small talk.

BEA: I don't know. Why?

His response comes seconds later:

NRB: Because they want to find a Czech mate.

I snort.

Sula peers out from the back room. "Doing all right?" she asks, a grin on her face.

"Fine." I wave my hand and pocket my phone. When she disappears back into the office, I pull out my phone again and set it on the glass counter.

> **BEA**: You're going to get me in trouble at work. You made me laugh.

> **NRB**: Did I really? I wasn't counting on making you laugh. But I was told we have chess as a common interest. A relevant pun seemed like a solid opening move.

I smile.

> **BEA**: It was. That's a hard act to follow, NRB.

> **NRB**: NRB?

> **BEA**: Not-Really-Ben. NRB.

> **NRB**: NRB, I like it. We're thinking similarly. I have you in as PA. Pseudonymous Addie.

Another snort-laugh sneaks out.

> **BEA**: Pseudonymous? Fancy vocabulary.

> **NRB**: Too many hours reading in the weird and awkward young years.

> **BEA**: Well, you aren't alone there. I was weird & awkward as a kid. Still am.

> **BEA**: Speaking of weird, do you feel weird about not sharing real names?

> **NRB**: It's odd not to know your first name. Then again, this situation itself is odd. But, not bad. At least for me.

That said, if you're uncomfortable with this, we can
forget it. I have no idea how you got roped into it, but
I don't want you to feel obligated. And I can tell you
my first name if that helps.

I stare at my phone, weighing my choices. This is flowing easily so
far, maybe *because* we're not using our real names, because I have something safe to hide behind. Having a pseudonym makes a difference
mentally, because if things don't pan out, it wasn't really *me* he ditched.
It's Addie. I think I like him not knowing my name.

BEA: Let's keep the pseudonyms for now. Is that OK?

NRB: That's fine with me. We have plenty of time before
Saturday and can always revisit that decision. Assuming
we both feel comfortable meeting when Saturday comes
around.

I peer at my phone. This weird tension tugs inside me. I keep thinking about Jamie and that almost kiss last week. How ridiculous it is
that I got all hot and bothered for a stuffy starched shirt who ran out of
that closet like I was a communicable disease. Just goes to show how
badly I need to get laid, how badly *something* needs to change in my
love life.

The truth is, I'm a little desperate, and this is all I really have left. It's
not like I've met a bunch of other great candidates lately. I can't stand
the dating apps or small talk at a bar—all that socializing that rarely
pans out and even more rarely leads to sex that's anything to speak of. If
my sister and friends want to send me a preapproved date, should I really be looking a gift horse in the mouth?

BEA: That works for me. I do want to be upfront, I'm not sure how serious of anything I'm looking for. I know we're just starting to talk, but I don't want to mislead you.

NRB: Thank you for your honesty. I'm not sure what I'm ready for either. Let's take this one day at a time and stay open with each other about how we're feeling. It's a strange set up, and no one's to blame if it doesn't work out.

BEA: It's really strange. But strange can be good sometimes.

NRB: Is it too strange to say I already like talking to you?

I smile again and trace my finger across the words.

BEA: I hope not. If it is, I'm right there with you. ☺

I've decided I forgive my sister fifty percent. Enough to let her make me dinner while I sketch at the kitchen island.

"Your dino nuggets, madame." Jules lays down the plate with a flourish. "As Jean-Claude would say, bon appétit!"

"If he ever cooked," I mutter.

"Yeah, pot, that criticism only works if you're not just as guilty of relying on my culinary talent as the kettle. You're welcome, by the way."

I glance up and grimace at the four baby carrots she stuck on my plate, drowning in a runny puddle of ranch. "You foisted vegetables on me."

"Extra-crunchy ones," she says.

Sighing, I drag the plate closer. "Thanks, I guess."

"You're welcome, sunshine." Jules turns off the oven and sets down her garden salad next to mine, a colorful leafy terrain with dino nuggets prowling across it.

"I might have to take a picture of that," I tell her.

"Be my guest. It is kind of cute."

I find my phone, set it to portrait mode, and adjust the angle. Zoom in. Zoom out.

"Okay, Annie Leibovitz," Jules says. "Some of us are hungry."

I snap the shot, right before her fork crashes down, shattering dinosaur utopia. "Got it."

"So," she says around a bite. "Wanna tell me what's up your butt?"

I post the picture to Instagram with the caption *Might doodle this later*. It would be really fucking cute on a card, minus the dinosaur chicken nuggets. I could definitely hide a solo pleasure pose in the salad.

"BeeBee."

I drop my phone. "What's up my butt? The burden of existence? The cruel truth that to stay open, a business must be patronized by customers?" I plunge my dino nugget in a nosedive, straight to its pool of ketchup doom. "I had a long day at work. Too much peopling."

She shakes her head, spearing another bite of salad. "You really aren't made for customer service."

"Yeah, well, that's true. But if I stop working the desk at the Edgy Envelope, I'd have to go back to painting to make up for lost wages. And seeing as I can't paint to save my life these days, I'm kind of stuck."

Jules nudges my foot beneath the island. "It'll pass. Creative block happens to every artist."

Guilt hits me unexpectedly hard. It always does when she's being nice and I'm reminded that neither of my sisters knows the full story, that it's much more than creative block I'm weathering. It's the residue of a shitty relationship whose lingering grime I haven't quite psychologically cleared in order to be able to paint again.

Avoiding her eyes, I tell her, "I can barely even *draw* anything original the past few weeks. It's like my brain's just wiped clean of ideas. My greatest inspiration lately has been this chicken nugget salad."

"Maybe this date on Saturday, having a little romance, will kick your creative engine back into gear."

I snap a carrot between my teeth. "We are *not* talking about that."

"Have you been texting?" she asks, ignoring me entirely.

I pick up my T. rex nugget, stomp it across the table, and bash her diplodocus until its head falls off.

"Rude!" Jules flies her pterodactyl to my plate and smashes my triceratops.

"That one's my favorite, you butthead!"

She gestures to her decapitated nugget. "Excuse me. Did you take your hypocritical pill today?"

I dip a carrot in ranch and use it to paint her cheek buttermilk white.

Jules gasps. Then she fishes out a halved cherry tomato from her salad and wedges it onto my nose. "So there, Rudolph!" she crows.

"Juliet!" I screech. "I hate tomatoes!"

We're on the verge of a full-on food fight when our apartment's buzzer cuts through the air.

"I'll get it," she says, springing up while wiping her cheek clean with her napkin. I launch another carrot at her and miss by a mile as she presses the intercom button. "Hello?"

"Juliet?"

A chill runs down my spine. I know that voice.

"I'm sorry to bother you," Jamie says, "I was—"

"West, hi!" Jules says. "No explanation needed. Come on up!"

Heat rushes through me as my memory flies back to the closet. The almost kiss. His hands on me. The horrible embarrassment of him running off afterward. "Why is he coming up here?"

Jules shrugs. "I don't know. That's why I invited him up to fill us in."

"He coulda filled us in on the other side of that intercom downstairs."

She rolls her eyes. "I'm not making him stand outside like he's some suspect stranger. He's our friend."

"*Your* friend."

Unlocking the front door, she opens it a crack and grins at me. "You're blushing."

"Juliet." I fish out another ranch-soaked carrot, turn, and lob it at her.

Except it hits Jamie in the face right as he crosses the threshold. The carrot drops with a sad little *thud* to the floor, and a Rorschach splatter of ranch marks his forehead.

"Oh my God, Bea!" Jules lunges for a tissue, then hands it to Jamie.

Humiliation burns my cheeks. Standing, I sweep up the carrot and toss it in the garbage. "Sorry," I mutter.

"Quite all right," Jamie says, wiping his forehead clean. "I should have expected it. Seems like your signature greeting."

I whip around. "As signature as your terse condescension."

"Oh boy." Jules laughs nervously. "Be nice, you two. It was a little misunderstanding. That carrot was meant for me, not you, West. Bea's sorry."

Jamie and I stare at each other. How did I nearly plaster my mouth to his in a closet? That moment seems lifetimes away. He stands, mouth tight, eyes narrowed, everything so exact in his appearance that I want to tug his shirt until it wrinkles, ruffle his immaculate hair, and knock his glasses sideways on that perfect fucking nose.

Turning, he faces my sister. "I'm sorry for intruding. I seem to have misplaced my keys, probably left them back at the office. I'm locked out of my apartment, and I assumed Jean-Claude was here, since he didn't answer the buzzer."

"He got tied up at work," Jules says. "You can have my key for now. Let me go grab it from my purse."

She pinches my side, whispering, "Be nice." And then she walks down the hall to her room.

Leaving Jamie and me alone. Again.

Dipping my massacred dino nugget in ketchup, which frankly looks gruesome, I spin on my stool and face him. He looks around the room at anything but me, his jaw tight.

"You have some ranch on your glasses," I tell him.

He freezes, then slowly turns to meet my eyes. "I imagine I do," he says icily.

"You're not going to clean them? You just don't seem like a guy who wants buttermilk ranch rusting his hinges."

His left eye twitches. "I'll take care of it once I'm home."

"Gotcha." I pop the last nugget in my mouth.

"Are those dinosaur-shaped chicken nuggets?" he asks.

"And if they are?"

He clears his throat. "Surprising choice for an adult's meal. Then again, your vegetable is a solitary baby carrot drowning in ranch. Perhaps your regard for nutrition is like that of most Americans. Deplorable."

"It was *four* carrots!"

"Ah, but you only ingested three," he says. "Considering one of them hit my forehead."

"Here you go!" Jules singsongs, cutting through the tension.

Jamie takes the key from her and nods politely. "Thank you," he tells her. "Beatrice," he says by way of a goodbye.

"James," I mutter between clenched teeth.

When Jules shuts the door behind her, I whip out my phone, pulling up my text thread with Not-Really-Ben. We've messaged a little bit the past few days, but after this miserable reminder of how absolutely awful Jamie is, I'm ready to double down on our prospective date. I need to get that almost kiss and Jamie Westenberg's arrogant face out of my head. For good.

> **BEA:** I'm about to tear out my hair. I could use a chess pun right about now.
>
> **NRB:** I'd offer one but I'm so aggravated I can barely type.
>
> **BEA:** What happened w/ you?
>
> **NRB:** I don't want to get into it. Just someone who thrives on getting under my skin.

BEA: Dude. Same. I peopled for 8 hours at work, then just dealt with the last person I wanted to see. I have no bandwidth for bullshit after socializing all day.

NRB: Makes two of us. I'm sorry you had a day like mine, but it's nice to know I'm not alone.

BEA: I'm sry you had a day like that, too.

NRB: Well, let's salvage it a little shall we? Here's a new riddle: How does an Aussie tell you they're attacking your king?

I drum my fingers on the counter.

BEA: No clue.

NRB: Check, mate!

BEA: Wow. That was like dad-joke level bad, NRB.

NRB: It took your mind off your bad day for just a moment, though, didn't it? Maybe even made you smile?

I hide my phone as Juliet glances my way and wiggles her eyebrows knowingly. Damn it all if an outrageous smile isn't lighting up my face.

EIGHT

Jamie

Hours after my traumatic encounter with Beatrice and the Baby Carrot, my phone buzzes as I lie in bed with a book in my lap. Pseudonymous Addie's text lights up the screen.

> **PA:** Do you ever feel completely alone?
>
> **JAMIE:** Yes. Do you?
>
> **PA:** Yes.
>
> **PA:** But I feel like it's my fault.

I shift in bed, setting a bookmark in my book and devoting my full attention to my phone.

> **JAMIE:** How so?
>
> **PA:** I told you I'm weird, but it's like the kind of weird that doesn't have a home anywhere. It's like the way I am isn't enough of one thing & is too much of another. Sometimes I feel like I don't belong anywhere & if I was only more of this or less of that, I would. Does that make sense?

JAMIE: It does, yes. It feels like when I had a growth spurt and my pants were too short and my sleeves weren't long enough. All I could do was feel how nothing fit anymore.

PA: What did you do? How did you deal with that, I mean?

JAMIE: I figured out what parts of belonging fit me best, and now that's what I wear in the world. That's how I learned to fit in.

PA: Isn't that lonely, though? Don't you ever wish you just wore what you wanted? That you could belong no matter what you put on any given day?

PA: I'm a little tipsy btw.

PA: Actually, you can just ignore this. I'm sorry. I'm being like the texting version of the drunk stranger at the bar who sobs on your shoulder about their personal shit that you didn't ask to hear.

My heart beats hard as I stare down at her words. As I finally find my own.

JAMIE: You don't need to apologize. I like talking about this. Nobody wants to talk about it. Except me. And you, apparently.

PA: Promise you're not just saying that?

JAMIE: Promise. And to answer your question, it is lonely—wearing those clothes to fit in, that aren't necessarily mine but rather, something I've agreed to wear. But it's been a long time since I wore anything else. I think

I'd feel very strange if I did. I might not even know what else to put on.

PA: You don't know until you try, though, right? Maybe you'd feel free.

My heart beats harder, my fingers aching to pour out so much that I keep buried deep inside. I type my response but hesitate, deliberating if I'll send or delete it. My cats flop and stretch on my lap, one of them bumping me so that my thumb prematurely hits send. My humiliation unfolds as it pings a cellular tower, then lands in our messages.

JAMIE: I don't know if I've ever felt free. What does that even mean?

PA: I don't know. I guess when I'm misunderstood or lonely, I remember at least I'm true to who I am & I know who that is. That to me, is being free. That who I am is non-negotiable. That I am myself. Sometimes, I just wish that identity had a place among others.

I swallow roughly, my fingers tracing her words.

JAMIE: People don't like to admit to that kind of loneliness, but, for what it's worth, I think we're all a little lonely that way. Most of us just aren't brave enough to say it.

PA: Do you mean that? I haven't scared you off with my weeknight drunk existential crisis?

JAMIE: If you saw my face, you'd know you haven't.

PA: Why? What are you doing?

Bringing a hand to my cheek, I feel the forgotten lift in those muscles, the foreign upturn of my mouth.

JAMIE: Smiling.

———————

My phone buzzes as I turn off the shower. Running my hands through my hair to get the wet strands out of my face, I step onto the bath mat, then wrap a towel around my waist. My stomach does a somersault when I see who it's from.

PA: Notorious NRB. So, I told you I'm a creative-type.

JAMIE: You did. But you're frustratingly thin on details.

PA: Details are for 1 hr from now. There was a joke coming.

JAMIE: I'm all ears.

PA: Why are artists terrible at chess?

JAMIE: I don't know. Why?

PA: Because they love to draw.

A dry laugh leaves my chest.

JAMIE: Now who's devolved to corny chess puns?

PA: You started us off with them this week! I'm just bringing it full circle.

PA: Ack. I'm all wiggly knees & jitters. I'm nervous. Are you?

I stare down at my phone, scrolling through the past few days' conversations. Since my awful encounter with Beatrice and the Baby Carrot, and the late-night texts with Addie that followed, it's flowed, some days with more conversation than others, but always something meaningful. I've never seen her or heard her voice, I don't know her real name, but I feel an undeniable connection with the person on the other end of this dialogue.

JAMIE: I'm nervous, yes. Nervous-excited.

PA: I feel that way too ☺. I'll be in a bright yellow dress. You can't miss it.

JAMIE: I'm tall, but I'll likely be seated on the bench, so that's not much help. Navy blue sweater and glasses.

PA: Okay. I'm signing off. My hair looks like I touched a live wire. It needs to be subdued.

PA: Please disregard that last one & when you see me, imagine I always look this polished.

JAMIE: If it's all right with you, I'd much rather imagine the wild hair.

PA: In that case, maybe I'll show up au naturel.

A smile tugs at my mouth as I type.

JAMIE: I look forward to it.

NINE

Bea

Somewhere in the past five days, I started liking this Not-Really-Ben guy. NRB is a smart, funny, slightly-proper-sounding cutie who I'm almost skipping to meet. I'm even a few minutes on the early side. This is partly because I want to covertly-but-not-creepily scope him out from a distance. Also, because something about the way he articulates himself and how quickly he responds to our messages gives me an *I am severely prompt* vibe. I don't want to disappoint him by being late.

It's no hardship, the long walk from my place to the bench across from Boulangerie, soaking up the glorious morning, fall in her splendor. The world is a gemstone mosaic. Emerald grass. Amber leaves swaying in the breeze against a sapphire sky laced with diamond-white clouds. It's one of those days that I could sit down just about anywhere with my colored pens and paper and draw for hours.

But I don't have hours, I have minutes. So I keep on walking.

As I get closer, my gaze snags on a man seated on the bench where I'll meet NRB, a book splayed in his lap. A *zing* of awareness dances down my spine. He has a strong profile. Long nose, angular jaw, pronounced cheekbones. Lips that he tugs gently between his teeth as he reads the book cradled in his bent legs. He's really freaking hot.

Then again, he's reading a book, and that's always revved my engine. There are entire handles on Instagram devoted to candid shots of hotties reading in public. Humanity has spoken: reading a book makes a sexy someone even sexier.

I watch him as my walk slows, as I come closer to the bench. His posture is excellent, his clothing pristine—

Ohhhh no. It can't be.

But it is. *He* is.

Hottie with a Book is none other than Jamie Westenberg, parked on the very bench where, in five minutes, I'm supposed to meet NRB. My luck. My fucking luck. Of course, right before my nerve-racking date, I would bump into Jamie McJudgerpants.

I stop in my tracks just beyond the bench. Noticing someone staring at him, Jamie glances up, one finger holding his place in the text. His eyes drag up my body, widening as they meet my face.

"Beatrice?" he says hoarsely.

"James." I curtsy. Because I'm weird, and sometimes I do things like that.

He snaps the book shut and, without breaking eye contact, slides it into his messenger bag beside him. And then he does something I really don't think I'll ever forget.

He stands. Like I'm someone you stand for. I stare at him, so tall and straight, standing for me as my heart spins like a top. Trying to ignore that inconveniently swoony feeling, I hike my bag higher on my shoulder, but my eyes ignore the mental mandate and wander his body. Unfortunately, the great outdoors suits Jamie.

Very much.

Our interactions thus far have been indoors. I've never experienced him in the light of day. Never in the glory days of sun-dappled fall. And now I really wish I hadn't.

Because under the autumn sun, Jamie's dark blond hair is a stunning bronze, the faint promise of russet in the shadowy dips of his waves. His hazel eyes are emeralds slivered with gold, and everything about his tall, trim body seems even more statuesque. He's the stuff of sculptures I stared at reverently in European museums, of artwork that made me fall in love with drawing the human form. In nature's best lighting, Jamie Westenberg—I hate to admit—is nothing short of magnificent.

"Sit," I tell him, because *I* need to. My knees are doing their wobbly thing around him again. "No need to stand for me."

He doesn't sit. He stares at me, gaze wandering my body. I've been checked out before, but this isn't it. Jamie looks like he's trying to piece together a puzzle. "Your hair's . . . smooth. And your dress," he mutters. "It's quite yellow."

I touch my hair self-consciously, then peer down at my soft, swingy T-shirt dress, the color of goldenrod that's blooming all around. "Yes," I say slowly. "And?"

Jamie's gaze meets mine as he lifts a hand to his chest, splayed over his heart. "Tall but sitting on the bench. Blue sweater. Glasses."

The pieces snap cruelly into place as we both say, *"You!"*

Jamie grips my elbow when I sway, before tugging me down firmly onto the bench. His touch is gone before I can truly process it—the rough edge of his fingertips, the dry warmth of his hand.

"If you're in danger of fainting, put your head between your knees," he says.

I flop my bag onto my lap. "Holy. Shit."

Sitting after me, Jamie slides his messenger bag out of the way. He looks stunned, too. "So you're—"

"Pseudonymous Addie." I glance over at him. "And you're—"

"Notorious NRB."

"Ben?" I ask.

"Benedick," he mutters. "Family name. Addie?"

"Adelaide. Don't worry, I know it's awful."

"Beatrice Adelaide," he says. "Hardly awful. Try being a James Benedick and see where that gets you on the playground."

In very un-Jamie fashion, he slumps over, elbows on his knees, head in his hands, and rakes his fingers through his hair. "This is inconceivable."

A laugh jumps out of me. I picture the guy from *The Princess Bride* yelling, "Inconceivable!"

Jamie glares up at me, his hands falling. "You find this amusing? That we've been duped?"

"No. It was just that you said . . . Never mind." Staring down at my boots, I tap them together as emotions tumble through me, too many to name. One sticks out above all the rest—anger. I am *angry*.

"Those assholes," I mutter.

Jamie grunts in agreement.

"I can't believe it!" I tell him. "Jules is so dead."

"And Jean-Claude?" He turns, his thigh bumping mine. I grab two fistfuls of my dress, grounding the bolt of electricity that jumps from him to me. "I'm going to throttle him."

The last emotion, and by far the strongest, hits me like a wave from behind. I feel sad, knowing NRB doesn't exist. It's just Jamie. Prickly, persnickety Jamie. As the promise of Not-Really-Ben vanishes, so does my last bit of hope. After nearly two years of wanting to move on but not knowing how to, I had a chance of finally getting somewhere with someone. Now it's gone.

The final blow is Jules. My sister lied to me. Big-time.

"Why are they doing this?" I ask him.

"I'm not sure. I'm wondering that myself."

"How does pairing us up make any sense at all?"

"It doesn't. Unless . . ." He frowns. "No, never mind."

"Say it." I turn toward him, accidentally knocking our knees. "Tell me what you're thinking."

"You live in the same neighborhood as I do. You know how difficult it is to find an affordable rental. Jean-Claude's a very money-conscious type—"

"You mean a financial tight-ass?"

Jamie purses his lips. "I'd defend him, but he's not exactly my favorite person right now."

"So don't. Get to what you think they did."

"Well, they can't possibly believe we suit each other."

I snort a belly laugh. "Could you imagine?"

Jamie's eyes narrow. "You didn't have to laugh *that* hard."

"Excuse me? You're the one who just said there's no way in hell they actually thought we'd be good for each other."

"I didn't say it *that* way."

"Oh, sweet Jesus." I drag both hands down my face. "Can we talk without bickering for like . . . three minutes? I'm starting a headache already."

He sighs through his nose, jaw ticking. "Fine."

Silence stretches awkwardly between us. I pick at my cuticles and steal a glance at Jamie's wringing hands, his knuckles and fingertips, which are so raw, it hurts to look at them. If I wasn't on the cusp of giving him an epic wedgie right now, I'd offer him my grandmother's homemade hand salve, which works wonders.

Taking a breath, I rein in my temper. At least enough to ask, "So what do you think their reason is, if it wasn't matchmaking?"

Jamie throws a quick, fleeting glance my way. "Perhaps Juliet and Jean-Claude want us out of their hair. If you and I struck up a relationship, they could do something like ask us to swap places. You live with me. Jean-Claude lives with your sister."

"Wow. You're even more cynical than me."

He peers down at his hands and scrapes his thumb along a raw knuckle. "Worst-case-scenario thinking's my specialty." There's a long pause as he studies his palms. "I don't *want* to think that. It's just the most logical explanation."

"*Or* they think we're both too pathetic to find anyone else. We're like the last two kids in gym class, being paired off."

He sighs heavily. "I suppose I'd deserve that assessment. But you hardly do."

"What's that mean?"

Before he can answer, a car horn blares, startling us both. It draws my eye across the street toward the noise and the lazy flow of midmorning traffic—parents pushing strollers, partners walking hand in hand, the occasional cyclist and runner passing by. And that's when I spot them.

"Jamie."

His head inclines my way, washing me in that woodsy, morning-fog scent. He has a lot of nerve, smelling that good.

"What is it?" he says quietly.

I turn my head, nearly brushing noses with him. Neither of us moves away. "Across the street. *Don't* look. Just listen, then casually take a peek. Across the street, there are two familiar people wearing very poor disguises."

Jamie glances down at his hands, his thumb running over a crack at his fingertip. Then, slowly, he peers up from beneath his lashes across the street. A flash of irritation tightens his expression before he sits back and folds his arms. "What is wrong with people?"

"I really wish I knew. I don't understand them. At all."

Stealing another glance across the street, I observe Jules and Jean-Claude, arranged in a composition titled *Casual Betrayal*. Jules wears a ball cap, puffer vest, and leggings with fuzzy boots that she'd never be caught dead wearing otherwise. Jean-Claude's sporting a hipster flannel that's far from his usual preppy style and is almost unrecognizable thanks to—

"Did Jean-Claude dye his hair?" Jamie says.

"Spray-in white, like the stuff you use at Halloween."

"This is disturbing," he mutters.

"This is *unacceptable*, is what it is. They played us, Jamie. They played us like well-fucking-tuned instruments."

It's been years since Jules did something like this—pulled a stunt to get around my stubbornness. Everything she said at the Edgy Envelope on Monday rattles around my skull, and in some overly sympathetic part of my twinny heart, I want to just laugh this off and let it go, because I know Jules, and I know she thinks she's doing what she has to in order to help me.

But all I can focus on is the hurt. My sister and my friends, who Jules said were all in favor of this, playing Cupid—it feels like they're saying I'm undesirable on my own, that I'm helpless and hopeless without them throwing me at someone. I have to be manhandled—no, *tricked*—into coupledom.

And sure, I recognize I'm not the easiest sell. I'm not charming and sophisticated like Jules. I'm not adventurous and worldly like our little sister, Kate. I'm free-spirited in my ways and intractable in others. I'm a solitary daydreamer, often lost in my own world. I'm sensitive and easily startled. I have limits and boundaries that a lot of other people don't.

But I am capable of loving and being loved. I can share passion when the atmosphere is right. It just takes time. And after what happened with Tod, it's going to take someone special.

I'll admit that in my worst moments, I'm afraid that special someone isn't out there, and that looking too hard for them is going to confirm it. So, more often than not, I haven't looked. I've stayed in this holding pattern, tired of having so little but afraid of reaching for more. Which I recognize isn't particularly healthy.

But *this* is their solution? The people who supposedly love me best, understand me most, *trick* me into a date. And with someone who, just last week, reminded all of us how awkward and clumsy and terrible at socializing I can be.

The longer I think about it, the pissier I get.

"I can't believe they even tried it," I tell Jamie. "I mean, there are so many holes in this plan."

"Not if they counted on us being consistent, which . . ." He glances over at me, adjusting his glasses. Crisp paper-white button-up. Midnight-blue sweater. And those damn tortoiseshell frames that bring out the amber in his eyes. He's annoyingly attractive, and I don't appreciate having to acknowledge that right now. "I know *I'm* consistent. And I'd imagine, in your . . . way . . . you are."

I glare at him. "You have a talent for using very few words and still making them sound very not nice."

He has the grace to blush. "I only meant that your sister knows you well."

"Uh-huh."

"Honestly, Beatrice. Not everything I say to you is meant as an insult. I'm trying to convey that Juliet knew how to angle this so you'd go along. Same way Jean-Claude knew how to angle it for me. He knew I'd follow the rules he'd laid before me."

I see what he means now, even if I still don't like it. "Jules knew I'd be a sucker for the anonymity, to protect myself."

As soon as I say it, I want to yank those words out of the air and shove them back down my throat.

Jamie frowns at me. "Protect yourself from what?"

"Just ignore that."

"I don't think I will," he says. "Tell me."

We engage in a brief, intense stare-off. Jamie blinks first.

"Point for me!" I crow.

"Says who? No points awarded. I didn't know we were competing."

"It was obviously a stare-off. I won. The end."

He shakes his head. "I demand a consolation prize. The truth."

"Ugh, fine. If you didn't know my real name, and if you lost interest, it wouldn't have felt as personal . . . or as painful."

"I see." He glances down at his hands. "Well . . . Turned out to be a nonissue after all."

"Right. Since this is all one big joke."

Another stretch of quiet holds between us before he says, quieter, "I meant that, in talking all week, I didn't lose interest."

"Oh." My eyes widen.

Oh.

I'm still processing that when Jamie clears his throat, then glances my way. "This certainly is not what I was expecting or what either of us deserved." He stands and slides his bag over his head, onto his shoulder. "But I say we at least get a hot beverage and a game of chess out of it."

I stand, too, and peer up at him, stunned. All this shit our "friends" put us through, and he's going to let it slide over a game of chess and a cup of coffee? Like hell.

"I want more than coffee and chess, James." My eyes narrow at the matchmakers across the road. "I want *revenge.*"

TEN

Jamie

Bea sips her coffee from a bowl-sized cup cradled in her hands. I watch her through curling wisps of steam wafting from its surface, puffing a mouthful of air that swoops her long bangs out of her eyes. It isn't the first time I've thought this, but after realizing she's the one behind this week's messages, it feels riskier to admit the truth—Beatrice is very beautiful.

Even when she takes ten minutes to make a move.

"You really weren't joking about being a slow chess player."

She glares up at me. "I don't see the board easily. I have to think through my options."

"Take your time. I don't have hours of work to do or anything."

"James," she warns, finally advancing her pawn. "It's not my problem you're a workaholic. It's Saturday, for Christ's sake."

"Saturday is an essential day in my workweek."

"What do you do?"

Staring at the board, I consider my options in light of her move. "On the weekends? Everything that I can't get done during weekdays. Professionally? I'm a pediatrician." When I glance up, Bea's watching me. "What is it?"

"A pediatrician?" she says faintly. "Like babies and kids?"

"That is generally what indicates a physician is a pediatrician, yes."

"Smart-ass," she mutters, returning her focus to a paper napkin beneath her hand. She's been sketching, and I've been stealing glances, watching it unfold. It's unclear to me what it is beyond black slashes and curves drawn so lightly they don't tear the delicate paper. Even though its concept is a mystery, it makes me feel something sharp and intense. It makes me want to see more.

"What are you drawing?" I ask her.

She freezes, then slaps her hand over the paper napkin. It crumples inside her grip as she drags it off the table and shoves it in her dress pocket.

"No need to stop on my account."

A splash of color hits her cheeks as she avoids my eyes. "That's all right. My drawing isn't fit for public consumption."

"How so?"

She hesitates a beat, then meets my eyes defiantly. "I'm an erotic artist."

"A *what*?"

My expression must be amusing because a laugh pops out of her, bright and sparkling as confetti. "I'm an erotic artist. I celebrate the human body's sensuality through art. At the Edgy Envelope—Sula's place—I design card stock, stationery, and other paper-based designs that contain subtly interwoven erotic imagery. Is that a problem?"

"Ehrm." I blink at her. "No?"

I'm having a very hard time processing this information. Bea draws nudes. Erotic art. Does she draw herself?

Heat roars through me.

"That sounded like a question," she says, eyeing me critically.

"Apologies. No. It wasn't. And it isn't. A problem, that is." Except that my body's on fire and my mind's turned pornographic, picturing wet paint and bare skin and—

"Great," Bea says, wrenching me from my obscene thoughts. "Let's talk about why we're here. Because even after pounding a chocolate chip muffin the size of my head, I'm still pissed."

"I understand."

She narrows her eyes. "Do you? You don't seem upset."

I peer down at the board, advancing my bishop. "I'm . . . perturbed."

"You asshole!"

"What? Perturbed is what I'm feeling."

"I'm talking about your chess move, Jamie." She scowls at the board.

I take a long sip of gunpowder green tea, watching her examine her options. She's done for unless she—

Damn. She moves her queen out of danger.

"So." She sips her coffee. "You were saying."

I advance my knight. "I was saying I'm perturbed."

"Well, I'd be perturbed, too, if I'd just had a ginger scone with green tea." She makes a gagging noise.

"Excuse you. Ginger and green tea are a classic pairing."

She sips her coffee again, making a show of how delicious it is. "*Mmm.* Coffee is where it's at. Coffee and chocolate. Green tea? Ginger? They taste like hand soap and floor cleaner."

I pop the last of my scone in my mouth and wash it down with a long drink of tea. Bea watches me, revulsion painting her face, followed by a full-body shudder. It's so subversively enjoyable to make her writhe, I almost can't swallow without laughing.

"You're a strange man." Shaking her head, Bea analyzes the board. "So what's the strategy?"

"Well, you opened with a French Defense, so here we are."

"I'm not talking about chess, Jamie. I'm talking about the meddlers, who are entirely responsible for the fact that you and I are having a coffee date instead of avoiding each other like the plague."

"Coffee *and* green tea. Let's be inclusive."

She hovers over her pawn, then drops her hand, staring at the board. "I'm pissed. You're perturbed. But that doesn't solve our problem. My sister's so hell-bent on me dating again, she swindled me into going on a date."

"Same with Jean-Claude." Turning over the situation, I sip my tea. "What a maddening irony that we won't be safe from their pressure to date until we're dating again—"

"Oh my God." Bea's eyes widen. "That's it, you genius."

"What? What's genius?"

She bounces in her seat. "We have to convince them that their plan worked. We have to pretend we're falling in love."

"I'm not following. Why would we feign a romantic relationship?" As soon as the words leave my mouth, the logic slips into place. "Oh. To get them to leave us alone?"

"I mean, that'll be a nice perk." Her eyes glint mischievously. "We fake a romance to crush their dreams, James. Give them a taste of their own shitty medicine and show them how much being manipulated blows."

"How?"

Bea leans in, washing me with her soft, warm scent, which is unsettlingly pleasant. "We pretend to date, get them invested in us, convince them that we're blissfully happy. Then . . . ?"

A lightbulb pings over my head. "Then we break up?"

"Yes." She nods triumphantly. "Then we break up."

Sitting back in my chair, I run my palm against my jaw. "I don't on principle believe in revenge."

She rolls her eyes. "God forbid you step one tiny toe outside the line of your moral code, you curmudgeonly Capricorn."

"Would you stop with the astrological nonsense—"

She gasps. "Take that back. It's *not* nonsense."

I sigh heavily. "Beatrice—"

"You"—she jabs a finger in my direction—"could not be more of a Capricorn. Look it up. Prepare to be humbled, Mr. Rules and Regulations."

"Rules and regulations exist for a reason. They provide order and structure, they establish clear expectations and dictate appropriate behavior—"

"Which our 'friends' completely violated," she fires back.

"And because they crossed a line, we should, too? Two wrongs don't make a right."

"Whoever said that was never wronged badly enough. Rules serve the people who fit readily within their boundaries and gain an advantage in their being enforced. I'm not one of those people. I live by my own code, and I'm not taking this shit lying down."

I have nothing to say to that because we could not be more different on that point. Rules keep me safe. Rules are my security, the framework for my life.

An uneasy silence falls between us.

"I regret that I'm frustrating you," I finally manage. "I know we don't see eye to eye on this."

She glances back down at the board. "Understatement of the century. Whatever. It's fine."

I stare at her as she assesses the game, warring with myself. Should I consider this? Why would I bend my rules and agree to a plot for revenge—a plot that will routinely not only subject us to each other but require pretending to be in a relationship? Am I honestly entertaining a faux romance—a *fauxmance?*—with a woman with whom I've shared nothing but physical catastrophe and a dozen stinging verbal paper cuts?

Except this past week. Except those text messages. Ben and Addie got along, didn't they? Why can't you and Bea?

Damn that moment in the closet. Damn those messages and the smile I felt in them, the laughter I sensed in too many early-morning exchanges. Damn Jean-Claude and Juliet and their so-called friends for making this mess even messier than it was.

Suddenly, Bea's fingertip grazes mine. I nearly knock over my tea.

"Leftie?" she says.

"What?" I stammer. "Oh. Y-yes. Why do you ask?"

She lifts her left hand, revealing ink marks inside her knuckles. "Me, too."

Her expression is guarded, but this feels like an olive branch. I take it.

"It's a hard life," I tell her, "being on the wrong side of the paper."

"And door handles."

"Ten-key number pads."

"Ooh!" she says. "Bicycle brakes."

I raise my left arm, revealing the scar along my wrist from a fractured distal radius. I overused the left-handed brake that stopped the front wheel and sent me flipping over my bike. "Learned that one the hard way."

Our eyes meet for a moment, and a flush creeps up Bea's throat to her cheeks. She glances away, examines her ink-stained fingers. When her eyes drift toward the window, she goes unnaturally still. "Those gloating motherfuckers."

My gaze follows her line of sight. The meddlers are still there, now seated on the bench where Bea and I met. Jean-Claude's sprayed-white head is bent, thumbs moving over his phone. Juliet steals glances at Boulangerie behind dark sunglasses, her own phone in hand as if, not too long ago, it was subtly pointed our way.

"Was she *filming* us?" I ask.

"Probably," Bea says between clenched teeth. "Taking pictures. Telling the others."

"The others?"

She arches an eyebrow at me. "Last weekend at the party, you and I didn't cross paths as much as we did by accident. Margo, Sula, even Christopher—they're in on this."

I stare at her, stunned. "Seriously?"

"Very seriously, James."

My blood pressure spikes, a surge of rare righteous anger burning through me. I'm a chess player. I can appreciate the beauty of a winning strategy. But people aren't pawns, and their personal lives aren't games to be played.

"That's it," I tell her. "I'm in. I want blood."

Bea snorts a laugh, glancing my way. "Wow."

"I mean, that is, m-metaphorical blood. Emotional blood. Wait—"

Stretching her arm across the table, Bea rests her hand on mine. It doesn't escape me that it's our left hands, that it's rare for someone's touch to mirror mine. It's unnerving to have something in common with Beatrice.

"I knew what you meant," she says quietly.

Staring at our hands, I observe my actions as if I'm outside myself, not driving the command center. My thumb sweeps across her palm, tracing faded ink stains and calluses that are evidence of how much work art takes, how messy creating illusions can be. Bea sucks in a breath as my touch slides down to her wrist. She pulls away the same moment I release her.

"Perhaps it's unwise." I clear my throat and avoid her eyes. "Pursuing revenge like this. I can't remember the last time I've done something so impulsive or vindictive. But, God, will it feel good."

"Just think," she says, "the looks on their faces when we finally break it to them. It'll be worth it. It'll stop this meddling matchmaking bullshit once and for all. Now, what's our timeline? It has to be long enough to convince them, but not so long that we drive each other off the deep end."

"Sounds wise," I agree.

"We 'date' until . . . ?"

"Do you all have any traditional gatherings, where breaking up would make a real splash? Christmas perhaps? That might be too long, though."

Bea scrunches her nose. "Oh, God, no."

"I'm sorry," I say frostily, "would that be an insufferably long time to fake date me?"

"Honestly, a little bit. And don't act like you could stand fake dating me that long, either."

Fair point. "Thanksgiving? Do your friends have a gathering around then?

Her eyes light up. "The Friendsgiving party! Oh, that's perfect. Okay, so that gives us . . ."

"A little less than two months."

"Two months. That's doable."

"Agreed."

Leaning in, she says, "We're going to have to sell it. I want them eating out of our hands."

I steal another glance at the bench where our audience sits, texting their coconspirators, feasting on this elaborate joke. Soon, they'll realize the joke's on them. "I understand. I'm committed."

"Excellent. It's a deal." She offers her left hand and I take it in my own, the hand I've been taught my whole life is the wrong one to offer.

I try to ignore that it feels remarkably right. "Deal."

ELEVEN

Bea

Jamie and I step outside the coffee shop, blinking against the harsh late-morning sun.

While I've turned so that my back is to the road and our antagonists across the street, Jamie faces the sunlight head-on, squinting down at me.

"They're watching, aren't they?" I ask.

"They are." He hikes his bag higher on his shoulder. "I assume we should part on some kind of amorous gesture?"

"Yes." I can't hold back my smile. "An 'amorous gesture' makes sense."

He squints harder as the sun's light intensifies. "You're mocking me."

"I'm not, Jamie. When I didn't know it was you, I really liked your twenty-point Scrabble words. My vocabulary expanded *immensely* this week, thanks to Notorious NRB."

He glances down at the ground and slides his glasses up his nose. "Well. All right, then." A splash of pink darkens his cheeks.

"It doesn't have to be much," I tell him. "We're not going to make out or anything."

He peers up beneath smoky lashes that fade to a burnished bronze tip. "Good idea. Too much too soon would raise their suspicions."

"Okay. So." I clear my throat. "Here goes."

Taking a step closer, I sidle up to him until our toes touch. Slowly, I bring my hands to his face, cupping his jaw, the slight rasp of his facial hair tickling my fingertips. I shut my eyes, feeling with my sculptor's hands the angles and planes of his face. Then, while I have a sliver of courage still guiding my touch, I stretch up on tiptoes and press a kiss to his cheek. To his jaw. To the corner of his mouth.

Jamie's breath stills in his chest, tension coiling his body. And just as I begin to doubt what I've done, wonder if I've taken it too far, his hands slip around my waist, steadying me. Holding me close. He turns his face so slightly, until his mouth brushes the shell of my ear.

And for a moment, I forget why this is happening. I shut my eyes, imagining his mouth wet and warm against the sensitive stretch of my neck, his teeth grazing the line of my collarbone, leaving a long, blooming bite.

"They watched every second," he says, shattering the fantasy.

"Good." My voice is breathy and uneven, which of course has nothing to do with the fact that my skin crackles with energy, with the awareness of Jamie's body throwing heat and his despicably huffable scent.

He pulls away, eyes holding mine. "Goodbye, Bea."

"Goodbye, Jamie."

Turning at the same time, we part ways, back-to-back, armed and ready, like a duel in one of my hist-roms. Except while our personalities will always be at odds, now we're no longer in opposition, no *ready, aim, fire.* This fake relationship is our shot in the sky, weapons set down. Now, somehow, Jamie and I are on the same side. No longer *me versus you* but *us against them.*

I remember the brush of his thumb down my wrist, the warmth of his touch as I kissed the corner of that hard, uncompromising mouth.

Us against them is going to take some getting used to.

———

Walking down the street as fast as my legs will take me, I'm aimless and buzzing.

Where should I go, jittery from a flimsy kiss and hug goodbye, red-hot humiliation from being duped still burning in my chest? I could catch a train to Mom and Dad's. The house is empty. I'd have it to my-self. But the thought of a train ride right now—the foreign smells, the constant stops and starts, the threat of a crowded car—rules that out. I couldn't handle it, after such an upending morning. It's not like I can go to the apartment, either. I risk running into Jules, and I'm not ready to see her yet. I'm too upset.

My feet have a mind of their own, and soon I'm a block away from the Edgy Envelope. I come to a stop after crossing the street. Should I slip into work? Sula and Margo won't be coming back. Toni runs the place on the weekend along with a revolving door of college temps, so Sula and Margo can have some work-life balance.

That answers my question. None of the meddling matchmaker crew will be at work. The Edgy Envelope is the perfect place to be.

Opening the door, I'm greeted by the overhead bell's familiar tinkle as I step inside. Toni doesn't glance up, focused on a customer, with six more in line behind them. I glance around, searching for any of the col-lege weekend crew, but quickly realize Toni is on his own.

Crossing into the back area, I ask him, "Want help?"

"Are my white chocolate macadamia cookies the stuff of pastry legend?"

"That would be a yes."

Toni hands our customer a large paper bag, with one of his beauti-ful, intricate bows binding the twisted paper handles. Giving her one of his megawatt smiles, he says, "Thank you so much! I appreciate your patience."

I step in beside him and unlock the other iPad, punching in my employee ID, then password. After ringing up the remaining six cus-tomers between us, Toni and I slump against the glass display.

"Oof," he says. "Thanks for the help."

"Sure. Why are you here by yourself?"

"McKenna's out sick."

"Why didn't anyone text me? I would have come in to help."

Toni's cheeks pink as he pulls his ink-black hair into a small ponytail. "Well, you had your date and I didn't want to, uh . . ." He scratches his nose. Telltale signs he's hiding something.

I gasp. "You're in on this shit!"

"Okay. Just . . . listen." He stares at me very seriously. "They made me."

"They made you."

"Yes! Last night, Sula and Margo texted that you had a date and it was not to be disturbed. That's all, I swear. Does that make it any better?"

I glare at him. "It does not."

"How about"—he bends, then straightens with a plate towered in what I can't see but know by smell alone are the world's *best* lemon cookies—"now?"

"Oh," I say on a breathy sigh.

He whips away the towel that was covering them. "Made with love. And a little pinch of guilt."

"Yum." I pop one in my mouth and chew happily, buttery shortbread and tart lemon filling bursting on my tongue. "That little pinch of guilt really gives it an extra something."

Toni sets down the plate and takes one himself. "So." He waves his cookie. "How'd it go?"

I glare at him and shove another cookie in my mouth. I wasn't expecting to have to lie so quickly. I assumed he'd be out of the loop because he's the one person in our friend group who didn't originate with Jules. He socializes with us occasionally, sometimes for movie nights but mostly game nights, since his boyfriend, Hamza, loves to go out and makes lots of plans for them. On top of that, Toni's still very much involved with the local artists' circle. That's how he and I met, though we didn't really become friends until he got a job here to supplement his income. By the time he was working at the Edgy Envelope, I'd already stepped away from the art scene, thanks in large part to Tod.

The cookie catches in my throat. Just thinking about my asshole ex makes me choke.

Toni whacks me on the back. "Okay?"

"Yeah," I wheeze, extracting my water bottle from my bag and gulping until the knot in my throat clears.

Toni's eyes are tight with concern when I set down my water. "You seem upset."

"You would be, too, if you suddenly found yourself dating Jamie Westenberg."

"Who?" When I give him a disbelieving look, he says, "I told you, I know almost nothing, just that your date today was do-not-disturb."

I pull out my phone and hop on the web browser tab that may or may not already have Jamie's photo in it. What? So I did a little rudimentary internet search of the guy who felt me up and almost kissed me in a broom closet. Never hurts to make sure he's not an ax murderer.

"Oh, he's hot." Toni stares at Jamie's LinkedIn profile picture. And smiles. Broadly.

"Stop it."

"I can't." He smiles wider. "He's *so* cute. He's giving me straight-laced, starchy bachelor meets eyeglasses-model vibe. And I'm definitely getting a total-gentleman-in-the-streets, freak-in-the-sheets energy."

"What?"

"You know, he's all manners and politeness in public, but the moment that door closes, he throws you over his mahogany desk, flips up your skirt, and spanks your ass."

"Antoni Dabrowski." I scissor my thighs and flush from head to toe. "Behave yourself."

Toni takes the phone from me, zooming in on Jamie's photo. "Ugh. So adorable. He's totally uptight and wrinkle-free. *But* he also clearly hits the gym. Just look at those shoulders inside his dress shirt. Bonus point, glasses means he reads."

"Glasses do not mean he reads. They mean he has less than 20/20 vision. His wildly impressive vocabulary means he reads."

"Whatever. You get my point."

I steal my phone back, pocket it, then grab another cookie. "I do.

He's bookish-looking and hiding a rocking bod in the wrinkle-free dad slacks."

"So." Toni wiggles his eyebrows. "You said you're dating? Does that mean going on more dates and feeling things out? Exclusively dating?"

I take my time chewing another cookie, then swallow. "Definitely exclusive," I tell him, tasting the lie on my tongue along with that last buttery lemon bite.

"Well, I can't wait to meet him! I have a feeling he's going to be a keeper."

A wave of unease crests inside me. I force a smile and pop another cookie in my mouth. "Me, too."

TWELVE

Jamie

I'm not a violent man, but after what he's done, if I saw my roommate today, I'd be tempted to throat punch him. Thankfully, avoiding Jean-Claude is easy. He practically lives at Juliet and Bea's place, so I return home and spend the remainder of the day at the apartment, well into the evening, catching up on continuing medical education, burning through a few seminars and a lengthy article, until the laptop screen gets blurry and my stomach starts to growl. That's when I realize I haven't eaten since my scone and tea this morning, and there's nothing in the refrigerator.

This isn't my typical time at the store, but then again, nothing has been typical today. Not since this morning, when it was Bea who showed up at the bench across from Boulangerie.

I pause halfway down the grocery aisle, my hand hovering where my phone burns a hole in my trouser pocket. Anxious thoughts crowd my brain. Was I cold when we left? Should I have sent her a message since we parted ways? Why am I horrible at all this? And why is a ten-hours-old *fake* relationship already on track to be more of a headache than the last real relationship I was in?

A voice on the overhead speakers announcing a sale on ground beef snaps me out of my overthinking.

"No texting," I tell myself, pushing the cart. "No need to overcompensate. No reason to act like an overeager, lovesick boyfriend."

Because I'm not, obviously. Lovesick. Or her boyfriend. Not really.

"Talking to ourselves in the middle of the grocery aisle, are we, James?"

I nearly crash into the canned goods when I whip around. "Beatrice?"

She curtsies slightly, her grocery basket thunking with its contents behind her back.

"What are you doing here?" I ask her.

"Well." She leans in conspiratorially. "Probably the same thing as you. I unfortunately spent the day working after all, and now I'm buying what I need from the only grocery store within walking distance of my apartment."

Right. Our places aren't that far apart. This is most likely the store we've both always used. I just typically come early in the morning.

I don't say any of that because my brain's capacity is maxed out on her very distracting outfit. Bea fills the silence. "Maybe we've never crossed paths because we're on opposite schedules," she says. "I like a late-night run. It's quieter."

"It's a ghost town at seven in the morning," I finally manage. "I'm an early-bird shopper."

"Of course you are. Early riser. Early shopper. You probably crush a marathon's worth of miles, then pound a zero-carb smoothie before purchasing all-organic produce."

"One look at the open cadaver of someone who suffered from poor nutrition and you'd eat clean, too."

"Yuck," she says. "I'll pass. I prefer to live in ignorance."

I can't take my eyes off her leggings. They're covered in platypuses—platypi?—with little text bubbles coming out of each one. The first one I see says, *No nipples? No problem.*

Beatrice realizes what I'm staring at. She glances down. "Yeah, wasn't expecting to bump into someone I know. These are my repellent pants."

"Repellent pants?"

"Tend to keep the creeps away."

"Ah." I can't stop staring at them. "Platypi are mammals, aren't they?" I point to the text bubble I read, near her hip. "How do they nurse, then?"

She beams, all white teeth and sparkling blue-gray-green eyes. The world swims a little. That smile's a dangerous thing. "Instead of nipples, females nurse their babies through folds in their abdominal fur."

"I see." Bea said *nipples*, and I'm blushing like a schoolboy. I clear my throat, cheeks heating. When I tear my gaze away from the platypus leggings, I see she's still holding her arms harshly behind her back, concealing her shopping basket. "Bea, why are you hiding your basket?"

Pink splashes on her cheeks. "Basket? What basket?"

"The one you're holding behind your back."

"Oh!" She shrugs. "Pfft. Nothing."

"If it's processed food, I promise I won't say anything. I'm off the clock."

She arches an eyebrow. "Really? I can't see there being off hours from a lecture with you."

"Ah yes. It's a Capricorn thing, right?"

Another winning smile sneaks out. "Ha! You caved and looked yourself up, didn't you?"

"No."

I might have. Briefly.

"You totally did." She shifts the basket behind her back, wincing at how it's straining her shoulders. "Well," she says, performing an awkward sideways shuffle that keeps the basket hidden. "This has been fun."

Because her eyes are locked on me, Bea misses the free-standing tiered baskets of snacks. Tripping into it, she stumbles forward, but I lunge and catch her wrist before she hits the floor. When I pull her my way, momentum sends her tumbling into my chest.

"Shit," she yelps, her hands landing on my waist as she steadies herself.

A wave of her scent washes over me, and her warm hands burn through my clothes. I swallow roughly, begging my body to cool down. It's been a year since anyone's touched me. That's all this is.

"Are you all right?" I ask.

Straightening, she steps back quickly and nearly slips on one of the spilled snack bags.

I catch her again, this time by the elbow. "Easy."

"Right." She nods, breathing unsteadily. "Right. I'm okay."

"Good."

Our eyes hold for a long moment before Bea glances away. My gaze follows hers and freezes on the sideways basket, its contents spilled across the store's laminate floor.

A dozen cupcakes. Midol. Overnight pads. Two cans of Chef Boyardee. And—

Sweet *Christ*. That's the largest bottle of lube I've ever seen.

Bea yelps again, diving for her goods. I bend in time to recover the cupcakes and the Chef Boyardee as she shuffles the items she's clearly most self-conscious about deep into the basket.

"Thanks," she says, quickly taking my handful, trying unsuccessfully to cover the lube, pads, and PMS meds. "Well, this has been humiliating—"

"Bea." I step closer, dropping my voice. "I'm a physician. I'm not going to have a conniption at the signs of your menstrual cycle."

She turns bright pink. "Oh God, Jamie. You had to say it."

"What? It's a perfectly natural . . ." She's turning pinker by the second. Embarrassment floods me. "I'm sorry. I didn't mean to make you uncomfortable. I only wanted you to know—"

"It's okay," she blurts. "I'm not sure why I got embarrassed. I'm not ashamed of my period. I just get flustered around you—" She takes a slow breath in, then exhales. "It's fine. Let's just . . . move on."

Before I can respond to her, both our phones blare in tandem. Mine's a crisp trio of rotary telephone rings. Bea's is M.I.A.'s "Bad Girls."

We unearth our phones and stare at them.

Bea's knuckles turn white. "My sister is on such thin fucking ice."

Juliet's text to the group reads: Bowling at The Alley this Friday—9

P.M. sharp! I have 2 lanes reserved. Bring money for shoes & lots of competitive spirit ☺.

The replies pour in. Everyone is magically available, responding immediately.

"Well." I pocket my phone. "They certainly aren't making it hard to want to get revenge, are they?"

"Definitely not." Sighing, Bea rubs her eyes. "Before we got interrupted, I interrupted you. I'm all turned around. What were you saying?"

"Just that—" It takes a bit of courage, a slow, deep breath before the words cooperate. "Even though you and I are pretending, that's for everyone else. You can be honest with me. Frankly, it's easier if you are."

She arches an eyebrow. "You don't strike me as someone who wants Bea Wilmot levels of honesty."

"I realize I'm not the warm, fuzzy type. I come across as harsh when I don't mean to. I know that we got off on the wrong foot, and I seem constitutionally incapable of not offending you, but I'm not trying to, I promise."

She bites her lip and stares at the ground. "I just feel like you're judging me."

"I feel the same way about you."

"I'm not." Her eyes meet mine. Bea takes a step forward, then stops herself. "I'm really not. Live your best, clean-eating, wrinkle-free life. I don't knock it. Just don't look down on me for being different."

"I don't. Maybe that's hard to tell because I'm a bit uptight, but—"

She snorts, then schools her expression. "Sorry. Go ahead."

"But if we're going to do this, I want you to be comfortable with me. You can tell me you have your period and buy pads in front of me. You don't have to hide canned ravioli or grocery store cupcakes or anything else, Bea. And I promise I will do better at making sure you don't regret your honesty."

Silence stretches between us. "Okay," she says finally. "That's . . ." Sniffling, she dabs her nose. "That's cool."

Oh God. I made her cry.

The physician in me takes over, reasoning that if her purchases are timely, her hormonal pattern makes this the part of the month she's most likely to cry about anything. It's the time when comforting things—a cozy couch, a heating pad, a warm meal she doesn't have to make—are most welcome.

"Why don't . . ." The words die in my throat.

"Hmm?" She glances up at me, eyes watery, her nose red with the threat of crying.

"Why don't you . . . come over for dinner?"

THIRTEEN

Bea

I'm starting to worry that I hit my head when I got out of bed this morning. Maybe I haven't woken up and the whole day has been one big trippy dream.

Except that when I came home from work to my sister singing in the shower, the ache in my chest because of her dishonesty was painfully real. When I hid in my room after slapping a highly mature, handwritten DO NOT DISTURB sign on my bedroom door, and wallowed in self-pity, that was real, too. And then, when a twinge of pain started in my stomach followed by the familiar discomfort of Aunt Flo paying her monthly visit, that was definitely real. Real enough to send me to the grocery store in platypus pants, embarrassing myself in front of Jamie Westenberg.

Jamie Westenberg, who's offering me dinner. Being . . . *nice*.

It's hard to deny that everything else has been real up to when I tripped on the snack stand. Maybe *that's* when I knocked my head.

"You're inviting me . . . to dinner," I repeat skeptically.

Jamie clears his throat, then slides his glasses up his nose. "Well, yes. Late dinner, unfortunately, but dinner nonetheless." He searches my expression. "Don't look so horrified. I can cook, you know."

"Okay, cool your breeches, Sir West. I just have a little whiplash. This is a one-eighty."

His jaw tics. He adjusts his watch until the face is equidistant between his wrist bones. "I'm just being practical. If you come back with me now, you can put up your feet while I make some dinner. Then we can discuss fake relationship strategy, in light of this"—he pats his pocket where he stashed his phone—"latest development."

I stare down at my platypus leggings, nerves knotting my stomach worse than any period cramps. I'm a disaster magnet who'll sully his spotless kitchen. We'll bicker. He'll make me feel even crappier after this crappy day. I don't even know why he's inviting me in the first place. Maybe he feels bad for me, traipsing around with period essentials in leggings covered with talking aquatic mammals.

Yeah, I don't need that energy in my life.

"You don't have to have me over," I tell him. "I'm sure you're beat. You worked all day."

He removes a microscopically small piece of lint from his sweater. It's as pristine as it was this morning. Does he exist in a vacuum of perfection? Does he change into fresh duplicate clothes halfway through the day?

Shit, now I'm imagining him unbuttoning his shirt. Crisp cotton slipping off his taut pecs and rounded shoulder muscles—

"You worked, too," he says, popping the bubble of my lusty thoughts.

I did. Toni and I nearly collapsed when we locked up the Edgy Envelope. "Yeah, but I sold stationery. You saved babies."

An almost smile cracks his mouth. "I stared at a screen for nine hours."

"Paperwork? Don't you have admins for that?"

"I do, and they're invaluable. But this is CME—continuing medical education—that I have to log in order to maintain my license and remain qualified to practice medicine." He clears his throat. "At any rate, this coming week is incredibly busy for me. With the bowling outing ahead of us, which I assume we'll be attending—"

"Oh, we're attending," I tell him. "Are you any good?"

He lifts a shoulder. Lord, even his shrugs are neat. "I'm passable."

"Excellent. Then we won't have to cheat."

His mouth twitches with another almost smile. "We won't have to cheat, no. Not that I know how one cheats at bowling. But if we want a prayer of passing as a burgeoning couple and not just a solid bowling duo, this might be my only night to solidify our approach because of the busy week ahead. I apologize, it's not always this way."

"Jamie, it's okay. I'm not . . ." I glance around and lower my voice because knowing our luck, if I were loud, Jules and Jean-Claude would jump out of the canned goods shelf and bust our plan. "I'm not really your girlfriend. You don't owe me time or explanations."

He glances away. "Right. I only meant . . . That is . . . What I meant—"

I don't know why I reach out toward him, except that I feel guilty, like maybe I misread him, or he's misread me. He's struggling with this conversation. If anyone can empathize, it's me.

As an autistic person, I work my ass off to function in a social system that is not intuitive. A system whose patterns I have had to learn and do my best to observe without breaking myself. It's harder with new, unfamiliar people, but it's even hard sometimes with the people I know and love. Some days, no matter who it is, I struggle, not unlike the way it seems Jamie's struggling now.

So I reach out, and my fingers brush his. I clasp his hand in mine, squeezing gently. "Sorry. I didn't mean to shut you down there. You were being considerate, explaining yourself. I shouldn't crap on that."

The tension in his shoulders dissolves. "I don't want you to think I expect you to bend around my schedule. It's not always this demanding."

The kindness of his words jolts me. I pull away and form fists with my hands, as if that will extinguish the sparks dancing beneath my skin. "Thanks, I appreciate that. But so you know, everyone at the stationery shop is pretty nice about changing shifts and covering each other in a pinch, so I have flexibility. I don't mind working around your schedule when you need me to."

He blinks rapidly, a deep groove etched in his brow, like I've confused him, saying that. "Well . . . thank you." He returns his hands to the shopping cart. I watch his knuckles turn white. "Right. Shall we check out, then?"

I cannot get enough of his speech. *Shall we?* He sounds straight from the tower of historical romances on my nightstand, and it makes me smile in spite of myself. I hoist the basket tighter in my arms, value-sized lube and overnight pads for all to see. "I believe we shall."

As Jamie shuts the door to his apartment behind me, two hefty furballs amble toward us, emitting *meows* that are more like howls of the dying. Or maybe they *are* dead. And haunting us. Zombie cats. That's it. They have that undead sway going on.

"What's up with the fur babies?" I ask.

Jamie strolls past me, arms laden with reusable bags—of course—and sets them carefully on the counter. The cats lumber past me and twine around his legs, throwing me suspicious feline glances.

"What about them?" he says.

I watch them warily. One is gray with misty pale blue eyes, the other with mint green irises and long white fur. Their stares bore into me. "They seem a little . . . hostile?"

"Hardly. They're easygoing seniors." Unpacking a bag of produce, Jamie sets everything in a neat pile by type on the counter.

"Have you had them since they were kittens?"

"Not as such. They're fairly recent additions."

"So they're the old cats from the shelter that nobody wanted and were about to get euthanized." Sweet Jesus, if he rescued these cats—

Jamie clears his throat, then says, "In a manner of speaking, yes."

Dammit. First, he's a baby doctor. Now, he rescues zombie cats in their hour of undead need. Ugh.

Then it gets worse. He grabs the back of his sweater and drags it off, temporarily ruffling those tidy bronze waves. He smooths down his hair, then unbuttons his cuffs and proceeds to roll the sleeves up to his forearms. Flicking on the water, he scrubs his hands in a way that I can tell is his habit, staring off, following an order of operations that reveals veins and tendons beneath a faint dusting of bronze-blond hair. My knees wobble a little.

Jesus Christmas, fortify, Beatrice!

Marching up to the sink, I step in and wash my hands after him, then reach to take over rinsing the produce. "I'll handle this," I tell him. "You do your culinary thing."

He frowns at me. "You're sure? You're feeling unwell and—"

"Jamie." I nudge him with my hip. "I've dealt with this every month for fourteen years. I'm a pro. Doing something is a good distraction. And I promise, I won't blow anything up. No glass to shatter, no liquids to spill. Just vegetables to wash. I'm fine. Go. Chef away."

Searching my eyes for a moment, he does another one of his gentlemanly nods. "If you insist." Then he turns with an armful of perishables toward the fridge.

I do not stare at his butt, tight and round and high inside his wrinkle-free dad slacks.

Well, not too long.

The gray cat hisses at me. I'm totally busted.

I've got to cool it. I need to stop getting swept up in this bizarre attraction I feel for Jamie. So what if he's my wet dream of a jock's body with silver-screen Gregory Peck glasses and good looks? So what if he takes care of babies and rescues geriatric cats and says adorable shit like *Shall we?* And *If you insist?*

He's my inverse, so unlike me it's comical. I have no business daydreaming about getting on my knees and turning Mr. Prim and Proper into a swearing, disheveled mess. The fantasizing has to stop.

While my mind has decided it's time to cease and desist with ogling Jamie, my eyes have not gotten the memo. They travel him hungrily. His broad shoulders. The muscles in his back, straining against his shirt as he reaches inside the refrigerator. His awesome butt, and those long, strong legs.

"Ouch!" I glare down at the white cat, whose nails have sunk into my platypus leggings. "Okay," I tell it. "Hint taken!"

Hissing at me as it retracts its claws, the cat levels me with a menacing green-eyed glare. If it could lift its paw and do the *I've got my eyes on you* move, it would. I stick out my tongue in retaliation. Turning with a flourish, it lifts its tail and flashes me its asshole. It's one hundred percent intentional.

"The cats are seriously territorial, James."

He shuts the fridge door and gently crouches. Oh, for shit's sake. His leg muscles press against his slacks. I have to turn away not to stare at the juncture of his thighs.

With my back to Jamie, I hear the soft purr they give him, the quiet sounds of him scratching under their chins.

"They're just old and settled in their ways," he says, straightening and rejoining me at the counter.

"And you adopted them why, again?"

Jamie's brow furrows as he concentrates on unpacking the last of the groceries. "There are too many cats without homes, and ethically, it reasons that the first to be adopted should be the ones whose lives are on the line. It's a practical thing to do."

I fight a smile. "Of course. Very practical."

"Precisely." A beat of silence holds between us as he sorts through the items he's set on the counter. "And . . . I was a little lonely."

My stomach knots. I peer over at him, water pouring over my hands and the green pepper I'm holding. "I got my hedgehog because I was lonely, too."

He glances my way but avoids my eyes, gently taking the pepper from my hand. "A hedgehog? Sounds dangerous. All those needles."

"On the surface, Cornelius might seem daunting. But prickly things often turn out to have the softest insides."

Jamie's eyes meet mine. "How did you figure that out?"

"Time," I tell him. "And patience. And bubble baths."

He almost laughs, but the sound stays subdued, warm and rumbly in his throat. "Bubble baths, eh? I wish that worked for me, but these two won't hear talk of a bath."

"Do you and the cats get along?" I ask.

The gray one gives me death eyes. Then she bares her needle teeth. I shudder.

"We do," Jamie says, calling me back from his cat's telepathic death threats. "They don't seem to mind that I have long hours periodically. I keep the heat on the high side and they have cat beds set in the south-facing windows, so they get as much sun to nap in as possible. They seem happy enough when I'm home."

"They totally sleep with you, don't they?"

An almost smile tugs at his mouth. "We may cuddle in bed some-times."

As I set the last of the rinsed produce on a towel to dry, I watch Jamie sorting his ingredients, the exact, ordered manner of his move-ments. Everything about him feels precise and deliberate. It makes me curious if there's a wild side tucked away in one of those crisp emo-tional pockets. It makes me a *teensy* bit determined to find out.

"You look like you're plotting," he says, selecting a cookbook from a thin shelf overhead. "Strategizing for what's ahead?"

"Something like that."

Our gazes snag. Jamie breaks eye contact first, clearing his throat. "Well. Why don't you go relax now?"

"I'd rather have a cupcake."

He bites back something, then clears his throat again. "If you must. Though, fair warning, if you take it to the sofa, Sir Galahad and Mor-gan le Fay will probably come meowing for it."

"I'm sorry, *what* are their names?"

Then it happens. It actually happens. Jamie smiles. It's soft and small and crooked, but it's there. I watch it unfurl, and my heart morphs into a gilded balloon that bursts, a shower of gold-leaf glitter sparkling in my chest.

"I was fascinated with Arthurian legend as a kid," he says, leafing through the cookbook. "I always wanted cats to name Sir Galahad and Morgan le Fay. But we were only allowed dogs named boring things like Bruno and Jasper—"

"*Jasper?*"

"Don't look at me. I didn't get to name them. With these cats, this is my first chance."

I peer up at him, the last golden flurries settling beneath my ribs. "That's adorable."

"It's a bit juvenile, but it made me happy." He shrugs. I've decided it's called a Jamie Shrug. One neat lift of his shoulder.

Opening the cupcake container, I pull out two, then set one in front of him. "Cheers to that." I knock our cupcakes together before taking a hefty bite. "Better late than never to make childhood dreams come true."

He frowns at the cupcake. "I don't eat sweets before dinner. No judgment, facts. You shouldn't, either—it's hard on the endocrine system."

"I make my endocrine system earn its keep." Smiling around my bite, I lick icing caught at the corner of my mouth. "They're pretty delicious if you want to keep your pancreas on its toes. No pressure to bend the rules a little, but if you do, I won't tell a soul."

Jamie stares at my mouth before his gaze dances up and meets mine. I watch hesitation play out before he makes his decision.

"Well," he finally says, carefully peeling back the paper, "I suppose one predinner cupcake won't hurt."

"That's the spirit."

He grins. A crooked, soft Jamie grin that once again fills my heart to a shimmering, golden *pop*. "I have a feeling you're going to be a bad influence, Beatrice."

"Ah, James," I tell him through the buttercream sweetness lighting up my tongue. "Now you're catching on."

· FOURTEEN ·

Jamie

God's looking out for me on Friday, because no patients arrive too late, no evening appointments run long, and when I finally make my way home, my wristwatch reassures me that I won't be late to bowling.

After sanitizing with a scalding shower and a change of clothes, I gather what I need, throw on a jacket, and rush downstairs. I check my watch again—eight thirty. Enough time to walk over to Bea's and catch a cab to the Alley together.

> **JAMIE:** I'm on time. Headed your way. Can I order a cab?
>
> **BEA:** Yep. All set to go.
>
> **JAMIE:** As in truly, really, all ready to go?
>
> **BEA:** If you're implying that because I'm a chick, I can't get myself ready on time, that's pretty sexist.
>
> **BEA:** On second thought, why don't you schedule that cab for 8:50.

Once I've ordered the taxi, I pocket my phone and enjoy the walk to Bea's, taking in dusk's cool lilac and pale pink streaks. As soon as I buzz, she lets me in.

Two flights of stairs later, I cross the landing. Her door is wide open, mellow funk music wafting from it, along with a faint thudding

sound whose origins I honestly can't begin to guess. I shut the door behind me and quickly have my answer.

"Hi," Bea says around something clenched in her teeth. She hops on
one foot before she sets it down and slams her heel. "Damn boots."

I'd like to say I'm looking at the boots, but I'm not. I'm staring at
her legs—pale skin, long muscles. The curve of her calf, her flexing
thigh muscle that disappears beneath a fluttery black dress covered in
tiny flowers.

"Don't worry," Bea says, misreading my speechlessness. "I'm wearing shorts underneath. Your fake girlfriend won't be flashing anyone
tonight."

"Right," I croak.

Bea doesn't notice. She's grumbling around her food, still stomping
her foot.

"Here." Closing the space between us, I kneel and pat my thigh.
When she does nothing, I glance up at her. "Bea?"

Ripping from her teeth what I now recognize as half of an everything bagel—judging by the sesame and poppy seeds raining down on
me—Bea blinks slowly. "I, uh . . . don't want to get your jeans dirty. *Are*
you wearing jeans? For real? Or are these jean-look-alike chinos?"

My eyes narrow to a glare. "Very funny."

"I'm serious! Whoa." She squeaks as I lift her foot and plop it on my
thigh. "I couldn't even picture you in jeans until now. Jamie in jeans is
like Bea in polyester. It doesn't exist."

"I wear jeans, Beatrice," I mutter, undoing the laces. "These are a
mess. How did you expect to actually get your foot past them?"

"Sheer determination," she says around the bagel.

"Mm-hmm. Clearly that was working well."

"Ah, there he is. Señor Sanctimony."

I tug on the laces harder than strictly necessary, making Bea wobble
and slap a hand on my shoulder to steady herself. Suddenly she's closer,
splayed wide as her foot rests on my leg. My face is level with the juncture of her thighs, and it's much too easy to imagine it. Hiking her

dress past her hips, wrapping one of those long legs over my shoulder, then burying my face in her—

"You okay down there?" she asks.

Averting my gaze, I pray my cheeks haven't turned red-hot as I loosen the laces. "Just shocked you didn't break something, jamming your foot like this," I tell her as the boot now slips on easily. "Some things shouldn't be forced." Setting one foot down, I pick up the other, repeating the process. "For example, combat boots with as much give as my dress shirts."

"Well, at least you know yourself," she says. "Were you rushing to get here? You're breathing heavily."

I'm breathing heavily, I almost tell her, *because I'm on my knees in front of you and not nearly uncomfortable enough about it.*

"I worked late," I tell her. "So I had to rush a little. But it's fine."

"Don't doctor offices close at dinnertime?"

When I hesitate, Bea tries to pull her foot away. Stopping her progress, I grip her ankle and fail to ignore the warmth of her skin beneath my touch.

"I rotate with a handful of physicians who offer care, free of charge, at shelters around the city on weeknights. This past week was my rotation."

Her eyes widen. "Oh. Wow."

I hold my breath, waiting for some backhanded compliment about my moral superiority. But nothing comes. When I glance up at Bea, she's staring at me curiously. She pops the last of the bagel in her mouth and dusts off her hands. I brush away the poppy seeds that land on my jeans.

"My bad," she says, wetting her finger, then using it to catch errant crumbs on her chest.

I force myself to look away.

"Why didn't you tell me?" she says. "About the medical moonlighting? Seems like one of the essential facts you should have shared over cupcakes."

I thread the laces quickly up the hooks on her first boot, setting it down, then alternating the other foot onto my thigh. "It didn't seem pertinent to our arrangement."

My hand curves around her ankle, sliding along the tight stretch of her Achilles tendon as I straighten her boot.

She sucks in a breath. "Getting handsy there, Doc. I'm not here to be examined."

"Probably wouldn't be a bad idea," I tell her as I lace her up. "As I said, you might have sustained podiatric trauma when you slammed your feet repeatedly into a boot that wasn't open wide enough to take it." I curve my fingers further, circling her ankle. "Posterior malleolus feels intact. Fibula. Medial malleolus as well. Lateral malleolus." My thumb presses the tender front of her foot and slides up to her shin. "Talus. All right as rain."

She narrows her eyes at me. "Show-off. I bet that's how you rope all the ladies, with that Dr. McDreamy act."

I finish her laces with tight double knots. And before I can tell her I've never touched a woman this way, never wanted to feel the paradoxical strength and fragility of the bones that make her being, my phone buzzes. I pull it out of my pocket and check the notification.

"Taxi's here," I tell her.

Bea slides her foot off my thigh. "C'mon, James," she calls, stomping toward the door and flipping off the switch to her speakers. She sweeps up a black moto jacket and then a canary-yellow purse as I follow her out. "Let's go kick some matchmaker ass."

The Alley is thankfully one of those old-timey establishments, not the glow-in-the-dark techno-bowling variety. I couldn't take one of those. I don't have the bandwidth for spaces like that. They're a trip wire for my anxiety.

"Remember," Bea whispers, shoulder to shoulder with me. "Stick to the truth as much as possible. Keep answers short. We're both annoyed with them."

"That won't take any acting," I mutter.

She throws me a knowing grin. It's bright and genuine, and it makes a rush of *something* thunder through my veins.

When I glance up, I see Jean-Claude coming toward us.

"Going to get myself a pair of shoes," Bea mumbles, slipping away.

Not quite ready to face my betrayer, I turn to my bag, sit down, and lace up my bowling shoes. I sense Jean-Claude watching me, but knowing lying isn't a forte of mine, I remain quiet, waiting for him to make the first move.

"You brought your own," he says.

I glance up, laces in hand. "Of course I brought my own. Don't get me started on the dubious hygiene of shoe sharing."

He clears his throat. "How are things with Bea?"

I stand. "You mean the woman you tricked me into dating?"

"Oh, come on. 'Tricked' is a little strong. More like—"

"Manipulated?"

"I was going to say 'maneuvered.'" He shrugs. "Either way, you're here with her, aren't you?"

"Yes, Jean-Claude. I'm here with her." I search the bowling balls next to us, on the lookout for a good fit for Bea. She's not short, but she's not tall, either. She needs the right size for her grip. There's hot pink, classic black; then I find one that's marbled—cream with swirls of aqua, coral, and canary yellow, the colors of the little flowers on her dress tonight. I select that one.

Just as I peer up, Bea strolls back with her shoes to a chorus of balls connecting with pins. She has a fast, no-nonsense stride that makes me smile for no good reason. Eyes narrowed, arms swinging, she's off in thought somewhere else.

"I know that look," Jean-Claude says.

"What look?" I mutter, eyes still on her.

"The look of a man falling hard," he says, as if I should know this. "You don't have to play it cool with me, West. I know how alluring a Wilmot girl is."

"Woman," I correct him.

He waves a hand. "What difference does it make?"

I'm distracted from answering him as I watch Juliet approach Bea when she sits, then roughly kicks off her boots and slips on her bowling shoes. Juliet speaks to her, and Bea's shoulders hitch higher as her sister continues. When she glances my way, her expression is tight. I have no idea if this means she wants me with her or not, but I'm erring on the side of caution.

"Excuse me," I tell Jean-Claude.

In a few long strides I'm next to Bea, bringing the conversation to a standstill. Awkward silence stretches between the three of us.

"Here." I offer Bea the marbled ball. "Juliet." I nod to her sister.

Juliet looks at me intently. "Hi, West."

"You brought me a ball?" Bea asks.

"Yes. It should be the right size, but give it a try."

She stands and peers at the ball in my hand. "Thank you, Jamie."

"If you'd like another one, I can get you—"

"No." She takes it from me, running her fingers along its surface. "It's perfect."

I search her eyes, sensing tension radiating off her in waves. "Doing all right? Need anything?"

Her expression falters for just a moment before the smooth front is back. "Yeah. But I could use a drink. Vodka cranberry? Thank you," she adds, nudging me gently with her shoulder.

Juliet stands quietly, staring at her shoes as Bea white-knuckles the ball.

"Be back soon," I tell her, hoping that's a reassurance.

We're in this together, I told her in the cab.

And now I realize how much I meant it.

FIFTEEN

Bea

Jamie strolls away, but not before stashing his bowling ball, then setting his hand, warm and heavy, against my back as he passes me. It's a fleeting touch, but it makes me feel better. It reminds me that when we pulled up to the Alley, he turned my way and bumped knees with me, making me stop from opening the door as he said, *Don't forget, when we get in there and we're bombarded by everyone. We're in this together.*

My heart squeezed at his sincerity, and I threw open the taxi door before I could do something ridiculous, like hug him when there wasn't an audience for it. Because that would be a completely wrong reason to hug Jamie Westenberg.

Now, watching him disappear around the corner to the bar, I'm doubly glad I didn't do that. Our dynamic needs to stay clearly defined in my head. This is pretend. It's built on deception. The last relationship I had was built on deception, too, and God, did I do so much fucking pretending. Pretending to be happy. Pretending that I felt loved. Pretending I was okay. Deception was Tod's bread and butter. He twisted things and warped the truth, and to sustain our relationship, I had to believe those lies. This time is different. This time I know the truth. This time the lie is on *my* terms.

"BeeBee?" Jules's voice pulls me back to the present. "Are you listening?"

I glance her way, shifting the ball in my grip. "Sorry, no."

"I said, you've been distant all week. We didn't bump into each other once."

That was on purpose. And I'll have you know that it takes skill to avoid your twinny roommate when you live in a nine-hundred-square-foot apartment. "I was busy," I tell her.

"Okay. Well, I was hoping we could have a conversation now, since we haven't been able to before this."

Sighing, I set my ball next to Jamie's. "Come on." I jerk my head toward the ladies' room. "I have to take a leak. Let's walk and talk."

Trailing after me, Jules hustles to catch up. "You're mad at me."

"Yes, Jules. I don't like being lied to."

Her cheeks flush. "I'm sorry, Bea. I know it was twisty. But I didn't know how else to get you to give West a chance. I tried talking to you at work, but you were so against him, this was all I could think of—"

"So you and our 'friends' manipulated me?" I say sharply, whirling around and bringing us to an abrupt stop in the hallway leading to the restroom. "The group deception is really fucked up—"

"Whoa!" Jules throws up her hands. "No, no. Our friends had *nothing* to do with this."

"Yeah, right. You were all throwing us together at the party."

"Okay, at the party, yes," she concedes. "But after Jean-Claude found you in the closet, everyone saw how embarrassed you both were, and they felt awful. Since that point, it's just been me—well, me and Jean-Claude."

"I am so fucking confused."

Staring down at the ground, Jules rubs her forehead and sighs. "What I said at the Edgy Envelope last week was true, that the friends approve of him. But they haven't been involved in anything since the party. Once I got you two set up for Boulangerie, I told them you had a date but not the circumstances. I didn't want anyone to call you in to work or invite you to do something else and give you a reason to back out Saturday. That's it. I promise."

My stomach drops. A cold sweat prickles over my skin. "So . . . they weren't in on the text-and-date trickery?"

"No," Jules says firmly, meeting my eyes again. "They weren't. No one knows except Jean-Claude and me. And they never will, I swear. I acknowledge I went a little far, but geez, Bea, give me a little credit?"

"You *tricked* me. You don't get credit."

She throws her arms up. "Because you wouldn't listen to reason!"

"That was my choice!"

"Fine," she yells. "You're right. Okay? I should have just let you stay pissed and miserable."

"Better than passive-aggressive and manipulative," I fire back.

Uncomfortable silence stretches between us as I absorb this. All my friends think Jamie and I voluntarily went on that date. This isn't some epic group manipulation. This is my pushy sister and her equally pushy fiancé, meddling where they shouldn't.

For a moment, I think about saying to hell with this revenge scheme, but you know what? I'm tired of being a doormat for this bullshit. After Tod and I ended, I swore I'd never let someone mow me down, toy with my emotions, the way he did. I am sticking to my guns. It's time for these fools to learn their lesson.

Jules doesn't get a pass simply because she didn't rope other people into the worst of her meddling. And, fine, my friends weren't in on the date setup, but they nudged and pushed and meddled at the party, and they've spent the past year—despite my protests that I'm not interested in dating right now—throwing prospective partners in my path.

Maybe my grievances aren't as extreme as I originally imagined. Maybe my revenge won't be as grand. But this group still needs to get it through their thick skulls that they don't get to disregard my wishes, even if their ultimate desire is for my happiness. The path to hell is paved with good intentions. Not all of them went as far as Jules, but they went far enough.

"BeeBee?" Jules says, pulling me from my churning thoughts.

Leaving her behind, I storm into the restroom, take the first stall that's open, and slam it shut behind me. The restroom door swings open a moment later, before Jules enters the stall next to me.

"You're really pissed," she says, like I've stunned her.

I take a long slow breath before I say, "Jules, I know you love me. I know that in your warped way this was you doing what you thought was best for me. But I don't need that. I need honesty. I need you and everyone else in our social circle to respect that I live my life my way, and it might not look like yours, but it's still valid."

In the neighboring stall, her feet tap on the tiles. Jules does that when she's nervous. "We had good intentions," she says quietly.

I barely swallow an empty laugh. Of course they did. And now they're going to learn what "good intentions" get them.

When I leave the stall, my sister is already washing her hands, examining her reflection. Our eyes meet in the mirror.

"I really am sorry, BeeBee," she says. "Are we okay?"

"Eventually we will be."

After a beat, she nods, staring down at her hands as she dries them. "Can I ask, if you're so angry, why are you and West here?"

"Because"—I grit my teeth, hating to say this even when I'm lying—"you were onto something. The texting worked and we clicked, okay? We're giving it a chance. That's all you get." I shoulder open the restroom door and wave her ahead of me.

"Eek! Yay. I knew it. I *knew* it!" Jules spins so she's backtracking, performing an obnoxious happy dance as we reenter the main room. "Okay. I'm calm. I'm cool." Her eyes widen as they lock on something over my shoulder. "Wow."

"Wow, what?" I ask.

"West is coming toward you looking super intense. He's—I think he just shoved someone out of the way and—"

"Bea." Jamie's arm is around mine, tucking me against him.

"Jamie!" I frown at him over my shoulder. "What are you doing?"

His cheeks are pink. There's an intense glint to his hazel eyes as he sets my drink on a neighboring bar-height table. "Stand still for a second."

Of course, because he just told me to be still, I fidget in his arms. "Jamie. Let go of me."

"Bea, please. Your—"

I pull out of his arms and storm away. "Yeesh," I mutter.

Sweeping up my ball, I hustle to the end of the lane to cool off. I don't do well being unexpectedly touched. It startles me like a jolt of static electricity and makes me desperate for personal space. It's a sensory thing, but Jamie doesn't know I'm on the spectrum. I haven't explained my sensory issues. Clearly, that has to happen, considering this is our first public outing and I already almost lost my shit on him.

"Bea!" Jules hisses, shuffling toward me, careful not to slip in her bowling shoes. "Wait!"

"Juliet," I snap, bringing the ball to my chin. "Just give me some space."

Swinging back, ball in hand, I hear Jamie's voice calling my name too late. My bowling ball–weighted hand slams right into his groin, sending a hoarse rush of air whooshing out of him. I spin around, dropping the ball clumsily as Jamie crumples to the ground.

"Oh my God, Jamie! I'm so sorr—*Ack!*"

His hand wraps around my wrist and yanks me down with him. In one smooth move, his body rests over mine, pinning me to the dusty floor. Nearby pins clatter as a ball crashes into them. I stare up at Jamie, stunned.

"Sorry," he wheezes. He drops his head to the crook of my neck, gasping for air. I recognize his stuttered breathing as the universal sound of someone whose nuts are in agony. Even as he's suffering, he holds himself so that his full weight doesn't crush me. But it's not enough. I still feel warmth seeping from his clothes, those long legs and their hard muscles. Every time he inhales, his ribs brush mine, and a shiver of heat ripples through me.

I try very hard not to focus on the thick weight at his groin that's nestled against my pelvis, but it's really hard not to. He's big and heavy, breathing roughly against my skin, and my runaway imagination insists on imagining that's just how he'd sound and feel right after he pounded me right into a glorious, screaming orgasm.

I'm stunned. And super turned-on.

When Jamie finally speaks, his voice is marginally closer to normal. "Are you all right?"

"Uh, Jamie, I'm the one who just crushed your nuts with a bowling ball. I think *I'm* the one who should be asking that. But if you want to explain why you turned into a stage-five clinger and tackled me to the floor, I'd love to hear it."

He clears his throat, lifting his head slowly. His cheeks are pink again. "Your dress, Bea. It was . . ." He swallows. "Tucked into your shorts."

A rush of heat floods my face. My shorts are cheeky boy shorts. Half of my butt is visible in them.

Awkwardly, I try to reach back, but I can't do that with his weight over me. Our eyes meet as I whisper, "I can't get to it. Can you—" I gasp as his hand slips between my back and the floor, the heat of his touch seeping through my dress. He slides the fabric from the band of my underwear until it flutters around my hip, covering me from anyone who's looking. Which, as I glance around, I realize with embarrassment is half the bowling alley.

"You're covered now," he says. "I fell on you like that because with you on top of me—"

"Everyone and their grandma in the bowling alley could see my butt?"

His blush deepens. "Well, yes."

Sighing, I pat his cheek. "Thank you for straightening me out. You're a true gentleman, James. But you're also heavy. Now, get the hell off of me."

Jamie was lying out of his glorious ass when he said he's passable at bowling.

He's a fucking beast.

And I am *wildly* competitive.

With Jamie in my clutches, I'm Gollum hoarding the One Ring, Emperor Palpatine with Anakin in his grip, Thanos wearing the Infinity Gauntlet.

I am despicable.

"Okay." I stand on one of the seats by the machine that spits our balls back to us, massaging Jamie's shoulders like a coach psyching up her prizewinning fighter. "You can do this. You can *do* this."

He glances up at me and sighs. "You're disturbing."

"*Competitive*, you mean." I squeeze harder. "I'm *competitive*. Eyes on the prize, James."

Turning back, he sweeps up his ball. Long gone is the prickly bespectacled pear I met. Before me is a man who's loose and warm, devastatingly invested in this game, and deliciously rumpled.

Jamie is so goddamn fine right now, I'm having explicit thoughts about dragging him into some dust-bunny-riddled corner of the Alley and kissing him into next week. His waves are tousled, an errant bronze lock falling on his forehead. His sleeves are cuffed just past his elbows, a few sexy wrinkles creasing his shirt. Perspiration beads his forehead and I have to stop myself from picturing him sweating, head thrown back in pleasure as he pins me the way he did against the floor but with a mattress beneath me instead.

"Bea," he says.

"What?" I peer down at him, breathless, a mighty flush to my cheeks. "Nothing."

"*Nothing?* I just said your name."

"Right." I clear my throat. Jamie cannot know I have the hots for him. We have an agenda to stick to, and having emotionless sex would absolutely compromise it. Maybe with someone else it could work, but not Jamie. We're *fake* dating, and everything about Jamie screams six *real* dates before making slow, fervent love to his partner. He stares into their eyes and holds off orgasm for forty-five minutes. He is the consummately selfless lover. I think I'd traumatize him if I put on the moves. I'd be wild. I wouldn't be ladylike with Jamie. I'd throw him down on a sofa with our clothes halfway off and ride him like a rodeo pony.

"You're holding things up!" Margo calls.

Sula tugs Margo onto her lap and blows a raspberry against her neck. "Chill out and leave them alone. You remember the early days."

Toni and his boyfriend, Hamza, trade knowing looks. Jules has the audacity to nudge Jean-Claude, throwing him a beaming conspiratorial smile. My rage is rekindled, bursting to fiery life after a fresh hunk of their gloating fuel is thrown on its embers.

"Jamie," I squeeze his shoulders again. "We *have* to win."

"We might have a chance," he says, "if you don't snap my collarbones with your death grip."

I retract my claws. "Sorry."

"Forgiven." An almost smile peeks out. "Do *not* follow me this time. We barely avoided a repeat performance of your ball-meets-body fiasco earlier, except this time I nearly knocked out your teeth."

I drop from the chair I'm standing on with a jazz-hands flourish, shuffling alongside him. These floors are slippery. I keep almost wiping out. "I'm just trying to boost morale—"

"Boost morale," he mutters. "Back *up*. I don't want to hurt you."

"I can't help it. I'm too excited."

He gives me a long, hard stare that sends a frisson of devious delight zipping down my spine. "Beatrice."

Oh God, his voice when he gets extra stern. It's lava, straight through my ears, down to the pit of my stomach, where it lands, molten between my thighs. I swallow thickly. "James?"

"Do you want to win or not?"

"Are you honestly asking me that?"

"No," he says, facing the lane. "I'm saying it to make a point. It's called a rhetorical question."

I roll my eyes. "Such an arrogant—"

That's when I realize he distracted me on purpose, long enough to snap his arm back and send the ball flying down the lane, where it lands with a crash.

Strike!

I scream like we've won the World Series, like we're the Cubbies after their 107-year losing streak. Adrenaline roars through my veins. My ears ring. My heart's pounding as I shuffle my way toward Jamie and launch myself at him like a koala that just found its first eucalyptus tree. "We did it!" I yell.

Jamie's arm muscles flex, steadying me as I lock my legs tight around his lean waist. Our eyes meet, and if his smile turned my heart to gold-leaf glitter, his laugh makes me see stars. It's honey warm and blazing bright, rich and deep and so unexpected, I throw my arms around his neck and crush my body to his.

Jamie's grip tightens, his hand cups my face, and then he does the absolute last thing I ever expected from Mr. Prim and Proper.

He kisses me.

And it's good. No, not good. Better. Best. A world-tipping, never-forget-this kiss.

His mouth brushes mine, fleeting, faint. Our eyes lock for just an instant before I meet his mouth hungrily again. His thumb slides along my jaw, his mouth savoring mine with deep, slow kisses, a faint nip of my bottom lip that makes my thighs tighten around his waist. Doing that brings our bodies closer. It makes Jamie suck in a breath and slide his hand lower down my back, tucking me against him. It makes my fingers thread through his hair as his hands wander my body.

His tongue strokes mine, and he groans, rough and low in his throat, as a gasp rushes from my lungs. Jamie slants his mouth and nudges mine gently—*More*, his kiss says. *Open up, give me more, give me everything*—

A crash of pins startles and tears us apart.

Jamie stares at me, wide-eyed.

"Ah, young love," Jean-Claude says. Jules sighs dreamily.

I ignore them, staring up at Jamie, who wears a vacant expression I can't read. "Doing okay?" I ask, so quietly I think he relies on reading my lips.

"Yes," he says. Slowly, he sets me down.

But as we pack up and say our goodbyes, as we wait in the cool night air for a cab, then share a quiet ride that stops outside my apartment first, I have the funniest feeling Jamie isn't okay at all.

SIXTEEN

Jamie

I've been a terrible fake boyfriend the past three days. I'm avoiding Beatrice.

Because that kiss was *not* supposed to happen. Well, it was, but not like that. It was supposed to be emotionless. Rehearsed. Like two actors going through the motions, playing their parts. *Not* an adrenaline-soaked crush of bodies, not a desperate kiss that made my heart thunder, that made every part of me that she touched ache for more.

Being in a fake relationship isn't supposed to be complicated. Kissing isn't supposed to make me think foolish, ridiculous thoughts about Bea actually wanting me when she kissed me, too. This situation is terrifyingly beyond me.

"Dr. West!" Luca, a seven-year-old patient of mine, waves as Ned brings him back into the office and starts his vitals.

"Hey, Luc." I smile at him and pocket my phone. The phone I definitely wasn't holding as I considered texting Bea for the eightieth time since we parted ways on Friday. "Catch any bad guys lately?"

"Ten!" he says emphatically. "I used my villain-destroyer machine." He lifts his shirt, revealing the insulin pump that he was fitted with just a few weeks ago.

"Whoa!" Ned says, wrapping the blood pressure cuff around Luca's arm. "Better keep that safe. Can't let the bad guys get anywhere near your destroyer machine."

Patting his pump like a cowboy with his holster, Luca grins. "Trust me, I've got it under control."

"He's done a great job taking good care of his villain-destroyer machine," Luca's mother says. "And *I've* felt much better now that Luca's got it. Now I know he's safe."

"And you're safe, too, Mama," he reassures her, legs swinging from the chair as Ned takes off the cuff. "Don't you worry."

A smile tugs at my mouth. There's nothing like kids. Their innocence and warmth. Their guileless transparency. I find them so much easier to connect with than adults. Because with children, there's no hidden agenda, just their honest thoughts and feelings. Unlike the matchmakers and many adults, who seem to have no problem manipulating people and situations to suit them.

Guilt sours my stomach. Am I treating Bea any better than the meddlers with my radio silence? Three days after the Bowling Alley Kiss, is she wondering why I've been so quiet? Then again, she's been quiet, too. Maybe she's relieved that I haven't texted.

Worse, maybe she doesn't care at all.

"Okay, buddy," Ned says. "Everything's good. Let's get you back to your room and settled in."

Glancing up, I give Luca my attention. "I'll see you soon, okay, Luc?"

He smiles as he walks by with his mom and Ned. "Okay, Dr. West."

Just as they turn down the hall to our exam rooms, my phone buzzes in my pocket.

> **BEA:** We're not even *actually* dating and you're ghosting me. I'd say I'm disappointed but honestly I'm just impressed.

A groan leaves me. I can't ignore that. I *shouldn't* ignore that.

> **JAMIE:** I'm deplorable.

> **BEA:** Nah. You're just freaked out because the best kiss of your life was your fake girlfriend.

She has no idea.

Staring at my phone, I comb my brain for a response that won't send her running for the hills. Because if I were honest, I'd tell her, *Well, now that you say it, Bea, the fact is you were the best kiss of my life. Kissing you, I wanted to do things I've never allowed myself to even consider. I was thirty seconds away from dragging you into some germ-infested corner of that dusty old bowling alley, hiking up your dress, and—*

My phone buzzes again.

> **BEA:** Okay, I freaked you out, didn't I? Jamie, I'm just kissing.
>
> **BEA:** KIDDING. Dammit.
>
> **JAMIE:** Beatrice, I'm sorry. This is entirely my issue.
>
> **BEA:** What do you mean? What issue?

I owe her more than that vague, incomplete explanation. I owe her more than an apology. But this isn't a strength of mine, knowing what to say and how to say it.

I suck in a breath and clutch my phone, begging my brain to unjam everything tangled inside it. My heart rate accelerates. I break out in a sweat. Every second that ticks by does more damage, but I can't—

"Dr. West," Gayle calls.

I startle and my elbow bumps the computer where I've been taking patient notes, coloring the screen with a stream of random letters. I select them, delete, then save the file.

A quick stroll brings me to my side of the front desk's opening. "What can I do for you, Gayle?"

Our head administrator glances my way with a wide smile and warm brown eyes. "You can explain this lovely young lady here."

After following the direction of Gayle's nod, I freeze. "Bea?"

There she stands, knocking the toes of her boots together. The boots that she wore to the Alley, which I laced up as her foot rested on my thigh, legs wide open before me—

Bad train of thought.

I clear my throat, then hit the hand sanitizer pump three times and rub it in. Tugging open the door from the waiting room to my side of the practice, I gesture her my way. "Come here, Bea."

She marches forward, flashing one of those dangerous smiles at Gayle. "Nice to meet you," she says.

"You, too, honey!" Gayle wiggles her eyebrows at me once Bea's facing my way.

When Bea stops just inside the door, I stare down at her. In her hands are—

"You brought me tea?"

She lifts a small bag. "Gunpowder green, or whatever you got at Boulangerie. And that floor-cleaner scone you liked."

"Why?"

Bea glances toward the front desk. All three admins whip their heads back to their computers.

"We should talk somewhere private," I tell her. Setting a hand low on her back, I guide her in front of me. "Straight down that hall, then the first door on your left."

I try very hard not to stare at the sweet curve of her backside as Bea strolls ahead of me, her long, purposeful stride punctuated by the thud of her boots.

I am miserably unsuccessful.

When I shut the door behind us, she hitches herself onto the exam table, paper crinkling beneath her legs. Glancing around, she admires the decorative border on the walls littered with woodland creatures, including hedgehogs, which I know she loves, seeing as she has one for a pet. "Nice."

"I figured you'd appreciate the décor."

"They don't hold a candle to Cornelius," she says, "but they'll do."

Then she holds out the tea and the small parchment bag for me to take. I set down the bag but keep the tea, popping off the lid. It's gunpowder green all right. Earthy and bitter. It smells incredible.

"Thank you for this," I tell her, sipping it carefully. "What brings you here . . . with tea?"

She grimaces, scrunching one eye shut. "I have a confession to make. And an apology."

"That sounds grim."

Taking a deep breath, she straightens and says, "Jules told me something in the restroom Friday. The friends weren't in on the date setup."

I nearly drop my tea. "What?"

"I mean, they definitely played with us at the party. But Jules said setting up that date was her only recourse, according to her, and only she and Jean-Claude coordinated that. So we haven't been made *complete* fools of. I should have told you right when I found out, but I was selfish and the thought of letting go of my chance to get back at them . . ." Her voice trails off, and she scrubs her face before letting her hands fall to her lap. "I'm angry at my sister, and honestly, I'm still pissed at my friends. They didn't take it as far as her, but—"

"They were still pushy at the party."

Bea blinks at me in surprise. "Well, yeah."

"You didn't think I'd see your side of things?"

She shrugs. "I guess I thought you seemed pretty willing to forgive them when we first found out. I figured once I told you the truth, you'd want out."

"And . . . you don't want out."

"No," she admits. "I want to make a fucking point. I want them to back off on me and my dating life for good, but you're part of this fiasco, and you deserve the truth and a say in how we go forward."

It takes a moment for her words to sink in, for me to formulate my own. "This doesn't change things for me. I hardly know your friends. When I agreed to it, I was in it to stick it to Jean-Claude and get him off my back."

"So, we're still on?" she asks carefully.

"We're still on."

A smile brightens her face before she tamps it down. "Thanks," she says quietly. Then, after a beat: "So are we okay? We haven't really talked. Which is fine. Obviously. I mean, why would we? I know the bowling alley got a little away from us. I promise I won't climb you like a tree on our next outing."

Guilt hits me like a sucker punch. I hate that I've made her uneasy.

"Bea." Rubbing the bridge of my nose, I sigh. "I'm sorry I've been acting odd. I've been stuck in my head since the Alley. I wasn't sure what to say. So I didn't say anything. But that's unfair to you."

Bea searches my eyes. "So you weren't freezing me out because I jumped you like a koala in heat after getting us so worked up over a friendly Friday night bowling match that it felt like life or death by the last frame? You're not pissed?"

I take a step closer to her, setting down my tea on the nearby counter. "Not at all."

"Oh." She peers down at her skirt, running her hands across the fabric. Black again, this time with tiny rainbows all over it. "Okay."

"I think . . ." The words catch in my throat, but I take a deep breath, then force them out. "I think we should talk about what we need to make this more comfortable, to make this work."

"Right," Bea says slowly, frowning. "Why does it sound like you're suggesting we get our toenails ripped out?"

I wrinkle my nose. "The things you come up with."

"Well, I'm looking at your gorgeous face, twisted with disgust—" She freezes. Eyes wide. "Wait. Forget I said that."

Heat blooms in my cheeks, floods my veins, until every corner of me burns hot and curious. I stare at her in shock. *Does* she find me attractive?

God, it's tempting, that thought. It's also dangerous, because then I'd want to tell her the truth. *I think you're gorgeous, too. I've stroked off every night and told myself it's not your body I'm wanting, your mouth I'm dying to taste again.*

I can't tell her that. There's a big jump from "your face is gorgeous" to "I've masturbated to the thought of you every night since we met." Especially if she didn't mean it.

Did she mean it?

"Seriously, ignore that," Bea says, flustered. "I-I-I think I blacked out. Had an aneurysm."

Ouch.

"An aneurysm, you say?" Leaning past her for the otoscope, I catch a trace of figs, the sensual undertone of sandalwood. That perfume she wears could bring a man to his knees.

Her pupils dilate as she stares up at me. "What are you doing?"

Dislodging the otoscope from its wall mount, I flick on the light. "Examining you for signs of intracranial aneurysm. Some doctors minimize a patient's self-diagnosis like it's their job, but I've found people are quite capable of knowing their own body. I take your concerns seriously."

Her eyes narrow. "James."

I step into the space between her legs until her knees brush my thighs. "Beatrice."

Our eyes hold. She blinks away first. "Okay, I didn't have an aneurysm."

Flicking off the light, I reach past her again and return the otoscope to its wall mount.

"I just . . ." Groaning, she slumps against the wall and frowns up at the ceiling. "I might find your face a tiny bit kissable. Purely sexual, I promise. That's all I meant."

Lust slams into my system as her words fragment and, like drops of long-awaited rain, drench my parched thoughts—*face, kiss, sex* . . . I picture holding her hips, kissing my way up the smooth, warm skin of her thighs, finding her wet and hot—

Christ. This abstinent streak is going to be the death of me.

Bea exhales slowly, her cheeks still bright red. "Okay. Let's pretend the last two minutes never happened."

"Excellent." My cheeks feel as hot as hers look. We avoid each other's eyes entirely.

"You were saying?" Bea offers. "About making this setup run smoother?"

"Right." I clear my throat. "So, I made things awkward, falling off the grid after a little harmless fun on Friday."

She glances up at me, silent for a beat. "That's okay."

"It's not. We'll have to kiss and act cozy again. It can't be uncomfortable like this every time afterward. We'll wear ourselves out."

That last phrase hangs in the air, a Freudian slip of massive proportions.

"True," she finally says.

"I think our task would feel easier if *we* felt easier around each other." I press my glasses higher up my nose before shoving my hands into my front pockets. "I think we should try to be friends."

"Friends?" She frowns.

"Yes?" Why am I suddenly doubting everything, from the words that just came out of my mouth to the tie I picked this morning, based on one little word from her mouth?

"Friends," she says again. This time it sounds less incredulous, more exploratory. Like sipping a new wine and tasting its subtleties. "So . . . you mean if we're friends, pretending to be more won't stress us out as much."

"Exactly."

"Makes sense. I'm in." Her expression flips to a smile as she hops off the exam table, her skirt fluttering as she lands.

"Right. Well . . . good." I'm honestly a bit stunned she didn't push back, but I'll take it.

"I'm going to hit the road. Leave you to your tiny patients," she says, marching toward the door. "Keep doing the good work. Saving babies. Curing disease. Solving world hunger."

I sweep up my tea and scone in one hand, then catch the door with the other, holding it open for Bea.

"Off I go," she says. "Ooh! Wait. I almost forgot."

Rummaging through her bag, Bea unearths a glass jar with a screw-top lid.

"Maybe this is weird," she says, "but this is my grandma's home-made hand salve. I thought—" She nods toward my raw hands. "Maybe it would help give you some relief. Cracked fingertips are painful."

"You're . . . giving that to . . . me."

"Yes," she says slowly. "Is that okay? If it's not, no worries. I'll use it eventually—"

"No!" That came out louder than I meant it to. "You can just . . . set it in my coat pocket."

Bea takes a step toward me, then slips the jar inside my pocket. Suddenly, I'm aware of every inch of her body. Every inch of mine. She stands beneath my outstretched arm, close and warm, her soft scent wrapping around me. Our eyes hold as I stare down at her.

"Thank you," I finally manage. "For the hand salve, and my tea, and the scone. No one's . . . no one's ever done something like this for me. It was very thoughtful."

She frowns, as if perplexed. But then the frown dissolves and she's smiling again as she takes a step back. "That's what friends are for, right?"

Friends.

Right.

SEVENTEEN

Bea

I can't lie. This newfound power I have over my friends and the traitorous twin is kind of priceless. Even at work, I have leverage like never before. Jules keeps making my favorite meals, trying to coax details out of me as I chow down. Sula and Toni butter me up with favors at work while fishing for juicy details. They're all hopelessly curious about how things are going with Jamie, and while I thought I'd have to lie out of my ass to get these fools to believe he and I are the real deal, turns out being mysterious works even better.

I am keeping them in total suspense. Revenge is glorious.

"Another raspberry thumbprint?" Toni offers, sweeping a plate of still-warm cookies under my nose.

"Probably shouldn't," I tell him. Eyes on my sketch, I elaborate the concept, creeping wisteria along a weathered wood trellis. But my pen keeps deviating from gossamer flowers to the tall silhouette of a man leaning inside its arch. Shirtless. Lithe. Tidy waves mussed in the wind. Tortoiseshell glasses.

"Bea," Toni groans. "I'm dying. Won't you tell me *anything*?"

"Maybe." I slip another cookie from the plate and pop it in my mouth. I'm going to ruin my dinner appetite, but I can't stop. "Only because these cookies are damn good."

Toni lets out a whoop of victory, hands over his head.

"*And* if you take the delivery today."

His arms fall. "You are evil."

"Better get your booty moving. Lots of boxes due in"—I glance at my phone to check the time—"negative three minutes."

Groaning, he stomps to the back, where the delivery truck is blasting its heinously loud moving-in-reverse beeps.

And now I won't have to stand there, listening to it at close range, *or* get super sweaty from unloading before my first *let's be friends* dinner with Jamie.

Glorious, beautiful revenge.

The truck finally stops beeping, followed by the sound of its door rolling up. Toni swears foully in Polish, then continues muttering to himself. My name's definitely in the mix of words that I can't begin to translate.

"Just because I can't understand it," I yell, "doesn't mean I don't know it's nasty!"

"Ask me if I care!" he hollers back.

Savoring the ensuing quiet, I go back to drawing again. I'm given only a two-minute reprieve before the overhead bell dings and Jules sweeps in.

"Hi, BeeBee!" My sister smiles, gliding her way around the circular front display table that Toni just reconfigured.

"JuJu." I focus on my sketch pad, letting my pen go where it wants. But what it wants is a little unsettling.

Jamie. Jamie. Jamie.

Argh! This has to stop.

"Whatcha drawing?" she asks sweetly, leaning her elbows on the glass top.

I slam my sketchbook shut, then slide it into my messenger bag. "Nothing."

Jules watches me gather my pens and phone, then swipe on some tinted lip balm. "Almost time for your date?" She wiggles her eyebrows suggestively.

I scowl at her, caught in a twisty tangle of aggravation and begrudging love. I want to grab her shoulders and shake sense into her. I know she only wants to see me on my way to happiness, but I wish she hadn't done such a shitty thing to try to get me there.

It's weird, feeling vindictive toward someone who—despite how angry she's made me—I still love deeply. I want to punish Jules for going too far. And I also want our old closeness, so I can tell her everything. But I can't have both. I've chosen to teach her a lesson, and that requires emotional distance.

"Bea," Jules says impatiently, frowning at me. "Where'd you go?"

I pop another of Toni's raspberry cookies in my mouth. "I was, uh . . . daydreaming."

"About *Jamie*?"

About revenge.

Her smile is so self-satisfied. I barely stop myself from lobbing a cookie at her head. Toni's baking is too precious to waste. "Mind your beeswax, Juliet."

"Since when do I do that? Ooh, those look good." She reaches for the plate of cookies, but I slap her hand away.

"No sweet treats for meddlers."

"Well-meaning older sisters," she corrects, dodging my next slap and stealing a cookie. "Sisters who see your chemistry with someone even when you're too stubborn to acknowledge it and give you the nudge you need."

"*Nudge?* That's what we're calling it?"

"I'm sorry—" She pops the cookie in her mouth and dusts off her hands. "Are you or are you not going on a date with the guy I *nudged* you toward?"

My scowl deepens.

"What are your plans?" she asks. "Going somewhere fancy? You're dressed up."

"No, I'm not." Am I?

I peer down at my jade-green pleated skirt with its wide stretchy waistband, and my favorite cobalt-blue sweater featuring a knit bow at the shoulder. Maybe I took a smidge more care with my appearance when I got ready for work, knowing I'd head straight to dinner with Jamie afterward. But as always, I dressed based on the fabrics and seams that felt comfy when I woke up this morning.

"I'm having dinner with Jamie. Nothing fancy."

"That's it?" She narrows her eyes. "I don't like this new private side of you."

"You made the monster, Frankenstein. Don't blame me."

The overhead bell sounds again, and the doorway is filled with six foot many inches of Jamie Westenberg, who, despite nearly always wearing dress slacks and a button-up, somehow looks even more put together tonight. His shirt is crisp canvas white, undone an extra button, which reveals the hollow of his throat. His chinos are casual, a complex deep olive that reminds me of oil paints and long, dreamy hours in my studio. He holds a heather-gray sweater in the crook of his arm, and a sleek metallic watch winks from his wrist, reminding me how despicably hot his forearms are.

A wolf whistle breaks the silence.

I give my sister a look. "Back off."

She shrugs. "Jean-Claude's got my heart, but come *on*. You look great, West!"

Besides a splash of pink on his cheeks—I'm hooked on how easily Jamie blushes—and a hearty throat clear, no one would know how much it knocks Jamie on his heels to be appreciated. I've only just realized he's self-conscious, after I let it slip the other day that his face is gorgeous, and he looked at me like I'd told him the moon's purple.

"Ah." He clears his throat again. "Well, thank you."

Throwing my bag on my shoulder, I call toward the back, "I'm heading out now, Ton!"

"Fuck you very much!" Toni yells. "How am I supposed to haul the delivery and man the storefront?"

"Sounds like a personal problem to me."

"And I didn't even get the juicy deets about Sexy Westy!"

Jamie turns pink.

Jules snorts. "I'll go help him. Get out of here, you two. No, wait." She stops me, fussing with my blouse beneath my sweater.

"Jules." I try to spin and escape her touch. "Stop it."

"The bow," she says, nosing her way back in. "You did it wrong. And your hair, Bea. Just a little beach-wave spray and—"

"I think," Jamie cuts in, eyes glued to mine, "Bea looks spectacular just how she is." Then he steps forward and takes my hand, pulling me away from my sister. "Let's go."

Jules gapes as he leads me out of the store and into the evening air. The sun settles against the horizon and drips down every surface in a dozen dreamy watercolor shades of coral, peach, and tangerine.

"Wow." I stop to watch the sunset because I simply can't miss nature's finest work. Jamie seems content to watch the sunset, too. He's quiet beside me, gaze narrowed against the sharp low light, and when the wind picks up, he shuts his eyes, as if drinking in the moment. When he opens them, he offers me one of his gentlemanly nods, then turns us to walk.

I notice he's still holding my hand, that his fingertips aren't cracked, and his knuckles are less red. He used the salve I gave him. I try not to think about why that makes the tiny pilot light inside me burn brighter.

"Nicely done back there," I tell him. "Thanks."

"She mothers you, doesn't she?"

I glance around as we walk. I have no idea where we're going, but Jamie seems to, so I amble along. "Yes. She's older."

He does a double take. "What? You're twins."

"Twelve minutes. Could be twelve years for how she sees it."

He rolls his eyes. "Sibling dynamics."

I don't know about Jamie's place among his siblings, just that he has three of them, which he told me the night of the platypus pants and PMS essentials. Jamie and I ate cupcakes, then, while he cooked, shared a few details to be sure we could pass muster around the meddlers at the bowling alley. I would have stayed and learned more, but then I realized he was making pasta primavera, which is, you might say, a bit of a problem food for me, given nearly all vegetables are my textural night-mare. So I pled cramps and fatigue and made an early exit.

I knew enough to get by on our first outing in front of others, and it's probably enough still. But even though I probably don't *need* to know more about Jamie . . . I want to.

"What's your place in the Westenberg clan?" I ask.

"Second son," he says. Jamie's expression seems darker, as if a shadow just crossed his face, and there's an unfamiliar flatness in his tone that raises my awareness. I'm very quick to observe a person's facial or vocal changes, but making sense of those shifts is a struggle. It takes courage to ask for help understanding them. I'm not quite there with him yet.

I don't know exactly what's wrong, only that something is. So I give him what often makes me feel better. A firm hand squeeze of reassurance. My fingers brush over his healing knuckles.

"The salve's helping?" I ask.

Jamie peers down at our hands clasped together, a notch between his brows. "Pardon me? Oh. Yes. Very much. I have to wash and sanitize them so often at work, they dry out, and I've never found something that works this well. Thank you again."

"I'm glad. And you're welcome."

"Sorry." He loosens his grip on my hand. "I hadn't realized I was still holding your—"

"That's okay." I tangle our fingers tight again. "Besides, we should practice. For . . . plausibility's sake."

"Plausibility." When his eyes meet mine, the shadow darkening his expression is gone, and an almost smile slips out. "Right."

———

"This is the best pho I've ever had." I swallow a mouthful of rice noodles, hoping I'm subtle as I navigate around the vegetables.

Jamie makes a hum of agreement as he ladles broth past his lips.

Which I definitely don't watch.

In too great detail.

He just looks so good in here, under ideal lighting for a chiaroscuro sketch. My hands itch for my charcoals as inspiration nags my brain, begging to be drawn. I shove the impulse back in a mental closet already brimming with too many Jamie items. His kisses. His addicting scent. His warm, solid grip when we hold hands. The way light plays on his features and makes his eyes glow. I can't crack open that door and safely pick even one of those things. It'll send an avalanche raining down on me, and when I dig myself out, I'm not going to like what I see—how many things I actually *do* like about Jamie Nary a Wrinkle in His Pants Westenberg, even if he talks like he's on *Jeopardy!* and silently judges me for straining my pancreas with too much sugar.

Acknowledging how much I like Jamie is a risk I can't afford to take.

So I throw a shoulder into that mental closet, lock it up, and move on. After a sip of my lemonade, I tell him, "I can't believe I've never heard of this place before."

"Well-kept secret," he says. As he sets down his spoon, his eyes fasten on my bowl, and I know I'm busted. "You're not eating your vegetables. Do they not taste right to you?"

"Um." My legs bounce under the table. "You might say that."

Jamie's brow furrows. "What aren't you telling me?"

I really wish I didn't care so much about disappointing health-conscious physician Jamie, but for some annoying reason I do. That's why I've kept this to myself as long as I could. "I don't . . . exactly . . . eat . . . vegetables?"

He blinks at me. "You don't eat . . . vegetables."

Shifting in my seat, I clutch my fidget necklace, a soft leather chord with small polished wood and metal shapes for me to slip my fingers through when my hands need something to do. "Mm-hmm."

I brace myself for judgment. A lecture on balanced nutrition and healthy eating habits. But it doesn't come.

Instead, Jamie says, "I see. Is it a textural issue?"

Wow. Not what I expected. "Uh. Yes."

"That's why you hightailed it when I made pasta primavera at my place." He sighs and pinches the bridge of his nose. "I should have asked you what you liked. I've gotten so used to solitary cooking the past year, I'm out of the habit. I'm sorry."

"It's okay, Jamie."

"It's not," he says firmly. "It was unspeakably rude."

I nudge his foot with mine under the table. "Please don't beat yourself up."

He meets my eyes. "I feel terrible. I could have made something else you'd like. What about vegetable puree soups?"

"No luck so far. They're lumpy or they feel too thick. They just won't go past my throat. I can manage the occasional very crunchy raw broccoli and carrots and that's about it."

"Ah yes." His mouth twitches. "I remember your fondness for baby carrots."

I cackle. "I'm sorry. Not my finest moment, but the look on your face when that carrot hit your forehead."

He arches an eyebrow, trying for a stern look, but his mouth keeps twitching like he's fighting a smile. "My glasses smelled like ranch for days."

"Oh God." I grimace. "I really am sorry."

He nudges my foot back. "I'm exaggerating. It was only until I got home and washed them."

"Do you forgive me? Now that you understand how much I hate veggies?"

"Forgiven." Jamie smiles before having a spoonful of pho.

"Dammit, James. Way to show me up. I give you shit for your clean eating, and here you are, being nonjudgmental about my vegetable aversion."

"I'm familiar with it, medically," he says. "Plenty of people of all ages have sensory-processing issues like that. There's nothing to judge."

A smile warms my face. Nonjudgmental Jamie is kinda cute.

"You like your pho otherwise?" he asks. "The broth and noodles, at least?"

"Love it. I wasn't exaggerating, it's the best pho I've ever had. How'd you find this place?"

I glance around at the hole-in-the-wall eatery that seems like the last type of restaurant Jamie Westenberg would ever come to. I pictured him eating fancy fine dining amid classical piano music and clinking crystal. Instead, we're at Pho Ever, a place I can only describe as happy chaos, with its mismatched tables and vibrant tapestries on the walls, the soothing scent of cooking spices and incense thickening the air.

He sits back in his seat, crossing his arms. "Is it so impossible to believe *I* found a fun spot like this, all by myself?"

"Yes," I tell him honestly.

That gets me a solid-gold Jamie smile, small and crooked, hard-earned. "Well, you're right. I found it through Anh at work. Her uncle owns the place, and she treated the office to a delivery lunch from here a few months back. There was no going anywhere else for Vietnamese after that. Usually I order takeout, but tonight seemed right to make an exception."

"Why?"

Jamie removes his glasses, pulling a small fabric square from his shirt pocket and meticulously wiping the lenses. "I thought it was something you'd enjoy."

"You picked this for me?"

Replacing his glasses, he meets my eyes. "Yes."

He says it so simply. Why doesn't it *feel* simple? Why does it turn the world cotton candy pink as happiness hums through my limbs?

"*Do* you like it here?" he asks.

"I do." I smile. "It's exactly something I'd pick."

"Good," he says quietly. Peering down at his pho, he glides his spoon through the broth.

After a moment of silence, I clear my throat and set down my spoon. "So we're here to get familiar. Should we swap some more core info? Since I ducked out early last time?"

"That's fine," he says. "You first."

"Why me?"

He peers up at me and presses his glasses up his nose. "Because it's your idea."

I roll my eyes. "Fine. Okay, so you know about my sisters. You know I went to school for art."

He nods.

"I've lived in the city my whole life," I continue. "I like city living, its familiarity, but I traveled some of Europe for a stretch with my younger sister, Kate, and it was the most stressful, fun thing I've ever done, so I think I'd like to travel more down the road. My favorite season is fall, my favorite food is sugar—"

Jamie sighs and shakes his head.

I give him a winning smile. "I love blasting music and drawing. Oh, and I'll throw in a fear. I'm terrified of bats."

"Parents?" he prompts.

"My dad, Bill, is pretty mellow, a retired literature professor. My mom, Maureen, is a master gardener, volunteer librarian, and can hold her whiskey like no other—"

"Wait." Jamie leans in. "Your father's name is Bill Wilmot. As in—"

"William Wilmot." I have a spoonful of pho. "Yep. Isn't that cruel?"

"Cruel, yes. Unprecedented? No. I can't believe some of the names my tiny patients get saddled with."

"Ooh, tell me."

He gives me a *get out of here* look. "I can't. That's a HIPAA violation."

"HIPAA Schmippa. Come on. I want the most ridiculous, far-out name—"

"Not happening, Beatrice. Next."

I blow air out of my cheeks, sending my bangs fluttering up, then landing in my eyes. I brush them away. "Do you *ever* budge from your moral code?"

"Considering I'm eating pho in the least-me environment ever with a woman I'd have no occasion to otherwise, solely for the purpose of a revenge plot that I was adamantly against, yes."

"Okay, good point."

"Thank you. Now tell me more about you."

I give him the stink eye. "I think it's your turn, James."

"Fine." He sits back, hands folded across his flat abdomen. I really need to stop undressing Jamie with my eyes, but it's hard. I'm a nude portraitist by training. My default is to undress people with my eyes, let alone when they're smoking hot like him. "My father's a surgeon descended from a long line of surgeons, and that's his everything. He's English—well, his father was, his mother's American—so while he grew up in England, he has dual citizenship and had his medical training here in the States. My mother's French, old money, no career interest, does a lot of charity work."

That explains his speech. There's something adorably formal about it, a little crisper, more posh than that of typical American guys.

"I went to boarding school," he says. "Then college for premed, medical school, and here I am."

"Oookay. But . . . what about your interests?"

He peers up at the ceiling, brow furrowed as he thinks. "Exercise. Cooking. Reading. Work."

"Work's not an interest."

"It is to me," he says. "I love my work."

I bite back a smile. "Why kids?"

"Because they're the hopeful side of practicing medicine. Yes, I've made my share of bleak referrals to pediatric specialists for worrying symptoms, but by and large, I get to keep little people healthy and see them grow." He shrugs. "It's meaningful to me and a lot less depressing than many other medical specialties."

"That's . . ." I tip my head. "Very sweet."

Jamie blushes and focuses on adjusting his watch.

"What kind of reading?" I ask.

"I like it all. Fiction, nonfiction, poetry. Books are my kind of adventure—all that unknown from the comfort of my couch."

I smile. "That's a good way to put it. And a fear?"

He frowns in thought, then says, "I'm terrified of being caught in the middle of a flash dance."

I shudder and lift my lemonade in a cheers of sympathy. "Ditto." We clink glasses.

"Worst kiss?" I ask.

He blinks. "What?"

"Your worst kiss."

"And you need to know this why?"

Because I want a tiny crack in your armor. A sliver of vulnerability.

"Sounds like you're digging for teasing material," he prods.

I make a halo over my head with my hands. "Who me? Come on, it's bonding. And a girlfriend would know that."

He tips his head, examining me. "Sarah Llewlyn. At the eleventh-grade spring formal. It was awful. *I* was awful. And yours?"

"Heidi Klepper. Heidi was great. I was not. I was way too gung ho with tongue. It was a disaster."

Jamie laughs, then goes back in on his pho.

I realize I just inadvertently outed myself to him. And he's . . . un-fazed. "Uh. So, obviously, given what I just said, it's clear I'm not straight—" My voice dies away as Jamie's foot nudges mine.

He holds my eyes. "I might have a stick up my ass, but give me a little credit," he says gently. "I've made no assumptions about your sexuality."

My heart's drumming against my rib cage. My social circle is pre-dominantly queer, my twin is bi, I'm pan. My little world is especially welcoming and affirming of who I am, and I treasure that. And sure, the city's a pretty progressive place, but you never know when someone's going to disappoint you with their attitude toward it. "I thought you might be surprised."

"That," he says, sipping his green tea, "would be despicably hetero-normative of me, wouldn't it?"

I smile. He smiles. And the room feels a little warmer. "Yeah."

He sets down his tea. "If you want to talk more about it, I'm listening. Tell me what you'd want me to know as your boyfriend. Well, fake boyfriend. That is—you know what I mean."

I smile as he blushes and presses his glasses up his nose, then tell him, "I'm attracted to people for who they are, not what's under their clothes." I point to the banh bao. "And I like dumplings."

Jamie's smile deepens as he nudges the plate my way. "All yours."

I slide my pho bowl aside and pluck the last dumping with my chopsticks. "What about you? If you want to talk about it. Totally cool if you don't."

He tips his head, eyes down on his green tea. "I've only ever been attracted to women, but I tend to be a slow mover." He hesitates, then says, "Relationships seem to take time for me to feel . . . comfortable."

"Do you . . ." I swallow nervously, knocking his knee gently with mine beneath the table. "Do you feel comfortable with me?"

He glances up, and when our gazes connect, warmth spills through me. "Yes. Despite the grief you give me for being a curmudgeonly Capricorn."

I snort a laugh, throwing back my head. "It's my prerogative as a cantankerous Cancer!"

"Yes, I know. I did my astrological research and read up on Cancers." He shakes his head. "Sounds exhausting. I hope you sleep well at night."

I laugh harder, and a soft rumbling laugh leaves Jamie, too. Our laughter dies away, then silence falls between us, new and peaceful. Jamie's eyes hold mine. It feels like looking down at a receding wave and completely losing my orientation.

"So . . ." I scramble to stay upright, to pull myself back from whatever it is that's caught me like a violent undertow, dragging me nearer and nearer to him. "How do you think we did at the bowling alley? Besides being badass bowling champions."

As I set down my chopsticks on the empty dumpling plate, Jamie signals for the server. "I'd call it a success. I think we were convincing."

That kiss sure as shit was convincing. It flashes through my mind, flooding me with heat. His hands gripping my waist. His mouth slanted over mine, each brush of our lips deeper, hungrier than the last. I squeeze my thighs together. "Yeah." It comes out half squeak. "I think so, too."

Our server sets the tray with our receipt on the table, and before I can reach for my bag, Jamie's wallet is out, crisp bills—of course he has cash—nestled beneath the clip. Then he's standing, pulling back my chair.

"Jamie, I wanted to split the tab."

"Please, Bea. I have to spend money somewhere. Otherwise, I go on shopping sprees for Sir Galahad and Morgan le Fay. I can't burn all my hard-earned money on cat towers, battery-operated fake fish, and hand-knit mice from Etsy."

With a resigned sigh, I tug out a crinkled ten-dollar bill and add it to his neat twenties for an extra tip. It's Jamie and Bea in a nutshell.

"So tell me," I ask him, as we weave through the tables and step out into full-on night. I clutch my sweater tighter around me. "Do you iron your fifty-dollar bills before or *after* your underwear?"

A low, deep laugh bursts out of him as we start down the street. "Please, Beatrice. I pay someone to iron my money. *And* my underwear."

I stop in my tracks. "Did you . . . ?" Turning, I face him. "Did you just make a joke?"

He faces me, too. "I believe I did."

Night wind stirs around us, and the first fallen leaves tap-dance down the sidewalk. Jamie's rare playfulness warms the air between us.

It gives me the courage I needed to be brave, like he just was, to tell him the one thing I was too nervous to share over dinner. "Jamie?"

"Yes, Bea."

I force myself to stare up at him and take a deep breath. "I'm autistic. I didn't tell you right away because I never tell anyone right away. I've just learned it's best not to bother with the work of explaining until I know someone's really in my life. Now that we're doing this . . . fake relationship, trying to be friends, it's real and I want to be honest about who I am."

Jamie immediately steps closer and slowly clasps my hand, squeezing once. Silence holds between us. The kind of silence that I'm starting to realize he likes as much as I like it, silence that makes space for daydreams, for time and patience to find the right words.

"Thank you for telling me," he says quietly. "For trusting me."

I smile, relief buoying me up until I'm floating on the sidewalk. "You're welcome."

"If there's anything I can do to make things easier between us, will you tell me?"

My heart tumbles. Dammit. Why is my fake boyfriend so perfect?

"I'll tell you, Jamie. Promise." I take the first step down the sidewalk, his hand still in mine. But on my next step, my arm extends and then goes no farther, making me stumble back. Jamie stands rooted to the pavement.

"Beatrice?" he says.

"Yes, James."

Gently, he tugs me closer, until we're nearly chest to chest, his eyes holding mine. "That means a lot, that you told me."

"It means a lot that you didn't act like you see me differently now."

He tucks a strand of hair behind my ear as the wind whips it across my face. "I don't see you differently. I see you better."

My heart leaps and clatters against my ribs. "That's a nice way to put it."

Swallowing thickly, he squeezes my hand. "I . . ." He clears his throat. "One good turn deserves another: I have anxiety, compulsions. I take medication and go to therapy."

I squeeze his hand again, my thumb sweeping in soothing circles. "Thanks for trusting me, too. Just how you said—tell me if I can do something to make things easier with us."

Jamie peers down at me seriously, his gaze traveling my face. "I will."

I smile. "Good."

It's quiet as we stand facing each other, seeing the other with fresh eyes. It feels like the first time in front of a lover, right after peeling off my clothes. Naked. Nervous. Thrilled. I'm as fascinated as I am self-conscious. I think Jamie is, too.

But as we resume our stroll, I find myself relaxing. And also glancing up at him more than I should, seeing him in this new light.

When I met him, I had no idea what to do with Jamie, because he was so cold and terse and difficult to read. He gave me so little to work with. But now I know how funny he can be over texting, and when the moment's right, in person. I know that he's a good cook and kind toward animals. That periods don't weird him out, and that he's willing to bend the rules and sneak a cupcake before dinner. That knowing my sexuality, that I'm on the spectrum, he doesn't see me differently, he simply sees me better. That he has anxiety and compulsions, that he struggles in ways many people are ashamed to admit, but he feels brave and safe enough to trust me.

I don't like that what I'm seeing makes me like him even more than I've begrudgingly begun to. I don't like that it's comforting when his hand holds mine and gives it a gentle squeeze. But I can't deny it, either.

That mental closet groans ominously as I shove my weight against it. I can't go there. Not even a quick peek. It'll all come tumbling out. *Then* what?

"Here we are," he says.

I look up, stunned as I realize it's my apartment building. "We're home?"

"*You're* home." He throws a thumb over his shoulder. "I'm five minutes that way."

"I live this close to the city's best pho?"

He arches an eyebrow and leans in. "You do. If by 'close' you mean a twenty-minute walk."

"We walked twenty minutes?" I'm starting to sound like a disoriented parrot. My cheeks heat. "Oh, Jamie. I'm sorry I zoned out. It's nothing personal, I swear. I just get lost in my head sometimes and—"

"Bea." One of those soft, crooked smiles warms his face. "It's all right. It was quiet, but it was mutual. I enjoyed it immensely."

He pulls away, taking his warmth and that woodsy scent with him. Reaching past me, Jamie opens the outer door to my building, gently guiding me in. Then he offers one of those nods. A Jamie Nod. Deep and a little chivalrous.

"Good night, Bea."

"Wait."

He pauses, catching the door before it falls shut between us. "Yes?"

"Want to come up for a bit?" I swallow nervously. "To . . . meet Cornelius?"

Silence stretches between us. "Well," he finally says, stepping into the foyer, "I can't say no to meeting a hedgehog, can I?"

EIGHTEEN

Jamie

Bea stops abruptly when we step inside her apartment. Juliet and Jean-Claude sit side by side on the sofa, Jean-Claude on his laptop, a pile of papers beside him, Juliet curled up reading inside one of his arms.

"Oops," Bea mutters, as I shut the door behind us. "Forgot about them."

Juliet looks up, her expression morphing from concentration to glee. "BeeBee! West!" She snaps the book shut and bounds our way. "Come hang out. Jean-Claude, put work away."

He frowns, throwing a brief glance over the back of the sofa, then gives us a polite nod. "Can't. Christopher's got me in work up to my eyeballs." There's a tinge of resentment in his voice.

"That's what you get for being excellent and earning a promotion," Juliet says, smacking a kiss on his cheek, then turning to face us. "Want a drink? A snack—"

"That's okay," Bea says, tugging affectionately at one of Juliet's loose ribbons of hair falling from her bun. "I'm just introducing him to Cornelius. Thanks, though."

Her face falls. "Oh. Are you sure?"

"Juliet," Jean-Claude says sharply. "Leave them alone and come sit with me."

Bea frowns his way, but her sister only rolls her eyes affectionately and smiles. "We're working on Jean-Claude's appreciation for double-dating."

He sighs and sips his whiskey, broadcasting annoyance. Jean-Claude's never been one to socialize when he has a girlfriend. The longer the relationship lasts, the less I see of him.

"I appreciate the offer," I tell her, "but I have to work tomorrow. I can't be out too late. Thank you, though."

"All right," she says, glancing between us, her smile widening.

"Stop it," Bea tells her. "Your gloating is intolerable." Taking my hand, she tugs me down the hall. "Have you ever held a hedgehog?" she asks over her shoulder.

"I have not."

She opens a door at the end of the hall. "No big deal. I'll show you the ropes."

I come up short at her threshold. Her room is beautiful. Dark blue walls, a white duvet on her bed with a turquoise blanket on top that looks weighted. A table littered with rainbow shades of art supplies, and an egg-shaped orange chair hanging from the ceiling that brims with colorful clothes.

"Don't mind the mess," she says, grabbing the pile of laundry and quickly tossing it inside her closet. A pair of dark purple panties falls and lands with a splash on the warm wood floor. Bea doesn't notice.

I do. They're simple. No lace. Nothing fancy. And yet, the mere sight of them makes my chest too tight for air, sends blood rushing south.

Turning away, I shut my eyes and suck in a deep breath. This does not help because Bea's scent is concentrated here, soft and sultry. Sun-ripe fig and rich sandalwood wrap around me in a caress, torturing me with thoughts of pressing her into her bed, breathing her in as I kiss my way down her body, then taste her, where she's sweet and warm.

"Jamie?"

My eyes snap open. Bea's standing in front of me, looking concerned. "You okay?" she asks.

"Sorry. Eyes are bothering me."

"Want drops? I have them everywhere. My eyes get sore when I'm in a drawing zone. Not that I've had many of those lately."

"Thank you, no."

"Okey-doke." She marches toward a multitiered structure made of natural wood and mesh screens.

"You say you haven't had many 'drawing zones.' Have you been too busy?" I ask while following her.

She doesn't answer me at first, approaching what looks like Cornelius's living quarters. "I haven't had much success drawing lately," she says quietly, peering down through the top level, which is a screen as well. "I have a creative block right now."

"I'm sorry. That has to be frustrating."

"It is. But it'll be fine. It's happened before. I've gotten through it."

"How?"

"Patience. Waiting for inspiration to find me. And lots of Toni's cookies."

Bea slides open the structure's top screen, revealing a small hollowed log with a round opening. There's a pile of rocks nearby, a tiny tent with a birch-bark pattern, and a small pocket of fabric at the other corner that looks like—

"Is that a *doughnut*?"

Bea smiles up at me. "From Kate, my younger sister. She has a very serious relationship with doughnuts, and she likes to sew." Bea turns back to the structure, still speaking to me but eyes on the log, which she bends toward, lowering her voice. "She's a photojournalist and almost never home, so she sends us things that make us feel like she's around. It works. Every time I look at that little doughnut sleeping bag for Cornelius, I think of her."

I watch Bea, the concentration on her face as she makes a soft noise and peers inside the log. "You're close," I say. "The three of you."

"Yes."

"That must be nice."

"It is. But with closeness comes conflict. You've seen how Jules and I are. It has its ups and downs. Ooh, there he is!" she says, her voice turning sweet and melodic. "Hi, buddy!"

A tiny hedgehog peeks from the log, sniffing around before he hops out into Bea's hands.

"Cornelius," she tells him seriously. "I have some news, and you might not like it, but you deserve to know. You're not the only man in my life anymore. There's someone else."

Cornelius's head pops up tentatively, small dark eyes locked on me.

"Thanks a lot. Telling him I stole you out from underneath his nose. Now he's going to *love* me."

"Eh. He'll get over it. After a few mealworms, it'll be water under the bridge." She slides her hand down his quills. "Or should I say, sand under the tiny log."

"Is that what it is? A sandbox of sorts?"

"Mm-hmm," she says softly, eyes on Cornelius. "He loves it in there."

I watch Bea, tenderly holding this thorny creature, touching him fearlessly. She loves something prickly, a bit daunting to approach at first. It unravels the ever-present anxious knot in my chest, a ball of relief unspooling through my limbs. If she can love that little creature, quills and all, maybe she could—

No, not love. Of course not. But perhaps . . . understand me. How rare that would be.

She catches me watching her and smiles. "Sorry, I space out holding him. Some people have therapy dogs. I have a therapy hedgehog."

"You're very comfortable with him. Was it always this easy, handling a ball of needles?"

She laughs quietly. "They aren't *that* sharp. Not like a porcupine or anything." She kisses the tip of his nose. "But no, it wasn't always easy. He needed time and patience. And he balled around my finger once—not fun."

"How long did it take, becoming comfortable with each other?"

She tips her head, examining Cornelius as he starts to root around her hands, as if looking for something. "I can't honestly remember. I know it took a while. He'd been with someone else before, someone who liked the idea of a hedgehog but wasn't prepared for the work."

"That happens sometimes with pets."

"Too often. People shouldn't take on something to love and expect it to be convenient for them. You have to meet a living creature where they are, and love them for who they are, not who you want them to be."

A faint smile tugs at my mouth. "I don't think most people come at other *humans* that way, Bea, let alone animals."

"Well, they should," she says, turning toward me. "Want to hold him?"

I steal another glance at his quills. "I think perhaps we should start as hands-off acquaintances."

"Jamie Westenberg. You aren't *scared*, are you?"

"Bea Wilmot, you aren't trying playground intimidation tactics, are you?"

She smiles wide, one of those big Bea smiles that sends me off-kilter. It turns her eyes the color of the ocean on a sunny day. "Maybe."

"Well, congratulations. It's working." Tackling my cuffs, I unbutton both and roll them carefully up to my elbows. "All right. Tell me what to do."

She comes closer. "Now, relax and stay nice and still, holding your hands just like that." Gently she sets her hand next to mine, so our fingers brush, the backs of our hands touching. "Just wait," she says softly.

Cornelius sniffs from Bea's hand to mine, startling as he smells my index finger.

"Sorry," I tell him. "I do a lot of hand sanitizing. I probably smell like antibacterial soap and isopropyl alcohol."

Cornelius huffs like he agrees. But then he sets the tiniest paw on my hand, sniffing more, stretching until the other front paw joins, too. After a moment's deliberation, he crosses over into my cupped palms. He's surprisingly light, and the sensation of his paws almost tickles.

Bea moves away, crouching beside the hedgehog structure and opening a minifridge. She shuts it with her heel, then snaps open a container. "Let's reward him, shall we?"

"By all means."

She sets a few pieces of food in my palm—diced apple, judging by the sweet-tart scent. He quickly nibbles them and settles deeper into my hands.

"What do you think?" she says.

I meet her eyes and feel myself smile. "He's no geriatric cat, but he'll do."

———————

Stepping out of my hands onto the top floor of his home, Cornelius surveys his surroundings before he toddles off to his rocks.

"Well," I tell Bea, "I think that was a good bonding session."

"Absolutely. But you need to understand, this is a responsibility now. He knows you. He's going to have expectations. No being in and out of his life."

"Am I getting the commitment talk already?"

She smiles. "My hedgie deserves the best."

I peer down just as Cornelius disappears into his tiny tent. "I think he already has it." Unrolling my sleeves, I glance down at my wristwatch. "I should go. Work bright and early tomorrow."

"Sure thing." Striding past me toward her bedroom door, Bea reaches for the handle, then freezes.

Long enough that I ask, "What is it?"

She turns to face me and leans against the door. "Just remembering," she whispers, "we're going to need a romantic goodbye out there."

Unease rolls through me. I'm not exactly sure what "a romantic goodbye" looks like, but I'm fairly certain it involves my mouth on Bea's.

My heart starts racing, remembering what a disaster the Bowling Alley Kiss was from a performance standpoint. Because it wasn't a performance at all. It was pleasurable, and it wasn't supposed to be. It was only supposed to be a premeditated step on the path of revenge.

This is different, though. At the Alley, I wasn't prepared. It was spontaneous. This time it's planned. That should make it better, easier. Less . . . affecting. Right?

"Right," I tell Bea as much as myself. "That's fine."

I follow her out of the room, down the hall, until we're once again in their main living space, Juliet and Jean-Claude just as we found them.

Juliet peers up from her romance novel. "Hey!" She makes to sit up, but Jean-Claude's grip on the back of her neck tightens, holding her there. He leans in and presses a kiss to her temple. "Just relax. Bea can see him out. Stay with me."

Bea scowls at Jean-Claude as she opens the apartment door. "Next thing you know, she'll be on a leash."

"Bea!" Juliet chides. Jean-Claude's eyes narrow to slits as Juliet turns away from him and gives Beatrice a *What the hell are you doing?* look.

"We'll just be going." I nudge Bea out the door.

She shuts it behind us and rounds on me. "*How* are you friends with him?"

"It's complicated," I mutter. "He's more forced pseudo-family than friend."

"Yeah, well, I'd disown him."

My mouth quirks, almost smiling. "They're not watching, so I can say my goodbye here," I tell her, warming to the idea. Then I don't have to kiss Bea, while trying—and failing—not to enjoy it. "You don't actually have to see me out."

"Oh yes, I do," she says, strolling past me toward the stairs down to the first floor. "Twenty bucks says Jules is in her room, peeking through the curtains like a nosy poke as we speak. Well, assuming Jean-Claude lets her get up off the couch. He's so intense with her. I'm not overreacting, am I?"

I shrug. "He's always been like that. When he's in love, he's obsessed."

"It's weird," Bea says. "You two, even as pseudo-family or whatever, is weird."

"We've just always been together. Our mothers are like sisters, so it's been family vacations, holidays, then we ended up at the same university. He just sort of . . . stuck."

Bea makes a noncommittal noise.

"So." I clear my throat. "Assuming Juliet's escaped his clutches to peek from her balcony, what's this . . . romantic farewell we're thinking?"

"Definitely a tongue tangling for the books."

I miss a step and grab the railing just in time.

"Okay?" she asks.

"Yes. Fine."

I'm not fine. Not at all. My mind is snagged on "tongue tangling."

"I swear these stairs are a death trap," Bea says. "I trip on them at least once a day. I'm permabruised. Then again, I'm a walking accident."

"You shouldn't say that about yourself."

She arches an eyebrow, glancing over her shoulder as she opens the foyer door and bursts out into the night. "It's true, though."

Taking me by the hand, she glances casually toward her apartment's windows and brings us to the edge of the curb. "Right here," she says.

"She's watching?"

Bea nods, searching my face. "Both of them are. You have a queasy look. Is kissing me that terrible?"

"No, Bea. Not in the least . . ." Stepping closer, I strain for the words to tell her, but they stick in my throat, a traffic jam that builds to a brutal pileup.

What's "terrible," I almost tell her, *is how much I want to kiss you. The ways I want to kiss you. The ungentlemanly things I want to do to your body when you stand there, blushing as you peer down at the ground, swaying your skirt.*

Bea's thumb softly sweeps over my palm.

"Listen," she says, oblivious to my spiraling thoughts, "we don't have to kiss. Not if you don't want. You never have to do something with me that makes you uncomfortable. I just figured, since the bowling alley kiss, you didn't mind—"

"I *don't*. Mind, that is." I stare at her mouth, the line of her collarbone, the curve of her shoulder, and the edge of her tattoo, a swirling dotted line whose composition I can't figure out. Brushing my fingertips against her cheek, I slip them into her hair. "It's just . . . different this time. Last time, at the alley, was . . . impulsive."

She strokes my other palm with her fingertips, her eyes searching mine. "You know, it was a really great kiss," she says quietly. "In case you were doubting that, or anything. At least, you know, from my side of things."

Pleasure hums through my body. "I thought so, too."

"Definitely convincing," she says, her eyes on my mouth. "We had them eating out of our hands."

"Definitely."

"So." She clears her throat, blinking away. "You kissed me last time. How about this time, I'll kiss you? It's only fair."

"You'll kiss me?"

She nods seriously, her eyes meeting mine again. "And you better kiss me back."

I feel the rare impulse to smile as an odd pang of affection thrums in my chest. "I promise to kiss you back. For plausibility's sake, of course."

"Plausibility." Bea smiles. "Of course."

The air's warmer, the space between us heavy with silence. I break it, taking the final step that sets us toe-to-toe as the wind sends her skirt billowing against my legs. "Ready?" I whisper.

Slowly, she presses up on tiptoe, her eyes on my mouth. "I hope so."

I bend, closing the distance between us.

When our mouths meet, plausibility is the last thing on my mind.

NINETEEN

Bea

Jamie leans closer, warm and tall, his hazel eyes glowing as he peers down at me. My knees weaken a little, and I don't mean to grab his shirt, wrinkling the fabric inside my fists, but I do. I need something to hold on to, something to anchor me as the world fades around us.

His hands rest gently at the base of my throat, both thumbs sweeping across my collarbones. A shower of sparks beneath my skin follows in their wake as my heart pounds against my ribs.

I'm reminded forcefully that I got the short end of the stick. It's much easier to kiss someone in the heat of the moment, the way Jamie did at the bowling alley. But now? Now I'm the one who has to kiss him while moonlight bathes his beautiful face in an otherworldly glow and the wind throws my skirt his way, as if nature itself is urging me toward him. My determination dissolves. This doesn't feel safe or fake.

It feels dangerously real.

"Beatrice," he whispers, dragging me back from my spiraling thoughts. My eyes find his. "Hmm?"

Our gazes tangle, then draw us closer. I breathe him in, the scent of sage and cedarwood and foggy air. When I exhale, it's deeper, a little easier.

"It's me," he says, as if somehow Jamie knows I need the reminder that I'm not repeating history. That with him, I'm transposing what was done to me nearly two years ago.

Back then, I thought I'd found love, and it turned out to be a lie. Now I'm living a lie that has no chance of turning out to be love. That's what I want, and that's what I get with Jamie—boundaries and trust, maybe even a little friendship. With him, I'm safe.

As I press on tiptoes, clutching him for courage, I wonder if what we share, this inversion of what broke me apart, might be the very thing that puts me back together.

My lips brush his, faint and soft. He draws in a quick, rough breath, retreating so slightly, I almost miss it. But I notice. And I wait. Patient. Still. Jamie's gaze wanders my face, his hands slide up my throat, and air rushes out of me, following the path of his touch.

When his fingertips graze my cheeks, I shut my eyes, lost as his mouth meets mine again, deeper and reverent. He sighs as I release his shirt and wrap my arms around his waist, holding him close, chest to chest, pounding heart to pounding heart. I taste the green tea he drank with dinner, the whisper of peppermint, something warm and dizzying and perfectly *him*.

My legs turn liquid as his tongue sweeps against mine. All I've known of Jamie is his restraint, his control, yet here he is, tasting me, groaning roughly, losing himself in me, even for just a fleeting moment. It makes tears prick my eyes.

I was right. And I was wrong. Kissing Jamie, I feel that while I'm safe . . . I'm also in danger. No, he won't hurt me the way I've been hurt before, but he might make me believe again. In something I lost. Something I wasn't sure I'd ever feel again. Something I'm terrified to hope for and risk the chance of those hopes being dashed.

His hands drift from my face, down to my hips, tugging me close against the hard, heavy length of him, straining against his slacks. My head falls back as his lips trail my throat, as his touch drifts up my ribs and his thumbs sweep the tender curve of my breasts, teasing closer and closer to my nipples. I lean into his touch, pressing every part of me into every part of him.

"Please," I whisper.

Jamie smiles softly against my neck, his hands slipping down my body, curving over my ass, moving me against him. "Please, what, Beatrice? What do you need?"

That voice. Low and ragged, like he's hanging on by a thread, when all I want to do is make him snap.

"I need..." But I'm helpless to speak, as Jamie palms my ass, notches the hard, thick length of him tight against me where I'm desperate for relief, chasing something aching, sweet, and torturous—

BAM BAM BAM.

My eyes fly open, taking in the world around me. Bedroom. Sunlight. Warm sheets. Air whooshes out of me as I sit up, the pulse of unfulfilled release sharp between my thighs. My door rattles again with three hard bangs.

That's when I realize my phone's alarm is playing a thirty-second stretch of acoustic guitar music. Judging by the time and when I set my alarm for, it's been on repeat for an hour. And here I thought my dreams were just capable of epic soundtracks.

"I can't take it anymore!" Jules shouts.

"Sorry!" I yell back. Reaching for my phone, I shut off my alarm, then throw myself back in bed and bury my face beneath the pillows.

That dream. Wow.

Except it wasn't *all* a dream. Up until the moment Jamie's hands began wandering my body, his mouth branding my skin, that's exactly what happened last night—a kiss that left me wanting everything my subconscious took and ran with in my dreams.

Of course, Jamie was restrained, gentlemanly as ever, seeing me inside, standing beyond the door as I locked myself in, a foyer between us not nearly enough.

Heart pounding. Kiss-stung lips. For just a moment I drank him in, framed by the doorway and starlight, wishing for his silky hair and warm skin and long, hard body moving over mine.

Then I turned and walked up those steps, not once looking back.

I have a serious problem.

I want Jamie. I'm not sure how far that wanting goes, but the wanting itself—whatever it is—it's too much.

Whipping back the sheets, I wince as my feet hit the cold wood floor. I pull on a robe, nab a hair tie to make a quick high bun, then throw myself down at my desk, opening a sketch pad as I locate my charcoal tin.

I stare at the paper, creativity buzzing in my fingertips, resolve flooding my veins. I'm going to draw Jamie Westenberg out of my system. I'm going to bleed this *want* dry until it's poured out onto paper and I have something new, even if I burn it all, even if none of it ever sees the light of day.

My heart got the best of me last time.

That's not happening again.

———————

I'm where I've been since I woke up, no sense of time's passage. My headphones ooze string music, the raw slide of a violin, the cello's carved-out ache. A spasm in my back, the fact that I've lost feeling in my butt, gnawing hunger pains dwindled to dull cramps, all indicate I've been here for a long time.

More banging on the door means I've been here too long. At least according to mother hen Juliet.

BAM BAM BAM.

The banging is quieter than it was this morning, muffled by my sound-canceling headphones and the string music. I hit pause and slide them off my ears. "Come in."

The door swings open. "How nice to do this twice in one day," she says tartly.

"What would I do without you, Juliet? Draw until I'm done? Have some peace? Live blissfully unaware of people's capacity for biting sarcasm?"

Helping herself to my room, she attacks my sheets, quickly making my bed. "You'd be bored. And lonely. Now, get up. Movie time."

I blink at her, stunned. Movie nights have been rare since she and Jean-Claude started their whirlwind romance, but not so rare that I forget when they start. "It's eight o'clock already?"

Done with the bed, Jules strolls past me and throws open my curtains to . . . darkness.

"Huh." I spin on my chair and take in the smoked-glass sky, sparkling with city lights.

"Shower, please," she says, softening the remark with a gentle tweak of my messy bun. "You're ripe."

"Yes, Mother." I set my charcoal in its tin and close the sketchbook. But once Jules is out of my room, I open it again for just a moment, lifting the pages and fanning through them. It's a slow movie unfolding, the way they used to draw cartoons. Each frame a different study of Jamie, some part of him or the whole. Those long, rough-knuckled, yet elegant fingers. His strong profile. Drinking tea over a chessboard, a disobedient lock of hair fallen on his forehead. Cupping my face in his hands, his mouth a whisper away from mine.

I stare at the last drawing. Last night's kiss. My stomach knots with more than hunger pains.

Drawing didn't help. Drawing made it worse. No, drawing can't do that. My art's always been tangled up in complex emotions, especially after Tod, but I've never believed art could make anything worse. Art can only reveal, only make us more truthful. It's just that sometimes being truthful *feels* like it's made things worse. Because when you face the facts, then you have to live with them. Eventually, you have to *do* something about them.

I have no idea what to do.

To cope, I'm going to distract myself until some epiphany comes crashing down on me like a piano from the sky. For now, I'll drink a bowl of wine and drown my worries in fermented grapes.

After a distracted shower and a change of clothes, I have a name for my problem, and that's a step. I'm calling it the Jamie Paradox. I need Jamie to carry out my revenge—and I *will* have my revenge—and I need distance from him so I don't fall down the slippery slope of infatuation straight into dangerous territory that I won't even name.

"Love!" Margo hollers from the kitchen, a spatula pointed in my direction. I wince like she's thrown me a curse. "I can see it in your eyes already."

"You are not playing it cool like we agreed," Sula says over her shoulder from a corner of the sofa. "Hey, Bea." She raises her wineglass in greeting.

"Hey, yourself," I tell her. "The hair's purple. I like it."

She smiles up at me. "Needed a change. Well, I was going to be subtle, but Margo blew that, so I'll just ask: how are *things* with the tall and dashing West?"

"*Things* are just fine with Jamie, thank you very much."

Sula lifts a purple eyebrow. "Seemed more than fine when you kissed at the bowling alley."

"You should have seen them after their dinner date last night," Jules calls from inside the fridge, pulling out a fresh bottle of white wine. "Freaking adorable. We all said it at Jean-Claude's party, and we were right: how adorable would they be together?"

My teeth grind. Lovely. I get to freak out about my Jamie infatuation *and* endure group gloating.

"I know things started off a little rocky," Sula says, "but I still think it's romantic."

"Hmm." I fold my arms across my chest, annoyance clawing at my skin. "I need wine for this."

"You're not going to tell us anything?" Margo offers me a taste of snack mix and watches me expectantly.

"More salt. And nope."

She frowns and adds a few shakes of sea salt. "This new tight-lipped version of Bea is not working for me. I reject this upgrade."

"That's why we're having a romance movie night," Jules tells her. "We're getting BeeBee boozed and heart-eyed with some wine and rom-coms, then she's going to tell us everything."

"Rom-coms?" I wrinkle my nose. "Give me angst. I want suffering. "Give me *Shakespeare in Love. Atonement. Blue Valentine*—"

"God, stop," Toni says, strolling out from the bathroom. "Next, you'll be calling for *Titanic*. Those aren't romances. We are here for happy endings, am I right?"

I accept his hug begrudgingly because I'm still miffed at all these meddlers, no matter their varying degrees of guilt.

"Hug me back, you goober," he says.

My compromise is a noodle-armed pat. "You're very needy tonight."

Once Toni's done squeezing the pulp out of me, Jules hands me a brimming glass of white wine. "You'll have to wait and watch Keira Knightley cry on your own time," she says. "Happy endings only. I can't take the heartbreak."

"You know what I *hate*?" Sula says as Margo plops onto the sofa next to her, snack mix in hand. "I hate those movies that get you thinking you're in for a romance. That make you feel all happy inside, give you hot sex, great character development, all the emotions, and then—boom—they don't end up together."

"Or one of them *dies*," Toni says darkly. "Those are *not* romances."

"They aren't?" I ask.

The whole room tells me, "*No!*"

"Okay," I mutter, tail between my legs as I settle into an armchair. "Just asking."

"You read romance," Margo says. "How do you not know this?"

"I guess I never noticed that they always end up together."

Jules sighs. "I loan her my beloved historical romance novels, and this is how she repays me. She doesn't even grasp the best part of the genre: happily ever after."

Sipping my wine, I shrug. "I'm in it for the fucking and the fancy talk."

"Fair, but let us be clear," Toni says. " 'Romance' means happy endings. 'Love story' means they took a romance novel, cut out the back ten percent, and replaced it with misery."

"Preach." Sula knocks his wineglass in cheers. "I'm Team Romance.

Otherwise, I'd rather watch something grim from minute one. It's awful starting happy and ending sad."

"Same." Jules grabs the remote and turns on the movie, then has a sip of her wine. "There's nothing worse than thinking you're in for a romance, getting invested in a couple's happiness, then watching outside forces tear it apart, or worse—watching two people in love destroy it themselves."

As their words seep in, I freeze with my wine halfway to my mouth. That's my solution to . . . everything. Not just getting the best revenge but solving the Jamie Paradox.

The root of my problem in the Jamie Paradox is that there's nothing disingenuous between us, no act, no script. Having tentatively agreed not to assume the worst in each other, we're now winging it gently, careful of each other while figuring out how to be friends. I'm not sure how far our behavior—beyond those kisses—is going to go in convincing the group we're falling in love. It's definitely not going to help me keep my feelings in check, either.

I need a manual, guidelines for how to make this so clearly a performance for me when I'm with Jamie. That way, my emotions won't get carried away, and it will still be believable enough to the meddlers that we have them eating out of our hands. What better material to work from than these schmaltzy movies that my friends love?

It hits me, as inspiration always does, suddenly, overwhelmingly, consuming my thoughts. I scramble for my phone, pull up the notepad, and type:

—Rom-com movie study session

—Rom-com-style dates. Document on social media

—Use rom-com material liberally in front of "friends"

"Who are you texting?" Jules asks, giving me a knowing glance. "Jaaaaamie?"

I don't glance up from my phone as I open my messages and find my thread with the man in question. "Yes."

"Ooooh," they all croon.

I roll my eyes. "Start the movie, you weirdos."

As the opening credits begin and upbeat pop music fills the room, I set my plan into motion.

> **BEA:** James. How many rom-coms have you watched?

My phone dings thirty seconds later.

> **JAMIE:** 3.

Of course he has. And of course he knows *exactly* how many.

> **JAMIE:** I enjoyed 2 of them. The third was a 90-minute cliché. Why?

> **BEA:** Those flicks are our first-class ticket to Revenge City.

> **JAMIE:** I'm confused.

> **BEA:** This Wednesday is blocked off for our next "date." My turn to plan it. It'll be clear then.

> **JAMIE:** I have a strong premonition I'm not going to like this.

I send him my favorite evil-grinning GIF.

> **BEA:** No idea what you're talking about.

TWENTY

Jamie

"Hands down best?" I peer over my shoulder and tell Bea, "*10 Things I Hate About You.*"

She grips a fistful of my jacket and shuffles behind me. We've been separated by crowds at the conservatory twice and we're both over it. "Yeah, it's rom-com excellence. But how much can we take from that? No paintball." She tugs my jacket. "Too messy for Mr. Tidy."

"Too *hazardous*," I tell her.

"Why, Jamie, whatever are you referring to? Me with a paintball gun—couldn't be a better combination."

I throw her a skeptical glance. "I was thinking more like paint by numbers. Isn't that a thing the kids do these days? Throwback activities from our youth? Sounds Instagrammable. Much less stressful than carnivorous flowers."

"You're such a grump. That Venus flytrap barely nipped you."

"It nearly ate my hand!"

"Shh," she says. "You're scaring the children. A pediatrician like you should know better."

"Beatrice."

"James." She stops me in front of a towering trellis of wisteria. "Stay right there."

"I still don't understand the need to go this far with our date planning. I thought we were doing fine."

She huffs impatiently. "You weren't listening to those hooligans blubbering about their love of happy endings. You didn't listen to them gloating about their matchmaking excellence."

"I still feel like it's a bit extreme."

"How hard is it to derive a little rom-com inspiration? Come on, don't wimp out on me. What else does *10 Things I Hate About You* teach us?"

"That the bad guy always gets the girl," I tell her. "Patrick Verona is a duplicitous jerk to Kat Stratford for far too long. And we wonder why toxic masculinity thrives. We romanticize it!"

She sighs. "You're terrible today. Absolutely terrible."

"Fine. You want ideas? I have an excellent paintball-adjacent activity. Jean-Claude was whining last month when Juliet dragged him to one of those painting classes specifically for couples. They're built-in date nights."

Bea opens her phone and sets up the camera mode. "I think *that's* a little extreme."

"Oh no, you don't. If I have to suffer through a near reenactment of *Little Shop of Horrors*, then by God, you're going to an amateur painting class for couples."

Her jaw drops. "This is *not* that bad."

"Neither is painting. You had your idea. This is mine."

Bea glares at me. "Give me a minute. I'm thinking of a stunning reply."

"I'll wait."

"Fine," she moans. Stomping over to me, Bea leans in and snaps a selfie. My head's cut out of the frame. "Dammit, James, be useful, will you?"

"I beg your pardon." I frown down at her. "I get two weekdays off per *month* and I'm spending one of them slowly poaching in my skin while sneezing to death, thanks to you. Then you have the audacity to lecture me about usefulness. *How* is this useful?"

Bea shoves her phone into my hand, well on her way to shouting. "We're being Instagrammable!"

A man gives us a concerned look and herds a group of children away.

"Conservatory." Bea gestures around her. "Flowers. Romance. Chess and tea."

"Chess and tea?" I ask. "When did you mention that?"

She scowls at me. "That *was* going to be your reward, if you were nice. You are not being nice, Jamie."

Exhaling heavily, I fix my cuff sleeves until the buttons bisect my wrists and spin my watch until it's in its rightful place. "I apologize."

"Accepted. Now, take the damn selfie of us so I can Instagram it."

Angling the phone, I snap a picture of us: Bea, her arms around my waist, eyes squinted in a forced but convincing happy grin. I'm peering down at her, a faint smile tipping my mouth. It's actually a grimace.

Somehow, it all looks quite romantic. It makes me wonder how many photos of couples on social media are complete lies.

"Damn, James," she says, examining the photo on her phone. "We're both pissy as piss, and you still took a good picture."

"It's the staggering height. Great angle."

Pocketing her phone, she peers up at me. "How tall *are* you?"

"Six four." I clasp her elbow and pull her out of harm's way, just as a herd of rambunctious elementary school kids bolts past us.

"Whoa." She glances over her shoulder. "Who knew it was field-trip day?"

"Somehow I guessed, based on the many yellow buses outside."

Bea yanks her elbow out of my grip. "I don't want to do this any more than you, but this is the price of revenge. Why are you so goddamn cranky today?"

Glancing around, I spot a small alcove with a bench by the window. Tucked away from shrieking children and cloying hot air perfumed with flowers, it looks calm and quiet. "Follow me, please."

Grumbling, Bea trails me, arms folded across her chest. When we're in our alcove, I sit on the bench. Bea doesn't join me. "I'm being terrible," I admit.

"Yep."

"I'm stressed. And when I'm stressed, I get anxious and cranky, and I don't want to be in noisy, crowded, hot spaces like this."

Bea's arms fall to her sides. "I didn't know, Jamie. You could have told me."

"I should have. I didn't think it was going to bother me so much." Sighing, I shut my eyes and drop my head against the wall. "It's my father's sixty-fifth birthday party two weekends from now. My mother keeps calling me and asking me if I'm coming."

"And . . ."

Slowly, I open my eyes and stare at the ceiling. "I caved and said yes."

"Is this bad?" she asks.

"My family dynamic is . . . unpleasant."

"Okay, then. Um—" She scratches behind her ear, shifting on her feet. "Would it help if I came?"

I meet her gaze, blinking in disbelief. "What?"

She shrugs. "It's a birthday party for your dad. I'm your girlfriend—I mean, I'm supposed to be. It would look weird if I *didn't* go, right? Plus, very Instagrammable."

I stare at her, turning over the idea in my head. Colorful, honest Bea in the stuffy, cold halls of my childhood home. She'd be miserable. "That's nice of you, but not necessary."

"Oh, come on, Jamie. How bad can they be?"

"Bad, Beatrice. Very bad. Arthur and Aline. My brothers except Sam. You'd despise them. They're the worst parts of me."

"Wow." She lowers herself next to me on the bench, patting my hand. "You're a little hard on yourself, aren't you?"

"It's the truth."

"Let me come. It's no big. I'm sure I can hold my own with them." She knocks shoulders with me. "Look at you. I don't mind you too much."

A wry smile tugs at my mouth. "I don't mind you too much, either."

"Great. It's a deal. I'll come."

"No, Bea. I don't want you to meet them."

"Let's solve this like adults." Standing, she grips my hand, tugging me upright.

"Where are we going?"

"Chess and hot beverages, duh."

"I thought I lost those privileges."

She smiles over her shoulder. "You've earned chess and tea *provided* the winner gets to decide if I come to the birthday party."

I glare at her as she tugs me through the crowd. Bea's a good chess player. There's a distinct chance I'll lose and then have to suffer subjecting her to my family.

And then she'll have seen me at my worst.

Perhaps that wouldn't be so bad. Because then the far-off, foolish chance I've entertained in weak moments, the possibility that she might actually like me, might actually one day want this odd friendship to become something more, would be entirely wiped away.

"Fine," I tell her.

Spinning and backtracking, she shakes our hands up and down. "That's the spirit."

———

Bea's phone clicks with the sound of a photo being taken. I lower my tea. "Was that really necessary?"

She snorts as she stares at her phone. "You looked just like Cornelius when he's blissed out in a bath."

I nudge her foot under the table. "Stop laughing at me."

"I'm sorry! It's cute. I swear I'm not laughing *at* you."

"That's exactly what you're doing." I sip my tea and exaggerate whatever expression I was already making. Hell if I know what it was; I just know it entertained her.

"Stop it!" She laughs harder, clutching her side.

Now I'm laughing, too. Boulangerie is mellower than it was when we were last here, perhaps because it's a weekday afternoon, so our laughter easily echoes around the space. We earn a few amused glances before we quiet down.

"Oh man." Bea wipes her eyes. "So good."

I stare at the chessboard and shake my head. "You slaughtered me."

She grins. "I did. And now you've got a partner in crime for the awful party." She tidies up the pawns, setting them into their drawers. "Do you want to talk about your family?" she asks, eyes on her task.

I swallow my tea and set down my cup. "Not really."

But maybe I should. Maybe getting it out is better than bottling it up where it builds like a pressure cooker right beneath my sternum.

Bea says nothing, eyes on her task. It's almost like she knows it helps, when the whole weight of her focus isn't on me expectantly as I search for words to explain.

"My father's a world-renowned cardiothoracic surgeon. My older brother's a surgeon, the younger ones are surgeons in training. That's what you do when you're a Westenberg. As the only pediatrician in the family, I'm a disappointment."

Bea shuts the pawn drawer and peers up at me. "A *disappointment*? You save babies, Jamie."

"Generally, I just make sure they grow up healthy."

"Don't downplay your work," she says fiercely. "Don't make yourself small just because someone else has."

A piece of hair falls in her face and swings precariously close to her coffee. I tuck it back, behind her ear. "Objectively, what I do requires fewer elite skills, less time in residency. A surgeon is a more prestigious career in my family's eyes, except for my brother Sam. I've made peace with it. It's just that my father hasn't. Arthur doesn't let me forget."

Bea frowns. "I don't think I like Arthur."

"That makes two of us, but I've learned it's easier to ride the waves of his disapproval rather than argue with him."

"Can I just say something?"

I nod. "Of course."

Bea leans in. "I hope you know this without me saying it, but you are the farthest thing from a disappointment that I have ever met, Jamie Westenberg. The people who matter know that. As my mom says, anyone who can't love you for you doesn't deserve your heart."

Her words seep in and warm me better than the best cup of tea. "That's kind, Bea. Thank you."

She smiles as she sits back, tugging apart her chocolate croissant. "So. Game night coming up. Are you prepared?"

"It's board games. I'd imagine so. Why?"

"Not the games. The cuteness. It's got to be next-level acting in front of them. We've been together—you know, *fake* together—for a few weeks now. We have to canoodle, like we're really starting to get into each other."

"I think we can handle it. Are you worried?"

Her gaze dips to my mouth, then dances away. "Well, no. I mean, I think we've got the kissing thing down. Right?"

I try not to stare at her mouth, but it's hard. It's very hard not to think about how easy it is—how pleasurable it is—to kiss Bea. "Right."

Eyes down, she pops another bite of croissant in her mouth, then picks up her pen and draws on the coffee napkin to her left.

"Solid kissing, that's in our favor," she says. "But it's different than spending hours around people, pretending like you're into me. The real question is, James, can you canoodle?"

"Oh, Beatrice, I can canoodle."

And I'll enjoy it more than I should.

"What about you?" I ask. "Are you bringing your canoodle A game?"

She peers up and narrows her eyes. "You bet your ass I am."

The door opens to Boulangerie and my heart lurches into my throat. My ex-girlfriend, Lauren, walks in, hair back, scrubs on, most likely after a morning of surgeries.

Thankfully, Bea's unaware, lost in her sketching.

When Lauren steps up to the counter and glances around, I angle away from her as much as possible, pointing to Bea's paper napkin and the dark lines she's drawing. "Still creatively blocked?"

She glances up, pen in hand, then back down to the napkin. "It's getting a little better. Thankfully Sula's chill and doesn't rush me. I've come up with enough designs that we have a pretty solid variety in our stock as is."

"Are you happy, working at the Edgy Envelope?"

"I love working there," she says, sketching still. "I mean, Sula and Toni drive me up the wall, but I enjoy designing, being creative. It's a good place for now, even if it's not my forever place."

"And did you always want to be"—a blush heats my cheeks—"an erotic artist?"

"I studied art in college, and my favorite work was with nudes. I was fascinated by how beautiful humans are. You know?"

My heart drums against my ribs, something deep and foreign unfurling in my chest. "Yes. The human body is beautiful. Terrifyingly complex beneath the surface, but beautiful."

"Exactly!" she says, brightening, her feet wedging between mine under the table. "I was hooked. How original and singular each person is. The parts of our bodies that diet culture and photoshopping tell us we should try to erase and hide—human 'imperfection'—they were what I thought, and still do think, make us works of art. Stretch marks. Wrinkles. Freckles and fine lines and rolls and curves. I realized I wanted to make art celebrating that, defending that belief."

Glancing up at me, Bea frowns, then peers back down at her napkin, her pen flying over the delicate paper. "I realized it's even more powerful," she continues, "when I can show the *sensuality* of those so-called imperfections. How we can appreciate ourselves and desire each other not when we're perfect but when we're *us*. So I started drawing, then painting, lovers together, individuals loving themselves. That was my art career before the Edgy Envelope—commissions and selling paintings through exhibits."

"What made you stop?"

She pauses her sketching and hesitates for a moment. "I . . . had a really toxic relationship. My partner fucked with my head, personally and professionally. He's a very talented artist, and I valued his opinion. So when he started critiquing my work, I internalized a lot of doubt. I didn't realize he was jealous of me, that instead of seeing our successes as compatible, he felt threatened."

I nearly drop my tea. "That son of a—"

"It's okay, Jamie." She nudges her foot against mine beneath the table.

"It's not."

"You're right, it's not. It's in the past, is what I mean."

"And is it to do with him, why you haven't painted since?"

She bites her lip. "It's complex. How Tod treated me, how bad it was, that was hard to recognize at first. I spent some time in therapy, working through it after he broke up with me. He got some advantageous career offer and moved to a different city, thank God, and I know now that he was full of shit. I've still struggled with painting, though, not so much to get his voice out of my head but to find my own again, if that makes sense? Painting is so personal. It's emotional for me. I haven't been in the right space for it."

Her pen falters. And my heart plummets.

I'm not the most emotionally advanced person, but even I can see how Bea's "spinsterhood," as Juliet's teasingly referred to it, has been just like her painting—that dating is something she had to set aside while she healed, until she could feel safe and ready to move forward. "Your sisters know this? How he treated you? What happened?"

She stares at the paper napkin. "He and I mostly hung out just the two of us, or in the art scene. Kate's barely been home in years, and the little bit of time he was up for hanging out with Jules, he was on his good behavior. So my sisters didn't know the real Tod, and I . . . I never told them what happened because I didn't want to admit to them who he really was, that I'd fucked up so bad in picking a guy like him. I wanted to move on. It's embarrassing."

"Bea. There's nothing to be embarrassed of. He was cruel to you. That's not your fault. It's all his."

She bites her lip. "Yeah, I know. I want to tell them. I will soon, I hope. I just have to find the guts." Clearing her throat, she rolls her shoulders, as if shaking off a chill. "Anyway, since the breakup, I've been in a bit of a holding pattern. It won't last forever. I know that I want to try again. With art. Maybe with a relationship, too, eventually. But, starting with painting. I haven't been able to do more than pick up a brush. I just stand there, staring at a blank canvas. I'm sick of it."

"You'll paint again," I tell her.

Bea throws me a peeved look. "Yeah, thanks to you and this horrible paint date you came up with."

"Perhaps it's serendipitous. That could be your fresh start."

"Maybe," she says quietly, taking a bite of chocolate croissant. "I've just been stuck in this rut for so long."

I brush a crumb off her cheek, where fine, dark tendrils of hair have fallen and kiss her skin. "All of us get stuck sometimes, Bea. I know I've been."

A milk steamer screeches and pulls my eyes toward the front, just as Lauren takes her coffee, then turns. Our eyes meet.

I give her a polite nod and, without waiting for her to acknowledge me, refocus on Bea. A moment later, the door swings shut, and Bea steals a quick glance over her shoulder at Lauren's retreating form. "Who was that?"

I sip my tea. "My ex."

She lets out a long whistle. "I only saw the back of her, but wow. You downgraded."

"Stop it. You're beautiful."

A blush warms her cheeks. "I wasn't fishing for a compliment."

"I know that. And I wasn't being disingenuous. You are."

Craning her head to the side, Bea groans. "Shit. I messed something up when I rubbernecked. Can you just press right there—" She points to the offending spot.

I slide my thumb carefully along the knotted muscles at the base of her skull, then down to her shoulder. Too quickly, my mind travels a dangerous road. How little it would take to cup her neck, angle her mouth, and meet it with mine for no reason other than the sheer pleasure of it.

Bea sighs as I rub the taught muscles of her neck. I remind myself of their anatomical names, desperate to check my body's longings, my thoughts' hopeless direction.

Splenius capitis. Semispinalis capitis. Longissimus capitis.

"Jamie," she says quietly. "That feels so good."

Her eyes fall shut, allowing me to look at her without giving everything away. "I'm glad."

She smiles dreamily. "Be careful. Keep it up and your fake girlfriend is going to demand real neck massages every time we hang out. You might get more than you bargained for in this fauxmance."

I watch Bea as she melts under my touch. As her head grows heavy. As I push aside the disconcerting thought that "more than I bargained for" might be exactly what I want.

"Did you and the ex end on good terms?" she asks.

"Not really. She connected with my father and his practice through me, and when he offered her a place on his team, he told her he didn't work with family. She chose the practice over me."

"Jesus," Bea says. "That's shit."

"It is and it isn't. I felt used, but honestly she's incredibly capable, and she would have gotten that spot with my father whether or not she'd met him through me. It's just regrettable that it had to happen like that."

I don't tell her that when Lauren did that, it reinforced the feeling I'd spent my whole childhood battling, that once again, no matter how hard I tried and excelled, I wasn't enough. It's too raw, too exposing. Even though some part of me aches to entrust it to her.

Instead, I tell Bea, "It's ultimately better. We were similar but not well suited. I understand that now, and I try not to hold it against her."

"Even if you have your head wrapped around it, that's still hurtful." Bea's eyes flutter open and meet mine. "I'm sorry it happened."

My thumb drifts to her jawline, the soft skin beneath her mouth. "Thank you. But I'm glad it ended."

Because if it hadn't . . . well, where would I be? Living that tidy, neat life I have for so long. A life, I've realized recently, that I wasn't nearly as content with as I'd told myself I was.

"You're glad?" Bea asks.

I search her eyes, my touch savoring her warmth, her softness. "I am."

Our gazes lock, and Bea leans in. I lean closer. And then she cups my jaw and gives me a long, deep kiss that turns my blood hot, makes me grip the table's edge so I don't topple over as I breathe her in and take our kiss deeper. She tastes so damn perfect, like her mouth was made for mine, like we were designed to do this. A soft sigh leaves her as my tongue strokes hers, as I slip my hand into her hair and fist those soft, dark waves. When she pulls away, there's a satisfied smile on her face.

I stare at her, stunned. "What was that for?"

Picking up her pen, Bea resumes drawing on the paper napkin. I realize she's drawing *me*. She nods slightly toward the outside, where Lauren stands waiting for a cab, directly in our line of sight. "That was what all our kisses are for, James. Revenge."

TWENTY-ONE

Bea

"Game night has commenced. Where are you?" Jamie's voice is on speakerphone as I shimmy up my panties and smooth down my dress.

"Work still. Almost time to close, though. You're there already?"

"Jean-Claude said he got tied up at work, so I came early to help with setup."

My heart does a tiny backflip. "That's nice of you."

"It was nothing. Christopher was here, too, being useful, so all I ended up doing was setting out a few condiments and tidying up a certain someone's colorful trail of socks, hair ties, and fine-tipped markers. Ahem."

"It's like Hansel and Gretel's bread crumbs. They lead you straight to my room."

"Which is where I remain. Cornelius and I are bonding."

I catch my reflection in the mirror as I wash my hands. I'm smiling. "He's a good morale booster. He'll help you get psyched up for our performance tonight."

"Oh, we're staying busy. I just explained your rom-com plan and gave him the *10 Things I Hate About You* one-sentence synopsis."

"Which was?"

"Broody stare-downs, singing in bleachers, poem reciting, making out with paint. But don't worry," Jamie says. "Our paint date is as far as I'm taking my inspiration. Poetry's not my strength. And serenading you would be cringey. I can't carry a tune to save my life."

"No more broody stare-downs, either. Meeting you was one long lesson in the pain of a broody stare. It was *not* romantic."

"What is she talking about, Cornelius? That was our meet-cute."

I snort, throwing open the door of the bathroom and looking both ways to ensure there aren't eavesdroppers nearby. "Tell Cornelius, try meet-disaster."

"I refuse. He's on my side now. I gave him apples."

"Wow, buying his love, huh?"

"Fortifying our bond." I can see his eyebrow arching, his serious expression holding until mine cracks. "Cornelius told me, ten years from now, our meet-disaster will be cute, the trauma dimmed by time and nostalgia. We'll tell the kids how I could barely string a sentence together and you spilled alcohol on me—not once but twice in one night. You'll tell it better, so I'll listen while you do, covered in paint splatters from your latest masterpiece, love for me still shining in your eyes."

I come to an abrupt stop in the store, stunned by the picture he's drawn with one of his rare forays into playfulness. Panic squeezes my chest. How is that so easy to envision? Why does it sink into my thoughts and settle with a heavy sigh of *If only*?

"That . . ." I bite my lip. Hard. Long enough so I don't blurt something absurd like, *That sounds absolutely perfect.* "That's cute. You should say that later around everyone. When you're looking at me all moony-eyed and someone decides it's socially acceptable to ask when we're having kids."

"Talking kids already!" Sula calls from the office.

"Gotta go," I tell Jamie. "They have ears everywhere."

"Cornelius reminds you that on your walk home, please stay with your friends and watch out for uneven pavement."

I smile. "Tell Cornelius I'll be careful."

"Good," he says. "See you soon."

When I set down my phone on the display table, Toni snatches it up and stares at the home screen, featuring the photo of Jamie and me at the conservatory. "I can't handle you two."

Sula appears through the doorway in her rolling office chair. "Is there a new pic?"

"No!" I tell her. "You two need to get lives."

Toni just wanders over to Sula with my phone, so they can gush over my pictures again.

The swoony photos are working like a charm. The meddlers are more invested in us than ever. Jules keeps fishing for juicy details. Margo told me I'm glowing. Christopher texted me his big-brother *He better take good care of you or else* proclamation. And Sula and Toni keep pulling up Instagram at work and making smoochy noises.

Sighing dreamily, Sula says, "He's a good kisser, isn't he?"

"Yes." Faking it or not, the man can kiss.

A funny sensation fizzes beneath my skin when I remember that kiss across the chess table at Boulangerie. The way he breathed me in and groaned with pleasure. Like he really meant it. Like all of this was *real*.

Which, of course, it isn't. That kiss wasn't for kissing's sake. It was for revenge, and yes, also possibly because kissing Jamie is never a chore. I loved kissing him while knowing his shitty ex might be watching, a prick of jealousy burrowing in her shriveled-up heart.

And yet, I didn't *just* kiss him to punish his ex. I kissed Jamie because I *like* kissing him, because we don't often speak the same language, but nothing gets lost in translation when we kiss. Because I can show him with my mouth and touch what I don't always know how to say or worry I'll mess up with words.

But those feelings are not fake-relationship territory, so back in the ominously full Jamie closet they go, slipped beneath the door.

Distracting myself, I flip open my sketchbook to the night sky I was drawing and run my finger over the design. I savor its secrets and the delight of having finally found some inspiration.

"*Yes?*" Sula says. "I ask about kissing and that's all I get?"

Toni sets my phone back on the display table and pokes my waist.

"Cough it up. I gave you a fifty-page report on my first kiss with Hamza."

"Ursula, you nosy little horndog. Back up out of my business. Antoni, the kiss report was *your* idea. I was happy to listen, but you would have told a mailbox about your first kiss with Hamza. I'm not giving either of you a blow-by-blow of my love life with Jamie. Not even our kisses."

Toni drops his elbows onto the desk and leans in conspiratorially. "So you *are* on to blowing?"

I shove him halfheartedly. "Go away."

Sula cackles, rolling back into the office. "I just love watching her blush."

"Especially when she's drawing her muse," Toni says.

I scowl, protectively covering my drawing of the night sky woven with stars and meteors. It's a lacework of constellations that conceals and—if you look hard enough—reveals lovers in a tangled embrace. The man's legs are long, his hair wild waves, and the woman's body is painted with stars. I'm trying not to read into the abundant parallels between Jamie and me that my hand decided to create.

"Oh God," Sula yells. "I pressed a button. The screen's turning colors. Mayday, Mayday! IT help, Toni!"

He sighs and turns toward the office. "I don't get paid enough for this."

I'm about to power off the iPads we use for checkout when the overhead bell jingles and in walks a woman who is the definition of chic. Tall, leggy, with rich auburn hair and honey-colored eyes. She wears just a touch of makeup and a luxurious camel wool coat.

There's something vaguely familiar about her.

"Are you—" Her eyes widen as she looks at me. Then she glances away, clearing her throat. I peer down at myself. Nothing on my clothes. Covertly, I touch my face. Do I have ink on it? I just looked at my reflection in the bathroom and didn't see anything. I examine my hands.

No fresh ink on my skin. I have no idea why she acted like that when she saw me, but then again, some people find all the tattoos a little alarming. Jamie definitely did when we first met.

Seeming to have recovered, she asks, "Are you still open?" She avoids my eyes. "I'm sorry for slipping in right before closing."

"You're fine." I shut my sketchbook, discreetly sliding it to the side. "Let me know if I can help you find anything this evening."

She tucks a glossy ribbon of auburn hair behind her ear. "Thank you."

Back to drawing, I'm peripherally aware of her as she wanders the store. She picks up our most expensive blank stationery, decadently thick card stock featuring an opalescent border, and two top-of-the-line fountain pens. Then, slowly, she wanders toward the wall of individual greeting cards. She bites her lip and frowns as she adjusts her armful.

"Want me to take that from you?" I ask.

"Oh." She glances down and smiles tightly. "That would be nice."

Stepping out from behind the counter, I smooth my skirt and quickly check the back of it. I've been paranoid about hems being caught in underpants ever since the bowling alley.

I snatch up a basket next to the display table and take her items, carefully setting them in the basket. She seems distracted, her eyes scouring the wall of cards. "Looking for something else?" I ask.

"I'm not sure . . ." She bites her lip. "Perhaps something romantic but subtle?"

"Gotcha." My work is the obvious choice. I point to a few popular designs. "These are good options for your purposes."

Her gaze follows my direction and she frowns, stepping closer. "How so? Their designs seem abstract."

"They are." I pull one from the thin shelves. "And they're something else." I trace the hidden design. "This one, for example, they're lovers. See, one's lying down, arms back, while the other—"

"Oh," she says quickly.

I glance up and notice that her lips are pursed, her expression a little shocked. "Sorry, if that's too much, I can show you something else."

"No," she says quickly again, stepping closer, taking the card. "No, that's the right idea. But perhaps . . ." She peers up the wall of shelves, spotting one of my favorite designs. "Is that a heart?"

"It is."

She smiles. Her teeth are toothpaste-commercial white. They make me squint. "How perfect."

"A heart is, of course, a classic symbol of love and—"

"No," she says over me. Reaching it easily, she plucks the card from the shelf and stares at it. "Not that. I'm a heart surgeon. But what's the lovers' design? I can't see it."

"That's not uncommon. Sometimes it's a matter of perspective. Approaching the image from a different angle can reveal it." I wait a moment, watching her grow irritated as she frowns at the card. "Do you want me to tell you?"

She sniffs, straightening. "Thank you, yes."

I point to the way I drew the heart—its ventricles and chambers, the flow of oxygenated and deoxygenated blood, all shaped as richly detailed flowers. "Those flowers' tone and shape," I tell her, "if you let your eye follow it, you'll see two people entwined together, in the position of mutual pleasure."

Her eyes widen. "Ah. I see it now. Well. This certainly is something."

"It is the *Prurient* Paper Collection."

She stares at the card. "It is, isn't it? It's perfect. I'll take it."

"Right this way. I'll ring you up." I glance over my shoulder as she follows me and catch her critically examining me again. "Can I help you find anything else today?"

"No, thank you."

It doesn't take long for me to charge her, then place the card and envelope in a petite bag with a bow that will never be as good as Toni's.

"Thank you again," she says, stealing one more curious glance at me before she reaches into her coat pocket for her ringing phone.

"You're welcome. Have a nice evening."

She steps away from the counter and turns, eyes on her phone. That's when it clicks. It's her retreating form that I recognize.

That was Jamie's ex-girlfriend.

Halfway to the apartment, I rush ahead of my friends with the excuse of needing to pee. I nearly face-plant twice, but I have to get home as quick as I can. I'm spiraling. I need answers.

"You made it!" Jules calls from the kitchen. "Tacos are here. Let's get some sangria in you."

Our apartment brims with Mexican food and mellow music, clusters of people talking, laughter on their faces. Jules knows my sensory threshold, and she's pretty great about not exceeding it. Not too many people or too many sounds. Just enough to be enjoyable but not overwhelming.

I can't even enjoy it, though. I can't stop fixating on Jamie's ex at the shop. That card she bought couldn't be for him, could it? Was seeing us at Boulangerie enough to make her jealous? To make her want someone she can't have anymore?

A small corner of my mind—the rational one—keeps telling me that I'm being ridiculous, worrying about my *fake* boyfriend being unfaithful to me or, worse, using me with this fake relationship to win her back. My rational brain is telling me you don't make up with someone who treats you the way he said she did.

And to my rational brain's credit, I'm pretty sure it's right. What's messing with me is how much I feel, how much I *care*. I've realized that if my fears about his ex were true, it would hurt. Deeply. And it shouldn't. It shouldn't matter to me what my fake boyfriend does. The man who's the epitome of wrong for me—quiet, wrinkle-free propriety to my haphazard, daydreaming chaos, who uses five-syllable words and saves babies and eats four carbs a year, while I half-ass a career, spin my professional tires, and subsist on refined sugar and canned ravioli.

This is what has my hands shaking, my heart tripping inside my ribs. Despite my best efforts to rein this shit in, to keep our dates purposeful, our every touch solely for this fake relationship and the goal of revenge—I'm still invested, vulnerable, barely holding back tears.

"BeeBee." Jules offers me a big glass of sangria. "What's wrong?"

I take a giant gulp, hoping the alcohol will numb the pain. "What do you know about Jamie's ex?"

She wrinkles her nose. "Uh. Not much. Why?"

"Tell me what you know." I glance around the room and don't see Jamie. He must still be hiding in my room with Cornelius.

"Okay," Jules says slowly. "I remember Jean-Claude saying she's a physician, too. But a surgeon. Cardiothoracic, maybe?"

Jamie's ex is a heart surgeon. And I doodle hidden genitals on card stock for a living.

That faintest, silliest fantasy of Jamie Westenberg ever seeing me as more than the clumsy girl who hates vegetables and walks around with her underwear stuck in her dress dissolves, leaving a hollow ache beneath my breastbone.

"It's whatever all his family does," Jules says. "I know his dad's famous for some procedure. And yeah, I think it's for hearts. Why?"

It's her. The woman at the Edgy Envelope has to be his ex. How many women look like Jamie's ex from behind and are cardiothoracic surgeons? That explains why she looked at me weird. She must have recognized me from Boulangerie.

"Bea, what's going on?" Jules asks.

I blink, leaving my thoughts as I force a smile. "Nothing. Thanks. Just curious."

She steps closer. "Are you sure—"

"Jules!" someone calls. "The oven's going off."

My sister sighs.

"It's okay, JuJu. I'm fine. Go be hostess."

"Don't go far," she says, taking my near-empty glass. "I'll be back with more sangria."

As soon as she steps away, I see Jamie at the end of the hall, shutting the door to my room quietly behind him. My heart drops in a bungee jump free fall, begging the line of trust to snap and save me. But right now it's only gravitational fear dragging me down, whistling-air dread drowning out all other sounds.

He glances up and, when he sees me, smiles a real Jamie smile, eyes holding mine as he closes the distance between us. I watch his mouth form the word *Hello*. I stare up at him, wordless, as he lifts my messenger bag off my shoulder and sets it on his.

"Bea," he says, gently wrapping his hand around my back and guiding me in, away from the door. "What is it?"

Margo curses at the stroller as she steps behind me into the apartment. "Ever seen her just stand there in a doorway and gape at someone like that?"

"No," Sula says, releasing their daughter, Rowan, to Jules, then taking over and smoothly collapsing the stroller. "But it's very reminiscent of how you looked when you first met me."

"I did not gape," Margo says tartly.

Sula snorts as she stashes the stroller against the wall of coats. "Sure, okay. Let's leave the lovebirds alone."

Once they've escaped for drinks and food, Toni and Hamza follow, hanging up their coats, then slipping by, too.

Jamie stares down at me, hand still on my back. "Are you all right?"

My breath catches in my throat, a watery hitch that means tears are coming. "I'm not sure."

"What's the matter?" The concern etched in his expression makes the ache even worse.

"I . . ." My eyes blur with tears.

"Bea." Jamie pulls me against him, a hard hug I didn't know how badly I needed. His strong arms wrap around me, one hand cradling my head. Gently, his fingers slip through my hair, a comforting touch that makes the first tears spill over.

"What do you need?" he asks, his voice low and warm next to my ear. "Want to go somewhere quiet?"

I shake my head, locking my arms around his waist. He's so lean and solid. He smells like a morning walk in the woods. And when I close my eyes, I picture it so easily—our hands tangled, nothing but the sound of wildlife hidden in the trees, twigs snapping beneath our feet, the dim roar of the nearby sea.

Sighing, I whisper against his chest, "Just this."

TWENTY-TWO

Jamie

Something is happening to me. Something frightening.

When I saw Bea, looking lost and too close to tears, a force I've never known in my life roared through my body. It was raw and base and *violent*. Something had hurt her. Something just beneath the surface of that tough exterior, those sharp tattoos and fierce eyes and shocking blond-tipped hair. And I wanted to crush it.

To the outsider, I imagine I looked calm as always, unruffled as ever. But inside, when I tugged her against me—now, as she grips me like a life raft—I've never felt so primally protective.

"Thanks," she whispers.

I swipe my thumbs beneath her eyes to wipe away her tears, cradling her face in my hands. Then I lower my head and meet her eyes.

Over chess on Wednesday, we made a plan for game night: we'd kiss thoroughly in greeting, stay handsy throughout the night. Give them something to talk about. But Bea showing up in tears, clinging to me like this, is as far off script as it gets. I won't risk the chance that she's no longer all right with what we planned, so I ask, "Do you still want me to kiss you?"

"Yes." She nods, her touch resting at my waist, fingers tracing my ribs. Her eyes slip shut as she sways closer. "For plausibility's sake."

I stare at her. Dark lashes, the freckle just beneath her left eye. The delicate upturn of her nose and those rosebud lips.

The truth snaps into place.

I don't want to kiss Beatrice Wilmot under false pretenses. I want to kiss her simply for kissing's sake. No angle to it, no vengeful intent.

And I have no idea if Bea will ever want what I want. Real, not fake. Just us.

Anxiety tightens its bands around my chest, pinches my lungs. What if, once again, I'm not enough? What if, when I tell Bea what I feel, she looks at me with the same frustrated discomfort that tightened Lauren's expression when I realized how little I'd actually meant to her?

I can't risk that, can't face the possibility that Bea will tell me this means nothing more than what we agreed it would.

So, like a coward, I stay quiet and savor holding her tight. I hate that Bea's upset, but I love that she needs *me*. That somehow I became safe, the person she leans into. Breathing her in, I shut my eyes, resting my cheek on the crown of her head. For a moment, the world is only her, close and warm and soft, the scent of figs and smoky sandalwood. Her fingers clutch my shirt as I bend and brush my lips against hers.

She draws in a breath, pressing on tiptoes to bring us closer. A groan rolls up my throat as she wraps her arms around my neck, her fingers slipping through my hair, scraping along my scalp. My mouth falls open as I draw her tight against me, my hands settling along the swell of her hips, showing her what she does to me, how urgent *everything* becomes when Bea and I kiss.

Time compresses and bends and dissolves, until all that exists is Bea's hands and Bea's mouth, and every sweet give and curve of Bea's soft body against the hard planes of mine. Until it's all just her.

Bea.

It's the word my thoughts beg, the sound of need singing in my veins. It's all there is until a wolf whistle breaks the moment, making us wrench apart.

Bea stares at me. A soft, careful smile tips her mouth.

"Cornelius take good care of you?" she asks.

I nod, smoothing back a strand of hair I tugged loose from her bun while kissing her. She watches me as I fix the damage, as my thumb trails her jaw. "Yes."

"Good." The smile tightens as I hitch her bag higher on my shoulder. "I'm going to go put this in your room, so it's safe."

She nods. "I'll come with. Say hi to the hedgie."

We walk down the hallway, into her room, where I enjoyed sitting on her bed before she arrived, taking in the countless colorful details, trying to figure out why I like Bea's brand of chaos so much.

"Hi, bud," she says to Cornelius, stroking along his back. He waddles across his tiny home and crawls onto her hands. "Sorry I was such a mess when I came in."

"You don't need to apologize, Bea. But I wish you'd tell me what's upsetting you."

She swallows slowly, eyes still on Cornelius. "Are you seeing your ex at all?"

"What? No. God, no." Worry cements in my stomach. "Why are you asking me that?"

"I think I met her tonight. And after we saw her at Boulangerie, it just . . . made me nervous."

I step closer, wanting to reassure with more than words but unsure if I should. "I promise you, Bea. It was pure coincidence. I have no interest in being with her."

"I figured that." She sets down Cornelius gently and slides the rooftop screen of his home shut. "I think I needed to hear it from you again."

With another step closer, I stop myself right behind her. Tiny wisps of chocolate brown hair kiss her skin. I trace one, drifting my finger down her neck. Her head tips back, exposing her throat for me.

"Would it matter to you?" I ask. "If I did want her? If I wanted . . . anyone?"

Her hands fist her dress. "Don't make me answer that."

"That kiss at Boulangerie." I lower my mouth to her shoulder, knowing I'm being reckless. Knowing I'm taking us somewhere that will be so hard to come back from if I'm wrong. I press one long kiss against her tattoo. "Was that really revenge?"

Bea leans into me, her head thumping against my shoulder. "Don't make me answer that, either."

I wrap an arm around her waist, then slowly turn her to face me. Her eyes shine as she bites her lip. Fear paints her expression, and I want so badly to wipe it away. To make her feel safe. To show her that she's not alone. That I'm right there with her.

Our hands brush, like a first, frightened kiss, before they meet, tangling tight. I bring her hand with mine, against my chest, searching her eyes. "Bea—"

"Oops!" Someone I don't know hovers on the threshold, red with embarrassment. "So sorry! Thought this was the bathroom."

Pulling her hand away, Bea smooths her dress. "Second on the left," she says, guiding them out, leaving the room behind them. I follow in her wake, unsure, worried I've completely misread it. But as soon as our intruder disappears into the bathroom, she spins and grips my hand, meeting my eyes. Then she presses a soft, lingering kiss to the corner of my mouth.

"It wasn't *just* revenge," she whispers.

Without another word, Bea draws me into the bustling kitchen that mirrors my frenetic thoughts.

"West!" Christopher calls, and grins. "Come play Risk. And bring Bea. It's her favorite."

Releasing my hand, Bea accepts a brimming glass of sangria from her sister. "Chill your boxer briefs," she tells Christopher. "I need alcohol first if I'm suffering through Risk."

"Beer?" Juliet asks me.

"Thank you, yes." God do I need it. "Something light."

Bea rifles through the ice bucket. "I'll get it. He likes those citrusy wheat beers, don't you, James? Something Pine-Sol-y."

Juliet wrinkles her nose, adjusting Sula and Margo's curly-haired daughter, Rowan, on her hip. "What?"

"Inside joke," Bea says. "Y'know. Coupley stuff."

Rowan reaches toward me, letting out a demanding shriek.

"You and me both, Ro," Bea calls over her shoulder, still digging around the beers. "It's been a long-ass day."

"Hey." Juliet pulls her close and presses a kiss to her dimpled cheek. "*I'm* your favorite. Not the big guy who's all over Aunt BeeBee."

Rowan hollers, reaching for me again.

"It's nothing personal," I tell Juliet, accepting Rowan from her and holding her high up against my chest. She goes for my glasses, like all babies do, and I let her. "They sniff out the pediatrician in me."

"Fair warning," Sula calls, "my child will go to great lengths to bust your glasses!"

I smile down at Rowan as she bends them. "These are flexible frames. Virtually unbreakable."

When I glance Bea's way, she's watching me. "You wear a baby well, James."

I feel a rush of pleasure at how she's looking at me. My cheeks heat. "Comes with the job."

Her gaze lingers a minute longer before she turns and pops off the beer bottle's lid against the counter. I'm mesmerized, watching the sweeps of color and black ink delicately curled around her arm, dancing as she moves. I think about my tongue tracing their path to her collarbone, down to the swell of her—

"Goo!" Rowan yells, jamming my glasses lopsidedly back on my face and helpfully breaking me from my lustful thoughts.

"Thank you very much," I tell her.

She gives me a wide smile. Then her face goes red, followed by an ominous rumbling in her diaper.

"Ah." I pat her back. "Just needed a fresh pair of arms to poop in, didn't you."

Margo steps up, setting her sangria on the counter. "I'll take care of that."

"I'm happy to handle it. I'm used to soiled diapers."

She blinks at me, like I've stunned her, then turns toward Bea. "If you don't marry him, I'm talking to Sula about being a trio."

Bea glares at Margo. "Back off my man. And use Jules's bedroom for the diaper change."

"Rude!" Juliet hollers.

"Yeah, yeah." Margo sighs. "Here I go. Off to glamorous diaper duty." Taking Rowan, she disappears with her down the hall.

"Come on, James," Bea takes my hand. "Time for a nap—I mean, to play Risk."

"A nap? What?"

She makes a miserable face. "Risk is such a snooze. It's booorrrriiing."

"It's strategic." There's only one seat left, across the table from Christopher, Toni, and Hamza. "It takes patience. Please," I tell her. "Sit."

"Nope." She shakes her head. "I'm not playing. You sit."

We engage in a stare-off before I finally drop down with a sigh, then tug Bea onto my lap. Time suspends for a moment as she nestles on my thighs and stares down at me. My hand wraps tight around her waist.

"Ready to get your butt kicked?" Toni says from across the table.

Bea turns and sticks her tongue out at him, crossing her legs and leaning into me. I have an unfairly good angle to see straight down her dress. It takes Herculean effort to set up my Risk soldiers instead.

"I'm pretty confident James is about to execute world domination on my behalf, Antoni." She sips her sangria. "And then we're going to annihilate you at Pictionary."

"Ooh." Hamza laughs. "Shots fired."

"She's not joking," Christopher says, before he takes a pull of his beer. "The only time I've ever seen her lose at Pictionary, she flipped. Threw the marker straight at Jules, who purposefully guessed wrong." He mimes the action. "Like a javelin."

"I still have a scar!" Juliet calls from the kitchen.

"You guessed wrong on purpose!" Bea yells back before she drops her voice and says to me, "You'd think she'd have learned her lesson about getting on my bad side."

I smile and draw her closer in my arms. "I pity the person who underestimates you."

Bea breaks our gaze first, a blush pinking her cheeks as she sips her sangria. I catch Christopher's eye right before he glances away from watching us and see something like curiosity. I realize he's the only one in the group whom I've never observed partnered. No one's trying to pair him off, like they were Bea and me. Which strikes me as odd, given how nosy they all are. Not everyone wants to date or be romantic, of course, so it might simply be that, but the way I caught him looking at us, it seemed almost . . . wistful?

"It's a long story," Bea says quietly in my ear. "But the short version is, he has his reasons for avoiding relationships, and they're serious enough that even Jules doesn't have the guts to try to interfere."

I sip my beer. "Did you just read my thoughts?"

"I figured you were curious why he gets a singles pass. And it looked like you caught him watching us. Like you cared." She pats my thigh gently. "It's funny, I know you came to us through Jean-Claude and Jean-Claude came through Christopher's firm, but it feels like it should be the other way around. You seem much more like Christopher's type of guy. Like you two would be friends."

I shift beneath her and stare at my beer bottle, knowing where this is going.

"Who *are* your friends, Jamie?" Bea says softly.

"I . . ." Clearing my throat, I take a drink of my beer. "I haven't really gotten the knack of friends since college. I was absorbed in my studies, then I was busy with medical school and residency, now working." I set down the beer bottle and adjust my watch until it's in its rightful place. "I get along with my colleagues, but that's about it."

"Except Jean-Claude?"

"I told you. He's stuck around. Like a bug on fly paper."

Bea snorts. "That might be the closest thing to an insult I've ever heard you say."

I smile up at her, relieved to see there's no judgment in her eyes that I have virtually no social life. "I'd like friends," I admit, because she's made me feel safe to say it. "I just haven't ever really known where to start."

Her smile's soft and warm. "I think you start here."

A crash makes Bea startle on my lap and nearly spill her sangria all over us.

"Close call," she says shakily, setting down her glass.

I glance over my shoulder to the source of the noise, where Rowan toddles across the room and plows down the Pictionary easel again.

"Bea," I mutter, hoisting her closer in my lap.

She turns and faces me, our mouths scant inches apart. Her gaze flicks to my mouth, then back to my eyes. "What is it?"

"Pictionary? Must we?"

"Jamie. You remember how I was at bowling."

My hand slides down the swell of her hip, to the line of her panties beneath her dress. "How could I forget?"

She pokes my side. "I don't mean the panty fiasco. I mean the *game*. My deranged competitiveness. I like to win, that's what I was trying to get at. And I will win at Pictionary."

"But, Bea, how is that possible when *I* can't draw a stick figure? I'm even terrible at coloring."

"How can you be terrible at coloring?"

"I just am."

She smooths the collar of my dress shirt, her eyes traveling me. My body feels so hot, I'd swear I'm fevered. Bea sitting on my lap, nestled in, touching me affectionately, is testing my limits. "We'll figure it out. You kick butt at Risk. I'll pick up your slack at Pictionary. Team effort."

Sensing eyes on us, too hungry to stop myself, I close the distance between us and kiss her until she's wide-eyed and gasping. "I like the sound of that."

TWENTY-THREE

Bea

Jamie was not exaggerating. He is *terrible* at drawing. I have never seen him this frazzled, even after we decided a shot of tequila was a super-good idea. Dutch courage, et cetera.

He points at the paper again, jabbing it with his marker.

"Jamie, pointing doesn't help!" I tug at my hair. "I've guessed every possible thing I can think of."

"Shocker," Toni says, "they were all genitals."

I throw a pillow at his head.

"We're leaving," Margo calls as Sula hauls the stroller past her. "Our spawn is over all you fools."

Rowan's shrieks confirm this. I blow the three of them a kiss, then turn back to face Jamie as he stands, head thrown back, shaking his fists at the gods of Pictionary, who do not hear him.

Tipping my head, I squint.

"Time's almost out!" Hamza says.

I start to see *something*. Something that my head tipping, eye squinting, gradually reveals.

"Wheelbarrow!" I scream.

Jamie spikes the marker, a receiver who just caught my answer for the touchdown. Then he crosses the space and crushes his mouth to mine.

I gasp against his lips as he hoists me up and wraps my thighs around his waist.

"Hey!" Christopher calls. "Get a room!"

"Gladly," Jamie says, half laugh, half growl as he kisses me harder. Laughter and jeers fill the room, but I barely hear them as his hands slide up my thighs, sinking into my skin. He walks us into the shadows of the hallway and pins me to the wall.

"That was the worst wheelbarrow I've seen in my entire life."

His hands drift higher until his touch slips beneath my dress and curves around my ass. "I'm sorry," he groans. "I shouldn't take it this far—"

"Not complaining." I run my hands up his solid arms, feeling every muscle flex as he holds me. "Definitely not complaining."

"I thought it was the tequila," he says after a deep, long kiss, "but I'm drunk on victory. Adrenaline. Endorphins. Lots of them."

"Me, too," I whisper, leaning back, offering him my throat.

Someone thinks they're funny and puts Barry White on the sound system, as a fresh wave of laughter breaks through our haze. I stare up at Jamie, breath sawing sharply in and out of our lungs. "Jamie?"

His eyes are on my mouth, heat high on his cheeks. "Yes, Bea."

"Let's get out of here."

Reality hovers at the fringes of my thoughts, but I push it away. We're only supposed to do this in front of an audience. To pretend, ham it up, lure the meddlers into our trap. But I don't want to think about them right now. I don't want them to watch what I want next.

Jamie kisses me one more time, then sets me down. "Let's."

Maybe it's the tequila or our Pictionary victory, but I'm all shaky limbs and nervous laughter. Jamie slides my coat up my arms, sets his messenger bag across his body, then bends and throws me over his shoulder, whipping open the door.

"Where are you going?" Jules yells.

"Getting that room you told us to!" he calls back before he slams the door shut behind us.

"Wow." I have a great view of his butt as Jamie carries me down the steps. "You're fit, aren't you? How often do you exercise?"

"Nearly every day."

"Geez, James!"

Jamie tightens his grip on my legs. "Exercising helps."

"Helps what? Oof. I need to be upright. Sangria and tequila need gravity on their side to stay put."

At the bottom of the steps, Jamie crouches and lowers me to the ground. It involves a painfully delicious slide along his body that leaves me a lot more breathless than I should be, seeing as all I did was get carried down the stairs like a sack of potatoes.

"It helps lots of things," he says, picking up where our conversation left off. "Sleep. Anxiety. I'm restless if I don't exercise."

"What kind of exercise?" I ask.

He stares down at me, then starts backing away, opening the building's front door. "Running and weights. What does Beatrice do to burn energy?"

"Beatrice walks. Does yoga. And swims sometimes."

An almost smile tips his mouth.

I poke his stomach. "What are you grinning about?"

"Nothing," he says.

"What's so funny about my exercise? I'm sorry I'm not an ultra-marathoner like you, James."

He coughs a laugh. "I didn't say anything!"

I lunge for his side, trying to find a tickle spot. An inhumanly high shriek leaves him. "Oh shit." My eyes widen with evil glee. "You're ticklish."

"Beatrice, no." Jamie puts up his hands, increasing his backtracking pace. "No tickling."

"You laugh at my baby exercises, you pay." I lunge and tickle him more, making him shriek again. I'm cackling. Jamie's tickle-shriek is the best sound ever.

"Beatrice! Stop!"

I lunge for his other side, which he barely dodges. "Make me."

Jamie narrows his eyes, then takes off in a sprint down the sidewalk.

"James!" I yell, huffing and puffing. "I do not run! I am not fit like you! I'm going to break my face!"

Jamie stops and spins, but I'm not quick enough to pump the brakes so I bounce into him. "Oof."

"Can't risk you breaking your face," he says. "Even to escape the tickle monster."

I giggle. He laughs. We're a little buzzed. And something's different now. Something unspoken.

"Come on," he says, wrapping his hand around mine. I don't miss that this makes tickling him virtually impossible unless I twist and try with my far hand, which, with my limited reach, is not going to happen.

"I think I want pizza," Jamie mutters.

"Pizza!" I gasp. "Who are you and what have you done with the real James Benedick Westenberg?"

"Ha!" He gives me a playful glare. "Boring Jamie isn't so boring after all, is he? Hmm? He can order a pizza on a Friday night when there's a little too much tequila in his system."

"One shot, James."

"I'm a lightweight," he admits.

"And that's wood-fired, artisanal pizza you want, isn't it?"

He grins and tucks me under his arm. "Maybe."

Hustling through the chilly night air, it's like a time warp—the speed with which we power down the sidewalk, laughing like goofs about nothing, before we're safe at his place.

Inside the apartment, I kick off my boots, take the six steps to his couch, and flop over the side.

"Oh shit, yes," I groan. "Sofa all to myself. Quiet. So much better than my place. Why did we do that? Socializing. Bleh."

"Revenge, Beatrice!" Jamie says. "Hmm." He peers around the apartment as if he's looking for something.

"Doing okay there, big guy?"

He frowns. "I need my phone."

"To order pizza?"

"Not yet. Good pizza takes time. *Deciding* whether or not to order good pizza takes even more time."

"You are delightfully strange."

"Likewise," he says. Removing his glasses, Jamie sets them on the kitchen counter, then he starts emptying his pockets. "Aha!" He lifts his phone, which glows with an unread message. "I needed my phone to stop buzzing. With a message from my roommate." He squints. "Saying he's not coming after all. Tell me something I don't know, Jean-Claude."

I blow a raspberry. "We didn't miss him anyway. Though it was kind of weird he wasn't there tonight. He's *always* there."

Dropping his phone on the counter with very un-Jamie-like carelessness, he says, "He was sulking about something. He does that when he doesn't get his way."

"What does he have to be mad about? How didn't he get his way?"

"Who knows." Jamie wanders into the kitchen. "Your sister looked like she'd been crying when I showed up. I imagine they had a disagreement, which generally means Jean-Claude didn't get exactly what he wanted and blew his top."

Unease prickles my spine. Why wouldn't Jules tell me that?

"Want something to drink?" Jamie asks.

I'm about to dig further into the Jean-Claude thing, but his ass hijacks my brain when he crouches and pets the sleeping zombie cats on their little beds next to the window.

"Bea?" he asks, snapping me out of it.

"What? A drink? Yep. Sure."

"What have we here? Liquor?" Jamie opens the freezer door, then slams it shut. "Nope. No liquor there."

I stare over his shoulder, processing what I just saw in the jam-packed freezer. "James, what on earth was in there? Are you preparing for the end-times? Are you a secret survivalist?"

He won't look at me. "You weren't supposed to see that."

"Well, now you *have* to tell me."

"Let's have tea," Jamie says. "At first I was thinking tequila, but given how my stomach feels, that's not such a good idea."

I slip off the sofa and sneak behind him toward the freezer. Just as I'm about to open it, his hand lands on the door, holding it shut. I stare up at Jamie, pinned between him and the refrigerator. "What's in the freezer?" I ask.

"It's . . ." Glancing away, he stares at the floor. "It's soup."

"Okay? Well, there's no shame in bulk soup making."

Eyes still on the floor, he says, quieter, "For you."

"For me?" My heart twirls in my chest. He made soup for me?

Jamie's cheeks pink as he clears his throat. "I made four different kinds of veggie puree soups with my fancy blender and froze them. I was going to give them to you, but then I didn't know if it was too much, or if you'd even like them. So they're just . . . sitting in there. Making me feel like a presumptuous weirdo each time I get ice. Which is every morning. For my breakfast smoothie."

"Jamie." My heart feels like something just woke up inside it and stretched, demanding more space.

Jamie doesn't say anything, but the blush on his cheeks grows.

A thick wave's fallen onto his forehead, half covering his right eye. I brush it back, then slide my hands through his hair, enjoying its silky softness. "You made four kinds of pureed veggie soup. For *me*."

"You need your veggies," he says quietly, his fingertips drifting along my neck, tracing my bumblebee tattoo. "And my state-of-the-art blender just might actually make them texturally palatable for you."

"My fake boyfriend isn't supposed to ruin me for everyone else," I whisper.

Jamie's eyes fall shut as he drops his forehead to mine. "Sometimes, Beatrice, I want to ruin you for everyone else."

My heart vaults out of my body, dancing in the star-studded sky. "You do?"

He nods. "And I know I shouldn't."

I stare up at him, terrified of what he's saying. Even more terrified that it's precisely what I wanted to hear.

"I shouldn't want to be here, just the two of us," he says, slowly wrapping an arm around me, then clasping my hand. "I shouldn't want to hold you like this and dance in the kitchen while the kettle's on for tea. But I can't stop myself."

On the first turn he tries to take, I trip on his foot and knee him in the thigh, rupturing the romance of the moment. "Well, try, James," I say testily, brimming with embarrassment, "because this woman does not dance."

Jamie peers down at me, unfazed. "You were doing fine. Just let me lead." Resuming our sway, he sets his chin on my head and sighs. "It's good practice for my father's birthday party."

"What's that mean?"

"It'll be a stuffy affair. The usual. Black tie. Live orchestra. A waltz."

I freeze. "Jamie, I'm not joking. I can't dance."

"Not at all?"

"Not at *all*. I'm not coordinated."

He pauses and stares down at me. "A waltz doesn't require coordination so much as memorization. Do you want to learn?"

"Yes?" The word leaves my mouth before I can swallow it as successfully as I have all the other absurdity I want to spew.

I want to laugh like this every night and have kitchen-counter sex and cuddle in bed and play chess and share cupcakes and never stop.

In the grand scheme of things, maybe a rogue *yes* isn't the worst thing that's ever happened.

Jamie takes me by the hand and walks me into the living room. Reaching for the TV remote and syncing his phone, he turns on a classical music playlist.

"Hoo-boy," I groan. "We're really doing this. It's going to be a disaster, I'm warning you."

"I'm not worried." String music fills the apartment. He draws me close. "Shouldn't take long at all."

Not that I doubted Jamie's competency as a pediatrician, but now there is officially no debate that he's good with children.

Because I'm being one.

I stomp my foot and let out a high-pitched whine that gives the string instruments a run for their money.

"Bea, it's all right. Dancing takes time and practice—"

"We've been time-and-practicing for thirty minutes, and I'm worse than when I started."

Jamie is not a good liar. Which is why he pinches his mouth and says nothing for long, awkward seconds. "You're not *worse*. You're—"

"Terrible. Clumsy. Awful. I've crushed your feet countless times. I probably broke a toe—"

"Beatrice."

Stern-Jamie voice makes me freeze, but it also makes certain parts of me very, *very* warm. "Y-yes?"

His hand rests heavy and low on my back. "Take a breath. More than one, preferably."

I do. A long, slow inhale, then exhale. Followed by another.

"Good." He clears his throat. "Right. So, I'm going to make this both easier and more difficult."

"What? That makes no sense."

"It will." He tucks me tight against him, so that our bodies touch. Chest. Hips. Thighs.

And now I'm aware of *every* inch of him.

"Ah. Okay. I'm following."

Jamie breathes in deeply from his nose, his eyes holding mine. "Think of it like lovemaking."

"What?" I squeak.

A deep blush stains his cheeks. "I told you. Easier and more difficult. Bear with me. When two people are together..."

"Yes," I whisper.

"It's like that," he says quietly, his hand splayed wide on my back, drawing me closer. My fingers sink into his shirt. I am five foot seven inches of longing. "Their bodies find a rhythm, a give-and-take that's right for them. Understand?"

I nod quickly. "I think so. I mean, yes."

"So let me lead at first. Follow my rhythm, then you'll find your own, I'll adjust to that, and then we'll be . . . dancing."

My grip tightens on his shoulder. "Promise?"

His eyes hold mine as he sweeps his thumb in a soothing trail along the base of my spine. "Promise."

Jamie seems to be waiting for the right moment in the music, and we stand still. Staring at each other. Bodies fused.

"It's not normally this close," he says as if reading my mind. "But it'll help you learn."

His left thigh presses into my right leg, and I step back, trying to remember the pattern. *Back, side, close. Front, side, close.*

"Bea."

My eyes snap up and meet his.

"Don't think about it," he says softly. "Just follow my body."

"Right." I grip him tight, nervously anticipating the moment I'll misstep and stomp on his toe again. But as Jamie holds me close, sweeping me into the rhythm, I find it harder and harder to think, easier and easier to feel . . .

Jamie's hand spread across the curve of my back.

Those long, strong legs guiding mine.

His solid arms drawing me forward, side, back.

Staring at his mouth, I feel my control slipping. I want dancing to become *more*. I want Jamie to want me the way I want him. But I can't risk sabotaging everything—not just our revenge but this fragile friendship we've grown.

So I try to distract myself. Besides looking at Jamie, all that's left is looking down, where I see our bodies moving in a steady, undulating rhythm. That does not help.

Jamie doesn't help, either. He's silent. And when I meet his gaze, it's intense, locked on me, and so hot I nearly step on his foot. He senses it and pushes me through to the next step, eyes never leaving mine.

"Any, um . . ." I clear my throat. "Any other dance etiquette I should master?"

He tips his head so slightly, searching my face. "Well, when it's an intimate dance like the waltz, you can hold each other's eyes. But I know that's not always comfortable for you. So you can look elsewhere."

"Elsewhere?" I tease, wiggling my eyebrows.

Jamie doesn't smile as his gaze roams my face. "Yes. So long as it's me."

The world glows rose-gold iridescent as those words sink in, as Jamie moves us in the steady grace of the waltz.

"I think I can do that." My gaze settles on his mouth.

"Sometimes," he says so quietly I can barely hear him. "Sometimes when you dance, you kiss."

I wet my lips, my hand drifting from his hard shoulder to the base of his neck. My fingers slip along the tidy silken strands of his hair. "I think you should show me that, too."

His lips brush mine, so gentle at first that I almost doubt they were there. But then his mouth meets mine again, deeper, hungry. When I part my lips, his groan fills my mouth, his hand drifting lower down my back, pulling me against him, until there's no mistaking how dancing has affected us both. My breasts press into the hard breadth of his chest, my nipples tight and sensitive as they rub against him. A sweet, hot ache fills me. Desperate, restless, I lean into him, wanting so much more.

I bring us to a grinding halt, throwing my arms around Jamie's neck, and like it's simply our choreography, his hands wrap around my waist, pulling me tight against him. Our mouths open, and our tongues dance how our bodies did—a sensual, rhythmic glide that makes me melt in his arms.

"Bea," he mutters into our kiss.

I kiss him harder, tangling my fingers in the beautiful waves of his hair. "Jamie."

"What do you want?" he says hoarsely.

The question knocks me sideways. Not because I don't know but because the answer is on the tip of my tongue, daunting and undeniable. When it's just a single word, you'd think it would be simple. But it takes courage, a brave tug of air to fill my lungs before I paint the space between us with one luminescent word. "You."

It's barely left my lips when Jamie sweeps me up and starts walking us toward the sofa, easing me onto the cushions. My legs fall shamelessly open as he drops his weight over me and kisses me slowly.

Oh God. This. *This* is what I needed. To kiss Jamie. To feel his long, heavy body pinning me down. I sigh into our kiss, moving as he moves, until we're tangled together, hands wandering, kisses deep and wet.

These are new Jamie kisses, uninhibited and hungry. He slants his mouth over mine, his tongue taking my mouth the way I want every inch of him moving inside me—deep, steady thrusts that make my toes curl inside my socks.

"Is this all right?" he whispers.

"So all right." I drag my hands down from his thick waves, along his back, all the way to his hard, firm ass. His moan echoes in my mouth as I pull him tighter against me. "Don't stop," I tell him. "Please don't stop."

"God, Bea." He scrapes one hand up my thigh, pouring my dress into a wine-red puddle at my hips. "I want you so badly."

"I want you, too."

Wrapping my leg around his waist, he gives me the exquisite feel of his erection—hard and thick, straining against his pants. I roll my hips, dying for friction, for touch, for every inch of me to find every inch of him. Reaching for his shirt, I wrench it from his pants and run my hands beneath that crisp cotton, sighing when I feel him—warm, taut skin, the hard ridges of his stomach.

I push him back on his heels and unbutton his shirt frantically, shoving it off his shoulders, yanking away his undershirt, too. Before I can even fully appreciate his body, he whips off my dress, then lays me back down against the sofa, latching his mouth over my nipple through the soft cotton of my bralette. His teeth drag gently, maddeningly perfect as they draw my nipples to hard, sensitive peaks.

The ache I feel is everywhere. My fingertips, my toes, deep inside and exquisitely close to the surface. Concentrated between my thighs, it's a steady, thrumming pulse that makes my hips seek his. Our mouths meet again, and when our tongues touch, my back arches, my breasts brushing against his chest.

And from there, release is a matter of *when*, not *if*.

I lean into Jamie as he moves steadily against me, the thick head of his cock rubbing my clit through our clothes. I reach between us and rub him through his pants, too, savoring how hard and big he is, lower where he's tight and heavy. I'm too busy enjoying myself to beg him for more than this, but I make myself a promise. Next time, there'll be nothing between us.

This is frenzied, exactly what I pictured the night we got a little wild at the bowling alley. It's rushing air and frantic thrusts, uncorked lust that's been bottled up between us for too long. Laughter and longing overflow as we kiss, as I taste his jaw, his cheek, his lips.

"You're close," he says, his mouth softly nipping down my throat.

"Y-yes."

"I want to make you come." Oh God. Such simple words, but they make my clit swell, turn my breasts shamelessly needy for his touch. "Tell me what you need."

I blush as I say it, not because I'm ashamed but because it feels hot to command him. To know he's going to do it. "More. Rougher."

He groans like my words are unraveling him as much as my hands that wander his body, coaxing rasped breaths when I catch him by surprise and make him rut against me harder.

Jamie sighs into our kiss before he drags my bottom lip between his teeth. An inhuman noise of pleasure leaves me when he lets it go, then bites right over my tattoo along my neck. He scrapes my nipple with his thumb, then soundly pinches it. It's like a switch flipped, how quickly I'm scrambling on the precipice, panting for air.

"Jamie," I gasp.

I taste his smile as he whispers, "Bea."

Desperation morphs into shattering relief as I come, and Jamie watches me, eyes dark, mouth open. I slip my hand between us, gripping him hard through his pants so he can thrust into my touch, until he comes, too, in warm, wet juts of release that seep through his clothes and soak my stomach.

Panting for air, we stare at each other. Then Jamie drops his head to the crook of my neck and presses a long, slow kiss right over a sweetly throbbing bite mark.

"Just so you know," I tell him breathlessly, "if you'd said this is what waltzing leads to, I would not have put up such a stink."

His laugh dances over my skin. I wrap my arms around him, a smile lighting up my face. I can't see how bright it is, but I know from how he looks at me.

I am incandescent.

TWENTY-FOUR

Jamie

We might be two mature adults who consensually brought each other to orgasm last Friday, but I can't say we've handled it as such. I woke up to an empty couch, no Bea in sight. I texted her to ask if she was home safely. She said yes. Then nothing else.

And then I doubted everything that happened, if I'd read her wrong, if she regretted it.

Since then, our messages have been brief and minimal. We agreed to meet for our paint date separately, straight from work. For the first time since this began, Bea and I are tiptoeing around each other.

I'm unhappy about it.

But not as unhappy as Bea, when she stops short outside of our destination. "Why are we doing this again?" she asks.

"Because an hour with cheap wine and amateur painting captured on Instagram will go a long way in our quest for revenge." I press my glasses up my nose and turn, facing the storefront.

She's quiet for so long, I peer over at her again. And when I do, I notice Bea's staring at me. She blinks away. "Right," she says. "Get in, paint, photograph, get out. It's Instagrammable."

"Precisely."

Even if that isn't the only reason I want to stick with this outing. Bea's been creatively blocked. She hasn't painted since she parted ways with that bastard of an ex-boyfriend. Since she told me about what he did, how he hurt her, I've almost offered to cancel this outing a dozen times.

But then I thought, if she could pick up a brush with me in the silliness of the exercise, it might help her feel safe to try again and experience joy for something she deeply misses.

Have I been too pushy? Maybe this is too much. Just like *I* might have been too much last Friday. Does she regret it?

Me?

All of this?

"Bea." I stare down at her, finally saying what I've been debating for days now. "If you don't want to, we don't have to do this. If I'm pushing—"

"Oh God, Jamie, *please* don't feelingly apologize. I can't take it." She sighs, staring up at the hand-lettered cursive sign boasting a paintbrush *t* with a heart-shaped red flourish at the end: PAINT TO YOUR HEART'S CONTENT. "I could have said no," she says bleakly. "And I didn't. So here we are."

My gaze travels Bea as she pulls out her lip balm and sweeps it over her mouth while still staring at the sign.

"What is it?" she asks, meeting my eyes. "Something in my teeth?"

Her jacket is canary yellow, her dress a deep blue-green that makes her eyes sparkle like gemstones. She's wearing purple tights with tiny golden pineapples printed on them. It's all so . . . *her*, it makes my chest ache.

"No, Beatrice. You just look very lovely."

She cocks an eyebrow. "You're not buttering me up by telling me what I already know. Teal's my color." Swooshing by me, she throws open the door. "They better serve more than one glass of wine during this shit show."

As soon as we enter, she stops abruptly, sending me tumbling into her. "Honestly, Beatrice. One of these days we're going to manage a public outing without a bodily incident."

She wears a horrified expression on her face as we're greeted by what I'm hesitant to call music, it's so earsplitting. "What *is* that?" she says.

I listen, trying to make sense of the odd sounds echoing from the speakers around us. But before I can catch more than a few seconds, a woman appears from the back of the shop, smiling brightly. "Halloo!" she calls loudly.

"Oh God, no," Bea mutters.

Carefully, I nudge her a few feet inside. "I'm sure she's just excited to see her first customers of the night."

"James, I cannot handle people like this—"

"Welcome!" the woman says brightly, waving us in. "Come in. Come in. I'm Grace, owner of Paint to Your Heart's Content. Oh, you two. What a beautiful couple, what radiant erotic energy. I feel it already."

Grace strolls ahead of us in head-to-toe Valentine red and pink. Her silvery hair is swept up in a bun with matching heart-shaped barrettes peeking out. When she smiles at us over her shoulder, her red cat-eye glasses sparkle with pink hearts at the hinges.

"Here," she says, sweeping her hand. "This is your station. We'll wait a few more minutes for the rest of our guests. I hope you don't mind?"

Bea blinks around the paint shop and former bakery, judging by the lingering scent of bread yeast and sugar-rich frosting that outstrips the faint odor of acrylic paint. Taking in the abundant art covering the walls, the empty easels, and the odd sounds echoing around us, Bea seems at a loss for words.

So I take over. "Thank you," I tell Grace. "And no, not at all."

"Aren't you sweet?" she says, blinking up at me and fluttering her lashes. "And so tall. My oh my." Sighing, Grace takes a step back. "Well, excuse me. I'll be back in just a moment to take your wine order. For now, please get comfortable."

Once Grace is gone, I pat Bea's stool. "Sit. You look stunned."

She lowers onto her seat. "Jamie, what *is* that noise?"

I peer up at a speaker right above us. "Whatever it is, it's pretty terrible."

"I can't take it." Bea's hands creep up over her ears. She shuts her eyes and rocks forward.

"Hang tight. I'll be right back."

Weaving through the empty paint stations, I find Grace in front, setting up an easel that looks like it will be hers for demonstration. "Grace."

She glances up and drops her paintbrush. "Oh! Goodness. Yes."

"I was wondering. The . . . music."

"The whale-mating sounds?" she says.

"Ah. So *that's* what it is."

"Yes," she says, sighing deeply. "Aren't they majestic?"

"Majestic. Yes. Most certainly. However, they are a bit . . . How should I say it? Hard on the ears after a while?"

She frowns. "You've been here for three minutes."

"Very true. The thing is, my . . . girlfriend." I try, and fail, to ignore the rush of pleasure that floods my chest when I say that.

Pretend, the voice of reason says. *It's all pretend.*

"The music," I continue, "is hard on her ears. It's nothing personal to the whales or you, but very high- and very low-pitched sounds are painful for her, so unless you can change it, we'll have to leave."

Grace blinks at me. Her eyes fill with tears. "She doesn't like my music?"

"It's not a matter of liking," I explain gently. "It's just that certain sounds hurt, physically. And the sounds of—"

"The Northern Pacific humpback calling to his mate? Filling the sea with the echoes of his passion?" Grace offers. "It's *painful* to her?"

"Yes. Again, this isn't a matter of preference. It's a matter of the space being inaccessible while it sounds like this. I know you don't mean any harm in it, and it's your choice whether or not you decide to alter your"—I glance over my shoulder at the empty easels—"client experience. However, we'll have to leave unless you can find something equally 'romantic' but gentler on the ears."

Grace sighs heavily. "Well. I suppose I can scrounge up something a bit less inspired but still appropriate for a night of impassioned painting."

"Wonderful. Thank you." I turn, then pause. "Do you happen to have that wine somewhere nearby? I think the lady could use a glass."

"Welcome," Grace says, "to a night in which we will touch into the tenderness of our hearts and allow art to bond us deeper to our partners."

Bea takes a large gulp of wine.

"This evening is a special one," Grace says to us and to the other couple who joined us right before we started. They sit up front, a late-in-life duo who can barely keep their eyes off each other. "Paint to Your Heart's Content is a unique guided artistic experience. You aren't here simply to mimic my masterpieces—"

Bea chokes on her wine.

I arch an eyebrow.

"Come on," she whispers hoarsely. "*Masterpieces?*"

Thankfully, we're in the back, and Grace doesn't hear us over the melodramatic string music that I've had to ask her to turn down. Twice.

"You're here," Grace says, "to paint from your heart, to express its vision of your lover's likeness, with my help. I will be assisting your technique while modeling the process with my own inamorato."

This time I almost crack, straightening my face just in time to hide it behind a fist, then a throat clear. Grace's inamorato strolls out. If he's older than me, I'll eat my glasses. He also looks like an underwear model.

"Damn," Bea says.

"Hey." I drag her stool closer. "You're with me."

She glances back my way. "What?"

"I said"—I drop my voice and lean close, breathing in her soft scent and barely resisting the urge to press a kiss to her neck—"you're with me."

"Oh." She smiles. "Don't worry. He's not my type."

I narrow my eyes. "What *is* your type?"

"Tall, dark blond, and stuffy." She looks me up and down. "Obviously."

My heart stutters before my mind snags on that last word. "I am *not* stuffy."

"You're stuffy," she says, sipping her wine. "And starchy. And so buttoned-up. It's precious."

"Precious," I mutter, tugging her stool even closer to mine.

"And now," Grace says, "we will begin."

We've clearly missed her opening remarks, because Grace has opened her paints and is discussing blending colors. As she speaks, her model glances out and smiles, his eyes lingering on Bea.

I clear my throat. Loudly. He meets my gaze, sees the murder I'm glaring at him, then looks away.

Bea pokes me gently in the side.

"What?" I snap.

She lifts her phone and takes a picture, then turns and shows me the screen. "Look at that and tell me you're not stuffy?"

"That is grumpiness," I tell her. "It's different."

"Oh really? You're not jealous, are you, James? May I remind you that you are on a *fake* date with your *fake* girlfriend?"

"You mean the one whose clothes I tore off last Friday, then brought to a stunning orgasm?"

Her jaw drops.

Mine does, too.

"Excuse me?" she whispers. "If you have something to say, *James*, then say it."

"Fine, *Beatrice*, I think I will. Why have we barely talked in the past five days? Why, after we came together, cleaned each other, and put on our clothes, then you curled up in my arms, *why* did I wake up alone?"

Bea blinks at me. "I . . . I didn't think you'd want me to stay."

"Not want you to stay?" I hiss as Grace rambles on. "You think I'd do that with anyone on a Friday night, then kick them to the curb at God knows what hour of the morning?"

"I don't *know*," she snaps back. "You didn't exactly make yourself clear."

"What wasn't clear about holding you in my arms and kissing you until we fell asleep?"

Her cheeks turn pink. "I didn't know what that meant, okay, Jamie? We were both a little slaphappy. One thing led to another. It was impulsive, and you are a lot of things, sir, but impulsive is not one of them. I had no idea how you'd feel in the morning, and I was *not* waking up in your arms, risking the sight of anything close to regret."

"Bea." I swallow roughly. "I would never regret that."

She seems stunned by this. "You wouldn't?"

"I wouldn't and I didn't." Leaning closer, I lower my voice. "Did *you* regret it?"

Her eyes drift to my mouth. She bites her lip. "No. I didn't."

"And you're not upset?"

"Jamie, no. I . . . I thought *you* would be."

"Well, I'm not," I tell her, failing to hide how offensive that assumption is.

"Um . . ." She swallows nervously. "Okay. Good."

I nod. "Good."

The air between us thickens with silence.

"Are we following?" Grace calls.

Bea and I snap upright, spin on our stools in tandem, then face forward. I adjust my canvas. Bea fiddles with her paintbrushes and zones out as Grace demonstrates building our palettes by blending colors.

"Beatrice, aren't you going to follow directions?" I ask.

She drops the paintbrush and gives me a nonplussed look. "I think my humble background in studio arts will see me through on the basics of color theory."

"Ooh, now who's stuffy?"

She gasps. "Am not!"

"Elitist, then. Same thing, really."

"I'm not elitist." Bea flicks open one of the small paint bottles that came with our setup and squirts it on the palette board. "I just know what the hell I'm doing without some woman who looks like a Valentine Little Debbie cake and has a baked good's worth of knowledge about art—given what's on the wall—telling me what to do."

I squirt my own paint on the palette, following Grace's example of blending colors to make skin tone and eye color for each other's portraits. "Sounds like elitism to me."

Bea growls, squirting more paint out onto her palette and struggling when she gets to blue. "Dammit," she mutters, smacking the bottle on the side of our shared table, which holds her wine.

"Bea, careful."

"Jamie," she snaps. "I've got this—oh!" Blue paint flies out of the bottle and lands with a splat on the left side of my chest. "Shit. I'm sorry."

I peer down at it. "A lethal strike. Straight to the heart."

"Hold on. I'll get some paper towels." Bea jumps off her stool, takes one step forward, and trips on the table leg. I try to catch her, but her momentum sends her hurtling over my lap, straight into my palette, which flips into her face.

Eyes scrunched shut. Lips sealed. Dripping with paint.

Instinctively, I sweep her into my arms and carry her between our easels, past the other couple, past Grace and her muse. Shouldering open the bathroom door, I snap the lock in place behind me, then start running water.

Bea is silent as I set her down.

"Hang tight," I tell her.

Once the water is tepid, I step behind her, sweeping back her hair. "Two steps forward and you're at the sink. You can start rinsing."

Bea shuffles forward and bends, which has the inconveniently pleasant effect of placing her backside right against my groin. I grab a fistful of paper towels with one hand, wiping the paint from my shirt. After I toss them, I try to step farther back, but I almost lose her hair. "Dammit, Beatrice. You couldn't have Rapunzel hair."

She spits as she rinses, keeping paint from slipping into her mouth. "Why would I have Rapunzel hair?"

"Because that way I wouldn't be standing behind you in a highly suggestive position, trying not to respond."

"Jamie." She squints one-eyed at me in the mirror. "I have blue acrylic paint all over my face. I look like a Smurf. You can't honestly—" Her open eye widens. "Okay, maybe you can. Wow."

I clear my throat, feeling my cheeks heat. I have no explanation. At least, not one I'm sure she wants to hear.

Leaning over the sink, Bea splashes her face, getting soap from the dispenser and scrubbing her skin. "I'm a little concerned you have a hard-on when I look like a Smurf."

I catch a few silky, dark hairs that have slipped out of my grip. "A very pretty Smurf."

"Keep talking to me like that and I'm going to get ideas."

I wish she would. "What kind of ideas?"

"Ideas in the vein of Friday. Without the painful awkwardness afterward, because it would have been discussed and agreed upon."

"What does that mean?" I ask.

"It means we're in a fake relationship, but there's no rule against *real* sex. We could sleep together."

My heart stalls like an engine on its last legs. "Sleep together."

But not *be* together. Not move past pretending and actually be a couple. A real couple who doesn't tick off a list of Instagrammable to-dos or limit themselves to the occasional fool-around on the sofa. A real couple who evolves beyond unlikely circumstance and unexpected friendship into something deeper, a connection I've felt strengthening between us, begging to be named.

Silence fills the bathroom as Bea shuts off the water and snatches a handful of paper towels. "Forget I said that," she mutters inside the towels.

"Bea—"

She's past me in a blur, but I catch the blush on her cheeks, her expression downcast as she unlocks the door and throws it open.

"Bea, wait." I stop her in the hallway when I catch her wrist.

"Jamie," she whispers, spinning her hand so it grips mine, too. "Please. I shouldn't have said that. Sometimes I speak before I think."

"Bea, sometimes—" Words stick in my throat, thicken my tongue as I stare at her. It takes longer than I want, but she's patient. She waits. "Sometimes," I finally manage, "I don't speak *after* I think, but I wish I could. I'm not always strong at spur-of-the-moment dialogue, but I want to talk. Right after this. Please?"

"Okay," she says quietly. "After this. Now, come on. Let's go be Instagrammable."

TWENTY-FIVE

Bea

I had to do it. Blurt what I've been thinking since Friday night in the worst possible way. I didn't mean *only* sex, but I wasn't exactly sure what else I meant, either. Because I'm scared to admit that I daydream about being with Jamie, about him really being mine. Not just on Instagram or at house parties, not just during painting dates and in over-heated conservatories and at the bowling alley. Twenty-four seven. For real.

Thank goodness I stumbled on my words. Thank goodness he reacted the way he did. Because when we talk after this, he'll explain that he doesn't do casual. And he certainly won't ask me for more, which will suck. But at least I'll have been spared making a fool of myself for a man who's all wrong for me. Again.

Honestly, you'd think I'd have learned by now to see an arrangement for what it is rather than what it could be. I blame this terrible lapse in judgment on Grace and her romantic aura, which thickens the air more than the heady jasmine and amber incense wafting around us.

"Stare deeply into your lover's eyes," Grace calls, as if we're in Carnegie Hall instead of a narrow shop front.

Jamie peers over at me, pressing his glasses up his nose.

I stare back at him.

"Excellent," Grace says. "This is a vital step in our evening. Now we open ourselves wide and forge the bonds that deepen our erotic energy."

Jamie's eyes widen, then shut as he inhales slowly through his nose.

I bite my lip and remind myself of the time my little sister, Kate, stuck hot sauce in the ketchup on my plate, and my tongue was on fire for hours. It barely keeps me from laughing.

"We open ourselves," Grace says, "to our partner's love by breathing fully from our heart chakra." She puts a hand over her heart and holds her partner's gaze. He might have glanced my way earlier, but he only has eyes for her now.

"The heart chakra," Grace says, "or anahata, translates roughly to 'unhurt.' This is the place within us that unlocks our capacity for love, compassion, and forgiveness—for ourselves and others."

Jamie's eyes meet mine, and every drop of hilarity drains between us.

"Examining our love," Grace says, "contemplating how our heart will guide our brush, we open ourselves to a fuller appreciation of the one before us, for the healing energy they bring to our lives. Old wounds have no place in our hearts now. No place for hurt in the *unhurt* space.

"Surely, we are none of us strangers to pain," she says. "But tonight, we create and connect from the newness of an open heart that does not beat for fear but instead finds itself stretched as a fresh canvas, ready to be altered by the beauty of the one we love. Let us begin."

Breaking our gaze, Jamie and I turn to face our canvases.

A blank canvas is always a daunting thing. But right now, that white rectangle feels more than daunting. It feels like a rip in the universe, about to suck me in to God knows where. This newness Grace talked about, this fresh start, it's staring back at me. And I'm scared shitless.

My heart beats faster, then even faster. A cold sweat dampens my skin.

"Bea?" Jamie asks. "Are you all right?"

I nod, staring at the canvas. "I'm . . . envisioning my . . . approach."

Lie. Such a lie. I'm being petrified, is what I'm doing.

I sit there for long minutes, fiddling with paint colors, mixing countless shades of amber and peach and green. Anything but putting paint to canvas. I try a few times, swirling my brush, wetting it with paint, and lifting it in the air. But then my arm freezes, and my heart starts pounding again. So back to color mixing I go, until I have more colors than room on my palette.

By this point, I'm holding my breath, waiting for Jamie to ask what's going on, to take offense that I'm not participating or prod me for an explanation. But he only glances my way a few times before his eyes swiftly return to his canvas.

"And how are we doing?" Grace asks. "How is our heart's expression on canvas progressing?"

This woman. She is something.

Jamie's right. I am a little bit of an art snob, but I'm not cruel. Grace clearly loves her business and its heartbeat for bringing people together through painting. I don't fault her for that. Hell, I admire it. I've just turned into a cynic who hasn't touched a paintbrush in almost two years and is now *really* scared to do that, because then what?

What if painting makes me feel the way it used to? Like my heart's in my hands, pouring itself out with each stroke of my brush. Like life's deepest meanings and truest truths can be captured in light and shadow and the daunting work of good perspective. What if that feeling turns my heart as soft and tender as it once was? And what if someone once again crushes it in their grip?

"Going fine, thank you," Jamie tells her after my awkward silence, because the guy is constitutionally incapable of being rude.

"Your efforts are . . ." Grace clears her throat and tips her head, staring at Jamie's canvas, which is hidden from me. "Very commendable."

Jamie adjusts his glasses and frowns at his painting. "You can say it. Visual art is not my gift."

"No," Grace agrees. "But your heart is there, in every stroke. That's the real gift. And you?" she says to me, stepping up behind my canvas.

My blank canvas.

"Oh." Her eyes widen. She peers at me over her red-framed cat-eye glasses, tiny bubblegum-pink hearts at the hinges winking in the over-head lights. "What is this, my dear?"

"It's . . ." A knot forms in my throat. "It's been a while since I did this," I whisper.

Her gaze searches mine. I'm not a big fan of prolonged eye contact. It gives me the sense that my soul's being excavated and my skin's been stung by a swarm of bees. So I let her look for only a moment before I stare down at my boots.

"Is there hurt tied to the act of painting?" she asks.

"It just kicks up . . . a lot of feelings."

"Ah yes," she says gently. "We paint from our hearts. And when our hearts have been hurt, our art can hurt, too."

"Yes," I manage, around the growing lump thickening my voice.

Nothing but melodramatic string music fills the air until Grace says, "Are you ready to try again?" Picking up the brush I have yet to do anything with but spin in three dozen shades of primary colors, she examines it.

I peer up at her, my eyes blurring with tears. "I think so. It's just that, starting, that first step . . . It's really scary."

"I know." She nods and smiles gently. "I know that very well. But if your heart wants it, then you can do it. I promise." She places the brush in my hand. "Blank canvas. Fresh paint. Courageous heart. You're ready."

Grace pats my shoulder gently. "Now back to *my* fresh canvas," she says with a coy smile.

"Thank you," I tell her.

"Don't thank me. Thank the person who knew exactly what you needed."

When she steps away, my vision fills with the man behind her, the man who was behind it all, every layer of this evening.

"James Benedick Westenberg."

He avoids my eyes, staring faithfully at his canvas. "At your service."

"You heard all of that, didn't you?"

He clears his throat. A blush hits his cheeks. "Rather hard not to. Grace has the lungs of an opera singer."

My laugh catches before it almost becomes a sob. "Jamie. Look at me."

He does. And when his eyes meet mine, my heart unlocks in a quiet, earth-tipping *click*.

"Is . . ." He hesitates, searching my eyes. "Is everything all right? Do you want to stop? We can, if it's too much—"

"No," I tell him, exhaling shakily. "And yes."

His brow furrows. "I don't understand."

How do I tell Jamie nothing is all right, not when I look at him and feel this?

How do I admit that I never want to stop, even though I'm afraid of what comes next?

How do I explain that this is too much? Looking at him, knowing that once again I have a blank canvas, that my heart is stretched wide open, begging for love to fill it with color.

I want to tell Jamie that I know so little about my life right now, but what I do know is that tonight, here, with him, is exactly where I want to be. I want Jamie to know that I need to paint him, to make him sit for hours in the apartment's studio, which I haven't used in much too long. To turn up the heat, strip him down, and capture the way he looks, like he sees straight to the heart of me. Just like he is now.

But first things first.

I lift my brush. I drench it with color. And with a shaky hand, I paint my new beginning.

———

"Bea," Jamie says. Posture perfect. Hands clasped between his long legs. A portrait titled *Patience*.

"Hmm?"

"Grace is ready to go. The workshop's over."

"Just two more minutes," I tell him, shifting on my feet. I've been standing since I started on the canvas. I never sit and paint. I move too much while I work.

"We'll bring your canvas home," he says gently. "But we need to leave."

"Don't worry!" Grace calls from the front of the shop. "Take your time!"

"I really am almost done," I tell him, eyes not leaving my canvas. "I mean for now."

Blowing out a slow breath, he glances my way. "I'm getting nervous."

"For what?"

"For the big reveal. You show me yours, I show you mine."

I smile, glancing between him and my easel. "Jamie. You have a *Jeopardy!* vocabulary. You bowl like a pro. You're a baby whisperer, and you adopt senile cats. You're a rock-star human. Allow me this one thing to be better at than you."

He blinks at me. "One thing? Bea, you're better than me at *lots* of things—not that this is a competition."

I snort. "Okay."

"Really!" he says. "You're not just a talented artist. You're seriously good at chess. You love the prickly creatures of the world. You're genuine and creative. You give people permission to be themselves rather than what the world tells them they should be. Maybe that's not summed up on a résumé or a test score the way my strengths are, but you have gifts, Bea, and gifts like yours matter."

My paintbrush falters as his praise sinks in and colors every corner of me, peacock-blue proud. "You mean that?"

"Have I ever said something to you that I didn't mean?"

"Uh. Well, I can't read your mind, but I feel like misleading me would violate one of your many Capricorn moral codes, so I'm going with no."

"Precisely. Now." He taps the easel with his clean and dry paintbrush, because of course he tidied up after himself. "I'm ready. But if you're not, that's all right. I can wait. Or if you never want me to see yours, that's all right, too. I didn't mean for this to push you, Bea. I thought it would be something you'd find fun, not that I'm an expert at that, but—"

"Jamie." I set down my brush, then cross the small space between our easels.

Slipping a finger beneath his chin, I tilt his face until his eyes meet mine. With him sitting on a stool, I'm taller than him for once, and I savor the fresh perspective it gives me. Light hits his cheekbones, the long, knife-blade line of his nose. That mouth that's so often tight and serious parts softly as he looks at me.

"Thank you," I tell him, sweeping my fingertips across the planes of his face.

He swallows roughly, eyes searching mine. "For what?"

I'm about to do something I shouldn't. Blurring our boundaries, not knowing what Jamie thinks or wants from me. But if now's my last chance to enjoy him like this, before he lets me down gently and we're back to behaving ourselves, I'm taking my chance, dammit.

"For this," I whisper, as I press a kiss to his temple. "For everything." A kiss to the sharp jut of his Adam's apple.

He exhales slowly as his hands settle on my hips. "Oh."

"I'm ready now." Pulling away, I force myself to let him go.

"You're sure?"

"Yes." Stepping back, I reach for my canvas and take a deep breath. "On the count of three?"

He nods, lifting his canvas from its easel.

In unison, we count, "One. Two. Three."

We flip our canvases, and as I stare at Jamie's, a shiver dances down my spine. His is mostly black, speckled with tiny white dots—stars?—his best attempt at my face in profile, staring up at the sky.

"Bea," Jamie says.

I tear my eyes from his painting and meet his gaze. "Yes?"

"This is . . ." He glances from my painting to me. "Incredible."

I peer around the side of my canvas, analyzing my painting of Jamie how I first saw him, minus the lion mask—glancing just over his shoulder, eyes beautiful yet serious, the promise of a smile hidden in his stern expression. "Eh. I'm rusty. It's nowhere near finished. But . . . it's a decent likeness of you. That makes me happy."

Jamie frowns at the canvas. "You really see me like that?"

"Like what?"

He's quiet for a long moment. "It just feels like it's a better version of me than I see."

"James," I sigh.

"Beatrice."

"You know it's okay, right? For someone to see the best in you. For them to like the things you're way too hard on yourself for."

He blinks as if confused, like I've surprised him. Like I've left him lost for words. I hate that Jamie doesn't seem to see himself how I do. I know he's not perfect, and yes, he has some quirks that make me bananas, but that just makes him human.

When did this happen? Was it his upbringing? His ex? I want to grab anyone who's made him doubt his worth and knock their heads together.

But for now, maybe it's just enough to *show* Jamie what he doesn't quite believe with words. It's enough to be here, together, doing . . . whatever this night is that feels different and special and scary all at once.

"I love your painting," I tell him.

He peers down at the canvas. "It's awful. Technically, I mean. But I was happy while I did it. I don't generally like doing things that I'm unskilled at, but painting you from memory, picturing you staring up at the night sky, made it an enjoyable exercise."

Carefully, I take his painting, and Jamie reaches for mine. We tip our heads at the same time, exploring each other's portraits. "You stretched yourself," I tell him.

"So did you," he says, staring at my canvas. "Simply by coming here. Seemed like the least I could do."

"Why the night sky?"

"Why do you think?"

I meet his eyes. "Because I like astrology?"

He tugs at his collar, a fresh blush hitting his cheeks. "It's a bit embarrassing."

"You're seriously worried about embarrassment in front of me? Do you know our track record?"

"Fair point. As I painted, I thought about when we took our walk home, after Pho Ever, and you disappeared into your own world. The way you looked at the stars, with wonder in your eyes . . . It's one of the loveliest things I've ever seen."

Tears blur my vision as I study his canvas again. "I don't know how lovely having my head in the clouds is when it means I trip while walking."

"That's why I'm here," he says. "To catch you. Take a drink to the shirt. Or pants."

"Stop bringing that up!" I reach for his side to tickle him. "That was mortifying."

"Wait!" Spinning away, he ducks my tickle lunge and holds my portrait like a shield between us. A shield he lowers slowly, then carefully sets on the easel. "I didn't say it to tease you. I said it because look where it got us." Searching my eyes, Jamie says, "Bea—"

Grace's delighted voice interrupts him. "Aren't you two just the picture of bliss!"

Jamie glances away, rubbing his eyes beneath his glasses. I want to shove Grace, as lovingly as possible, back to the other end of the store and demand Jamie keep talking *now*. But instead I face our interrupter, who's reminded me why we're here.

"Actually," I tell Grace, slipping my phone from my pocket and opening the camera. "If you don't mind taking a photo, we'll be exactly that."

Jamie dutifully wraps his arm around my waist for the picture, but the moment our photo is taken, his hand drops. Silently, we help tidy up and break down our stations—despite Grace's protests—then trundle outside with our damp canvases, braced against the wind.

Still quiet, Jamie pulls out his phone and orders a cab.

My nerves are shredded. I stare up at the sky and search for constellations, trying desperately to distract myself.

Will he ever finish saying what he started to when Grace interrupted us? Maybe he's regretting opening his mouth. Maybe all Grace's talk of heart chakras and deepening erotic energy warped his thoughts and now he realizes—

"Bea." Jamie wraps his hand around mine.

I glance up at him. "Yes?"

Please let this be it. Please let him put me out of my misery and tell me what he was about to say, so I stop hoping like a fool for something that isn't supposed to be.

"Before," he says. "When Grace interrupted us, what I was going to say was . . . That is, I don't want to make this awkward, or perhaps, more so than I already am—"

"Jamie. Remember, it's just me."

"*Just* you?" A beat of silence hangs between us. Jamie steps closer and carefully extracts his hand from mine, then cups my cheek. "There's no such thing. And I could have sworn I've been so painfully obvious that I feel that way."

"Feel what way?"

His fingertips trace my jaw, slip through the wisps of hair that tangle toward my face in the wind. "Like I'd take a cocktail to the chest, a half-dozen glasses of champagne to the pants, a hundred thousand times if that's what it took to end up here. Like I'd never trade our meet-disaster for anything because it set everything into motion."

Searching my eyes, he says, "Because if we'd just made small talk with not a spill in sight, then parted quiet ways, we'd have stayed exactly on our solitary paths. Our friends might not have interfered. And if they hadn't interfered, I wouldn't have ended up almost kissing you in a closet, staring at you over a chessboard and a cup of coffee, agreeing to the wildest and best month of my life."

I stare at Jamie as my heart turns into a firework grand finale, a sparkling cascade of thundering booms. "What are you saying?"

"I'm saying, you're the best kind of chaos I've ever met. And while chaos used to terrify me, you make me crave it. I'm saying, even though this is an absurd situation we've backed ourselves into . . . I'd do it again in a heartbeat because it's given me you."

The world turns peach-pink, glittering gold, as the pyrotechnics in my chest build to a fever pitch. "You would?"

"Yes, Beatrice. Because while I've found an unlikely friend in you, I've found much more than that, too."

I grab a fistful of his coat, so frightened he'll fade before my eyes and I'll wake up, heartbroken that this was some torturously vivid dream. "Jamie. Is this real?"

He curves his hand softly around my jaw. His eyes travel my face. "As real as it gets. That's how faking it with you has felt . . . real. Friday wasn't an outlier, Bea. It was a paltry expression of everything I want with you. I spend each minute I'm not with you scrounging up excuses to see you again. Trying to find another thing we can do together, and not because I want to teach a few misguided, albeit well-meaning, people a lesson but because I want to be with you."

"*Be* with me?"

"Yes. But I realize . . ." He swallows roughly. "I realize you might not want that. We can see this through exactly how we planned when it started. If that's what you want, I'll honor that. No, it won't be easy, but I can accept it if you don't feel the way I do—"

"Jamie." I tug him closer, holding him in place as I untangle my thoughts. "Jamie, I didn't know."

He smiles softly. "I get that now. I thought I sort of gave myself away on Friday."

"I thought I gave myself away, too. But I was scared it wasn't what you wanted."

"How could I not want you?" He bends and gives me the gentlest kiss, then whispers against my lips, "You're everything I never knew I wanted."

I savor that kiss, and I kiss him back. I want to drown in that kiss, to bathe in it and never come up for air. And yet, reality yanks me to the surface and whispers worries I can't seem to push away.

"But it hasn't been real," I tell him, pulling back, taking a deep gulp of cold night air. "What if we've tricked *ourselves* into this? What if we're just lonely? What if being on our best behavior's made us think two people as wildly different as us will work?"

Tipping his head, Jamie traces my mouth with his thumb, the rough callus of his fingertip brushing my sensitive skin. "I've considered that. I think that's the fear talking. We've been on our best behavior around the meddlers, but what about all the hours we've spent, just you and me, being ourselves? We were never trying to impress each other or win each other over. In fact, I think I've been my most insufferable self with you because it felt safe to do so."

Safe.

"Safe," I whisper. "You're right. But it's still . . . it's such a mindfuck."

"It is." His hand slides down my waist, drawing me close to him. "We don't have to run headlong into this. There's no rush, Bea."

My eyes slip shut for just a moment as I feel the pleasure of being tucked against his body, the heat and height and hardness of him. "I'm in a bit of a rush. I feel no reason to go slow."

His mouth tips in one of those almost smiles that make my heart crackle to life like a summertime sparkler. "Does that mean . . . you want this?" he asks. "To be real?"

"Yes." The truth lurches from the heart of me, leaving a raw tenderness in its wake that reminds me how vulnerable this makes me feel. "But I'm scared. I'm scared you're going to wake up tomorrow and realize that sure, we dry hump and kiss like champs and have a blast teasing the shit out of each other, but you don't really want someone as chaotic as me in the picture for the long haul."

"You're not alone. I'm scared, too. I'm afraid you'll get tired of me," he admits. "That you'll get sick of my neurotic rigidity."

Giving him a saucy smile, I run my hand down his chest. "I like your rigidity."

"Beatrice."

"James."

He sighs. "I'm serious."

"You are serious, Jamie. And I'm pretty gone for it."

Now it's Jamie's turn to look unsure, to hold me tight like he's worried I'll vanish in his grip and this moment will morph into a mirage. "What are you saying?"

I press on tiptoe and steal a long, slow kiss, then whisper, "I'm *asking*. If you want this to be real, too. You and me, together."

His eyes search mine, his expression serious, tense. "What about the plan to break up and get your revenge? *Our* revenge? You'll just . . . let that go?"

"Mmm . . ." I tip my head in thought. "I think our happiness is revenge enough."

"How so?"

A smile lifts my mouth. "The meddlers pushed us together, Juliet and Jean-Claude tricked us into texting, but . . . Jamie, *we* chose what to do with that. We chose to spend time together, become friends, become . . . more. We made this real on our own, not because of them but in spite of them." I cup his cheek, my thumb softly tracing his jaw. "That's vengeance enough for me."

He leans into my touch, his eyes holding mine fiercely. "Good."

"So . . ." My smile deepens. "Want to officially stop pretending with me?"

Jamie's smile is brighter than the stars above us. "More than anything."

TWENTY-SIX

Jamie

This cab ride is the best cab ride of my life. Bea keeps stretching her seat belt, leaning in and kissing me. I keep kissing her back. Because she wants what I want.

I feel like I can breathe again.

When the cab drops us off, Bea practically skips to her building and throws open the vestibule door. "Want to come upstairs and play with my hedgehog?" she asks.

It's hard to swallow a laugh, but I manage it, giving her my best poker face. "That's a disturbing euphemism."

"Hey!" She lets the door to her building fall shut behind her. "You weren't supposed to see through that."

I tug her jacket closer to her chin as she shivers against the cold. "It was a wild guess."

"I actually meant it. Well, I was hoping playing with Cornelius would be an enticement, then I'd seduce you with my wily ways."

"And what are those?"

"Um. Well, I was working on that. I thought maybe I'd tickle you to the bed and it would turn into something else."

"Tickling does not lead to seduction."

"What *does*?" she asks.

A smile wins out as I peer down at her. "If I tell you that, I lose my mystery."

Bea gives me sad puppy eyes. "You're not coming up, are you?"

"I want to, but no." My fingers thread through her hair, cradling her scalp. I watch her eyes fall shut. "When we're together, I don't want other people around, Beatrice. I want hours and hours, and plenty of privacy for you to be as noisy as you want."

Her eyes spring open. Her mouth parts as she stares up at me. "I've got time. I'll be quiet. Let's go."

"No, you don't. And you won't." I press a kiss to her cheek, then reach past her for the door, opening it again. "And I'll love it."

"Jamie," she whines, clutching my jacket. "Friday wasn't enough."

"It absolutely wasn't."

"So let's go fix that."

I kiss her nose this time, then her forehead. "Go inside and warm up."

"Oh, don't worry," she says, biting her lip. "I'll be thinking about you tonight, warming myself up in bed *plenty*."

A groan rolls out of me. "Stop tempting me and get inside. I've made plans that'll be our reward after the party. We can pick up where we left off." My stomach tightens anxiously. "That is, if you're still amenable to—"

"If you ask me one more time if I'm up for this party, I'm going to get offended. I am going, James. I am going for the fancy, tiny tapas, and the bougie bubbles, and the chance to step on your toes in front of two hundred strangers. I even got a new dress." She adds coyly, "It comes just past my butt."

"Not funny."

"It's a little funny. So—" She sashays closer and drops her voice. "You've got *plans*, you say?"

"Yes, you imp." I nudge her into the vestibule, swatting her softly on the bum. "Plans. Now, up you get."

Bea spins, then kisses me hard on the mouth. "I knew you'd be a spanker."

"Beatrice!" My cheeks turn red. "That was not a spank. That was a . . . a love tap."

She cackles as she jogs up the stairs, tripping halfway on the first flight. "It was a spank!" she yells. "And I liked it!"

My head falls back as I stare up at the sky. "God help me."

———————

I'm running late. Of course I am. Because today is my father's birthday party and Bea's waiting for me to pick her up at six sharp, and since I have somewhere to be, the universe dumped the longest line of folks needing care at the shelter that I've seen in months. Cold and flu season is ramping up, so it's not entirely unexpected to have an uptick in patients, but it was still an unprecedentedly busy day. And now I'm behind schedule.

"West." Jean-Claude tsks, making a show of glancing at his watch. "You're late."

I sprint by him toward my room, peeling off my sweater, unbuttoning my shirt. "Thank you for that astute observation."

His laughter's drowned out as I turn on the water, tear off the rest of my clothes, then step into the shower and scrub myself clean under near-scalding water. After a quick but thorough shave and applying the usual pomade to tame my hair, I'm in my tux, hopping into my shoe as I reenter the living room. Jean-Claude's pocketing his keys.

"Where are you going?" I ask him.

"Eh?" He frowns my way. "To the same party as you. Where do you think I'm going?"

I nod toward his keys, stepping into the other dress shoe and tying it. "We're riding together, with Juliet and Beatrice."

"You offered. I said maybe. I've changed my mind."

I straighten from bending over my shoe. "Why?"

"Because I'll be sharing my beautiful fiancée all night, and I want her to myself until then."

"Jean-Claude, you're practically glued to her. Would a limousine ride with us be that much of an imposition?"

"I've hardly seen Juliet the past few days." He adjusts his tie in the mirror and fiddles with his hair. "Thanks to Christopher. He has me crushed with work. Connard."

I raise my eyebrows. "Awfully nasty thing to call your friend."

"He's my boss first and foremost, and he's made sure I know it, with all he's given me to do."

"More responsibility generally seems to come with the territory of a promotion, doesn't it?"

He sighs at his reflection in the mirror. "As usual, you're naïve about these things, West. He's doing it on purpose because it separates me from Juliet. He's incredibly possessive of her."

"What are you talking about?"

Turning, Jean-Claude faces me. "He has a fucking picture of her on his desk."

"And I'd bet she's not alone in that picture."

His jaw tics. He glances away and pours himself two fingers of whiskey in a lowball glass. "That's beside the point."

"It's not, Jean-Claude. I'm sure he has photos of all the Wilmots because they're his family. Juliet and Bea are like sisters to him, Bea told me—"

"Of course she did. Because she doesn't want Juliet with me, either. She wants those two together."

"Are you *listening* to yourself?" I stare at him, nearly at a loss for words. "What's gotten into you?"

"She's mine," he says under his breath. "And I'll be damned if Christopher seduces her behind my back, while he has me killing myself with work like some pathetic underling."

"Jean-Claude. I think you're tired. Or stressed. You're acting paranoid."

He laughs emptily and swirls his whiskey. "It's not paranoid when you're right."

"How do you know you're right? Have you addressed these concerns to Juliet? Asked her how she sees Christopher?"

"It's not *her* I'm worried about," he mutters, eyes on his drink. "It's everyone else. When she's with me, everything's fine. It's—" He brings the glass to his lips. "It's perfect with her. She's perfect." He tips back the glass and drains it.

"You're already getting started, and you'll be drinking more at the party," I remind him. "You can't drive after that."

He rolls his eyes.

"Jean-Claude, I'm serious."

"As am I." He slams the glass on the counter and sweeps up his phone.

"Be sensible. Ride with us. It might not be your first choice, but Beatrice and Juliet *like* spending time together. At least Juliet will be happy—"

"Don't," he says, low, dangerously quiet, "tell me what makes my fiancée happy. You think I don't realize those two are thick as thieves? It's the entire fucking reason I wanted you dating Bea, to get her out of our hair."

I blink, stunned. "What about 'you're lonely and miserable, and it's time to find someone who makes you happy'? Or was that just a lie so I'd go along with your plan?"

He starts toward the door, bringing himself closer to me, but not too close. Jean-Claude's never liked that when we're close, he has to crane his neck to look up at me. He shrugs. "Your potential enjoyment of her was a plus, but not my primary motivation. My goal was to get Bea out of the picture, because you know what kind of shit Juliet was telling me when I met her, when I knew how much I wanted her? *Let's keep it casual. I need to go slow. My sister's been in a tough space, and I'm not sure how she'll take me having a serious partnership, not yet.*" He makes a face of disgust. "I'd be damned if some oddball sister who couldn't get over being dumped was going to come between me and what's mine—"

"That's enough," I snap.

Our eyes lock, and Jean-Claude arches his brows coolly. "Oh, is it?"

Suddenly, my tolerance for living with someone because our families are entwined, because he splits my rent and doesn't ask much of me, because the devil you know is better than the devil you don't, and I'm experienced in living with moody, sharp-tongued men—my father made sure of that—evaporates.

"You won't insult Bea like that again," I tell him coldly. "Are we understood?"

"But of course." With a smooth turn of his heel, he throws open the door of our apartment and slams it shut.

"Shit." I scrub my face, groaning. Part of me wants to run out and tell him to get his ass in that limousine waiting outside. The other part—the part that wins out—has given up on him.

Unearthing my phone, I text Bea, On my way. Can't wait to see you.

Her response lights up my screen just a few seconds later. Great! Got on my fanciest pair of sweatpants & I'm ready to go.

I roll my eyes, smiling as I stroll out the door.

———

I've watched three rom-com movies, which is three more than most cynical, unromantic souls like me can say for themselves. I know about the dramatic reveal moment, when the love interest dresses up and makes a grand, elegant entrance to the hushed awe of everyone around them; when the other love interest realizes in that heart-stopping moment, *this* is the one for them. So I should have been prepared.

I was not.

Nothing could prepare me for Bea wrenching open the door to her apartment, breathless and smiling, draped in midnight black silk that clings to every curve like spilled ink poured over her body.

Air rushes out of me. I slump against the doorframe.

Bea grimaces. "That bad, huh?"

"That bad. And worse." Pushing off the doorframe, I step closer, drinking her in. "God. Look at you."

She bites her lip. "What?"

I clasp her hand, tangling our fingers. And then I bring her hand to my lips, kissing each knuckle, tucking her palm against my cheek. "You're so beautiful. So impossibly beautiful."

A rose-pink blush stains her cheeks. "Thank you, Jamie." One step closer, and our fronts brush. Begrudgingly I let her hand go, so she can use both to adjust my bow tie. "You are devastatingly handsome. Leave it up to you to look like temptation in a tux, when I swear I've never met someone in one of these getups that didn't look like an oversized penguin."

A thick laugh bursts out of me. Bea tips her head, slides her thumbs carefully beneath my eyes. "Are you crying?"

I blink away the traitorous wetness. "Fall allergies."

"Of course." She nods. "The pollen count in this apartment is despicable."

"It is. I'll be having a word with your landlord." Pulling her close, I press a soft, slow kiss to her lips and breathe her in.

You're the best thing in my life, I want to tell her. *You're safe and real and perfectly imperfect. We started as a lie, and now we're the truest thing I've ever known.*

But I don't say it, don't speak those fragile words into the delicate space between us. There's time to tell her, soon enough. After we've survived tonight. When it's quiet and dark and just us, Bea wrapped up in my arms.

For now, I content myself with telling her every other way that I can—in my hands wandering her waist, the hunger in our kiss. I walk her backward, kicking the door shut, until I've pressed her against the wall, her fingers toying gently with the close-cropped hair at my neck.

"Jamie," she breathes, arching into my touch as I kiss my way down her neck and find the soft swell of her breast, the hardened tip of her nipple. Her hand slides down my back, then wanders between us, stroking me where I'm getting harder by the second. "I can't believe I'm the one saying this," she says faintly, "but we're going to be late if we don't—"

"Right. Yes." I pull back, breathing roughly. I straighten the strap of her gown and let my gaze trail her from head to toe.

"Seriously, though." Bea shifts a little, like she's nervous, hands dancing at her sides. "Is the dress okay? I have a wrap I can wear if you think the tattoos will be a problem—"

"Beatrice."

She stills. "Yes?"

I drift my fingertips along the high neckline of her gown, where it tapers to delicate straps; over her collarbones, her throat, the soft tendrils of her upswept hair. Bea leans into my touch and I lean in, too, my mouth brushing the shell of her ear.

"The tattoos are the antithesis of a problem."

Her throat bobs with a swallow. I press a kiss there and earn her gasp. "They unsettle people," she says shakily. "Not everyone knows what to do with them. *You* didn't, when I met you."

"Ohhh, yes I did." I trail kisses along the delicate dotted line weaving down her neck. "I knew my tongue and my mouth wanted to taste every place you'd marked with those enigmatic designs, to discover and savor every sweet, soft corner of your body, until you were writhing and gasping and begging me for more."

She clutches my tuxedo jacket and sways a little. "Definitely didn't get the memo that night."

"That's because I was a tongue-tied, anxious mess, looking at the most overwhelmingly beautiful, sensual woman I'd ever seen. Of course I was a first-rate ass."

A laugh jumps out of her, as effervescent and sparkling as the finest champagne. The kind I'll watch her sip tonight while I think about sliding that black dress off her body until it lands at her feet in a pool of midnight silk.

"Forget the wrap," I whisper against her neck. "I love the art you've put on your body. It's beautiful, and you're proud of it."

She smiles. "I am proud of it."

"I am, too."

Bea turns just enough to press a tender kiss on my cheek before she sets both hands on my chest and gently guides me back, placing a few feet between us. "Maybe I should give you one last chance to decide on the wrap," she says, starting to turn. "After all, you haven't seen the whole dress."

Frowning, I set my hands in my pockets. "I can't imagine—*fuck*."

"Language, Mr. Westenberg!"

My gaze is fixed on the back of her dress, or, more accurately, the lack thereof. It's nothing but a swooping curve of silk that drapes from her shoulder straps to the base of her tailbone. "I'm so very sorry."

She smiles over her shoulder. "No, you're not."

"No, I'm not. Come here." I clasp her hand, snatching her black clutch, wrenching open the door. "Bring the wrap after all, but only because it's chilly out."

"Eek!" She snags it just in time as I whisk her over the threshold. "What's with the sudden rush?"

I lock up with her keys, then sweep her into my arms, making her squeal and throw her arms around my neck on a happy laugh as I hurry down the steps. "Because if I spend one more minute with you, that dress, and your bedroom just down the hallway, there's no way in hell we'd make it out the door."

The limo is an exercise in restraint, a constant battle not to picture all the ways I could take Bea: bent over, on her back, legs spread, hands in my hair, hands on the glass, making her writhe and pant and come again and again.

I will temptation away by remembering we've already had one rushed, frenzied sexual experience. Next time, I want all the time in the world.

There's also the fact that I'd wreck her gown, and then I'd tell the driver to turn around, at which point we'd miss the party. Not that I'm dying to go. I'm just resigned. This is what I do—placate my mother, appease my father, smile, be all politeness and propriety, then disappear until the next time I'm drafted to show my face and pretend like my father isn't a heartless bastard and my mother's content to stay by his side.

Tonight, though, there's a faint kernel of joy inside me. This is going to be terrible in many ways, surrounding myself with my family and the parts of my upbringing that I loathe, and yet Bea's here, beside me in the limo, smelling like her sultry perfume, her legs stretched across my lap. When we walk in, she'll be on my arm. Smiling, curious, her unbridled self. That makes it bearable.

The driver opens my door, and I let myself out, smooth myself down, then hold out a hand for Beatrice; when she straightens from the car and her eyes widen like saucers as she takes in my family home, I feel happier, more hopeful, than I have in a long time.

"Okay." She threads her arm through mine and squeezes. "So your family home makes my parents' place look like a gingerbread house."

I laugh quietly. "I like your parents' 'gingerbread house.' It felt homey."

"It is," she admits. "I like their house, too. Oh Lordy. That's your mom, isn't it?"

I glance up to where my mother stands, serene and stately, in the doorway, greeting guests with continental kisses on cheeks. "Yes."

"She's . . . intimidating." Bea says. "And tall."

"We're all tall. But don't worry, I'll make sure you can reach the appetizers."

She elbows me, but she's grinning. "Very funny."

"James," my mother says in her thick French accent, wrapping me in her arms. "You're late. At least you look handsome, mon biquet." She turns, facing Bea. "And who is this magical creature?"

"Maman, this is Bea Wilmot, my girlfriend." Bea's grip tightens on my arm. "Bea, this is my mother, Aline Westenberg."

Bea smiles nervously. "Nice to meet you."

"Enchantée." My mother draws her in for a perfume-soaked hug and kisses her once on each cheek. Turning back to me, she says in French, "Please make sure you find your father first. He'll feel slighted otherwise. Speak to the appropriate people and make introductions. Otherwise, you're free. Have some champagne. Dinner is in an hour."

"Yes, Maman. I know what's expected," I tell her in French, because it's my default with her. "You don't have to worry."

She shrugs, eyes already on the guests behind us. "Just trying to keep you out of trouble."

Like that ever worked. I kiss her on each cheek. "Enjoy the night."

As soon as we're past her, Bea yanks my hand, earning my attention. "What the *hell*, Jamie?" she hisses.

"What?" I ask, utterly confused. "Is something wrong? Did I—"

"You speak *French*?"

My mouth parts, but I'm not sure what to say. "Ehrm. Yes?"

"And you never thought to tell me?"

"I'm . . . sorry?"

"Not forgiven." She drags me to the edge of the foyer for a kiss that melts every worry our confusing conversation's caused. "French on your tongue makes me want to do filthy, filthy things to it."

Oh Christ. Heat *floods* me. My tongue. Beatrice. I'm aching for it. "I—yes, let's. Absolutely. Let's go."

Bea laughs, gently pushing me away and threading our fingers together. "Champagne and a dancing disaster first. French later."

I kiss her again, hard, desperate. "As you wish, mon cœur."

TWENTY-SEVEN

Bea

"Mon cœur?" I frown up at Jamie as he brings my hand to his lips and kisses my knuckles. "What's that mean?"

He grins. "I'll tell you later."

"Tease."

His grin deepens as he slips an arm around my waist. "Takes one to know one."

A woman in a silver dress sweeps by me, suddenly reminding me of Jules, how anxious I am to find her and make sure she's all right. Before Jamie knocked on my apartment door, then nearly knocked *me* over with how good he looked, I was worried about my sister. We went from plans for more or less a double date—though I wasn't too keen on spending a forty-five-minute drive out of the city with Jean-Claude—to her telling me they'd be driving alone, on some bogus excuse about Jean-Claude wanting them to be able to leave when they felt like it.

She avoided my eyes when I got back from work and found her in the bathroom, wrapped in a silky red robe, her hair in a towel turban. It looked like she'd been crying. But before I could get a straight answer out of her about anything, she distracted me with makeup and samples of no-smudge, long-lasting red lipstick, then disappeared in a woosh of silver chiffon to Jean-Claude's douche-canoe car, and here we are.

"All right?" Jamie asks.

Smiling up at him, I feel my heart swoop. A solitary wavy lock caresses his temple, and I smooth it back, knowing he wants to be his tidiest. His hazel eyes crinkle handsomely as he peers down at me and light kisses his sharp cheekbones, his long nose, the strong line of his jaw. He's unbearably hot. "I'm okay," I tell him. "It's just that . . . I'd like to find Jules."

He nods. "We will. I'm sorry Jean-Claude was an ass about driving separately."

"Eh. Jules seemed excited enough to ride in the Porsche."

Jamie tightens his grip around my waist, gently pulling me to his side, out of the way of a fast-moving waiter bearing hors d'oeuvres. "Not for the wide world would I let that man drive me. He's a terror behind the wheel."

I stop short. "Why didn't you say something? I let my sister get in the car with him!"

He sighs, peering down at me as we walk. "He's not actually reckless generally, and I doubt he'd be so careless with Juliet in the car. He just used to act reckless to mess with me because he knew I hated it."

"Every time I learn something new about this man," I mumble, "I like him less and less."

"If he'd be cautious and restrained with anyone, it would be Juliet. And if not . . . your sister's gone driving with him before. She knows who she's with and how he acts."

"Does she?" I glance out into the massive space, scouring the crowd for my sister. It's an actual ballroom. Jamie has a *ballroom* in his house. Mansion. Whatever. "I'm not sure she does. Some people . . . they show you their good side first. That's how they lure you in, and then gradually, they change—well, actually they don't change, they show their true selves, who they always were. But by then, you don't know what to think. What do you trust? Are you imagining things? Are they just having a rough week? Doesn't loving someone mean putting up with their bad side?"

My throat thickens as shitty memories return. Memories of Tod that I've worked so hard to leave behind and move on from.

"Bea." Jamie's hand gently cups my cheek, turning me until our gazes meet. His eyes search mine. "That's what he did to you? Your ex."

I nod. "I know what I'm talking about. I think that's how Jean-Claude is. I've *never* felt good around him, even when he was all smiles and rose bouquets, whisking her away for dates, surprising her with gifts. He moved too fast. He's never wanted me around. That's how they work, manipulators, possessive types. They cut you off, one by one, from the people who love you, who know the real you and make you feel good. And then they break you down until all you want is their approval, their presence—until they're your whole world and you're alone."

Jamie's jaw tics. "I'm not a violent man, Bea. I swore an oath to heal, not to harm. But I want to *crush* him."

Leaning into his touch, I smile up at Jamie and wrap my hand around his as it caresses my cheek. "I know. And that's more than enough for me. Maybe I can put you on standby with Jean-Claude?"

He glances up, searching the crowd. "Tempting as that is, I'll likely have to resort to harsh words. But no matter what, I'm on your side, all right? And Juliet's, too, if it comes down to it." His eyes meet mine again before he leans in and presses a long, slow kiss to my forehead. "I promise."

"BeeBee!"

My sister's voice startles me, and I jump, nearly headbutting Jamie. After a month of my shenanigans, he's developed excellent self-preservation instincts and jerks away just in time to avoid what would have been a nasty bloody nose. "Look at you," I tell him, patting his chest in reassurance. "Reflexes like a mongoose."

He smiles, setting his hand on my back as Jules throws an arm around my neck. "There you are!" she says brightly, kissing my cheek. "You look incredible. Doesn't she, West?"

Jamie's thumb softly traces my spine in a sensual trail to the edge of my dress before he drops his hand altogether. "She does. Utterly breathtaking. You look lovely, too, Juliet."

Jules smiles and sparkles like a constellation, all smoky eyeshadow and silvery dress. "Thank you."

"Enough of that." Jean-Claude slides his arm around my sister's waist and tucks her close against him. I burn holes into his hand with my eyes. "I'm contending with too much interest in her as it is."

"Please," Jules says on a laugh. "Just because *you* like me this much doesn't mean everyone else does."

"You say that," he tells her, tightening his grip on her waist. "But then, you're not in my shoes, dealing with double the competition."

Oh, *hell* no. He did not just say that. My hands turn to fists. Jamie scrubs his face and groans.

"Jean-Claude." Jules arches an eyebrow. "I've told you that's ridiculous."

"Not to mention offensive," I mutter.

"Mathematically it's not," he says, ignoring us.

"Jean-Claude," Jamie warns.

He ignores Jamie, too, his attention fixed on Jules. "You like men *and* women. I only like women. Meaning you're twice as likely—"

"Stop it," I snap. "I can't listen to this for another—"

"Excuse us." Jules grabs me by the elbow and wrenches me with her through the crowd to a powder room, where someone dressed like the wandering waiters sits on a stool, holding a tray of towels and small toiletry products. Finding a small alcove with a love seat, Jules drags me to sit beside her. "Listen," she hisses. "You're not helping."

"JuJu, he just said—"

"I *know* what he said, Bea. And while it's not okay, it's not your place to jump down his throat and lecture him. Let me handle myself."

Hurt swallows up my worry. "Oh, like you let *me* handle myself? So you're allowed to meddle in my life, but I can't tell off your boyfriend for being a biphobic twat muffin?"

My raised voice echoes in the bathroom, and every other conversation in the space turns to a hush. Jules shuts her eyes, exhaling slowly. "Thanks, Bea."

"I'm sorry, I just—"

"Can we *please* not do this?" she whispers, opening her eyes and blinking away tears. "No person or relationship is perfect, okay? And no, he didn't behave like the most socially evolved person back there, and yes, we're in a bit of a rough patch, but Jean-Claude's stressed with work, and some people aren't their best selves under that kind of pressure. So please don't make this harder for me. Please?"

I want to talk this out with her. And I want to tell her everything about Tod. Because I wonder, if she knew how it started with him and how it ended, if she'd see as much of herself and Jean-Claude in our situation as I do. "Jules—"

"Bea." She squeezes my hands, giving me a teary, pleading look. "Please. Stop."

I swallow the lump in my throat, silent as I nod.

"Thank you," she says, taking a deep, calming breath and smiling serenely, her *I'm fine* mask firmly back in place. "Now, go on. Have fun with West. And good luck meeting his dad."

We stand, and Jules threads her arm through mine. "His dad's that bad?"

She lifts her chin as we leave the restroom, shoulders back, that beautiful confidence taking over her again. "Almost as bad as Jean-Claude's."

Out in the throng of people, it's crowded, the cacophonous space echoing with so much complex noise it's like a dozen people are standing in front of me, shouting. I feel the creeping aggravation that precedes a sensory overload. My skin starts to buzz and tingle, like a hive of bees dancing beneath my skin, and my chest feels heavy. I take a long, deep breath and eye the bar. I need a stiff drink, a few minutes alone in the quiet, cool air outside, and then hopefully I can hold out long enough for Jamie to see this shit show through.

"BeeBee?" Jules asks. "You okay?"

I squeeze her arm with mine. "Nothing some schnapps and a moment out in the fresh air won't fix."

She nods, weaving us through the crush of bodies to the bar. In her

Jules way, she smiles and conjures a shot before I've even had time to gulp the glass of ice water that she got for me first.

"Better?" she asks.

"A little." I set down the shot glass and exhale slowly. "I'm going to sneak outside for a minute. Want to come?"

I know her answer before she gives it to me. Her eyes lock with *him* over my shoulder and she blushes. "No." Blinking away, she meets my gaze. "I mean, as long as you're okay, of course, I'm going to rejoin—"

"I'm fine." I can't hear that asshole's name. Can't stomach how besotted she still is with him. I try to remind myself that's how I was, that it took until Tod was his absolute worst for me to truly see him for who he was, to realize how badly I needed out of our relationship. Once again, guilt sucker punches me. I wish I'd told her everything. I wish I could have warned her. Maybe she wouldn't be in this mess of a relationship. Maybe I could protect her—

"All right," she says quietly, pecking my cheek. "Text me if you need me, okay? I'm close by."

I nod, then watch her stride off toward him. "After this," I promise myself, weaving my way toward a pair of French doors that promises an escape into the cool October night. "After this, I'm going to tell her."

When I reenter the ballroom, I spot Jamie right away in a half-moon of middle-aged men, taller than most, his head bent like he's staring into his cocktail and wishing he could drown in it.

I'm coming! I want to shout, wishing I didn't have such an abysmal threshold for outings like this that I had to steal away and recharge the battery after I disappeared on him to the bathroom.

Then the strangest thing happens. It's like he's heard my thoughts. Jamie glances up and locks eyes with me. Then he smiles, slow and soft and a little crooked. It makes my heart thud violently against my ribs, makes each step toward him pound in tempo with my heartbeat.

And when I'm at his side, everything feels right. "Hi," I tell him.

He swallows roughly, then slides his arm around my waist, pressing a long, soft kiss to my hair. "Missed you," he whispers. "Doing all right?"

I wrap my arm around him, too. "Yeah. I'm good now."

He nods.

"Tell him, Hawthorne," a man says, and instantly I know it's his dad. Not only because of the posh British accent but because, God, Jamie looks *just* like him—tall, lean, neat waves; same long, proud nose. And yet he doesn't. When Arthur Westenberg's gaze lands on me, I shiver. There's a chilliness in it that makes me shrink against Jamie. Where Jamie's eyes are full of warmth and kindness, this man's gaze is calculating and ice-cold. His voice dies off. He cocks his head. "Who's this, James?"

Jamie softly releases my waist and sets a hand reassuringly on my back. "This is Bea Wilmot, my girlfriend. Bea, my father, Arthur Westenberg."

"Nice to meet you," I lie.

Arthur sniffs and doesn't say anything, just tips his head in the other direction, examining me. Jamie's grip on my back tightens as he introduces me to the rest of the group. "Bea, this is an old friend of my father's and his colleague, Dr. Lawrence Hawthorne—" The older man nods politely. "And my brothers, Henry, Edward, and Sam."

The first two, who are much more a blend of Jamie's parents, give me openly critical once-overs, but it's Sam, whose resemblance is more like Jamie's, his eyes just as warm, his hair cut much shorter, who offers his hand and grins. "Good to finally meet you. I've heard *lots* of great things."

"Behave yourself," Jamie warns, but he's smiling gently.

"Nice to meet you all," I tell them. *Except you, you, and you*, I think to myself, directed toward his prickly, cold father and the snobby other brothers. "Sorry I interrupted."

"Quite all right," Dr. Hawthorne says.

Swirling his cocktail, then draining it, Jamie's dad gives me one more critical glance before he sets his glass on a passing tray. "I was just asking Hawthorne here to talk sense into James."

Sam sighs and sips his cocktail. Jamie's stiff beside me.

Arthur leans in a little. "Well, aren't you going to ask what I'm talking about?"

"I think you're going to tell me whether or not I do."

Jamie's grip on my waist tightens. He hides a smile behind his cough.

His dad's eyes narrow at me. "I'm talking about James going into pediatric surgery. If he *must* bother himself with children, the least he could do is specialize in the family legacy."

Jamie tenses beside me.

"Hawthorne's a leader in the field," Arthur continues. "It would be the chance of a lifetime to work with him."

Dr. Hawthorne says to Jamie, "With your background, I'm sure you'd be a brilliant addition to our team. Of course, surgery isn't everyone's calling—"

"Nonsense," Arthur says. He picks up a glass of champagne offered by a passing server, his gaze locked on Jamie. "It's what Westenbergs do, isn't that right, boys?"

One of the brothers who gave me a chilly once-over when I joined the circle—Henry, the older one—raises his cocktail. "Cheers to that."

The younger one, Edward, clinks his glass with Henry's and smiles, but it's more like a sneer. "Damn right."

Sam pointedly doesn't join in. His gaze slides worriedly our way.

But Jamie's expression doesn't shift, calm and composed as ever, like what just happened is as ordinary as clouds in the sky and ground beneath his feet. It makes my heart hurt.

Clearing his throat, he directs himself to Dr. Hawthorne. "I deeply appreciate the offer, and I'm flattered you think I'd be qualified to work with you. I have the utmost admiration for what you do. But surgery isn't my calling."

Arthur's jaw tics. His expression is thunderous.

"Darling." Jamie's mother glides in, hooking her arm through his. Tall and willowy, she's like a silver-screen starlet, frozen in time. Dazzling in an ivory fashion-forward dress that would make me look like a misshapen meringue, not a pore in sight, skin glowing. Her glossy brown hair is a few shades lighter than mine, perfectly coiffed, not a single gray to be seen.

I glance around at the rest of the group making small talk, feeling my height difference around all these giants, my frizzy waves that Jules tamed for me into an artfully messy updo, the shine that's no doubt made an appearance on my chin and forehead. I'd never try or hope to look flawless, and generally I like my appearance well enough, but right now I feel like maybe I stick out like a sore thumb. And I worry that maybe I'm embarrassing Jamie, that I'm bringing him down with my tats and my obviously not-posh background.

When I glance up at him, he's peering down at me, the faintest smile tipping his mouth. He leans in and whispers, "You look magnificent."

"Mind reader."

He grins. "You wear it all on your face. I watched your entire train of thought— Ouch!"

I've elbowed him, and I'm not sorry. "Reminding me I make weird faces when I'm lost in thought is very ungentlemanly of you."

"They aren't weird, you hardheaded woman. They're"—he shrugs— "you. It's delightful."

"Hmph."

"Now," Jamie's mother says, "time for dinner—"

His father interrupts her. "A dance first."

She frowns. "Arthur, a dance? Why on earth—"

"A waltz, Aline." He turns toward her. "I want a waltz with my beautiful wife."

She preens under his compliment. "Well," she says softly. "I suppose one waltz wouldn't be the end of the world."

TWENTY-EIGHT

Jamie

As always, Maman goes along with my father's manipulations, apologizing to her guests that they're changing the order of ceremonies just a little, that now she'll give her toast, and we'll have one dance before going in to dinner.

I'm not sure what my father has planned, but I know it's a punishment. Somehow, he's going to humiliate me. Because in his eyes, I've humiliated him. No matter that I've only told him hundreds of times I can't be a surgeon. That I'm not meant to cut people open but instead keep them whole. To him, I'm an embarrassment, unworthy of the family name, and when he gave me yet another chance to rectify that, I obstinately refused him.

And now I'm going to pay.

"To Arthur!" my mother says, raising her champagne.

Bea and I raise our glasses perfunctorily. Neither of us drinks. She turns and faces me. "Hey. Do you want to—"

"James."

My father's voice cuts our conversation like a knife. String music starts up. I face him as he smiles coldly. "Why don't you lead us, son?"

Dread settles like cement in my stomach and seeps into my lungs. I tug at my bow tie, feeling my chest constrict. I hate being the center of attention, and he knows it. My punishment has been meted out. Bea glances between us, her eyes narrowing at my father.

I nod. "Yes, sir."

Bea's practically hissing as he turns away. "What the *hell* was that—"

"He wants to embarrass me," I tell her, tugging at my bow tie again, adjusting my cuffs until the buttons bisect my wrists, taking a deep breath as I mentally prepare. "He knows I hate being in the spotlight."

"So fuck him," she whispers. "Let's leave."

I smile down at her, clasping her hand. "Ah, but then he wins."

"Let him win, then. If it makes you miserable, I don't want to do it."

I search her eyes. "In the past it might have, but tonight it won't be so bad."

She tips her head, stepping closer and squeezing my hand. "Why?"

"Because I'll be dancing with you." I squeeze her hand back. "That is, if you don't mind."

"I don't," she says quietly, smiling up at me. "But I can't promise it won't be a disaster. And I'll definitely step on your toes."

I start backtracking toward the dance floor, her hand in mine. "Step on as many toes as you like." She gasps as I tuck her close and press a kiss to the tender spot behind her ear. "All I need is you."

The dance begins, one that I know well, that I've danced to more times than I can count. But this time it's different. Because Bea's in my arms.

I stare down at her. She's so beautiful, my heart aches.

She stares up at me, biting her lip, her hair arranged into delicately upswept strands. Gold earrings with an onyx-like stone sparkle almost as bright as her eyes. She has barely any makeup on except her lips, which are painted rose red. They make her skin glow; her blue-green eyes glitter in contrast. I could stare at her for years. For a lifetime.

"What is it?" she asks quietly.

I sweep my hand lower down her back, savoring the satin softness of her skin, its delicate warmth beneath my cool hand. "I'm glad you came. Even though I was stubborn and tried to stop you."

"Well, thankfully I'm as stubborn as you." Her eyes search mine and she slides her hand up higher, toying idly with the hair at the nape of my neck. "I'm glad I came, too."

We're alone on the dance floor, my father glaring from the sidelines, savoring his retribution, but I hardly notice. The world dissolves to only this—the two of us, Bea, warm and soft in my arms, her eyes seeing only me.

I love her. Oh God, I love her. With each pound of my heart, the swell of the string quartet as the music builds, that's the only thing I hear and feel—I love her. When haven't I loved her?

"You know what's funny?" she says, oblivious to my thoughts, smiling as I draw her closer, already terrified that somehow now, because I know I love her, I'll lose her.

"What?" I ask, sighing with pleasure as her fingertips drift higher into my hair, an affectionate, comforting touch.

"That this would be the ultimate occasion to fool Jules and Jean-Claude, to splash a dozen glamorous photos on Instagram and make the other meddlers so hopelessly in love with the idea of us."

My stomach tightens, dread filling it. Has she changed her mind about us? About abandoning our scheme?

Bea wipes away my fears as she curls her hand around my neck, guiding me down for a kiss. She flashes a bright smile as our mouths part. "All I wanted was revenge," she says softly, her hand settled over my heart. "And now all I want is you."

I kiss her. I kiss her again and again, and it throws off our timing and we stumble a little, and it's perfect. It's so perfect because it's her, here with me. Us. Together.

When I finally pull away and we find the rhythm of the waltz again, I'm aware peripherally that my father's decided I've suffered enough. He's out on the floor with Maman. My brothers join with their partners. Then Jean-Claude's parents, Jean-Claude, and Juliet. More and more couples fill the floor, but I don't see them. I see only Bea.

"You're staring at me," she says.

"Yes."

She smiles, blushing prettily. "Do I look like a red-mouthed clown?"

I laugh. "No. Why would you?"

"So Jules was right," she says enigmatically. "She swiped on that lipstick and swore I wouldn't be able to wipe it off if I wanted to."

Bea licks those red lips, and it makes my body burn awake. The thought of her lush mouth parted in pleasure as I taste and tease her, then traveling *my* body, wrapped tight around my—

"Jamie?"

I startle. "Hmm?"

Bea tips her head. "I just stepped on your toes. Twice. And you didn't say anything."

I smile and steal another kiss. "Didn't even feel it."

She eyes me suspiciously as I spin her in a tight, fast turn while the waltz builds to its dramatic end. "What are you thinking?"

"I'm thinking after we finish this waltzing nonsense, we get the hell out of here."

Her eyes brighten. "Really?"

I kiss her again, then lower her in a dramatic dip that makes her laugh. "Really."

We're giddy, delirious with laughter, as we make our escape and rush down the front steps of my parents' house to the limousine. I throw open the door, and Bea gasps as I haul her onto my lap. Pushing the privacy screen button, I kiss her frantically, my hands tangling in her hair, our tongues meeting in a frenzied dance that puts our waltzing to shame.

"Wait," she says, wrenching her mouth from mine. "Honk, please," she tells the driver, rolling down the window and yelling out of it, "Smell ya later, assholes!"

Laughing, I throw an arm out, middle finger high in the air.

Bea shrieks with delight at that and kisses me again, straddling my lap.

Then suddenly she's quiet as she slips her fingers inside my bow tie and undoes the knot. When she pops open the first two buttons of my shirt, I draw in a deep, calming breath, and a swell of tenderness fills me. She sensed it, how I was slowly suffocating in there, how hard it was to breathe.

"Better?" she asks, her fingertips tracing my collarbone, my throat, the line of my jaw.

My grip on her waist tightens. I pull her closer and nod. "Much better."

Her touch continues its journey over my cheekbones, my nose, my forehead, down my temple. When she traces the shell of my ear, I let out a groan of pleasure. "What are you doing?"

"Drawing you." Her eyes follow her fingertips' path. "I've drawn you so many times. In my mind, in my sketchbook. But this is better than all of that."

My hand slides down her back, sweeping along the fabric pooled just above her backside. "What do I look like, in these drawings?"

"Beautiful," she whispers. "Frequently naked."

I swallow roughly. "I hope the real thing lives up to what you've imagined."

Her eyes meet mine, soft and warm in the faint light illuminating the drive. "You won't. You'll exceed it."

"How do you know?"

She presses the gentlest kiss to my lips. "Because you're *you*. You're wonderful, Jamie. A truly good, beautiful, wonderful person who I can't get enough of." Her eyes search mine, reading my unease. "I hate that your asshole dad made you grow up doubting how incredible you are. I hate that your family, except for Sam, go along with it. Fuck them, okay? You are enough—more than enough—just as you are."

I swallow roughly. "Thank you, Bea."

As her mouth meets mine again, tender and reverent, my heart thunders in time with the words I can't stop saying to myself.

I love you. I love you. I love you.

We bump off the private drive onto the main road, snapping me out of it. "Beatrice. Seat belt."

"Jamie—"

"Safety first," I tell her, already lifting her off my lap.

"Fine," she pouts.

Gently, I set her beside me, buckling her seat belt. Then I slide my hand up her ribs, my thumb sweeping the soft underside of her breast through warm, ink-black silk. I tease her nipple with my thumb and feel it harden to a sharp, delicious point. "Doesn't mean we can't have fun on the way."

"Jamie Westenberg," she says on a coy, heated smile. "Wonders never cease."

I smile back and press a long, slow kiss to the hollow of her throat. "Just wait until you see what I have planned next."

TWENTY-NINE

Bea

"Karaoke?" I stare disbelievingly up at the dive bar, its neon light flashing against the night sky.

The limousine pulls away as I unspool my flimsy wrap and throw it around my shoulders. Jamie tugs open another button of his shirt and peers up at the building. "Karaoke is one of those universally fun things, right? I don't know who doesn't like karaoke."

I bite my lip. "I'm a terrible singer."

He laughs. "So am I."

"This is going to be iconic."

He steps closer, cupping my face and stealing a gentle kiss. "We don't have to. I just . . ." His thumb sweeps over my bottom lip. "I wanted to give you some fun after all that misery with my miserable family at their miserable house with all the miserable stuffed shirts."

"It wasn't *that* bad."

He arches an eyebrow. "It was. And I knew it would be. So I planned this."

My heart cracks and spills happiness through me like poured sunshine, painting the moment golden and glowing. "You did?"

He nods, tucking a loose wisp of hair back into my updo. "I could have asked what you'd find most fun, but I wanted to surprise you, and since I'm not precisely the fun expert, I went with a hunch and here we are. But we can go anywhere. Home. The movie theater. A diner. At least, until we're due at the tattoo parlor. Though I suppose I could reschedule that."

My eyes widen. "Wait, *what*?"

Jamie frowns. "*What?*"

"You. In a tattoo parlor. What are *you* going to do in a tattoo parlor?"

He bristles and rakes a hand through his hair, making the waves a little less perfect and tousled. "I don't appreciate your incredulity, Beatrice. What do you think's going to happen when I walk into a tattoo parlor? Am I going to vanish into a puff of prudish smoke?"

I laugh, then shiver. It's getting cold out here, and my wrap's a flimsy piece of sheer black fabric. "Maybe, after you give it a hygiene audit."

"Ha-ha." Jamie shrugs off his coat and wraps it around me. It's warm and heavy, and it smells like his cologne, a whisper of sage and cedarwood and foggy mornings. "There," he says. "Better?"

I nod. "Thank you."

"I'm good for something, at least." He sniffs, adjusting the jacket so it's wrapped tighter around me. "Apparently not tattoo parlors, though."

"Hey!" I shoot a hand out from beneath the jacket and yank him close by the shirt. "I was just teasing you. But seriously . . . why do you want to go to a tattoo parlor?"

He lifts his chin, playing at being miffed, but I can see a smile tugging at his mouth as he opens the door to the karaoke bar. The smell of fried food and cheap beer wafts out, chased by a raw, soulful voice belting Janis Joplin.

"Why, Beatrice," he says, guiding me ahead of him. "To get a tattoo of course."

"They booed us!" Jamie yells. He curls his arm around me as we shoulder our way out of the karaoke bar and into a misty October rain, our cab mercifully waiting at the curb. "They actually booed us!" Jamie is indignation personified.

I smile up at him, cheeks aching, tears and rainwater streaming down my face. I have never laughed so hard. "I mean, do we blame them? I can't tell a howling dog from a world-class singer, and *I* know what we just did was an offense to the human ear."

Jamie opens the car door and gently guides me in. "They could have at least been more gracious about our effort."

I wrap my arm around his waist as he settles next to me and buckles in, soaking up his warmth. He's a furnace. "To their credit, we *did* pick a six-minute song."

"'Bohemian Rhapsody' isn't even the longest song on that album," he says defensively, buckling me in, too, and wrapping an arm around me, hugging me close. "In my eyes, we showed them mercy."

A fresh burst of our laughter echoes in the car as the driver pulls out and speeds through a yellow light. Jamie's grip on me tightens. He double-checks my seat belt, an adorable frown knotting his features. His hair's wild from headbanging with me at the end of the song, those chiseled cheekbones flushed pink from effort. He smells like sweat and rain and Jamie, and it's that moment, right then, when I know, as surely as I know my name: I love him.

And I'm completely terrified. I'm terrified I'm every kind of wrong for him, that one day he'll realize the fun fades but my weird lasts, and it's not his kind of weird; that loving him will somehow end up hurting as badly as loving Tod did. That's when I get *really* scared. Because I never loved Tod like this. I never let him in so far, never trusted him like I've trusted Jamie. Loving Jamie is the highest height, but God, at least with Tod the fall wasn't fatal.

If anything happens to us, if this ends . . . it will crush me.

I squeeze Jamie hard, burying my face in his neck, hiding these new tears. Tears of relief. Happy tears. Terrified tears. It's a deluge of feelings that rivals the downpour that bathes our taxi's windows with sheets of rain.

"Bea," Jamie says quietly, his hand running up and down my arm. "What is it?"

I glance up and we brush noses. Then mouths. I look at him, white shirt plastered to his body from the rain, water glistening on his skin.

His eyes hold mine, then darken, his hand sliding down my arm, the slope of my waist, gently around my ass as he pulls me closer. I cling to his shirt, slide my leg over his. And then I pour into my kiss everything I'm too frightened to say. I tell him with my touch and my mouth and each breathless sigh what he makes me feel, how afraid and thrilled and wildly in love I am with him, the last person I would have ever thought would love me or that I would love.

When our mouths part, he peers down at me, squinting through the flecks of rain still marking his glasses. Gently, I slide the frames off his face and with the edge of my wrap, kept dry and safe under his tuxedo jacket, I polish his glasses before carefully returning them to his face. Then I sweep my fingers through his waves, savoring their rare untamed state, picturing all the other ways I plan to make him even wilder, more disheveled, lost to himself.

"Beatrice," he says.

I kiss the base of his throat. "Hmm?"

"You can't keep looking at me like that."

I smile against his skin. "Why not?"

"Because." He clears his throat and not so subtly adjusts himself as my hand wanders up his thigh. "I have plans. The night is young."

"To hell with the plans, Jamie." I dance my fingers low across his stomach, teasing his belt buckle.

His hand lands on mine, stilling my touch, but he softens the gesture, linking our fingers together. And then he nods over his shoulder as the car comes to a stop, toward the familiar sight of my tattoo artist's shop, a knowing grin lighting up his face. "You sure about that?"

I meet his eyes. "Wow. You were serious."

Arching an eyebrow, Jamie throws open the car door. "When am I not?"

I stumble out, catching myself on his arm as he shuts the door behind me and shields me as best he can from the downpour while we run. Safe inside the shop, we shake like wet dogs, wiping our feet on the welcome mat.

"Bea!" Pat opens her arms and hugs me, then turns and offers Jamie her hand. "And you're Jamie."

"Guilty." He shakes her hand. "Thank you for accommodating us."

I smile up at Jamie, stunned. "You're really going to do this?"

He pushes his glasses up his nose, then gives me a narrow-eyed scowl. "No, we're here for tea and crumpets. Yes, I'm seriously doing this. I told you already, and now I'm starting to get upset."

Pat's laugh is husky and unexpected. I've never heard her laugh. "I love him already. Okay, let's take you back."

I lean in and whisper, "It's just a little unexpected, that's all."

He frowns down at me. "And I can't do unexpected things?"

"Oh, all right." I link my arm through his. "I'll stop asking."

"Thank you."

We follow Pat down the hall, admiring the art on the walls, the beautiful prints of tattoo designs—some of them borne out on people's bodies, others simply sketched on paper. When we turn into Pat's room, I plop down on a stool next to Jamie, swiveling from side to side as he lies down on the fully reclined chair and starts to unbutton his shirt. With her back to me, Pat's humming to herself, setting up some apparatus I've never seen.

"What is that?" I ask.

She stops humming and glances up. "Huh? Oh, this is a drape."

"A what?"

Jamie clasps my hand. "Ever seen a C-section?"

"Uh, no. Thank God. Why would I?"

"Well, I don't know," he says. "Some people watch those birthing shows."

"Not me. Nope." I'm getting sweaty just thinking about it. "Birth's lovely and all—you know, more power to my fellow humans who further the species, but I'd rather stay blissfully ignorant."

Jamie frowns up at me. "But you said you like kids. You want kids."

"I do!"

"And were you planning on them arriving by stork?"

"I'll figure it out *then*. I just don't want to know a moment before." I fan myself, getting flustered. "I'll just . . . cross that . . . birthing . . . bridge when I . . . come to it?"

Jamie sighs and shakes his head despairingly. Pat bites her lip, trying hard not to laugh at us.

"Anyway," Jamie says, giving Pat an apologetic look as she sets up the drape across his sternum, shielding us from the rest of Jamie's body. "I asked Pat if she could work with this if I could procure it. Given my medical supplier contacts, it wasn't hard to pull some strings, and here we are."

I grin. "Your dealer hooked you up."

"He did. Drove a hard bargain, but in the end he got me what I wanted."

"Why do you want this? Are you scared of needles?"

He pushes his glasses up the bridge of his nose with his arm nearest to me that's free of the drape. "Not exactly."

Leaning my elbows on the edge of his chair, I softly toy with the lock of hair that's always slipping onto his forehead. "Why the drape, then?"

Pat shuts the cabinet and drops a pair of packaged sterile gloves, ready for use. "Need to restock gloves in here," she says before walking out of the room. "Be back in five."

When Jamie's shoulders fall with relief, I realize why she left. To give us a moment alone.

"Because . . ." He clears his throat, and a new blush heats his cheeks. "I wanted to get the tattoo with you, but I wanted to show you later, when it's not angry and red—I have very sensitive skin, is the thing." He sighs. "What I mean is . . . That is . . ." His eyes search mine. "I wanted to reveal it in a more . . . intimate setting."

My eyes fill with sudden tears. I drop my forehead to his shoulder, rolling my head from side to side. "Jamie," I whisper.

Slowly his hand comes to my hair, softly tangling in the half-out strands. "Is something wrong?"

"No," I tell him thickly, lifting my head, then meeting his mouth for a long, deep kiss that leaves him grinning with proud satisfaction. "It couldn't be more right."

"I'm invincible." Jamie stands like Superman outside the tattoo parlor, hands on his hips. "I am a badass."

I laugh and slip an arm around his waist. "You are. You're also soaring on endorphins and adrenaline right now, and unless you ate your weight in tapas while I was in the bathroom with Jules back at the party, I don't think you have enough food in your system. You're going to get shaky."

Jamie tugs at his collar, glancing between the curb where our cab is due any minute and me. "Hmm." As I predicted, he's looking a little sweaty and pale now. "I think you're right." He sways a little. "I need to eat something."

"Absolutely." I hold his waist tight, and this time it's my turn to open the car door as the taxi pulls in. "Food will perk you up. What'll it be?"

"A burger the size of my head," he says blearily, the back of his skull hitting the headrest with a *thump.*

My heart starts pounding. Not only am I a terrible cook, but I'm a total wimp for handling raw meat. Even if I attempted a homemade burger, I'd have a sensory freak-out, then probably end up burning down the apartment. And after a whole night out—the noisy, echoing party; the sheer chaos of karaoke; the monotonous buzz of the tattoo gun as Pat worked on Jamie—I absolutely do not have one more stop in me.

Which leaves only one option. One that I can't even believe I'm considering.

"You going to a burger joint now?" the driver asks. "Which one?"

"Actually . . ." I turn toward Jamie and link my fingers with his. "Hey, Jame."

"Hmm?" His eyes open only as slits before they shut again.

"So here's the thing. I know a place that makes the best burger in town."

His eyes are shut as he nods. "But there's a catch?"

I clear my throat nervously, ignoring our driver's huff of annoyance as I make him wait. "There definitely is."

When he hears the worry in my voice, Jamie opens his eyes fully, his mouth tipped in a frown of concern. "What is it?"

Squeezing his hand, I ask him, "How do you feel about meeting my parents?"

THIRTY

Jamie

"You're sure this is all right?" I stroke Bea's palm with my thumb, our hands clasped as we stand on her parents' front porch.

"Yep," she says brightly. *Too* brightly. Like she's nervous. Is she nervous for me to meet her parents?

But before I can say anything else—offer to swig a Gatorade, stuff a few saltines down my throat, and call it a night instead—she's slid her key into the lock and is opening the door of her parents' home.

A flood of memories washes over me. The last time I was here, that's when all this began. I see it perfectly—the milling crowd of people as I walked in and covered my face in that damn itchy lion mask, blending into the jungle mayhem as the cold prickle of anxiety slithered down my spine. I hear the noise of the room once again—laughter, small talk, clinking glasses, clattering appetizer plates—and then I remember it, the moment I heard her soft voice, caught the faintest trace of enticing, earthy perfume, when I saw—

"Bea!" It's unmistakably her mother, not just because it's her home but because she and her daughter have the same sparkling sea-storm eyes and wide smile. She crosses the foyer and opens her arms. "Come in! Come in! Ohh, it's good to finally meet you, Jamie."

I'm wrapped in a lavender-perfumed hug before Bea gets in a word of introduction. Our gazes connect over her mother's shoulder and Bea smiles, mouthing, *Sorry*.

I shake my head. There's nothing for her to be sorry for. Especially not the lump in my throat that makes it hard to swallow as Mrs. Wilmot releases me from her motherly hug and smiles between us. "Well?" she prompts Bea. "Aren't you going to introduce us?"

"Hold on! Wait for me," Bea's father calls, tugging a sweater over his head as he reaches the bottom of the stairs. He's tall and straight-backed, and he gave Bea his dark hair. His is now silvered at the temples, his smile kind, as he hugs Bea with a kiss to her hair, then offers me a firm handshake. "Welcome."

"Thank you, sir."

"Oh my." Mrs. Wilmot sets a hand on her cheek. "So delightfully proper."

Bea sidles up to me and threads her arm through mine. "Mom, Dad, this is Jamie Westenberg, my boyfriend." She blushes beautifully and squeezes my arm, meeting my eyes as she gives me a *don't you dare laugh* look. "Jame, these are my parents, Maureen and Bill."

My heart squeezes. *Jame.* She called me that in the car, too, and I thought I was dreaming as my head spun and I briefly wove in and out of awareness.

"Pleasure," I tell them. "I apologize for us barging in on such short noti—"

"Goodness," Maureen says. "Not at all! Bill and I were just sitting down to dinner, and don't you know, burgers were on the menu."

I glance at my watch, doing a double take. "It's . . . eleven thirty."

Bill steps behind Maureen, whose apron has come loose, and reties it. "Travel as much as we do, and you lose all sense of mealtimes."

Maureen smiles and shrugs. "We eat when we're hungry. And I'm so glad I have more mouths to feed, because you know me, I get carried away in the kitchen!"

Following them through the foyer, I feel an odd swoop in my stomach, worse than when the full pain of my tattoo came raging to the surface of my skin. This is . . . so foreign to me. An affectionate mother, a father who smiles kindly and fawns over his wife. Parents who *want* their grown child and her partner not to parade about, performing some societal duty, but simply to be together because they love her.

I glance at Bea, wondering how she could even stomach my father's party this evening. The proud posturing, the arrogant showmanship, the cold, impersonal, inane conversation. And a creeping fear grips my heart. Did she see how much I look like him? Does she remember what I was like when we met? Does she worry time will change me, that one day I'll resemble my father—all sharp prickles and frigid, cutting edges? Are her memories of the night we met, like mine, already turned fond by the passage of time, or is being here with me reminding her how horribly we began, the terrible first impression I made on her?

As if she's read my spiraling thoughts, Bea slides her hand down my forearm until our fingers lock tight. "I'm glad we came," she whispers.

I squeeze her hand and steal a quick, world-righting kiss. "Me, too."

––––––––

Not that I doubted Bea, but it *is* the best burger of my life. After our late-night meal, Bill sweet-talks us into staying for a few games of euchre, which becomes many games of euchre, thanks to Bea's brutally competitive streak and my absolute delight in all of it.

Now, somehow, it's four in the morning, and we're outside Bea's apartment door, slaphappy and exhausted.

"Shh," she whispers, putting the key in the lock and turning. "Or maybe I should say, cover your ears. Those two aren't quiet."

I shudder involuntarily. It makes Bea hysterical.

"Now *you* shh," I whisper.

She shuts the door behind us and smiles saucily. "Make me."

It's too tempting to silence her mouth with a kiss as she walks backward down the hallway, my hands on her face, her hair, her waist. But when we get to the threshold of her room, I let go. Bea frowns. Realization slowly seeps into her expression. "Not this again."

"Afraid so."

She whines and slumps against her open door. "Jamie, *whyyyy*? I don't need candlelight or rose petals or body chocolate—"

"Body chocolate?"

She shrugs. "It's a sexy-times thing. That I don't need." Pushing off the door, she sinks her hands into my shirt and tugs me close. "I need *you*." Her touch travels my waist, then drifts lower, lower—

"Whoa, now." I clasp her hands, then bring them together between us, kissing her knuckles softly.

Bea whimpers. "Jamie. I'm going to die of sexual deprivation."

"No, you're not. You're going to die a dozen little deaths tomorrow night when I have all the time I need and you deserve."

Her mouth falls open. "Back it up. How am I dying—"

I laugh quietly, kissing her, a soft flick of tongue that makes her sigh before I kiss a path along her jaw to the shell of her ear. "You said you wanted to hear me speak French?"

She nods, exposing her throat for more kisses.

I kiss her neck, behind her ear, then whisper, "En français, quand tu jouis, ça s'appelle la petite mort."

"T-translation, please," she rasps, as I run my knuckles faintly along her ribs, making her belly jump, her breath catch.

"I said, 'In French, when you come, it's called the little death.'"

She pulls back. Her eyes widen. "A *dozen*, you said?"

I grin as she throws her arms around my neck, wide-eyed, enthralled. "If all goes to plan."

"Let's make sure it does," she says against my lips, stealing a kiss. "What's the plan, by the way?"

A laugh rumbles in my throat. "You'll sleep in today."

She pouts. "Without you."

"I'll sleep in, too."

Her pout deepens. "Without *me*."

I console her with a kiss. "And then, you'll be ready at five sharp for me to meet you right here."

She smiles. "Go on."

"You'll pack an overnight bag."

"Oooh, now we're talking."

"And anything you need to sleep well in my bed."

She wiggles her eyebrows. "What if I said I don't plan on much sleeping?"

I kiss her one more time and make it last. "I'd say I'm very glad to hear it."

THIRTY-ONE

Bea

Both of our weekend-only college temps get hit with the flu, so only because I love Toni do I drag my ass out of bed at ten in the morning and cover their shifts at the Edgy Envelope. I've had a coffee and an espresso to make up for my lack of sleep, but I'm not sure if I even need the caffeine. I'm pure adrenaline, child-before-Christmas excitement.

At two minutes to closing, I stand at the counter, powering down the iPads and tapping my toes to Toni's Electric Funk playlist. Just as the iPad screens go dark, the bell dings over the door of the shop. I glance up and my heart does a pirouette in my chest.

"Jamie."

Toni pops out of the back office and glances eagerly between us. It's the most unsubtle thing I've ever seen.

My ultimate revenge plan might be set aside, but I'll still have my little moments of vengeance. I throw Toni a look over my shoulder. "You've seen him. I'm leaving. Now, showtime's over. Get out of here."

Toni shakes his head solemnly. "I even baked you cookies."

I pop one in my mouth just to make a point. "I upped my price. I demand cupcakes now."

"Rude!" he yells, before disappearing into the office.

I turn to face Jamie, who's watching me closely, a small, private grin warming his face. "What are you doing here?" I ask him.

He shrugs. A neat one-shoulder Jamie Shrug. "You told me you had to work after all. So I stopped by your place, picked up your overnight bag, then fed Cornelius and gave him some TLC. Now I'm here to walk you home."

"Oh." My heart's a puddle. "Okay."

As I finish tidying up the counter, my excitement over tonight dims a little, replaced by nervousness. Jamie's so precise and excellent at everything he does—what if he doesn't like how I do sex? What if we're so right in all these ways I've never been right with someone else, but our sex is all wrong? What if I have one of my super-clumsy days and I accidentally elbow him in the nose or knee him in the junk or—

"Spinning your gears, I see." Jamie's watching me closely, one hip leaned against the counter. He's getting almost Juliet-level good at intuiting my thoughts, and I'm not sure I like it.

"Sorry. I'm good. Fine. Totally okay."

He smiles, but maybe there's a little nervousness in that smile, too. Jamie stretches out his hand and pushes off the counter. "Come on."

I round the glass top, tug on my jacket, and call goodbye to Toni, taking Jamie's hand as we leave the Edgy Envelope.

He insists on carrying my messenger bag, and after he's set it on his shoulder, he clasps my hand again. We walk in silence, leaves dancing down the sidewalk, a cool October gale whipping my clothes. I huddle in close to Jamie and savor our wordless ease. I love how much he loves silence, how there's a silence that's ours, somehow, simply because we share it.

"How are things with you and Juliet?" he asks.

I frown up at him. "What?"

He nudges me gently. "Didn't take a rocket scientist to intuit things were strained between you last night at the party, after Jean-Claude flew his asshole flag nice and high."

"She was gone when I woke up. Apparently Jean-Claude 'whisked her away' for the day."

The wind picks up, and Jamie hikes his jacket collar tighter around his neck. "I'm sorry it's tense between you right now."

"Nothing I can really do. She told me to back off and let her handle Jean-Claude herself."

Jamie sighs. "Jean-Claude, I don't even recognize him anymore. I don't know if it's the pressure of the job or something else going on that I don't know, but he seems worse since—"

"He started dating my sister?"

Jamie's quiet for a moment before he says, "Unfortunately, yes."

"Yeah, I don't think he's good for her, but she doesn't want to hear that. So I guess for now I need to keep my nose out of her business."

Jamie wraps an arm around me. "That's hard when you're so close . . . and just a little accustomed to being very much in each other's business."

"Yeah, we are. It's our twinny way." Silence falls between us again, and I breathe Jamie in. His woodsy scent, the warmth of his body. "I don't want to talk about them anymore, okay? I want it to be just us tonight."

Jamie smiles down at me, then presses a kiss to my forehead. "You got it. Just us."

Warm air greets us as we step into Jamie's apartment. He shuts the door behind us, hangs up my bag, and takes my coat. Then he gives me a long, hard hug that I sag into like a rag doll. I need this hug like I need air.

When he gently rubs my shoulders, an inhuman noise leaves me. "Oh God," I moan. "Right there." Jamie digs into the tense muscles at the base of my neck. "It was a restock day. So much bending and unboxing. And sweating. I feel gross."

"Want to take a shower?" he asks. "Get comfortable? I have some things to do in the meantime."

I glance around his place, taking in the cool white walls, cognac leather furniture, and way more glossy, green-leafed house plants than I could ever keep alive. It's calm and lovely as ever, but no lights are on, nothing indicating we'll be spending time out here. My curiosity is piqued. "Okay?"

"After your shower," he says, "use the bathroom to change. If there's anything you need from my wardrobe, say, another alma mater hoodie like the one you stole—"

"Borrowed," I correct.

"Hmm." He arches a severe eyebrow, but his smile gives him away. "If you need anything, tell me, and I'll get it for you. You're not allowed in my room, all right?"

"Why?"

Jamie turns and starts rummaging in the refrigerator. "No more questions. It's just a little something. You'll see soon."

Curious but swayed by how gross I feel, I head to the bathroom and take a long, hot shower. I use his body wash and luxuriate in big Jamie-scented bubbles as I shave my legs with the razor I packed, then scrub my scalp until it tingles. Out of the shower, I brush the hell out of my teeth and change into sweatpants, fuzzy socks, and Jamie's hoodie that I stole—I mean, borrowed—just to stick it to him.

"I'm alive!" I call as I walk down the hallway toward the open-concept kitchen and living space.

Jamie laughs. "Just how I like you. In here, still."

When I turn the corner, I'm nearly incapacitated by the glorious sight that is Jamie Westenberg's ass in sweatpants, tight and round, stretching the material as he crouches down and rummages through a lower cabinet. Flabbergasted, I trip over my own feet, right into the counter.

"Whoa!" Jamie spins, lunges, and somehow catches me before I fall and bust my face open.

My palms slide up his chest. It feels like the broom-closet moment, the night we met, all over again—our bodies pressed together, heat pooling low in my belly—except this time there's no pretending, no wondering *what if*, only *when*.

His hands settle on my back, rubbing it gently. "What happened?"

I blink up at him. "You. *You* happened. You're in *lounge clothes*."

Jamie peers down at himself. "It's just joggers and a sweatshirt."

Just joggers and a sweatshirt. The absurdity of that sentence. I've seen what those navy-blue joggers do to his bounce-a-quarter-off-it ass, and now I see how they hug his long legs and the muscles of his thighs. His sweatshirt is a heather-gray crewneck with I ♥ MY CATS in bold font across the chest, perfectly pushed up to reveal his forearms. What's worse, he's oblivious. He has no clue how obscene this all is.

"You look so goddamn hot right now."

He turns beet red. "Beatrice. Honestly."

I step back and stare at him. He looks tousled and cozy and soft and so fucking mine I can't even breathe. "I might do you right on this kitchen counter."

"Hush now. Don't take the wind out of my sails." He scoops me up, making me squeak in surprise as he wraps my legs around his waist and walks us toward his room.

"Where are we going?" I ask, stealing a quick kiss.

He kisses me back. "Originally, I'd planned to whisk you away somewhere special, but we talked on the cab ride home last night— well, this morning—about how long of a day it had been, how good it would feel to just—"

"Stay in," I whisper, slipping my hands through his gorgeous hair, kissing his jaw. "And wear sweatpants that make your ass look spectacular."

Jamie somehow turns an even deeper tomato red at that compliment, but that's all the acknowledgment I get. "So I thought, rather than go somewhere special, why not bring 'somewhere special' to us?"

I peer over my shoulder as he opens the door, and my heart beats so hard it bruises my ribs. Staring in disbelief, I slide down his body, then turn and take in his bedroom. A picnic feast of dumplings and pho sits in the middle of the floor, with plush blankets and cushions arranged on the ground for comfortable seating. The fancy modern fireplace dances with silent, flickering flames, and a few lanterns glow throughout his room with tiny tea lights. The light is faint, but as I glance up, I know why. Projected onto his ceiling is every constellation you can see right now in the Northern Hemisphere. When it's darker, they'll be as bright as the stars outside.

"It's so romantic," I whisper.

Standing behind me, Jamie wraps his arms around my waist and sets his chin on my head. "I'm glad you think so. I wanted it to feel special, but not too much. Candlelight and a fire, but—not that you wanted them—no rose petals. I'll sneeze. And no body chocolate—"

"Too sticky."

I feel his smile as he hugs me harder. "Precisely. Hope that's not a disappointment."

I laugh through the lump in my throat. "Nothing about this could disappoint me, Jamie. It's perfect." Blinking away tears, I turn and face him. "*You're* perfect."

THIRTY-TWO

Jamie

I watch her eat, humming happily, licking her fingers. And when we're done, I unceremoniously dump our containers in the kitchen sink, then come back and tuck Bea close between my legs as I lean against the foot of my bed, her back to my front.

"Thank God for sweatpants," she sighs, rubbing her full stomach as she stares up at the constellations projected on the ceiling. "I ate *all* the dumplings."

She's taken off my sweatshirt because it's warm in here, revealing a soft emerald-green T-shirt draped over her body. I slide up the sleeve, tracing her elaborate flower tattoo on one shoulder. And for the first time, I see the flowers' leaves are actually pages of books. "What does this mean?" I ask her.

Bea glances down from her indoor stargazing, watching my fingertip swirl over her skin. "My parents. My mom's flowers she loves to grow, my dad's love of books. You should see my dad's library. That was locked up the night of the party, and I never got to show it to you last night."

"You and your bloodthirsty mother were too busy annihilating us at cards."

She snorts a laugh and peers up at me. "Mom's always been like that with games. Sorry if we got a little carried away."

I shake my head. "It was wonderful. I wouldn't have changed it for the world."

"But I should have shown you the library. You'd have loved it."

I tuck a loose strand of hair behind her ear, searching her eyes. "There'll be another time, other nights there . . . I hope."

Her smile brightens her face. She kisses my palm as it cups her cheek. "There better be."

Our eyes hold as my fingertip traces the dotted line down her neck, to her other shoulder, where more designs weave together. Among vines and flowers, I spy a stack of books, a camera, a palette and paintbrush, and three delicate bluebirds huddled on a branch.

I don't have to ask this time for Bea to know I'm curious.

"The books are for Jules. She's a bookworm like Daddy. Loves her romance novels. One day she'll write one." She arches an eyebrow. "Didn't see that coming, did you? The meddling matchmaker loves romance."

I laugh quietly, my finger tracing the tattoos' path.

"The camera," she says, "is for Kate. She's a photojournalist, got her first camera when she was five, and lives with that thing wrapped around her neck. The palette and paintbrush are for me, of course."

"And the birds?" I ask.

Bea smiles. "My sisters, all three of us. Our parents call us 'birdies.' I don't know why. They just always have."

My touch wanders from her tattoo to her shoulders again. I rub the taut muscles, making Bea's head fall against my chest with a contented sigh.

"When do I get to see *your* tattoo?" she asks quietly. Her hands slide up and down my thighs, weaving figure eights higher and higher.

"Tonight."

Bea glances up at me and smiles, barefaced from her shower and so lovely. "Really?"

"Really." I hold her tight, a surge of vulnerability and love knotting my heart.

She tips her head, examining me as I examine her. "What is it?"

"Just . . . watching you," I tell her.

Her smile deepens. "Why?"

"Because you're beautiful. And I want to."

Turning in my arms, she settles on my lap, then wraps her legs around my waist before she rests her hand over my heart. "Good."

"I want to do more than watch you," I tell her, as she runs her fingers through my hair.

"I want you to do more than watch me, too." Leaning close, she kisses me softly. "Though, watching could be fun sometime."

A groan rolls out of me. The thought of watching Bea touch herself makes me harden so quickly, I have no time to tamp down my response before she feels it.

She shifts on my lap, rubbing herself over my sweats as I drink her in. Her gaze roams my face, then my body. Her expression grows serious, her touch drifting beneath my shirt and sweatshirt. "I'm nervous."

Clasping her face, I kiss her cheek, the tip of her nose, the freckle below her eye. "Tell me what you're nervous about."

Her fingers sink into my shirt as she sets her forehead against mine. "I want it to be good for you, for us, and I'm worried I'll mess it up."

"You won't, Bea. You could never." After a beat, I tell her, "If it makes you feel any better, I'm nervous, too."

She frowns in confusion. "About what?"

"I'm nervous the moment you touch me, I'm going to go off like a rocket."

Laughter bursts out of Bea as she wraps her arms around my neck and kisses me, deep and slow. "Even if you do, there's always the next time. And the next time and the next time, until the sun's coming up and I've had my wily way with you so many times. You did promise me a dozen little deaths, after all."

"So I did." I kiss her deeply and draw her close, pulling her hips against mine.

"And if I happen to throw a rogue elbow," she says, "or make a really intense sound when I orgasm—"

"It'll be perfect," I tell her between kisses. "Because it's us. Nothing could be more right."

A happy hum leaves her throat. "See? Your theory was disproved after all," she whispers.

"What theory was that?"

"What you said the day we agreed to our revenge. Two wrongs don't make a right." She smiles. "I'd say we've proved they do."

I laugh as our fingers tangle, as I kiss her triumphant smile. "I have never been so glad to be wrong."

I tidy up my bedroom, dim the fire, then brush my teeth over the kitchen sink while Bea uses the restroom. I'm seated on the edge of my bed when she returns, and I watch her cross the room.

"Hi," she says.

My gaze travels her, still in her T-shirt and lounge pants, my hands aching to wrench them off and see her. To finally see *all* of her.

"I just realized," she says, "I haven't spent a night away from Cornelius since I got him."

"Well." I draw her closer between my legs. "He'd better get used to it."

"Or he could come with," she offers. "We could have sleepovers!"

I arch an eyebrow. "No."

"What? You don't want to get freaky in front of the hedgehog?"

I give her a stern look that doesn't last long before I crack. "I'm not making love to you in front of Cornelius, no. Not now. Not ever."

"So he's not an exhibitionist," she says to herself.

I tickle her and make her shriek. She twists away from me, landing with a splat on my bed. "No tickles!" she yells.

"Ah, so she can dish it out, but she can't take it!" I crawl over her on the mattress and press a long kiss to her neck. My kisses travel up her throat to her mouth. I settle in against her hips, rocking against her, because I've been hard and dying for her for what feels like years now, and she feels perfect beneath me.

"Jamie," she says timidly.

I freeze, easing my weight off her, meeting her eyes. "What is it?"

She clears her throat. "Um. So, before we—" She makes a hand gesture that I think is meant to indicate sex. "Now is when I give you the speech that just because I am an erotic artist does *not* mean I like it in the butt or that I can bend like a pretzel."

I sigh heavily. "Damn. That was the only reason I was up for this."

Her jaw drops as her color fades.

"Bea." I clasp her face in my hands. "Joking. Oh God, Bea, I was so entirely completely one thousand percent joking. Or trying. Very poorly. I'll never do it again."

She exhales and drops her head against the mattress. "Jesus. You pick now of all times to be a funny guy."

"I'm sorry." I kiss her forehead. "I was trying to put you at ease. Obviously I failed. This is why I don't joke."

She laughs faintly. "You're adorable. Even when you give me a heart attack and nearly break it all at once."

"I would never break your heart, Bea. All I want to do is protect it."

Bea searches my face, her hands drifting back up and hugging me tight. "What else do you want?" she asks.

"I want to kiss you. Everywhere. I want to know what you look like when you wake up. I want to make you pureed veggie soup and cupcakes for dinner." I steal a kiss and gently drag her bottom lip between my teeth, earning Bea's quiet gasp.

"I want to watch you paint," I tell her, "and light up from within. I want nights at home, holding you on the couch with nothing else to do. I want whatever you'll give me and then some, because I'm greedy. Because every time you show me a new part of you, I want more."

I hold her eyes, seeing my own vulnerability reflected back. "I want *you*."

"Well," she says unsteadily, slipping her fingers through my hair. "I meant sex-wise, but that was much more romantic."

We both laugh until laughs become groans at the profound pleasure of our bodies finding each other, even through layers of clothing.

I'm lost to the curve of her hips, the warmth between her thighs that I press myself into.

Feeling me, Bea groans. "Oh *wow*, James."

"Wow? What? What is it?"

"Just. Lube. I always need it, but with that bludgeon you've got, I am *really* going to need it."

A furious blush hits my cheeks. "Beatrice."

"What?" she says. "You have to know what heat you're packing down there."

I don't answer that. "I have lube, same kind I saw you buy at the store that night. I figured you'd need it."

"*Did* you?" She grins. "You sure you aren't here only for the butt stuff?"

"I'm going to kiss you if you don't stop saying things like that."

"That is not a disincentive, James."

I kiss her hard. Bea wraps her arms around me and kisses me back harder. I pull away, gasping for air.

"See?" she says. "Not a disincentive." Beaming, she clasps my hand and clutches it against her chest. "You are wonderful. You bought my preferred brand of lube just for tonight."

"Well." I reach to adjust my watch but frown, realizing it's not there. "I'd hoped not just for tonight. For many nights. And for both places. You have one at your place. This one's for mine."

Bea pushes my chest gently, and I let her guide me onto my back on the bed. She gets on her knees, straddling my lap, and slides her hands beneath my sweatshirt. "Have I told you how cute you are? How perfectly thoughtful and kind and obscenely cute you are?"

"Cute?" I wrinkle my nose. "I was hoping for a more robust adjective than that."

She laughs. "I don't have your twenty-point Scrabble word vocabulary, Jamie. But you're right. I'm sure I can do better." A kiss to my throat makes my hands tighten around her waist.

"Gentle," she whispers. "Strong. Caring," she says against my jaw.

Her hands find mine and lace them together, lifting them above my head as she rests her body over mine. "Handsome. Funny. Smart. Thoughtful."

She nips my neck, a quick drag of teeth, then chases it with her tongue, making my hips lurch off of the bed. "Really. Fucking. Sexy," she whispers. "How's that?"

Releasing my hands, her touch drifts beneath my sweatshirt. She teases my nipples with her fingertips, making my hips lurch again beneath her. "I want to see that tattoo, Jamie."

I smile against her kiss, and then I hoist us upright. Bea yelps in surprise, holding on to my shoulders until I reach behind my head, dragging off my sweatshirt but leaving a T-shirt beneath.

Bea scowls. "That was a cheap trick."

I grin. "Your face. You were so sure you were getting the goods—ack!" I shove her hand out of my armpit, which she's just tickled. "No more."

"Then stop torturing me," she mutters, squirming on my lap.

I pin her hips so she won't move again. "Do much more of that, and the rocket will indeed be launching."

Her laughter fills the room.

But once I've peeled off my shirt, Bea's not laughing anymore.

THIRTY-THREE

Bea

I stare at it, every drip of dark ink marking his skin, right over his heart. My fingertips hover over the delicate flower, the bee that perches on its petals, the words above that I can't translate. "La vie . . ." I peer up at Jamie, who watches me closely.

" 'La vie est une fleur dont l'amour est le miel,' " he says quietly. The words fill his throat and roll off his tongue, rich and soft. His French is beautiful. " 'Life is a flower of which love is the honey.' " His hands drift along my waist, lower down my back, bringing us closer. "I realized what was missing in that poem, between the flower and the honey . . . what was missing in my life."

Taking my finger, he brings it to the bee inked right over his heart. "You." Wordless, lost in emotion, I trace softly around the tattoo, careful of his still-tender skin. "You asked me what 'mon cœur' means. Why I called you that last night." Our gazes collide, his hand settles over mine as he pins it against his chest. "It means 'my heart.' "

"Jamie . . ." I press a kiss to his chest, my heart swelling. "That's obscenely romantic."

He makes a sound of quiet satisfaction, burying his nose in my hair and breathing me in, then gently guiding me back so he can see and touch me. I raise my arms, and he knows what I want. Slowly, watching me, he grips the hem of my shirt and lifts it off, over my head. And then his hand settles over my pounding heart, too, the tiny bumblebee above my left breast.

"I knew it." He grins.

"Quite the gamble," I tell him. "What if it was a cicada?"

"What can I say, you bring out the reckless side in me." Leaning in, he presses delicate kisses along the tiny dotted line of the bee's path that wraps from the base of my skull and around my neck, down my shoulder, over my ribs, then lands where my heart pounds. "And I might have gotten a little peek that night on the sofa. Tell me what it means."

I sigh at the heat of his body so close to mine, the part of him I want closer, frustratingly held away. "The bee's path journeys from the head to the heart. To remind myself what I learned in therapy—sometimes thoughts lie, but our hearts don't. It reminds me my heart knows best."

He smiles against my skin, then kisses the bumblebee. "I love that," he whispers. His lips trail lower, over the curve of my breast, before his mouth settles, warm and wet over my nipple, and sucks. I arch in pleasure. It feels so good to finally have Jamie here, knowing me this way. My exhale is shaky as pleasure floods my body.

"And what does your heart say?" he whispers, one rough hand sliding up my thigh. He reaches my ass and caresses it.

"That it wants you," I tell him. "More than it's ever wanted anything or anyone."

He spins us on the bed until I'm on my back, Jamie braced over me. "Bea?"

"Yes, Jamie."

His eyes meet mine. "I need to make you come. I've needed it . . ." His throat works as he slides his thumb along my bottom lip. "Ever since the last time. When I watched you beneath me on the sofa, gasping my name."

I bite my lip, drifting my hands along his back. "I need it, too. I need *you.*"

Our mouths meet as he cups my breasts, teases my nipples. I arch into his touch, rubbing myself against him—my hips and his, my bare breasts and the fine hairs covering his hard chest. Air leaves me in tight, desperate heaves.

Jamie slides an arm beneath my back and hoists me effortlessly higher up the mattress. I cup his face, then scrape my fingers through his hair. Our mouths drop open as he presses into me, hard and heavy. I wrap my legs around his waist.

"All I've been thinking about is having this with you," he whispers against my mouth. "I can barely function. I've been so distracted, I walked into a wall."

A breathy laugh jumps out of me. "What?"

"I went into the office today for just a few hours, but I couldn't stop thinking about you. I was so distracted, I walked straight into a wall. I kept remembering you, that night, how you moved beneath me, every gasp and hungry kiss. I kept remembering how warm you were, how good you smelled." He kisses my neck, the tender space behind my ear, his voice dark and quiet. "How badly I wanted to taste you, to drive you wild with my hands and mouth and feel you come all over my cock."

"Jamie." That stern voice, those rough words. It's my undoing. I slip my hands up his chest, savoring the sharp planes of his torso, the curve of his pecs. I'm restless, turned on, desperate.

"What is it, sweetheart?" he says quietly, his fingertips slipping beneath my pants' waistband.

"You know what," I whisper shakily.

"I want you to tell me," he says, teasing me, lower and lower, so close to where I'm wet and dying to be touched. "Tell me what you need."

"I need you so bad," I babble, rubbing myself against his hand. "I need to be naked, and I need you to touch me. Please, please—"

On a soft growl, Jamie shucks my sweats and fuzzy socks, then throws them over his shoulder. I don't have time to make a joke about his uncharacteristic messiness because his expression silences me.

"What is it?" I ask, after a long stretch of quiet.

His eyes search my body. "Jesus," he whispers. "You're so beautiful. It hurts." He sets a hand over his heart and pats softly. "Right here."

I hold his eyes, affection blooming in my chest. "Let me see all of you, too."

After one more deep kiss, he pushes off the mattress and stands at the foot of the bed. Taking off his glasses, he sets them on his dresser. He looks different and so impossibly, dearly, the same.

"Can you see me okay?" I ask.

"It's a bit fuzzy from here," he admits. "But closer, I'll see fine."

My heart pounds, staring at him, illuminated by the fire's flames and the soft glow of the tea lights. Just like the first night I saw him, all I can think is how I want to draw and sculpt and paint him, capturing every dip of shadow, every plane of light.

Jamie steps neatly out of his joggers, making the sharp muscles in his arms and torso flex as he moves.

I stare at him and feel my bare legs rub together. "You're a work of art, James."

A blush hits his cheeks. "I . . ." He clears his throat. "Thank you."

God, I love that he's a man who whispers filthy words in my ear yet blushes when I watch him undress, that there's a side of him that I see that no one else does—the wild side of someone the world only knows as serious and staid.

He stares at me, eyes roaming my naked body hungrily. His erection is massive, straining the fabric of his boxer briefs.

Launching myself off the bed because I can't go a second longer not touching him, I set my hands on him, travel the ridges and valleys of his body, all this bare, glowing skin. I press a kiss to the tattoo above his heart. Then, slowly, I slide my hands across his back and then down, beneath the waistband of his boxer briefs, over the hard curve of his backside. He breathes shakily as my hands cup him firmly, sweeping lower, where those tight, round muscles meet his thighs.

"Bea," he says, kissing me suddenly. Urgently. Tongue, teeth. Hot and feverish. "Don't tease me. Not now."

"Tease? Me?" I smile against his kiss, then step back enough to hook my fingers tight around the waistband. Gently, I lift them around his cock, watching it spring free as I kneel and drag the fabric to his ankles. Jamie steps out of them quickly, his hard length bobbing as he moves. It's thick and long and wet at the tip. I press a kiss there and sigh as I taste him, salty and warm.

"Shit," he groans.

I tsk. "Language, James."

He stares down at me, tension painting his face as I carefully fold his boxers and joggers, which are pooled on the floor. "Beatrice," he says tightly.

"Yes, dear."

"What the hell are you doing?"

I widen my eyes innocently. "Keeping things tidy. Speaking your love language."

"I don't care how my clothes look right now, Bea, and my love language is physical touch."

Setting aside the clothes, I slide my hands up his legs and enjoy the soft golden hairs underneath my palms as I press kisses up his thighs. Finally, I wrap my hands around his beautiful erection and slide it appreciatively through my grip. He hisses between his teeth as his head drops back.

"Okay?" I ask.

"Yes. No. I'm embarrassingly close."

"Is that so bad?"

He answers me by hoisting me up and tossing me onto the bed. I squeal with delight.

His hand skates up my calf, then my thigh as he kisses me, as he watches my body arch under his touch, begging for more. "I could look at you forever," he says roughly. "Learn what all of these little markings mean. Taste their path on your skin."

A hum of pleasure leaves me. "Please."

Finally, Jamie drops his weight over mine. When our bodies meet, we both gasp at the pleasure of hot skin and feverish touches, the places where we ache, warm and wet, finally meeting as Jamie moves over me. His tongue dances with mine in a sensual rhythm that feels like the way we've waltzed—dizzying and fast and just enough clumsy to feel human and safe and real.

"Jamie," I whisper.

"Hmm?" He kisses the corner of my mouth, then my jaw, before he starts slowly kissing his way down my body, his tongue swirling against my skin as he goes. His hands wrap tight around my waist as his mouth travels me hungrily. He drags his touch up, over my breasts, then rolls his thumbs over my nipples, teasing them to stiff peaks. He's so tall that when he reaches the foot of the bed and hikes my hips to the edge of it, he's kneeling but still bent over me. His mouth trails down my hip bones, over my pelvis, inside my thighs.

"I'm on the pill and STI-free," I tell him. "Test results are on my phone, if you want to—"

"Bea," he says against my skin, before he glances up and meets my eyes. "I believe you."

"O-okay."

He smiles, still thumbing my nipples. "I am, too."

"Can we not . . . I mean, I would like . . . no condoms. But if you're not comfortable with that—"

"I want that, too," he says, kissing lower. "But first, I want this. If that's all right."

I reach and clasp his face, my fingertips sweeping over his cheekbones. "It is, but it takes me a while for that."

His eyes darken. "Spending a good long while between your thighs is my idea of heaven."

I try to push away thoughts of the past, but the embarrassment I've felt when every partner I've had grew frustrated with how long it took is hard to forget.

Jamie seems to sense where my thoughts are going. His hand travels up my stomach to rest over my heart, his fingers tracing the bumblebee as his eyes hold mine. "I'm going to spare you statistics of the average time a woman requires to build to orgasm. Both because doctor mode is a mood-kill and because you don't need a man telling you about your own body."

A smile tips my mouth. "Thank you."

"But I want you to listen to me." There it is, that stern voice that makes my eyes snap to his, makes my heart pound. "With us, there's no long or short. There's what your body needs, and mine. No one gets to say otherwise."

Tears prick the corners of my eyes. I nod quickly.

Jamie's jaw tics. "Whoever made you feel that way, they're not here. It's *me*. And you. All right? Just us."

"Just us." Tears spill down my cheeks.

He wipes them away and crawls back up my body, tucking me tight against him. Jamie holds my eyes, his hand traveling down my stomach, softly parting my thighs. He presses a tender kiss to my mouth, as his fingertips gently travel my skin's stretch marks, tracing each spidery soft line. We kiss, then kiss more, while his hand wanders my thighs and my stomach, everywhere but where I know he's going to touch me next.

"Please," I whisper.

He smiles into our kiss. His fingers part me softly, cupping me gently, covering me with such cherishing touch, I have to swallow more tears. Jamie watches me, dragging my body's wetness up to my clit in soft, lulling circles.

His other arm hooked beneath my neck, he draws me close, tucked against him, warmed by his body. I search his eyes as he touches me. It feels so different from what I've had with someone before. Like it's not just touch and hormones and impending release, but something deep inside me recognizing something deep inside him. Like our bodies keep taking these tiny steps toward each other, and when there's nowhere else to go, it won't just be coming together. It will be the connection that I was always waiting for but never found in that perfect fit.

"Show me, sweetheart," he says quietly, before he steals a slow kiss. "Show me where it aches. What you need."

I watch my hand shakily travel my body until it slips over his, our hands entwined as I adjust him slightly. A little lighter, a bit faster. I guide one of his fingers, then two, inside me to stroke my G-spot.

Time is lost to me as Jamie touches me, as he watches me for every sign of pleasure, every indication of what makes me climb higher and higher.

"So beautiful," he says. Words pour out of him, French whispered against my skin. Deep and quiet, rich and dark. Their meaning escapes me, but it doesn't matter. They turn my body hot, make me melt in his arms.

Jamie groans, feeling me clench around his fingers, watching me ride his hand.

Pleasure blossoms rose red behind my eyes. His touch is smooth and warm, perfectly steady, and I release his hand, my arm flopping above my head. Jamie's free hand finds mine and locks our fingers together, pinning my hand against the mattress.

I moan, surrendered, held, weightless. My breasts brush the soft hairs of his chest. My cheeks warm against his gentle kisses. Breathing becomes harder, as a white-hot ache builds inside me and I writhe against his hand. Jamie's mouth meets mine again, first gentle, then hard and possessive, urging me on. The ache turns sharp and urgent, shivery and molten.

Release swells inside me. My toes curl, my feet slide frantically along the sheets. "Oh God, Jamie. Oh God, please."

"That's it," he says roughly, working me harder, kissing me, biting my lip and gently dragging it between his teeth. "Let go."

"Jamie," I gasp, moving desperately against him. And when he says my name against the shell of my ear, I shatter, wave after wracking wave making me pulse against his hand, around his fingers, which stretch my release until I can't take another second of it.

I beg for no more, and yet as soon as his touch leaves me, as I watch him hold my eyes, sliding one long, knuckled finger into his mouth at a time, tasting me, breathing harshly, I can't wait a second longer for him.

"I want you." I stroke his cock, which presses insistently into my hip.

He stills my hand and kisses me again. "And I want you to wait a little longer."

"Why?" I moan.

He kisses his way down my body. "For another petite mort, of course."

I laugh breathlessly. "You do still owe me eleven—"

My words are cut off with a gasp as Jamie wrenches me by the hips and drags me close.

Pleasure ripples through me like a pebble that's struck water as he lowers his mouth to where I'm exquisitely tender and wet. I gasp as he faintly tongues my clit, my hands slipping into his hair, knotting and tugging. "That's perfect," I whisper. "Gentle like that."

He hums in response, and his kisses, which were already soft, turn softer. His tongue swirls lightly around but never directly on the place I can barely stand to be touched, that place that's so terribly sensitive I have a love-hate relationship with it.

His reach is so long that Jamie's hands easily drift up my ribs and cup my breasts, kneading them tenderly.

I dissolve into the mattress, into the gold glow of the firelight turning his hair burnished bronze, into the quiet sounds of satisfaction that hum in Jamie's throat. He lets me guide his rhythm as his tongue learns the sweeps and swirls that make my thighs tighten around his shoulders, make my breath catch in my throat.

I try not to panic at how good this feels, how quickly it's building, because I think I might cry again. Because I've never been touched this carefully, never been listened to like this, never been . . . *loved* like this.

My orgasm knocks the air out of me, wracking my body as Jamie pins my hips to the mattress and makes me feel it all.

"Jamie," I plead, clasping his hand, tugging him my way. "I need you."

"I need you, too," he says quietly, kissing me, letting me taste myself and him and sighing with pleasure as my hands wander his body.

He pulls away only long enough to reach for the lube in his nightstand. I watch him, rubbing my thighs together against the ache that pounds there, and stare at his beautiful body. The breadth of his shoulders, tapering to a narrow waist; the sharp indent where his hips meet his backside; the powerful, long lines of his thighs.

Lube in hand, he slides back onto the bed and rubs it between his fingers, warming it. Then his touch slips softly over me, featherlight circles just like his fingers and tongue that make me bite my cheek before I moan so loud I'm sure the whole apartment complex hears me.

Reaching for my hand, Jamie guides my touch along his cock, iron hard and silken hot, pumping lube over every thick inch. His eyes search mine as he smooths my hair off my face, damp with sweat, as I touch him. I open my legs wider as he settles between them, guiding himself to my entrance.

Our eyes hold as he eases just inside me. But then his drift shut, and his head falls back, exposing the long line of his throat. His Adam's apple works roughly as he swallows and his mouth parts. "Oh God," he whispers.

Breathing slowly, I try to relax, but the feeling of fullness is almost overwhelming. "It's so t-tight." My breath stutters. I clasp his shoulders as a nervous shiver rattles my body.

"I'll go slow," he says softly, kissing me tenderly, his tongue sweeping against mine. One hand cradles my face as he rocks gently, each roll of his hips easing him in a little more. Restrained. Controlled.

Even as I hear how shaky his breathing is. Even as his heart jackhammers against my chest.

He's patient for me. Meeting me where I am. Like he always has.

"I . . . I . . ." *I love you*, I want to say. *I love you so much there aren't words to do it justice.* But as he fills me, air leaves my lungs. Tears spill down my face. Emotion knots my throat.

Jamie meets my mouth in a deep kiss as he seats himself fully inside me. "I know," he whispers.

I clutch him close, heart to heart, as he moves inside me in deep, unhurried strokes that make pleasure unfurl inside me, make my thighs tighten around his waist. Our mouths meet for slow, wet kisses. Our tongues slick and move like our bodies, our moans filling each other's mouths. Jamie's cock thickens, and a fine sheen of sweat gleams on his skin.

Our eyes hold, and his breathing turns harsh, ragged. I can feel his control, the raw power in his big body, pinning mine down, his weight anchoring me to earth even as each lazy roll of his hips turns me weightless.

"Feels so good," I whisper.

He nods, breathing roughly, bending for a kiss. "So good."

Need throbs inside me, and Jamie feels it, pressing my legs wider, grinding his pelvis against mine as he thrusts harder, faster, just how I need.

The bed starts to creak, and we laugh—the intensity broken for just a moment before our expressions turn serious again, our eyes lost in each other's. The headboard knocks against the wall as we kiss, as I clutch him tighter.

A new, tender ache begins inside me, so deep, where Jamie strokes into me. I pull him close, rubbing his hard, beautiful ass, tangling my fingers in his hair, calling his name as he moves faster, faster—

The ache blooms into a breathless, free-falling bliss as I come around him. I cry out, shaking, clutching Jamie tight as I call his name.

"Bea," he groans, pinning my hands over my head, lacing our fingers together. Finally, he lets go, hips driving into me. Fierce, tight breaths, hair wild. How I've always dreamed I'd see him.

On a hoarse shout, he buries his face in my neck, his arms like a vise around my waist as he fills me, hot and long, his hips pumping frantically, like he'll never get enough.

It's a moment, suspended in time—our jagged breaths, the soft, intimate sounds of our bodies moving, slowing, growing still. We sigh and kiss as our hands wander the other in newfound reverence. Wordlessly, we clean each other, then draw close, tangled limbs, naked, content. I kiss him until I can't stay awake any longer. And under the starry night sky Jamie gave me, sparkling on his ceiling, I sleep.

THIRTY-FOUR

Jamie

I wake up to sunlight burning through the curtains and roll onto my back. Bea sits, legs crisscrossed, eyes on her sketchbook, charcoal flying in her hand. I smile.

And when she glances up at me, she smiles, too. "Good morning," she whispers.

"Good morning." I tip my head, assessing her, naked but for a blanket thrown around her shoulders. "How'd you sleep?"

She arches an eyebrow. "This implies I slept at all."

I smile. "A dozen little deaths, as promised."

Leaning in, she kisses me softly on the lips. "You're a man of your word." When she straightens from bending over to kiss me, she tries and fails to hide a wince.

Guilt knifes through me. I sit up in bed.

"Dammit, James." She drops her sketchbook. "Now my perspective will be off."

"I hurt you."

She sighs, then sets aside the sketchbook and charcoal pencil, looking at me patiently, like she expected this. "No. I had sex after a two-year dry spell."

"It's my—" I gesture between my legs. "My—what did you call it?—bludgeon's fault."

"Jame." Bea shakes her head and then leans in for another kiss. "A pencil eraser would have made me sore, and all the lube in the grocery store wasn't going to prevent it. It's nothing to do with you."

"Still." I throw back the sheet, about to get up and do *something* about this, but she pushes me back on the bed, straddling my hips. My cock's eager and hard, jutting up between us. I cover it with a hand, pinning it against my stomach. "Ignore that."

"Impossible," she whispers, reaching over me toward the night-stand.

"W-what are you doing?" Her breasts brush my face. I kiss them because I have to.

"Getting lube of course," she says. Her voice is smokier in the mornings, and it's doing things to me, tightening my balls, making need pound through my cock.

With the lube, she strokes me, then rubs herself. And then she glides, soft and wet, over my length in slow, maddening rolls of her hips. I grip her helplessly, sinking my hands into the sweet roundness of her backside.

Bea presses a kiss to my bare chest and breathes in deeply.

"Are you inhaling me, Beatrice?"

"James." She sinks her teeth playfully into my skin, then chases her love bite with a kiss. "You smell so fucking good. What is it? I need it bottled. I'll spray it in the air to make me happy every time a customer comes in and wants to return something they clearly used."

"People actually do that? With stationery?"

"You'd be surprised. Seriously, Jamie, what makes you smell so good?"

I groan, throwing back my head. She honestly expects me to be able to talk right now. "My God-given natural essence."

"I'll get it out of you one day. Is it just your body wash? Do you wear cologne? I'll steal it from your place if I have to."

"It's just the body wash. Oh *God*—" She's rubbing herself right over the tip of my cock, making it throb and drip and ache so badly for her. "Stop depriving me."

Bea smiles a little wickedly. "I want to make you fall apart."

"You most definitely did that, numerous times, last night."

"I got close." Peering down at me, she touches my pecs, teases my nipples. "But you were still in control."

"I like being that way with you."

"I know." Bea slips a hand through my hair, twirling a lock around her finger. "And I like it, too. But sometimes it's a relief to set that aside for a while. And I want to give you that . . . if you don't mind."

"I'm not sure," I tell her honestly.

She stills her hips. "Want to try? If you don't like it, we'll stop."

I stare up at her, my hands drifting over her ribs, cupping her breasts. "All right."

Bea's smile is bright, one of those wide, beaming smiles that make my heart tumble in my chest. She scooches a little farther away and sits on my thighs before taking me in hand.

"Have you ever heard of edging, Jamie?" She presses a kiss to the base of my cock that makes my stomach flex.

"N-no."

Her breath is warm against me as she kisses my thighs and swirls her tongue closer, closer. "It's when I get you really close to orgasm, then back off. And I do it over and over until you're ionizing the air with swear words and begging to come."

A flush creeps up my chest and neck. "That sounds . . . like torture."

Bea laughs quietly. "Oh, it is. But it's the best kind. The kind of torture that results in orgasms lasting so long they ruin you for everything else. You did it with me that time last night when you bent me over the bed and—"

Another groan rolls out of me. I know what she means now. Each time I felt her start to come, I was so greedy to make it last, I'd pull out and touch her, tease her clit, her breasts, kiss my way up her spine, before I drove back into her and got her close. I did it until she was cussing me out and I couldn't take one more stroke inside her without detonating.

"Mm-hmm," she says against my stomach, planting soft kisses, teasing me with tiny scrapes of her teeth. "So really, I owe you. Tell me, Jamie. Yes or no."

"Yes," I breathe.

She tastes me with her tongue, teases me with her hands. It's the kind of torture I never dreamed I'd want. Time and again she works me up to the brink of release; long, hard sucks and pumps until I'm taut as a bow, sweat beading my body. I've lost track of how many times it's been. I barely know where I am anymore or what day it is.

This time, if I don't come, I'm going to lose it. Bea flicks the head of my cock with her tongue over and over. I groan and tangle my hands in her hair when she takes me all the way in her mouth, working me up to orgasm again.

I stare down at her as she kisses her way up my length and crawls higher, her sweet, beautiful body bared to me, and says, "I used to fantasize about you looking like this—disheveled and swearing and desperate. I made myself come over and over to this."

"Oh fuck," I hiss as she teases the tip of my cock with her body. I touch her, where she's silken smooth and flushed, where I kissed and licked and learned her for hours last night. "You're going to kill me."

Bea hums happily as she grips the base of me and sinks down an inch, then another. Then she stops. She stops, leaving me on an agonizing precipice. "Do you have something to say, James?" Her fingers sweep up my stomach, her muscles clench around me, and that's my breaking point.

I growl as I grip her hips. "Fucking hell, woman. Ride my cock *right* now and make me come."

"Gladly." On one steady thrust, she seats herself on me, braces her hands on my waist, and does what I've told her to, riding me hard. I thrust up into her, climbing a height I never have before, every inch of me more dizzyingly sensitized than it's ever been. Her hands on my chest, the softness of her backside as she lands on me with each roll of her hips. Her breasts, soft and delicate in my hands as they bounce with her movement. Her small, slippery clit swelling for me as I rub it with my thumb.

Our eyes hold as Bea works herself on me, as she brings us closer to what I already know will be the most intense come of my life. When she throws her head back and cries my name, clenching me in tight, rhythmic spasms, I grip her waist and thrust home, pouring into her.

When my hips finally stop moving, she falls off of me. "That," she gasps, "backfired on me a little."

"Don't worry," I pant, curling her inside my arms and kissing her deeply. "You still came out on top."

She snorts a laugh. "That was such a dad joke." Quiet settles between us as she runs her fingers through my hair. "You, sir, look thoroughly tupped."

"My thanks to you, madam."

Her eyes roam my face. "You're beautiful," she whispers. "One day I'll paint you like this."

Tracing her tattoos with my fingertips, I tell her, "You're beautiful, too, you know. The most beautiful."

On a contented sigh, she slides her leg over mine and curls up closer. I kiss her forehead, tucking in the blankets around us. "Let's never leave," she whispers.

"It's a plan. Except for one very important day that's coming up."

She lifts her head, frowning at me. "What?"

"Halloween, of course. Not only do I need help eating unconscionable amounts of fun-sized candy, but I have an artist girlfriend, and I need her help with my costume."

Bea squeals with delight as she hugs me so hard, it knocks me back and sends us tumbling off the bed. "I thought you'd never ask."

———

"Not too many kids out," Bea says around a bite of Milky Way, shifting in her crab costume. "Damn shame. More candy for me."

I glance her way, drinking her in, and smile faintly. I feel like blown glass. Light and transparent. Breakable in a way I never have been. It's been a week of lovemaking and dinners in, quiet nights on the couch with books and her art supplies littering my table. So many chances to tell her I love her, but it's died on my tongue every time, fear knotting my stomach. What if she loses interest? What if the novelty fades? What if I'm not creative enough or playful enough or fun enough? *What if, what if, what if.*

I can't listen to those fears anymore. From now on, I'm going to be brave.

"You okay?" she asks.

I blink. She's getting too good at reading me. "Fine." Glancing out at the houses across the street, swarmed with trick-or-treating children, I grimace. "Except for the fact that we're the most skipped-over building on the block."

"No, we aren't." Bea hides the barely touched candy bowl beneath her pincers.

"I told you these costumes were going to scare away the kids. Which might turn out to be fortunate, seeing as you haven't stopped eating Milky Ways since we parked it out here."

"I'm on my period, James. This is the one week out of every month you may not give me shit for my sugar addiction. Plus, if kids can't appreciate the sheer artistry in our costumes, I don't *want* them eating our candy."

"Hyperrealistic crabs the size of an adult are so approachable," I tease. "I can't think why the children are terrified."

"This is a failing of modern society." She lifts her pincer. "Because I am telling you what, our kids will not be scared of a little papiermâché."

Her eyes widen. Mine do, too. She groans and tries unsuccessfully to bury her face in a crab pincer.

My heart bursts with hope and love—sheer, blissful relief. Now. *Now* is my moment.

THIRTY-FIVE

Bea

I can't believe I said it. Of all the things to blurt as I sit in a head-to-toe crab costume, looking like an oversized seafood-house logo, it had to be that.

But Jamie's smiling, his eyes dancing in a way they weren't just a moment ago. He nudges my pincer out of the way, then kisses me, sliding his nose along mine. "You want my babies," he whispers. He sounds annoyingly arrogant and so perfectly vulnerable. I want to tickle him until he shrieks, then kiss him some more.

"How many?" he says.

"A couple? Siblings are annoying, but I couldn't live without mine. What do you think?"

He nuzzles my cheek. "Whatever makes you happy. That's what I'd want."

I stare up at Jamie, knowing I haven't said the words. That *I love you* knots in my throat every time it's about to come out. It's that final step, something that I'm ridiculously frightened will backfire the moment I speak it into existence.

But each day that's passed since I told Jamie with my body how much he means to me, in every way but those exact words, I despise myself a little more. I feel like even more of a coward. What's the point in fearing what I know is true? Of harboring some baseless suspicion that when I say it, the truth will somehow be compromised?

I love Jamie. I love him in a way I have never loved anything or anyone in my life. Not more than my sisters or my tiny pet or my parents, but *differently*, deeply, right down to my bones.

And tonight, while tiny witches and ghosts, warriors and dragons and pumpkins, have stopped and balked at me, then warmed to him the second he pushed up his knightly visor and smiled, I knew I was going to say it.

Glancing up at Jamie, while kids shriek in delight as they sprint down the street, costumes trailing behind them, I know I'm going to say it *right now*.

"'Scuse me!" a kid voice yells, shattering the moment.

God*dammit*.

"Happy Halloween," I grumble, holding out the bowl.

"Be nice," Jamie chides.

The kid, dressed as an old-school Power Ranger, rifles around in the bowl and frowns. "Where are all the Milky Ways?"

"Huh." I shake the bowl. "Who knows. Guess they're popular with the kids. You're a little late to the game, my friend. You know the saying, 'The early bird gets the worm!'"

He scowls at me, takes a handful of candy, and shoves it in his pillowcase.

"Kids these days," I mutter as he stalks off, pulling a fresh Milky Way from my pocket. "No gratitude."

Jamie belly laughs, adjusting his homemade knight's visor so it's up off his face. "I can't believe you. Depriving children of their beloved Halloween candy."

"You're the one lecturing me about how America's youth eat too much sugar!"

Reaching past me, Jamie plucks a Snickers from the bowl, tears off the wrapper, then pops it in his mouth. "Fair point, Miss Crabby."

"I'm not crabby." I nip him with my pincer. "I'm hormonal. And I have better boundaries with little people. You're a sucker for them, so I balance you out."

Jamie clasps the pincer and stares down at me. "Bea?"

I pause with a Milky Way halfway to my mouth, then lower it. Oh God. Is this it? Is he beating me to the punch?

"Yes, Jamie?"

He leans in, gently lifting the crab antenna that's flopped in my eyes. "Do you remember when we texted, before we knew who the other person was?"

I nod. "Yes."

"And we both said . . . it was 'strange' how much we liked it. How well it worked."

Tears turn my vision blurry. "I remember."

"And then you said, 'strange can be good sometimes.'"

I nod again and smile tearily. "Yes."

"I never thought . . ." He removes one of my pincers and clasps my hand inside his, softly tracing my palm with his thumb. "I never thought I could love someone so unlike me. That being so different from someone could make me feel right at home rather than every kind of wrong." He glances up and meets my eyes. "But each moment I spent with you, every time we pretended, the strangest thing happened . . . It became real. Every way you were my opposite only made me want you more, every secret part of you that you entrusted to me only made me ache to trust you just as much. And then I realized that difference that I couldn't get enough of . . . that strange, perfect intensity between us . . . it was love, beyond anything I'd ever known. I fell in love with you, so wildly, Bea. I love nothing in the world as I love you. And maybe you find that strange, but if you do . . . I hope it's the best kind of strange, the kind that you might one day feel, too."

Tears spill down my face. "Jamie." I kiss him hard as I throw my arms around his neck, breathing him in, my heart dancing in a maelstrom of color and joy and love. "Jamie, I—"

"Bea!"

We startle apart, but this time it's no trick-or-treater that's broken the moment. That was my sister's voice. I glance over my shoulder, instantly worried.

"Jules?"

She's trying very hard to smile, but her face is tearstained and her make-up's turned her into a sad racoon. "I'm okay," she says thinly. "It's okay."

I hug her, wrapping her in my ridiculous costume. I rip off the head-piece and the other pincer. "No, you're not. What's wrong?"

Her face crumples, and she finally gives in to tears. "Everything."

———————

It's been a while since I've been the caregiver in our twin dynamic, but I remember exactly what Jules needs. I stick her in the shower and set out her favorite tea, then I change the sheets on her bed and light a few lavender candles.

Jamie's an angel and helps me, putting on the kettle, teaming up with me to make her bed. We're both tense wrecks because we both know this has to be about Jean-Claude, whose rare absence we've obvi-ously noted, even though Jules hasn't said that yet. She hasn't said any-thing. She just cried the whole walk home, leaning into me, Jamie on my other side, supporting me as I supported her.

Shortly after the water for the shower shuts off, our apartment door opens, and air rushes out of my lungs. Christopher has a black eye and a split lip. He shuts the door, wincing at the movement of his shoulder.

Jamie's in doctor mode, walking up to him, gently clasping his other elbow. "What happened?"

Christopher groans as he slumps into a chair at the table. "Jean-Claude."

"What?" I sit across from him as Jamie goes to the freezer and makes an ice pack, then wraps it in a clean kitchen towel.

"Put it on your eye," Jamie tells him.

Christopher obeys, wincing again as the ice connects with his swol-len, bruising face. "Has Jules told you anything?"

I shake my head. "She showed up at Jamie's—she'd been trying to call while we were passing out candy, but I didn't have my phone on me, so she walked to his place—and then she just lost it."

He adjusts the ice on his eye. "I should let her tell you."

"She'll tell me her version of things." I clasp his hand and squeeze gently. "You tell me yours."

"Jules came in for our usual end-of-month strategy meeting." He turns to Jamie. "Hedge funds can't advertise in the traditional sense. It's all networking and shoulder rubbing, which I'm good at, but not the expert."

"Juliet is," Jamie says.

"Exactly. Her PR consultancy career is thriving for a reason," Christopher says. "So we were having our usual meeting, and I notice she seems subdued, not her usual upbeat self. I was worried, so I asked her if we could switch gears, talk as family. She said yes, and then she told me what was going on."

"What?" I ask. "What is it?"

"Well, *that* is her story to tell, but needless to say, she was upset, I was upset for her. So I hugged her. Which just so happened to be when Jean-Claude stormed into the meeting, took one look at us, lost his shit, and came at me."

Jamie stares at Christopher and his black eye, pained. "He did that to you."

"Yes. A few bruises, nothing major. And I'd like the record to show I only look like this because I wasn't going to pulverize Jean-Claude in front of Jules. I subdued him, which was upsetting enough for her. I would have been here sooner to check up on her, but I had to deal with the police."

"So you reported the assault," Jamie says.

Christopher nods emphatically. "Hell yes."

"Good." Jamie sighs bleakly. "God, what a mess. I'm so sorry."

Christopher waves his hand. "He's not yours to apologize for. He was my employee, and he clearly has issues I should have noticed by now, not limited to a violent temper and irrational jealousy. I mean, Christ, she's a sister to me. I would never—"

I pat his hand gently. "I know. But there's nothing rational about behavior like that."

"No, there isn't," he agrees.

"So . . . what now?" I ask.

"He's gone," Christopher says forcefully. "I fired his ass. Police have him."

I breathe a sigh of relief. "Good. That's the least he deserves."

"His father will bail him out," Jamie mutters, scrubbing his face, hands sliding beneath his glasses. "He'll get a slap on the hand and a new job somewhere working with some executive who owes his father a favor."

"Probably," Christopher concedes.

"But he's out of our lives, at least?" I ask.

Jamie drops his hands and meets my eyes. "Absolutely."

Christopher massages his shoulder and stares down at the table. "Without a doubt."

"Poor Jules," I whisper miserably, rubbing the ache in my chest, sympathy pain that's a shadow of what she must be feeling.

"Hey," my sister says from the other end of the room, her voice shaky. We all stand. She gets one look at Christopher and crumples, hiding her face in her hands as she starts to cry. "Oh Jesus, Christopher. He really hurt you—"

"Hey, no. Jules, I'm fine," he says, starting toward her.

"I've got this," I tell him, setting a hand on his arm to stop him before turning toward Jamie.

"Go," he says softly, his hand on my back. "I'll keep Christopher company. Give him grief for not getting that shoulder checked out."

Christopher narrows the eye that's not swollen shut. "I've been a little busy."

"Well, there's time now," I hear Jamie tell him as I cross the room toward my sister. "Let me take you. I have a colleague from the shelter who I know is working tonight at the nearest ER. I'll make sure you're seen by her. Come on."

Wrapping my arms around Jules, I walk her toward her room and bed, shutting the door behind us.

She's trembling as she crawls onto the mattress, and I join her, slipping off my shoes and dragging the blanket over our heads. I flick on the flashlight I stashed there earlier.

Fresh tears slide down her cheeks. "Just like the good old days."

"Jules." I clasp her hand carefully. "Did he hurt you?"

She burrows in on herself, hiding her face. "Not physically. But watching him go at Christopher was terrifying."

"Of course it was." I rub her arm gently. "He hurt you with words, though, didn't he?"

Jules glances up at me, wide eyes like mine wet with tears. "I was such a fool, Bea."

"No, you weren't." Taking her hand, I hold it to my heart. "You weren't a fool for believing the best in someone you loved. Someone who swept you off your feet with his best self and made you fall head over heels for him in just a few short weeks."

She sniffles. "It was so perfect. What happened? How did we end up in this nightmare?"

I smooth away a ribbon of dark hair stuck to her tearstained cheek, tucking it behind her ear. "Because Jean-Claude isn't well. Because he doesn't love in a healthy way. He may have started off with good intentions, or maybe his goal was always to possess you, but either way, that's what it became—possession, control. Not love."

She frowns at me, wiping away more tears. "Why does it sound like you're speaking from experience?"

I kiss her knuckles, blinking away my own tears. "There's . . . something I should have told you about Tod." I swallow roughly. "And I *hate* myself for not doing it sooner, because what if I had? Maybe you'd have known the signs, maybe you'd have found it easier to believe me when I raised concerns about Jean-Claude."

"Bea." Jules scoots closer, knotting our legs together, forehead to forehead. "Tell me."

I do. I tell her what I told Jamie, how it started so well and then I lost my bearings, how he gaslighted me, made me doubt myself, how, when we ended, I realized I hadn't been loved—I'd been manipulated.

"God, I'm so sorry," she says hoarsely. "Here I was, pushing you to date again, to open up, when you needed time, when you'd been hurt—"

"You didn't know. Because I didn't tell you. I was proud and embarrassed, and I wanted to move on."

She laughs tearily. "Yeah. I get the wounded-pride thing. I get that real hard. Along with the bruised heart and the *what the fuck can I trust?* feeling that just makes me want to bury my head under this blanket and not come out for a very, *very* long time."

Searching her eyes, I ask, "What happened? Since the party? All week, you were barely around, barely answering my texts."

"We did a day trip the day after the party, and he was so hot and cold. He was still pissed I didn't stick up for him in front of you. I told him I'd handled it, but it wasn't enough." She hesitates and wipes her eyes. "By the evening, it seemed better. I thought we'd smoothed things over, but then he asked me to go on his business trip this week. I had a pretty busy work schedule lined up, so initially I said I didn't think I could, and then he just . . . lost it, verbally exploded, saying I was withdrawing, creating distance, that I didn't really love him.

"So I went with him to try to reassure him, and it was just more of the same, hot and cold, amazing sex and then hours of stony silence, not answering my texts, no explanation when he returned to the hotel. By the time I got home, I was raw and sad and confused. Then I had my meeting with Christopher and he was just . . . my brother, you know? This good, safe, kind guy. The contrast couldn't be more pronounced, and I fell apart. Because I realized, what Jean-Claude had been doing, it was such . . ." She scrunches her eyes shut. "Such bullshit, that I believed and felt guilty for. That I did *not* deserve."

"No," I whisper. "You didn't. But it's done now. And you'll heal."

Tears streak down her cheeks. "How?"

"One day at a time. Therapy. Quiet nights in with your people. Mom's home-cooked meals."

A sob jumps out of her. "It feels like it'll never be better. Like I'll always hurt like this."

"It gets better, JuJu. I promise."

"How long?" she says through tears, burying her head in my neck. "How long?"

I wrap my arms around her and kiss her hair, dread seeping into my heart. New tears—tears for me and Jamie, for what I know we have to give up—prick *my* eyes. "As long as it takes."

THIRTY-SIX

Jamie

I let myself into Bea and her sister's apartment hours later, careful to shut the door quietly. I imagine after such a terrible, exhausting evening, Juliet's asleep.

As my eyes adjust to the darkness, I spot Bea on the couch, her back to me. When she turns and faces my way, my stomach drops. She's crying.

"Bea." I close the distance between us as she springs off the couch and throws herself into my arms. A wave of relief rushes through me. If she's leaning into me, everything's all right. It has to be.

"Juliet's safe from him," I tell her. "So is Christopher. His lawyer is working on a restraining order, and I've texted Jean-Claude, told him he has forty-eight hours to get out of my place."

Bea nods, then whispers, "Thank you, Jamie."

I kiss the crown of her head. "How is Juliet?"

"Awful."

I hug her hard, swaying her gently, because I know it soothes her. "What can I do?"

"Kill him," she growls.

"If only pistols at dawn weren't a thing of the past and I hadn't pledged the Hippocratic oath."

Her voice grows hard. "I hate him. I hate him for hurting her." She wipes her tears from her cheeks angrily. "I know my sister's not perfect.

I know she overstepped in what she did to bring us together. But he *hurt* her. He hurt her and Christopher, and they're my family, Jamie. And now we have to pick up the pieces. I wish she'd never met him."

I stare down at her, trying not to be wounded by what she's implied. Because if Juliet had never met Jean-Claude, how would *we* have met? How would we have ever found each other?

"I'm sorry," I tell her. "For all of this. I hate how much pain he's caused. I regret that he hurt Juliet and Christopher, and that he'll probably go on to hurt others. But I won't regret that they met, not when it gave me you."

Blinking away tears, Bea wraps her arms around my waist, then sets her head over my heart. "Jamie."

"Yes?" I hold her tight, swaying her how she likes.

"I—" Her voice breaks as she buries her face in my chest. "He hurt my sister, Jamie. And I can't let her hurt anymore."

Rubbing her back in gentle circles, I kiss her temple. "I know you can't stand for the people you care about to hurt, Bea, but you can't take away Juliet's pain. You can only be there while she weathers it."

"I can lessen it." Bea swallows thickly, clutching me tighter.

I frown, pulling back enough that I can search her eyes. "How? What are you talking about?"

Tears spill down her cheeks. "Jamie, we can't see each other anymore, not right now. Not when everything that happened with Jules and Jean-Claude is tangled up in our relationship. Every time she sees us—sees you—she'll be reminded of him. Even if I try to slip away to see you privately, she'll know where I'm going, who I'm seeing, and it'll dredge up painful memories and grief, everything she needs to forget so she can truly move on. I can't do that to her."

I stare at her in shock. "You're not serious."

"I've been in her shoes, and I know what she needs—comfort and safety, not constant reminders of the person who hurt her. I have to protect my sister, give her time to heal from Jean-Claude."

"I'm not Jean-Claude."

"I know you're not, Jamie." Bea wipes away her tears. "Dammit. I know you're not. Stop twisting my words."

"I'm not twisting them, I'm making a point. You're saying you can't be with me because of something someone else did?"

Her expression crumples with new tears. "I'm just trying to . . ." She groans and hides her face in her hands. "Please, I can't choose you over Jules."

"I'm not asking you to choose me over her. I'm asking you not to set me aside like a pawn that no longer serves your purposes."

"It's not like that!" Bea says defensively, dropping her hands. "This isn't a fucking chess game. It's people's hearts and feelings—"

"I'm aware! Mine happen to be involved."

"I know, Jamie!" she hisses, glancing at Juliet's shut bedroom door and lowering her voice. "You think I don't know that?"

"It doesn't feel like it. You're telling me I'm on standby indefinitely, that we can't be a couple because of my *roommate*—the man *your* sister chose to date. Do you know how terrible that feels, Bea? To be set aside so readily?"

Tears slip down her cheeks. "I'm sorry. I never wanted to . . ." She groans in frustration. "I'm trying to be honest about what I think my sister needs, and yes, it involves a sacrifice, but it feels like you're willfully misunderstanding me, Jamie. I'm not breaking up with you. I'm asking for a *break*, for some time."

"Time," I say, breathing through the ache in my chest. She's telling me *I'm* the one who's irrational here, but it doesn't feel like it. It feels like once again, I've been assessed as deficient and discarded. "How much time, Beatrice? For this 'break'?"

She throws up her hands. "I don't know, okay? I don't exactly have a schedule for my sister's recovery from emotional abuse, so I guess you'll just have to wait to hear from me, Jamie."

"A 'break' with no end date. Sounds an awful lot like a breakup."

Fire flashes in Bea's eyes, which fill with tears. "It certainly does, when you put it *that* way, Jamie."

"I'm sorry, how else exactly could I put it?"

"I—" A quiet, pained growl rolls out of her. She clutches her hair in two big fistfuls and tugs. "I don't know. It's complicated. And you're not making it any simpler."

"Well, my sincere apologies for being inconvenient, for wanting clarity and an actual answer about this." She's silent, her head hung as she tugs harder at her hair. "And that silence right there," I tell her, "that's all the answer I need." Yanking at my cuffs, I adjust the buttons until they bisect my wrists. My chest is painfully tight.

Turning on my heels, I leave her standing on the threshold.

When my feet hit the pavement, I run.

———————

Weeks feel like years. I go to work. I run until I'm exhausted. I feel hollow.

I avoid all places that I could cross paths with Bea. Meaning I go to the office, and then I go home. My apartment is empty of laughter and full of silence. The only calls I get are from my father, which end in a furious voicemail about "remembering where my loyalty lies," complete with insults and veiled threats because I didn't stick up for Jean-Claude's despicable behavior. Jean-Claude complied with my demands and moved out. I was gone when he left, and he was gone when I returned. Good riddance.

Now I have only my cats for company, and even they seem miserable. I throw out the tasty cat treats that Bea brought them on Halloween and fed them from her hand, saying they deserved a proper treat, too.

I feed them their healthy grain-free dental treats. They hate it. I hate it.

I hate that I did this again. That I let myself foolishly fall for someone who was never going to want me for the long haul.

I loved her. And I still wasn't enough. There's no thinking my way out of it, no changing the past. I just have to drag myself through the present each day and make it to bed.

Standing in my empty kitchen, I stare out the window, not tasting my breakfast smoothie, when my phone's screen lights up with a message from Christopher:

Any interest in coffee and catching up?

Guilt floods me. God, what an ass I've been. It's been weeks since I saw him safely in the care of my friend at the ER, and while I checked in on Christopher once afterward, I haven't messaged since. He's been nothing but kind to me, someone who, had things not blown up in my face, I hoped would become a good friend.

Nervous, hands shaking, I text him back. I'd like that. Time and place?

His response is immediate. This morning? If you don't mind coming here, my espresso machine is up and running.

My stomach drops. He's next door to the Wilmots. I have an absurd fantasy of seeing Beatrice when I get there. Our eyes meeting, the world dissolving around us, time in slow motion, until we're in each other's arms and it's apologies and kisses and promises to never again—

Meow.

I stare down at the cats, their heads tipped in twin expressions of concern. Morgan saunters toward the front door, pawing the handle. Gally nudges my leg.

"Should I?"

They meow loudly in unison. Swallowing roughly, I text Christopher and sweep up my keys. On my way.

Christopher's home is similar to the Wilmots' but a little rougher around the edges, tidy still, the yard immaculate, and yet I spot paint peeling here and there, older windows, brick that's begging to be repointed. With how successful he is, I have no doubt he could afford to pay someone to do the work. It makes me wonder what's stopping him.

I knock on the door and only have to wait a moment before one of the last people I expected to see opens the door.

"Jamie!" Maureen Wilmot opens her arms and wraps me in a hug.

She looks up at me and I'm at a loss for words. Bea's sea-storm irises sparkling merrily. A kind face warmed by a smile so familiar it hurts.

"Jamie?" she says. "Everything all right?"

"Well enough," I tell her, crossing the threshold. "And you?"

"Busy," she says briskly. "You caught me just as I was about to leave. I was dropping off some meals, since Christopher's been burning the candle at both ends at work, making up for that rat bastard's absence."

I bite my lip, oddly tickled by her language.

"It's been a cooking whirlwind, making comfort foods to tempt Juliet, because she's barely been eating, and now I have my other daughter coming home, and she has a hollow leg. I pulled out all the culinary stops, then came by to make sure Christopher got some of the bounty. You should take some with you, too."

"You're very kind, but that's all right."

"You sure?"

I nod.

"Suit yourself." She shrugs and shuts the front door behind me. "Come in, at least. Let's find Christopher. You know," she says, smiling up at me, "I still think about the note you sent, thanking us for hosting you that night. No one sends notes anymore, but you did. That's when I knew you were a keeper, and I told my Beatrice, 'That one's a keeper. A man who has impeccable cursive and knows how to write a proper thank-you? Don't let him get away,' I said. And then she of course said, 'You think I don't know how wonderful he is? How could I ever let him go?'"

I grip the doorframe so I won't fall over. "What? When?"

"Oh, just the other day," she says idly, leading us into Christopher's kitchen. He's nowhere to be seen, but a cabinet drawer is open, revealing an empty waste bin.

Maureen frowns. "He must be taking out the trash. Now, why don't you sit and I'll serve you one of my blueberry scones with fresh clotted cream."

I'm about to tell her I have no appetite for food, only for more news, more words, now that she's fed me this crumb of hope, but she sets the scone in front of me before I can.

"So, how are you holding up?" she asks. "This break between you and Bea must be trying."

"Mrs. Wilmot—"

"Maureen," she corrects gently.

"Maureen, it's not . . . a break."

She tips her head, perplexed. "Bea said that until things settled down with Juliet, you'd need to take a break."

I pinch the bridge of my nose, anxiety pounding in my skull. "Bea said we needed to take a break, yes, but she had no sense of when that break would end. I told her that was a breakup. And when I pressed her to refute that, to make it make some kind of sense, she didn't have an answer for me. So I left, and we haven't spoken since. Which means . . . That is, I don't think . . ." Sighing, I scrub my face. "We broke up. She didn't tell you that?"

"I think she told me what she wanted me to hope for . . . perhaps what she's still hoping herself." Her hand lands softly on my arm, its heat seeping through my sweater. She's so different from my mother. So warm and maternal. She tips her head again, as if reading my thoughts.

"Whatever's happened between you two, I think you should talk," she says. "I'm no expert, but I've picked up on a few things since marrying Bill. He and I are very different people who don't often communicate the same way, and we used to let that come between us. But we've learned it's the things that went unsaid, rather than the things we *did* say, that have hurt the most over the years. Once we talked, every time, it was always better, even if it took a little while."

I nod somberly. "I'll bear that in mind."

"And you know, you can confide in Christopher, too."

"Ah. Well." I frown down at my scone. "Yes, I suppose. I'm just not very . . . practiced at that."

She nods. "Neither is he, but you both would benefit from a good close friendship. He's an only child, you see. His parents passed when he was younger, so we're his family. The people he loves, his friends, they're his family. That's why he's hurting so keenly for Juliet. That's why I think he could use a friend like you. He speaks very highly of you. I know he considers you a friend already. When we're hurting, we need to lean on our friendships."

Before I can respond, Christopher rounds the corner into the kitchen. "Hey, West." He briskly washes his hands, then dries them. I stand and shake his hand when he offers it. "How are you?"

"All right enough, I suppose. And you?"

"Same. And what about *you*?" he says to Maureen, wrapping an arm around her shoulders and smiling coyly. "You badgering him? Meddling? Making mischief?"

She swats him away. "I'm serving scones and clotted cream, is what I'm doing."

"Mm-hmm." He eyes her suspiciously.

"And now that I've made my delivery, I'll be on my way."

"Stay for coffee," he says, pointing to the fancy machine behind him. "I can make you literally anything you want."

"Tempting, but no," she says as her phone buzzes and she pulls it out. Reading the screen through squinted eyes, she smiles.

"What is it?" Christopher asks.

"Katerina's just texted." Maureen pockets her phone. "She's here!"

Christopher blinks at her, shocked. "When were you planning on telling me Kate's home?"

Maureen winks at me, then turns back to Christopher. "Honestly, Christopher, I wasn't sure, considering I value my sanity. I have a lot on my plate lately, young man, and the last thing I need is to suffer through another one of those spats you and Kate have."

He gapes at her.

"All right, I'm off to the birdies' apartment and no riffraff allowed, so don't even think of following." She opens the side door off the kitchen and waves goodbye to me. "Toodle-oo!"

After the door slams shut, I turn toward Christopher. "Is she always like that?"

"What?" he says, watching her go. "A menace?"

For the first time in weeks, I almost smile. "I was going to say a bit of a charmer." A bittersweet pang knifes through my chest. "No mystery where Bea got it."

"Just wait until you meet Kate," he mutters darkly. "Then you'll know who got her menacing streak."

I watch Maureen through the door's windowpane, crossing the lawn to her home, until she disappears inside. Her words echo in my head: *It's the things that went unsaid, rather than the things we did say, that have hurt the most.*

"Christopher, you don't happen to have a pen and piece of paper, do you?"

THIRTY-SEVEN

Bea

A loud bang on the front door of the apartment jars me awake. I glance up and read the digital clock next to my bed. It's disgustingly early.

The door rattles with more bangs again. Knowing Jules is a light sleeper and how badly she's been sleeping, I stumble out of bed, then run down the hall, hoping to stop the noise before it wakes her up. I try to dodge the coffee table but stub my toe, biting my lip to stifle a cry of pain.

Hobbling, I make it to the door and wrench it open, about to have a few choice words with whoever thought it was cute to show up at my door at seven thirty in the morning. But instead my mouth falls open. "Kate?"

"Finally. Here, this was wedged in the door." My younger sister slaps an envelope to my chest, then breezes past me, massive suitcase clunking behind her. It wobbles dangerously, missing a wheel, as she drags it with one hand.

That's when I realize her right arm is tucked tight to her front. In a sling.

"What happened?" I ask. "Why are you here?"

Kate drops her suitcase with a loud *thunk* and heads straight for the kitchen.

"Oh, okay," I tell her. "Cool. Don't answer me. Just be gone for eighteen months, with five emails and two airmail packages constituting our relationship, then barge into *my* apartment and make yourself at home."

"Thanks," she says, fumbling with the cabinet door as she pulls out a glass, then knocks on the spigot, filling it with water. "I will."

I glare at her as she chugs the whole glass, then sets it down noisily.

"Katerina Wilmot. Answer me."

"Jules was supposed to tell you."

I wrinkle my nose. "What?"

"Jules. She didn't tell you?" She opens the refrigerator and noses around. "Oh, hell yes. Mom cooked." Shutting the fridge door with her hip, she sets down a breakfast casserole, finds a fork, and digs into it cold.

I nearly gag. Storming past her, I turn on the coffee maker, which wasn't programmed to brew for another hour. I need caffeine. "Stop being cryptic," I tell her. "Stop answering my questions with more questions."

"Fuck's sake." She drops the fork and looks genuinely pissed. "Why are you two so functionally dysfunctional?"

"Uh . . . what?"

"Forget it," she says around another bite. "Jules will tell you when she comes out of her room, the scaredy-cat. As for me, I'm here because I hit a rough patch."

"What happened to your arm?"

She pauses mid-bite and looks up at me. "A rough patch. Literally. I biffed it while hiking for a job in some really rough Scottish landscape and broke the shit out of my shoulder."

"Yeesh. Are you okay?"

"Splendid," she says. "Thrilled to be home."

I roll my eyes. "How long *are* you home?"

She shrugs her good shoulder. "Long enough to nurse a badly broken shoulder and recoup my income. Photojournalism with only your nondominant hand at your disposal is pretty impossible. And without photojournalism work, I don't have money. And without money, I don't have anywhere to live—before you say it, *no*, staying with Mom and Dad is not an option. I love them, but no."

"Ah. Now we're getting somewhere."

"Can I crash with you?" she says, a note of pleading in her voice. "I can't afford to split rent yet, but I'll take the sofa. Clean up after myself. I've got some photography friends here who I'm sure will pay me to do edits, enough that I can help with groceries and utilities until I figure out what's next."

"Of course, Kate. You know you're welcome here."

"Cool." She polishes off a row of breakfast casserole and starts in on the next. "So, what's going on with you? Mom said you and your boyfriend are on a break?"

Tears fill my eyes. Just thinking about Jamie hurts.

"Ah shit," she groans. "You're crying. Don't cry."

I wipe away my tears and try to smile, try to do what I have the past few weeks, which is focus on the good, even when my heart says nothing can be good without Jamie in my life.

But here's my sister, a splash of freckles on her skin and auburn streaking her hair from all that time in the sun, her threadbare clothes and banged-up body. I've missed her. Missing her tangles with missing Jamie. I'm a chestful of hot, sharp missing. "KitKat, have I told you you're a sight for sore eyes?"

She narrows her eyes and sniffles suspiciously. "Knock it off, Bee-Bee. Don't make me emotional."

I hug her hard, careful of her shoulder. "I need someone to join me. All I am is emotional."

"Why?" She pulls away, frowning at me.

Tears blur my vision as I try to hold back the need to cry. "How much do you know?"

"Nothing, beyond Mom saying your boyfriend was friends with the douche canoe who hurt Jules. So things were understandably tricky right now."

"'Tricky' is an understatement. That douche canoe did a lot of damage. He hurt Jules. He hurt Christopher. It was awful."

"Hmm," she says, stabbing the casserole. "I'm sure Christopher will land on his feet."

"One day, it would be lovely if you two shared a hemisphere not charged with electric hatred."

"That will be in another life," she mutters around her food. "I'd like to keep my appetite, so let's move on. Get me up to speed about your guy."

I tell her between sips of coffee and nose blows. Then I slump over the counter, thumping my forehead against it. "I'm so screwed and stuck and confused. I don't know when Jules will be past this, and until then, there's no way Jamie and I can be together. But . . . I miss him so much."

Kate frowns thoughtfully. "Yeah, that's a shitty corner to be backed into. But I will say, I don't like how he walked out on you. He shouldn't have turned a break into a breakup."

I shake my head. "No, he had a point, and I didn't recognize that. I got defensive and—"

"Lost your cool," she finishes for me. "I can see that."

I glare up at her. "First of all, look in the mirror, Miss Hothead."

Kate scoffs.

"I didn't say it *gently*. He's been through a bad breakup, KitKat, with someone who made him feel . . . disposable. Telling him he'd have to take a number and wait to hear from me, I made him feel that way all over again."

She grimaces. "Ouch."

"Yeah. I messed up," I whisper through tears. "I've wanted to call him a hundred times, but it seems so pointless to say, *Hey, sorry I treated you that way, but I'm still going to ask you to be on standby for now.*"

"That sucks, BeeBee. I'm sorry."

"Me, too." I stare down at my hands. And that's when I realize I've been clutching this envelope ever since Kate shoved it at me and blasted her way in. My heart takes off at a gallop as I read the single word scrawled across it:

Beatrice.

"What is it?" Kate asks.

"This envelope . . . That's Jamie's handwriting."

She leans my way. "Well, don't just stare at it. Read it."

"Can you give me a smidge of space?"

"Sure." She steps back. "My bad. My suitcase and I will just wander over to the couch and mind our own business."

"Thanks."

I stare at his handwriting. Then I tear open the envelope and stare some more. Letters neat as always, a bit jagged at the edges. A tear slips down my cheek as I read.

Bea,

It's taken me too many days to realize what you were asking wasn't easy for you to ask, but it was necessary to care for someone you love. What you asked for hurt, but just because something hurts doesn't mean it's wrong—it just means it's hard. What I should have said was that while it was going to hurt to wait, I understood.

That's a lot of words for what I've meant to say since I started writing this, so I'll say it now: I love you and I'll wait for you. However long it takes.

Always yours,
Jamie

"Okay over there?" Kate calls.

I clutch the note to my chest and ugly cry. "No."

Groaning, Kate pushes off the couch, then sidles up next to me, giving me stiff pats on my back that I think are supposed to be comforting before she pries the note from my hands.

"Be careful with it!"

"Cool your tits. Just let me see what he has to say for himself." Her eyes scan it quickly. "Damn. The dude can pen a letter. Short, sweet, and swoony."

I take back the note and wipe away the tears streaking my cheeks. "Yeah. And I have no idea what to do."

Kate gently squeezes my shoulder. "BeeBee. It'll work out."

"How?"

"Hey," Jules says. She shuts her bedroom door behind her and rolls a suitcase down the hallway in her wake.

I stare at my sister, who is looking much more like her old self than she has in weeks—dark hair lying in soft waves, the shadows under her eyes hidden with concealer. She wears a royal-blue dress that makes her eyes pop and her favorite black high heels. She looks ready to take on the world. Which makes no sense, seeing as she was in the fetal position, sobbing in my arms last night.

"Where are you going?" I ask.

Her expression is as close as she's come to a smile in weeks. "On a trip."

Kate seems surprisingly unsurprised.

"Did you know about this?" I ask her.

My younger sister pointedly avoids my eyes, suddenly very intrigued by the newspaper sitting on the counter.

"BeeBee." Jules takes my hand and threads our fingers together. "I'm going to miss you. What are you going to do without me sticking my nose in your business?"

"Stop it. You already apologized. I forgave you, JuJu."

"I know," she says, swallowing through tears. "But I still feel shitty about it. I shouldn't have pushed you. I'll always be in your corner, and I'll probably always fuss and worry more than I should, but you know your own path to happiness. I shouldn't have tried to make it for you."

I wipe tears from my eyes with the back of my hand, Jamie's note still clutched tight in my grip. "But why do you have to go?" I whisper. "Why now? And where?"

She smiles around her tears. "Because I *want* to. Because it's time. The universe says so. Kate had a place lined up for the next few weeks, but now with her accident, she's no longer using it. So that's where I'm starting, the-middle-of-nowhere Scotland, and I'll go from there."

My eyes blur with more tears. "I can't believe you're leaving. We've never lived apart."

"It's weird, I know. I'll miss you. But you won't be alone for long. You have Kate. And you have West. He's so perfect for you, Bea. I know I went about it the wrong way, but I'm glad it still gave you the right person."

"Jules—"

"Be happy," she whispers, kissing my cheek and throwing her arms around me. "Because when I come back, I will be, too. So you better be ready."

I wrap my arms around my twin, feeling our hearts beat against each other's chests. Same height. Same hard grip when we clutch each other. "I love you," I tell her. "I'm sorry everything ended—"

"Awfully?" she says through a teary laugh. "Me, too. But good fodder for the novel I've always wanted to write. That's what Grandma said—'You have nothing to say, Juliet, because nothing's happened.'"

"Grandma was harsh sometimes," Kate says.

Jules nods. "But I think she was right. Now, get over here and hug me goodbye."

Reluctantly, Kate curls her good arm around us both, towering over us and tugging us close. "Nothing like a good five-minute Wilmot sister reunion."

My twin's teary laugh echoes inside our little sister cocoon. "Love you both," she whispers.

Then, like a Band-Aid being ripped off, she shrugs on her coat and powers out the door. It thuds behind us, and I hear her thumping with her suitcase down the steps. Sprinting, I make it to my bed and rip open the curtains just in time. "Jules!" I yell, yanking open the window.

She squints up at me, taxi door open. "Goodbye!" she yells, trying hard to smile. "Parting is such sweet sorrow!"

I laugh through the tears as the door shuts and her cab disappears down the road.

Kate walks in slowly, looking as hesitant and allergic to tears as ever. "All cried out?"

"I guess," I croak, before blowing my nose.

She drops onto the edge of my bed, making me bounce. "I'm going to get unpacked. Mind if I take her room until you find a roommate?"

"I'm not getting a roommate, you weirdo. Obviously, you'll take her bed. Just pay what you can toward rent. We'll make it work."

Kate pats my thigh. "Thanks, BeeBee."

I swallow fresh tears. "Ugh. This is so weird. She's not supposed to leave."

"She's supposed to do whatever makes her happy and allows her to live a fulfilling life. Same for you. Why don't you take your mind off things, go sit somewhere and sketch. Clock some hours at work. Draw clandestine clitorises. Sell smutty cards."

"Can't," I tell her. "Store's closed for the holiday. Tonight's the Friendsgiving party."

"Friendsgiving?" Kate perks up. "Sounds like lots of good food. When do we leave?"

"I—" My voice dies off abruptly. Reality hits me.

I can see Jamie now. I can fix things with him. Jules is gone, safe from any sadness and pain that seeing us together would cause. What am I doing here, crying in my pajamas?

I push off the bed and am halfway to the closet when a text pops up on my phone. Scrambling back, I unearth it from the sheets, because what if it's Jamie?

But it's not.

> Is Kate really back or is your mom just messing with me again? It's been a while since she pranked me.

"Who is it?" Kate asks.

"Christopher," I mumble, tossing aside my phone, then darting into my closet. He'll just have to wait for an answer. I don't have time for anything but getting myself in Jamie's arms as soon as humanly possible.

Kate wrinkles her nose. "Will he be there? At Friendsgiving?"

"Yep!" I call from the closet.

"Ew. Never mind. I'll eat leftover breakfast casserole."

"Sure." I'm distracted, heart pounding. Inside my closet, I rip off my pajamas, drag on Jamie's sweatshirt that I stole and a thick pair of warm leggings.

"I don't recognize *that* sweatshirt," she says as I dart into the bathroom and frantically brush my teeth.

"Mm-hmm," I answer her absently, splashing my face with cold water and quickly running a brush through my hair, fixing my bangs.

"I think I'll go outside," Kate says, "and wear my underwear on my head, singing 'Yankee Doodle Dandy.'"

"Uh-huh." I rush back into my room, hopping into socks, stomping into my untied Doc Martens. "Gotcha."

Kate watches me with an amused smile as I tug on my jacket and grab my phone. "I'm assuming this mad dash has to do with that lovely little note you got. And the person whose sweatshirt you're wearing."

"Jamie," I say breathlessly. Unlocking my phone, I text him the way we started, no preamble, no flowery greeting. A chess joke. The corniest one yet. I hope it makes him smile. I hope it tells him everything he needs to know. That I got his note; that I'm sorry, too; that we're free to be together.

That I can't take another minute not running headlong toward him.

"Wish me luck!" I tell Kate as I sprint out of the room.

I barely catch her voice before I drag the door shut: "Good luck!"

———

Running is generally an unwise choice for me. Especially when my shoelaces are untied. But I don't care. I sprint down the sidewalk, cold air burning my lungs, sun-gold, bronze, and amber leaves swept into the autumn wind, nature's confetti swirling around me.

I'm one block away, my boots thudding into the ground, when the door to his building whips open.

Jamie. Sprinting toward me, totally disheveled. Tall and straight-backed, arms pumping. Perfect running form, I'm sure. And yet his buttons are one off, his glasses halfway down his nose. The waves of his hair are wet and loose, wild in the wind.

I don't stop as we get close. I leap at him the way I did that night at the Alley. Our bodies collide, and my heart clatters like bowling pins with the strike of our kiss. It's a *never forget this* kiss. A *best kiss of my life* kiss. An *I always want to kiss only you* kiss.

"Bea," he whispers against my mouth. His arms lock around me.

"Jamie." My hands are in his hair, cupping his face. I study him reverently, tracing the sharp, handsome planes of his face. The lines of his jaw, his cheekbones, his nose. The soft part of his mouth. The heat burning in his hazel eyes.

"I'm sorry," I tell him through tears. I kiss his forehead, his cupid's bow, the corner of his mouth. I want to kiss all of him and never stop. "I never meant to hurt you. I'm sorry for how I said it, how I asked for time—"

"Don't be," he says quietly. "I told you in my note, I understand now."

Our eyes meet. He's the most beautiful thing I've ever seen, until I can't see him anymore. The world is blurry as tears flood my vision.

"I missed you," I whisper, wiping my eyes.

His face warms with a soft, just-for-me smile. "I missed you, too," he says quietly. My patient, gentle Jamie, kissing my forehead, breathing me in. "So much. What's changed? Is Juliet—"

"She'll be okay," I whisper. "She's on a trip. Nothing's keeping us apart. Not now, not anymore. Never again."

Relief gusts out of him. "God, Bea." He kisses me, deep and slow, pained with wonder. I hold him so hard, I hope I imprint on his skin. I want him to wear me forever. I want him to be mine always.

"I love you," I tell him, because I can't keep it in one more moment. "I love you so fucking much."

"I know you do." He kisses me softly this time, breathing me in. "I knew that even before you said it. I'm sorry I doubted you."

"I didn't tell you," I whisper through tears. "Because I have never loved someone like I love you, Jamie, and it scares the shit out of me. But you deserve to hear it. You deserve to hear what I was about to tell you when everything blew up on Halloween: that I love you. That I want to kiss you when no one's watching and paint you for my eyes only. That I want to cuddle under my weighted blanket and watch snow fall and laugh about the weirdest things. Because you are exquisitely precious to me. You are everything I want, just as you are, no conditions or clauses, no end date or revenge, just you."

Jamie crushes me to his chest in a fierce hug, his mouth pressing sweet, soft kisses down my temple, my cheek, the bridge of my nose, and finally, my lips. When he pulls away, he tucks a lock of hair behind my ear. Our eyes search each other's as he tells me, "I have an answer to your riddle."

I bite my lip, remembering what I texted him. "And?" I ask shyly.

"Ah, not so fast." He slides his thumb along my bottom lip, freeing it from my teeth. "First you have to repeat it."

"It's so corny! Fine. Okay." I clear my throat, then repeat, "What did the lovers call each other when they played chess?"

His thumb trails lower, along my jaw as he kisses me. "Check*mates*."

"I'm surprised you came running *toward* me, not away, after that," I tell him.

"Just further testament to how much I love you." He sweeps me like a bride into his arms, making me squeal with delight.

"Where are we going?"

"My bed," he says. "Then the sofa. Then the shower. I'm feeling adventurous: maybe even a closet. We seem to do well in those."

"Ooh, a closet."

When we're inside his place, Jamie kicks the door shut, then walks us to his bedroom and shuts that door, too, turning the world soft and quiet. Sliding down his body, I step closer so I can see him and feel him and know he's real. He's here. He's mine.

Slowly, he peels off my jacket, tossing it aside. He meets my mouth with a gentle kiss that grows deeper, that promises more. Today. Tomorrow. Forever.

"Bea." His nose nuzzles my cheek, followed by a kiss. "You're so beautiful."

"So are you," I whisper. "Even if I almost didn't recognize you. You have wrinkles in your clothes."

"My phone went off while I was in the shower." Another slow, deep kiss. "Then I saw it was you. Which led to the world's fastest wardrobe change."

"My precious Capricorn." I straighten his collar. "You still ironed your underwear, didn't you?"

"I've *never* ironed my underwear, you gremlin."

"Did you know," I ask, as Jamie walks us back to his bed, sitting, then drawing me onto his lap, "that Cancers and Capricorns are ideal pairings?"

"Yes," he says, taking my hand and kissing my palm, slipping his fingertips beneath my sweatshirt, grazing my stomach, my waist. "Because they are opposing signs, they share a strong complementary attraction."

"Wow. First the wrinkles. Now you know your zodiac. Who are you?"

"The same man who loved you the last time he saw you and is so damn glad he's holding you now. I'm really holding you," he says, kissing my throat, cupping my breasts. I suck in a breath and squirm on his lap, where he's hard and thick inside his pants.

"You are," I tell him faintly. "And I love you. Did I mention that?"

His crooked grin fills my heart to the glittering brim, tints the world luscious, in-love lavender. "You did." My sweatshirt is peeled off, my body pressed back onto the bed. "But I'll listen to you say it all day long."

"I love you." I watch him remove his glasses, his button-up; yank a tight white undershirt over the back of his head and toss it aside. Watch him slip off my boots, then my socks, drag my leggings down my body. Marvel as he shucks his shoes and pants and briefs, as he crawls over me and presses our bodies together.

"Again," he says roughly, his breath hot on my neck as he kisses me, tastes me, the clean warmth of his skin heating mine, making me shiver. "Tell me again."

"I love you."

"How much?" His hands weigh my breasts, thumbs teasing my nipples. His kiss is harder, possessive. The man he is only for me, only with me.

"Hmm . . ." I bite my lip as he kisses his way down my body. "I love you a . . . reasonable amount."

His head pops up. He frowns. "*Reasonable.*"

"Mm-hmm." I'm teasing him, and he knows it. He knows how much I love him. I've told him. And now I've shown him. I'm here in his arms, and I'm never leaving them again.

His eyes narrow, but his mouth twitches like he's fighting a smile. "Beatrice."

"James?"

"Don't tease me." His hand slides along my hip, then curves lower.

"Or what?" I whisper coyly. "I'll earn myself another one of those 'love taps'?"

A low groan rumbles in his throat. Then in one smooth motion, he flips me on my stomach, hoists up my hips. His palm lands on a swift, sweet smack of my ass that makes me moan like I'm dying. If you can die of pleasure, I just have.

"That's what you needed, hmm?" he says, kissing his way up my back, his hand smoothing my ass, warming it.

I nod feverishly. "More."

"We'll see." His voice is rough, but his mouth is sweet, his touch sweeter, coaxing from me a sharp, glorious orgasm. I'm still dazed with bliss as I hear him behind me, stroking himself with lube before he eases himself inside on one slow roll of his hips. We both gasp when I'm filled with every inch of him.

"I love you," I whisper through tears, through joy that's a sunrise in my soul.

I'm spun again, his body plunging into mine, his arms around me. "Bea." His voice is hoarse, his hands finding mine and linking them together over my head. "Mon cœur."

The bed creaks. Air flies out of me as he takes me, with each deep stroke that sends pleasure racing through me, hot, shivering, sharp and needy between my thighs, aching in my breasts. Everywhere we touch and taste, sharing breath and pleas and promises.

The ache inside me coils tighter, leads me to a height so high I'm as terrified as I am thrilled to know that soon I'll fall.

I lock my legs around his waist, feel his rhythm falter, feel him swell inside me.

"Come for me, Bea." His teeth graze my throat, chased by a long, hot kiss. "That's it, sweetheart. Come for me."

As I bow off the bed and shatter, free-fall, soar, Jamie follows me.

———

"Your Pine-Sol tea, sir." I set Jamie's cat-shaped teacup on the nightstand, my matching coffee mug beside his.

He smiles up at me, still shirtless, hair mussed, glistening with sweat, a flush on his cheeks. A portrait I'll paint titled *Satisfied*.

Thinking of that reminds me—

"Where are you going?" he says. His voice is low and quiet and a little rough, how I'm starting to learn it turns when he wants me.

I glance over my shoulder from my bent-over position, rifling through my jacket for my phone. "I have something to show you."

"Whatever it is, it can't top my current view."

Smiling, I stand and tug down his undershirt, which I'm wearing and which barely covers my butt. "I don't know about that."

I leap onto the mattress, straddling his lap, and give Jamie a slow, hot kiss. "Here. For you."

He squints at the photo on my phone's screen. A close-up of a canvas still mounted to an easel in my studio at home. Carefully reaching past me, Jamie slips on his glasses so he can see it better. His eyes scour the painting, his face drawn tight with emotion. "Bea."

I slip off his lap and nestle in beside him as he wraps an arm around me. "I've been working on it for weeks. It's based on Grace's photo at Paint to Your Heart's Content, but I exerted some creative license. Instead of standing, we're sitting over a chessboard, which is for—"

"Our first date, of course," he says.

"In the background, beside the storefront of Paint to Your Heart's Content, the karaoke bar, the tattoo parlor, and the Alley for the most embarrassing night of my life."

Jamie laughs. "I just remember kneeling at your feet before we left, lacing up your boots." His eyes meet mine. "I didn't want to get up."

I blush spectacularly and press my thighs together, remembering how talented Jamie is with his tongue, his hands, his everything. "Stop tempting me. I'm being romantic."

"I love it," he says, sneaking a kiss before he studies the image again. His smile returns. "I'll finally have my own Beatrice Wilmot original."

"The first of many."

His grin is so deliriously wide it makes my heart sing. "What's it called?" he asks.

"*Two Wrongs Make a Right.*"

Jamie slowly lowers my phone. He blinks. Then blinks again, before he dabs the corner of his eye. That's when I realize what's happening.

My heart drops to the floor.

"Jamie? I made you cry. I'm so sorry—"

"Come here, you," he says, curling me tight in his grasp, setting my phone on the nightstand next to him. "Don't be sorry," he murmurs as he nuzzles me. "It's just those pesky fall allergies again."

Relief washes through me. "So mine isn't the only place with an astronomical indoor pollen count."

He laughs softly, then clears his throat, dabs his nose. I reach past him, looking for tissues, but don't see any on the nightstand or when I visually search the room.

"Be right back," I tell him, running toward the small storage closet in his hallway. I throw open the door and reach on tiptoe for the shelf that has tissue boxes, lined up in color-coded order, of course. That's when I feel him—that warm, tall body close behind mine, the glorious scent of cool, foggy mornings. Just like that first night in another closet, close and dark, our breaths echoing in the small space.

"You can't honestly run off in nothing but my shirt that barely covers this"—he says it in rich, soft French—"beau cul of yours and not expect me to follow."

I smile, turning and facing Jamie just as the door slips shut behind him and he crowds me, then lifts me onto a shelf. "I was just getting you tissues."

"I don't need tissues. I need you," he grumbles against my neck, trailing kisses across my collarbone, pressing my thighs apart, pulling me close until I feel how hot and hard and ready he is.

"Again?" I whisper.

"Again. And again. I'll always need you." He wraps my legs around his waist as I clutch his shoulders.

His kisses tease my throat, my breasts. I drop my head back in pleasure and smack it on the shelf. "Shit."

Jamie rubs the back of my head, cupping it in his big hand as he presses a kiss to my temple. "All right. No closet sex after all."

"It's a little bump on the head, not a concussion," I whine, tightening my grip around his waist.

"Considering I'm the physician, Beatrice, I'll be the one making diagnoses." He hikes me higher in his arms and kisses me before I can argue further. "Now, open that door."

Pouting, I reach around him for the door handle, then pretend to not be able to turn it, jiggling it for extra dramatic effect. "Damn. It's stuck. Guess we'll just have to stay here and have sex after all."

His smile is soft and amused. "That would certainly be poetic," he says, "seeing as this all started with us locked in a storage closet, and it is rather cozy away from all those meddling fools, the nosy, noisy outside world. But"—he reaches behind me and easily turns the knob—"I think we've proven we can hold our own out there, don't you?"

"Yes," I tell him as he walks us down the hallway, whispering kisses over his beautiful, dear face. "I do."

Jamie smiles and holds me close, heart to heart. His kisses whisper love. His arms are home.

If this is wrong, I will live long and happily never being right.

· ACKNOWLEDGMENTS ·

I figured when the time came to write acknowledgments for this book, this dream come true wouldn't still feel like a fantastical figment of my imagination: that the romance novel I wrote, marrying my lit-nerd love of Shakespeare and my conviction that we need stories affirming *everyone's* worthiness of happily ever after, somehow found its way into the heart of an agent, then an editor and a publisher, and will soon, I dearly hope, find its way into the hearts of readers, too.

It still feels like a dream.

So while I keep pinching myself, I want to express my deepest thanks to my stellar literary agent, Samantha Fabien, who loved Jamie and Bea from page one, whose heart for inclusivity in romance stole *my* heart, and who has made me feel beyond supported, heard, and advocated for. Thank you to Kristine Swartz, editor extraordinaire, for your enthusiasm for *Two Wrongs*, for believing in Jamie and Bea's story, for supporting my voice and my vision for romance that champions everyone's worthiness of love, for your wisdom and guidance that's shaped this story into its best self. Thank you also to everyone at Berkley who has worked on and supported this book, through design, editing, publicity, marketing, and beyond.

Thank you to my dear friends who I've found through my love of romance reading and writing. Helen Hoang, there aren't adequate words to express how much your books, friendship, guidance, and support mean to me—you're a gem, and I treasure you. Mazey Eddings and Megan Stillwell, my neurodivine queens, thank you for coming alongside me on this journey with lots of laughs, coordinated comfy clothes, Airbnb adventures, and so much love. Elizabeth Everett, Rachel Lynn

Solomon, Sarah Hogle, Sarah Grunder Ruiz, and Sarah Adams: each in your own way, you've cheered me on and offered wisdom as I dipped my toes into the world of traditional publishing, then took the plunge, and I'm so thankful for your friendship. So many more wonderful author and reader friends, I hope you know how much you mean to me: your kindness and support are gifts that I'll never take for granted.

Thank you to my family and friends in the everyday, not-so-bookish part of my life. You love me for who I am—someone who nearly always has one foot in a story she's writing or reading, the other in the world we share. You humor me when I ramble about tropes and first kisses and all those ideas for my next novel. You mourn my disappointments and celebrate my victories, and I'm so grateful to have you in my life.

To my two firecracker kids, you are the best things I will ever give this world. Thank you for stretching my heart and curiosity and putting a fire under my derrière to make the world a kinder place. I hope if you ever read my books (If you do, let's make that wayyy down the road, yeah?) that you will be proud of me, that you will recognize in my writing what I hope and dream for you: lives built on healthy self-understanding and self-love, on the love of friends, family, found family—and yes, one day, a romantic partner, if your heart so desires—who adore you for *all* of who you are, who want to learn you and wrap their arms around you and with whom you are safe and fully known.

Finally, to anyone out there whose brain and/or body, like mine, makes existing in this wild world just that much trickier, who feels relegated to the periphery more often than not, who's been hurt or misunderstood or overlooked, who questions whether or how they can belong: you belong, and we need you. I know we have a way to go in being the inclusive, accessible, empathic society that we need to be, but it is my deepest belief that we are going to get there. For me, compassionate fiction that doesn't shy away from human struggle while holding tight to hope is a comforting place to go while we wait, while change is made in too-tiny increments. I hope, if you're waiting like me, that in some small way this story has been a safe space for you, to see folks with struggles and vulnerabilities maybe a little like yours find loving belonging for exactly who they are. I hope that stories like mine and so many others, which endeavor to open people's hearts to empathize and reach out and make room at the table, make a difference— that one day, true inclusivity won't be the exception but the rule, that we'll feel right at home, welcome in the very heart of life's story.

· DISCUSSION QUESTIONS ·

1. If you're familiar with Shakespeare's *Much Ado About Nothing*, what are some parallels and departures that you noticed between the original text and this modern reimagining in plot, themes, character names, and relationships? If you aren't familiar with *Much Ado*, do you now find yourself curious to read it or watch a film adaptation?*

2. This story features a neurodivergent couple: Beatrice is on the autism spectrum, and Jamie has anxiety. What was it like for you to see the world through their eyes? For those who aren't neurodivergent, do you feel it has impacted how you might perceive and engage people who identify as neurodivergent? Are there some ways you relate to Jamie's and Bea's experiences?

3. In both *Much Ado* and *Two Wrongs Make a Right*, we have two main couples in love: Jean-Claude and Juliet (in the original play, Claudio and Hero), and Jamie and Bea (Benedick and Beatrice). In both stories, their relationships follow very different paths. What do you think is the commentary on what makes for healthy partnership and love in how differently Jean-Claude and Juliet's relationship progresses from Jamie and Bea's? If you're familiar with *Much Ado*, what do you think is the commentary on modern expectations for relationships in how different Jean-Claude and Juliet's relationship arc is from that of their parallel characters?

4. At first, Bea and Jamie seem like *very* different people, but they end up discovering a deeply compatible partnership. Do you think this is because they're more similar than dissimilar, or because they appreciate and complement each other's differences? Some of both? Have you had close friends or partners who are very different from you? What brought you together and connected you?

5. Irony abounds in both *Much Ado* and *Two Wrongs*. In *Much Ado*, Benedick and Beatrice are tricked by their friends into overhearing their rehearsed discussions of the other's feelings for them, but the irony is, while the specifics of what their friends say are lies, this deception leads Benedick and Beatrice to recognize the truth: they *do* have feelings for each other; they've just been terrified to admit or act on them. What do you think are the parallel situation(s) and irony in *Two Wrongs*?

6. In their friendships and family relationships, Bea and Jamie navigate complex dynamics. What do you think of Bea's relationship with her twin sister, Juliet, and its arc throughout the story? Of Jamie's relationship with his family and Jean-Claude?

7. Themes of right and wrong and making moral judgments come up a lot in this story. Do you think the friend group as well as Jules and Jean-Claude were wrong to meddle with Jamie's and Bea's love lives? Were Jamie and Bea wrong to plot revenge and to try to deceive them all in retaliation? Do how these relationships progressed and how the story ended shape your judgment of what was right and wrong of them to do?

*I cannot recommend enough the film adaptation of *Much Ado About Nothing* (1993), starring Emma Thompson, Kenneth Branagh, Denzel Washington, Keanu Reeves, Kate Beckinsale, and many more incredible actors. It's an all-time favorite and is sure to bring Shakespeare's language accessibly and vividly to life for modern viewers, while also making you belly laugh and fall in love.

Turn the page for a preview of

Better Hate than Never

Kate

My life has come to this: all my worldly possessions shoved into one trusty, albeit three-wheeled and wobbly, suitcase; seven dollars and fifty-nine cents in my bank account; and zero idea of what comes next.

This is what I get for heeding my monthly horoscope.

As the stars align, your path shifts. Change creates new chances. Old wounds offer wisdom. Your future awaits. The question is: are you brave enough to embrace it?

That damn horoscope.

Starfished on my sister Juliet's bed, I stare at my reflection in the nearby standing mirror and ask it, "What were you thinking?"

My reflection arches an eyebrow as if to say, *You're asking* me?

Groaning, I paw around the mattress until I find my dinged-up but still operational phone, then swipe it open to turn on music. It's too quiet in here and my thoughts are too loud.

Moments later, a song from my aptly named playlist GET UR SHIT 2GETHER fills the room. But it doesn't help—not even the most high-octane feminist anthem can change the fact that I am so prone to act first, think later, so easily goaded by a challenge, that one minor family crisis coinciding with a taunting horoscope, and look where I've landed myself.

Home, where I haven't been in nearly two years, or stayed for longer than a week at a time since I graduated college. Specifically, in my older sister Juliet's room while she flies over the Atlantic, headed for a stay in the quaint Highlands cottage I've been renting. A cottage, I quickly realized after breaking my shoulder and having to pass on my usual photojournalism gigs, that I couldn't afford (neither budgeting nor saving has ever been my forte).

I had a rental cottage I couldn't pay for, and my sister Juliet needed a change of scenery. Swapping places was a no-brainer at the time. Now, lying in my sisters' apartment, left alone to contemplate my choices, I'm not so sure.

As if she knows my thoughts are spiraling, my phone lights up with a text from Beatrice, my other older sister and Juliet's twin. I can feel her happiness in a few simple sentences, and a wave of calm crests through me, a reassuring reminder—I made the right decision in coming home.

> **BEEBEE:** Hey, KitKat. I'm really sry for dashing off so soon after you got here. I know you get why I needed to talk to Jamie right away, but I'll come back tonight & we can spend time together, OK?

I bite my lip, thinking through how to respond. Neither Bea nor Jules knows how much *I* know about the predicament they were in or the solution made possible by my return. That's because my sisters don't know Mom spilled the tea on our monthly phone check-in and told me everything I'd missed:

Juliet and her fiancé had matchmade Bea and Jamie, the fiancé's childhood friend. The fiancé turned out to be a toxic piece of trash, and Jules ended their relationship. Even though Jamie also cut out the piece of trash, Bea brought their relationship to a halt because she knew Jamie would be a painful reminder for Jules. Until Jules was in a better emotional place, Bea felt that, even though it crushed her, they had to stay apart.

As I listened to my mother explain what a pickle my siblings had gotten themselves into, her voice's speed and pitch escalating in tandem with her worry, I realized that for once I *wanted* to come home. I *wanted* to be of help. Even more bizarre, I felt like I could.

The solution I offered required a few . . . untruths. But they were worth it. Small lies of omission. Harmless, really.

Harmless, huh? Just like that horoscope? My reflection gives me a skeptical glance.

I flip it off, then refocus on my phone, typing a response to Bea.

> **KITKAT:** If you dare show your face tonight, BeeBee, I will spin you right around & send you back where you came from.
>
> **BEEBEE:** I just don't want you to be alone your first night home 😞.

A sigh leaves me, even as a twinge of affection pinches my chest. Older sisters.

> **KITKAT:** News flash, I like being alone. I get to eat all the food Mom stuck in the fridge & dance around naked to Joan Jett.
>
> **BEEBEE:** News flash, you'd do that with me around anyway.

I snort a laugh and roll off the bed, wandering out of Juliet's room into the hallway.

> **KITKAT:** I'll be fine. Seriously.
>
> **BEEBEE:** You're sure?
>
> **KITKAT:** Yes! I promise.
>
> **BEEBEE:** You could always go to Mom & Dad's for some company?

I scowl at my phone, picturing the man who lives next door to my childhood home, who's been a source of misery for as long as I can remember.

I will not go to my parents' and risk bumping into Christopher Petruchio—long-standing nemesis, bane of my existence, asshole of epic magnitude—because the universe is a jerk, and whenever possible, I always have the misfortune of bumping into Christopher.

> **KITKAT:** I'm good. Now get off the phone & go bang your boyfriend's lights out.
>
> **BEEBEE:** Done & doner.
>
> **BEEBEE:** OH! I forgot. Cornelius needs his dinner. Would you mind feeding him? His meal is in a container in the minifridge, labeled for today.

I peer into Bea's bedroom and spy her pet hedgehog waddling around his elaborate screened-in living structure. A smile tugs at my mouth as he perks up and his little nose wiggles, sniffing the air. I'm an animal lover, and while I've never looked after a hedgehog, I'm not worried about being able to handle it.

> **KITKAT:** No problem.
>
> **BEEBEE:** Thank you so much!!
>
> **KITKAT:** You're welcome. Now STOP TEXTING & GET BANGING.
>
> **BEEBEE:** FINE! IF I MUST!

I shove my phone into my back pocket and slump against the hallway, scrubbing my face. I'm jet-lagged, my system heavy with exhaustion yet humming with energy. I can't stand when I'm tired yet hyped, but such is life. Just because my body's wiped out doesn't mean my brain gets the memo.

Moaning pathetically, I traipse through the living room, then flop onto the sofa just as my phone buzzes again. I reach inside my pocket and yank it out.

> **BEEBEE:** Wait, just one more thing!

> **BEEBEE:** In case you change your mind, a reminder that the Friendsgiving party I told you about is 4–8. There'll be PUMPKIN PIE.

I roll my eyes as I swipe open the screen, then type my response. Yes, my weakness is pumpkin pie. But my hatred of Christopher, who will be there, is much stronger.

> **KITKAT:** Not a chance in hell, BeeBee. But nice try.

———————

Okay, so maybe my dependence on pumpkin pie is a *smidge* stronger than I care to admit.

Not so strong that I've decided to swing by the Friendsgiving party and chance seeing Christopher. Instead, there's Nanette's, a kick-ass bakery that I'm headed to, located a handful of blocks from the apartment. After some slight (read: thirty minutes of) social media scrolling, I discovered Nanette's was having a flash sale this evening on pumpkin pies—buy one, get one half off.

I might have seven dollars and fifty-nine cents in my bank account, but I do have a credit card for extenuating circumstances that I'm prepared to use. Thankfully, I don't have to—I found an envelope on the kitchen counter with my name on it in Mom's loopy cursive and five twenty-dollar bills inside. Not even the prick to my pride, that my mother had both inferred and fussed over my rocky financial status, could stop me from snatching up two twenties and powering out the door.

Clearly, the universe intends for me to have some pumpkin pie after all.

Strolling down the sidewalk toward my destination, I bask in a bracing November wind that whisks dried autumn leaves along the concrete in tumbling, percussive swirls. My WALK IT OFF playlist blasts in my headphones and I feel a swell of happiness. Fresh air. Two whole pumpkin pies, all to myself. No Friendsgiving required. No having to face—

Slam.

I collide with someone just as I round the corner of the block, my forehead knocking into what feels like a concrete ledge but is more likely the other person's jaw, followed by their hard sternum jamming my sore shoulder. I hiss in pain as I stumble back.

A hand wraps around my other arm to steady me, and its warmth seeps through my jacket. I glance up, assessing if I'm under threat, but we're caught in a shadowy patch of the sidewalk, late-evening darkness swallowing up our features.

Before I can panic, the strength of their grip eases, as if they've sensed I stopped wobbling. As if whoever this is understands something about me that I don't feel anyone ever has: that while I am fiercely independent, sometimes I want nothing more than a caring hand to catch me when I falter and just as freely let me go when I'm steady once more.

The rumble of a voice dances across my skin, making every hair on my body stand on end. I yank off my headphones so I can hear them clearly.

" . . . so sorry," is what I catch.

Two words. That's all it takes. Even if they're two words I've never heard him say before, they're all I need to recognize a voice that I know as well as my own.

Fiery anger blazes through me. Not because my shoulder's throbbing, though it is. Not because my head feels like a bell that's been rung, though it does. But because the person who I've been trying to outrun is the very person I just ran into:

Christopher Petruchio.

"What the *hell*, Christopher?" I wrench my arm out of his grip, stepping back and stumbling into the reach of the streetlamp's glow.

"Kate?" His eyes widen, wind whipping his dark hair, sending his scent my way, a scent I'd give anything to forget. Some criminally expensive cologne evoking the woodsy warmth of a fireside nap, the spiced smoke of just-blown-out candles. Resentment twists my stomach.

Every time I see him, it's a fresh, terrible kick to the gut. All the specifics that have blurred, carved once again into vivid detail. The striking planes of his face—strong nose, chiseled jaw, sharp cheekbones, that mouth that's genetically designed to make knees weak.

Not mine, of course. And strictly objectively speaking, merely from a professional standpoint. As a photographer, I spend a lot of time analyzing photogenic faces, and Christopher's is unfortunately the epitome. Slightly asymmetrical, the roughness of his severe features smoothed by thick-lashed amber eyes, the lazy sensuality of that dark hair always falling into his face.

God, just looking at him makes my blood boil. "What are you doing here?" I snap.

He rubs a hand along the side of his face, eyes narrowed. "Thank you for asking, Katerina. My jaw is fine, despite your hard head—"

"What a relief," I say with false cheer, cutting him off. I'm too tired and sore to spar with him. "Though if you'd simply been where you're supposed to be, we wouldn't have had this collision in the first place."

He arches an eyebrow. " 'Where I'm supposed to be'?"

A flush creeps up my cheeks. I hate my telltale flush. "The Friendsgiving thing."

Christopher's mouth tips with a smirk that makes my flush darken. "Been keeping tabs on me, have you?"

"Solely to avoid the displeasure of your foul company."

"And there she is." He checks his watch. "Took all of twenty seconds for the Kat to find her claws."

A growl rolls out of me. Hugging my sore arm to my side, I start to walk past him, because he has this infuriating ability to get under my skin with a few well-placed words and that aggravating tilt of his damn eyebrow. If I stay here, I might actually turn as feral as he's always accused me of being.

But then his hand wraps around my good arm at the elbow, stopping me. I glare at him, hating that I have to look up in order to meet his eyes. I'm tall, but Christopher's towering, his body broad and powerful, his arms thicker than I can get two hands around.

Not that I've thought about that. No, if I've thought about wrapping my hands around anything, it's been that neck of his, giving it a good hard squeeze—

"What happened to you?" he says.

I blink, yanked out of my thoughts by the sharp tone in his question. Feeling defiant, I lift my chin and dare him to look away first.

He doesn't.

My breathing turns unsteady as I realize how close our faces have become. Christopher stares down at me. His breathing sounds a little unsteady, too. "Lots happened while I was gone," I finally manage between clenched teeth. "Sort of unavoidable when you step outside your tiny world. Explore new places. Encounter obstacles."

Such as a bit of rocky Scottish landscape that led to a broken shoulder. Not that I admit that to him.

Still, his jaw twitches. My dig's landed where I wanted.

For all his sophistication and success, a corporate capitalist's wet dream, Christopher has never left the city. Without stepping so much as a toe outside his kingdom, he's simply crooked his finger and success has come to *him*. His world is contained and controlled, and he knows I judge him for it. Just as he judges me for how carefree and—in his eyes—reckless I am, for how quickly I walked away from my hometown and family the moment I graduated.

After losing his parents as a teen, he doesn't have a family of his own—my family is his, and he's protective of them, which is fine, but he doesn't see my perspective. He doesn't understand that I feel like an outsider in my own family, that I know I'm loved but don't often feel loved the way I need to. He doesn't get how much easier it is for me to feel close to those I love from a distance, that only my love would bring me home, because that's what it took for things to be okay.

Finally he glances down, once again frowning at the arm I hold against my side. My shoulder's healed—despite what I told my family—but it's still tender enough that ramming into the brick wall of Christopher's chest has it throbbing.

A notch forms in his brow as he examines how I'm clutching it.

"You do realize," he says, his voice low and rough, "that you don't *actually* have nine lives to burn through."

Before I can answer with some stinging reply, his thumb slips along the inside of my arm, making my breath hitch. My voice dies in my throat.

Releasing me abruptly, he steps back. "I'll walk you home."

My mouth drops open. The audacity!

"Thanks for the daily dose of patriarchal manhandling, but I don't need an escort home. And I'm headed there"—I point toward Nanette's over his shoulder—"to pick up buy-one-get-one-half-off pumpkin pies. I did not suffer a head-on collision with you only to be turned around by your high-handed nonsense and sent home without them, so piss off and let me by."

His jaw's twitching again. "Fine. Get your pies. I'll wait."

"Christopher." I stomp my foot. "I'm twenty-seven. I don't need to be babysat."

"Trust me, I'm relieved we've outgrown that. You were a holy terror to keep an eye on."

"Oh, har-har." There's six years between us, but for how conde-scendingly superior he's always acted, you'd think it was sixteen.

Brushing by him, I storm into Nanette's. The friendliness of the folks behind the counter, the soothing sweet scents of pumpkin and vanilla, chocolate and buttercream that wrap around me as I wait for my pies to be packed up, take the edge off my irritation, but not for long. When I walk back outside, clutching both pie boxes, he's still there.

Plucking the pies from my hand, Christopher nods his chin toward my sister's—now also my—apartment. "After you."

I try to snatch the pies from him, but he lifts them out of reach.

I glare up at him. "I can walk six blocks to the apartment alone, thank you very much."

"Congratulations. So could the woman who was mugged right here the other night."

"That's terrible," I say sincerely. "But I know how to handle—"

"You have *one* fully functioning arm," he argues. "How would you defend yourself?"

Totally beyond rationality, I swing my arm and wave it around, hat-ing myself as pain pulses in my shoulder socket. I definitely bruised it, if not something worse, when I ran into him. "I'm fine, okay? I'm fine."

The truth is I *am* fine. Or I was, until I crashed into Christopher. While I did break my shoulder back in Scotland, as I told my family, the truth is it happened two months ago. I had to pass on jobs while it healed; my finances dwindled; and when it came time to try to pick up work again, I couldn't seem to catch a break. So when Mom told me Jules and Bea's predicament, I had the perfect solution for all of us. I offered to swap places with Jules for a while; conveniently neglected to say *when* I busted my shoulder, only that I had; and made sure to wear the sling when I showed up this morning.

Yes, it's dishonest, and no, I don't like deceiving my family. But I knew without a legitimate injury as an explanation for my uncharacter-istic return home, Jules wouldn't take me up on my offer and Mom might get her hopes up that I was home for good, and then where would we be?

Christopher stares at me, eyes narrowed. Suspicious.

Dammit, I had to bump into him while not wearing the sling *and* I just flailed my arm around to show him I'm fine. Now I have to figure out how to keep him quiet about that when everyone else in the family thinks my shoulder's freshly busted.

I'm so tired, so annoyed, so sore, I can't think straight. This conundrum is for Future Kate to solve. Present Kate needs a hot shower, a cozy bed, and a pumpkin pie eaten straight out of the baking tin.

Catching him off guard, I wrench the pies out of Christopher's hand. "Now if you'll excuse me, I have a walk as well as a couple pies to enjoy *by myself.*"

Breezing by him, I round the corner and stomp the remaining five long blocks leading to the apartment. I don't once look back, but I feel his eyes on me the whole way.

As the foyer door of the building drops shut behind me, I scowl down at the pastry boxes in my hands. "You had better be the best damn pumpkin pies of my life." Wrenching open the inside door, I traipse up the stairs, anger a white-hot inferno burning through me. "Nothing less would make what I just suffered worth it."

Photo courtesy of the author

Chloe Liese writes romances reflecting her belief that everyone deserves a love story. Her stories pack a punch of heat, heart, and humor, and often feature characters who are neurodivergent, like herself. When not dreaming up her next book, Chloe spends her time wandering in nature, playing soccer, and most happily at home with her family and mischievous cats.

To sign up for Chloe's latest news, new releases, and special offers, please visit her website and subscribe.

CONNECT ONLINE

ChloeLiese.com
Chloe_Liese
Chloe_Liese
Chloe_Liese
ChloeLiese

Ready to find
your next great read?

Let us help.

Visit prh.com/nextread

Penguin
Random
House